Evangeline

Meghan Flewellyn

Published by Meghan Flewellyn, 2026.

This is a work of fiction. Similarities to real people, places, or events are entirely coincidental.

EVANGELINE

First edition. March 13, 2026.

ISBN: 979-8993304915

Written by Meghan Flewellyn.

Chapter One

As the earth stretches down into the bottom of the Delta, past the rolling foothills in Mississippi and Arkansas, small pockets of suburban quietude nestle into the arms of the waterways, rivers, and creeks of Louisiana. It doesn't seem quite possible that the land could flatten so quickly, the sky become so big.

Herons stretch their wings to soar over the interstates and highways to look for fish in the drainage ditches that run along the breakdown lanes. In the early morning and late evening, frogs croak and bugs whine, high and unrelenting. Oak trees droop with Spanish moss. The trees choke with kudzu, invasive and slowly squeezing the life out of the branches to which it clings. In the ditches there are crawfish that bury themselves deep in the mud, wary of the young boys and old men who set traps for them.

If there were a place where you might find ghosts, this would be it. The droop of the moss could be the shock of hair belonging to a woman whose head hangs as she cries. The branch of a Live Oak might by the accusatory arm pointing to the crossroads formed by two highways. *Wait at the crossroads and see who might be waiting for you*, it says.

In this part of the state, old women tell stories of the souls of a young bride waiting eagerly for her lover to return from some war and of the sad and vengeful spirit of a slave woman weeping for her stolen children.

The air is heavy with long ago violence. The humidity traps it. You can hear it in the creak of old floorboards in a shotgun house. Old death and new death mingle in the above ground mausoleums. In the afternoons when the oppressive air bubbles up to form angry thunderheads, there is no movement until the sky opens and drenches the earth, not to nourish, but to drown.

On a street with two streetlights and a bright moon visible as the red sun sets, a woman walks with her head down, phone in hand, ponytail moving in an arc. The woman is thinking, worrying, trying to sort through what she sees as a mess of circumstances and unknowns.

On the corner of the street where the woman walks, there is an empty lot covered with the same species of tall pines that cover most of the subdivision where she lives. A girl, not a child but not quite a woman, walks through the lot. Her head is up and she swings her arms, looking straight ahead. She is going nowhere and everywhere.

A mile away, a third woman sits on the patio below her raised house and rocks rhythmically in a glider, coffee in hand. She stares straight ahead, out past the slope of her lawn to the swamp behind it, her face a work of carved obsidian. She forces herself to breathe slowly in through her nose and out through her mouth.

They are connected by nothing and everything. As the sun begins its slow descent, all three women are drenched in the dying light, their faces masks of shadows and bloody glow.

Chapter Two

Missy Douglas tried to smile to herself a little as she flipped a pancake. She didn't feel much like smiling right now, even though her husband was home after being away for a month and was about to leave again in two days for another month-long stint working offshore. She felt like they had made the most of the past month, despite the circumstances in which they found themselves. They had lots of good days, not a lot of fighting, and Wes hadn't been drinking too much. Most days, Wes had worked on getting the yard cleaned up from all of the rain they'd had. Wes gladly watched the kids when Missy went to visit Evie in the hospital.

Missy closed her eyes and rested her palms on the countertop. She felt woozy and strange as she fed her children their pancakes. She forced a smile when Wes came into the house from the grocery store and dumped bags onto the counter.

With a smile, Wes pulled two kites out of one of the bags and waggled his eyebrows at Missy.

After pancakes, they took the kids into the center of the cul-de-sac in front of their house to take advantage of a light wind kicked up from a tropical storm in the Gulf of Mexico. A storm brewed there, swirling and angry, but it wasn't set to come their way.

Although it wasn't raining, the clouds overhead seemed pregnant with rain like they could rupture at any time.

"No lightning though," Wes shrugged.

Their children, John and Sophie ran happily in circles. The bright kites that Wes bought at Walmart mostly just dragged behind them, but occasionally the wind caught them and launched them into the air. Wes and Missy cheered each time the kites lifted and offered encouragement each time they fell. Missy sat on the side of the street hugging her knees, allowing Wes the space to play with the kids on his own. Beer in hand, he chased Johnnie around the circle of grass in the middle of the cul de sac.

"Daddy, look at me!" Sophie yelled over and over with the exuberance only a four-year-old can muster.

Missy felt the vague worry that had been with her for the past few days crawl down her spine like a spider and desperately tried to brush it away. Usually when she had this feeling it was something to do with Wes and his drinking. That he was going to have a bad day, that they would go back to how it was when he was drinking heavily. She eyed the beer in his hand, the only beer he'd had so far today and it was already past lunch, and didn't think that was it.

Since they had moved from Tennessee to Louisiana, Wes had kept his drinking under control, as promised. He went to a few Alcoholics Anonymous meetings when they had first arrived, but then his job working offshore in the middle of the Gulf of Mexico had started. Missy didn't care if he drank when he was offshore, she just cared if he drank when he was home, around her and the kids.

When they decided to move, Wes had promised her that if she didn't leave, he'd clean up his act. They could make a fresh start. When Wes had originally told her about taking a job offshore, she knew what an opportunity it was for their family: not just the financial opportunity but an opportunity to start fresh, away from Wes's old crowd, away from old habits.

He would be able to be promoted soon, he assured her. They could afford a bigger house, maybe even a boat. Missy could go back to school to get certified to teach in Louisiana and could substitute teach when she felt like it whenever Wes was home. They could hire a babysitter and go out to dinner. They could give Johnny and Sophie Ann a good life.

Missy watched the kids as they ran and laughed with the kites and wondered if the move had been a good thing. Wes's drinking seemed to be under control, but what would happen to her and the kids this month when Wes was away? This would be the first time he was gone, and she would be without Evie.

"Mommy, can we go get popsicles?" Johnny yelled.

"Sure, baby."

Missy's heart tugged with worry as she watched Johnny run down the driveway.

"I got it, Miss." Wes gestured to Johnny and Sophie and crushed the beer can he was holding. Missy vaguely wondered if he was going to help himself to another beer when he got the kids their popsicles but didn't say anything.

Evie's going to be ok, Missy told herself for the thousandth time. *Antibiotics that's all.* She looked up at the tall pines overhead and closed her eyes, praying silently to whatever God was listening.

Evangeline, beautiful, funny, her wonderful friend, her only support when Wes was working offshore, had been in the hospital for a week already. The police said the fall down the embankment was an accident, that she was lucky she didn't go straight in the water and drown, that she was lucky someone found her when they did.

Missy imagined Evie lying motionless by the side of the river, imagined the snakes and the alligators and the worms and the bugs and felt herself start to retch in her throat.

She squeezed her eyes closed and listened to her children laughing.

It had been lonely being so far away from everything she was used to when they first moved to Louisiana. Her new house was beautiful, her new car reliable, her children happy to have a huge yard and a new swing set, but she had felt totally isolated.

Missy thought about the play group she had found on social media and the disastrous time she took Johnnie and Sophie to a play date at a playground. One boy immediately pushed Johnnie off the swings and an older girl threw sand in Sophie's face. The other moms gossiped about women they knew, and Facebook, and their cheating husbands. Missy left disgusted and thankful for the quiet of her own backyard.

A week later Missy met Evie while out on a walk with Johnnie and Sophie. Evie, who was softspoken when she talked but laughed like a crow. Evie always with a gaggle of children surrounding her: cousins, nieces and nephews, friends' children. Missy had smiled hopefully as Evie got the mail from her mailbox, and Evie immediately waved her over.

"I've been meaning to come introduce myself for ages," Evie smiled and shook her head a little, eyes wide, "You must think I'm so rude."

Missy squeezed her eyes closed even tighter at the memory. Evie and her children, Raylynn, who was 12, and the twin boys Vincent and Michael, who were 3, welcomed Sophie and Johnny by handing them each a small spade and inviting them to come dig in their mud puddle.

In the months that followed, Missy spent every afternoon happily chatting with Evie about schools, husbands, potty training, mothers who won't listen but give advice- all of the worrisome, scary, happy, and silly pieces of life as a mother of young children. She confided in Evie her worries about how behind Johnny's speech was and it was Evie who encouraged her to get him some help.

"So, he needs speech class!" Evie waved her hands and shrugged, "Three of my nephews needed speech and now they don't shut up, right Ray?"

Raylynn widened her eyes and nodded solemnly, prompting her mother to throw her head back and caw.

Missy opened her eyes and looked down the street towards Evie's large Acadian on the opposite corner of the street. She squinted at the large figure walking toward her and raised her hand in a greeting. The feeling that her skin was crawling started again and she felt a deep dread in her chest.

Evie's husband, Paul, was tall and heavyset, a former linebacker at Louisiana State University. He had a low brow and a stern face and kept his blond hair cropped close to his skull. He stood in stark contrast in every way compared to Evie, who was barely five foot three, dark complected, with curly black hair to her waist, and whose round face gave her an almost childlike appearance. Paul's looks were deceiving though, and he was as kind and as easy to laugh as Evie. He and Wes had immediately gotten along and had spent a few barbeques drinking, cooking, and critiquing their neighbors' grass cutting techniques.

Evie had two sisters and two brothers and a host of aunts, uncles, in laws, nieces, and nephews, and Missy hadn't heard much from Paul since Evie went into the hospital and tried to respect the fact that she wasn't family, that she was just a relatively new friend.

Missy's heart beat faster.

Paul did not return her gesture, so she lowered her hand and started walking down the street to meet him. Johnny and Sophie still ran in circles with their kites, and Wes was too distracted with the kids to notice him.

"Hi Paul!" Missy tried to sound cheerful, but her voice sounded strange in her own ears as she spoke.

Paul's face was pulled into a strange smile, one that was too tight around the edges and looked more like a grimace.

"Is everything ok?" she called as she walked toward him, "We were just trying to teach the kids to fly their kites."

Paul shook his head and took a long shuddering breath. He stood there for a minute with his hands on his hips, looking off into the distance.

Missy watched him and waited for him to speak. The dread in her heart grew and spread and time seemed to slow down. Paul looked up to the sky, to where Johnnie finally had his kite up in the air.

"Evangeline died last night."

Chapter Three

To Missy, it seemed like every inch of Louisiana was teeming with things that were alive. Frogs, stick bugs, raccoons, stray cats. Every branch in every tree buzzed with insects. When you stepped outside at night, the noise from the bugs was a drone of repeating crescendo and diminuendo. Geckos climbed over the screens on the windows waiting for moths.

During the late spring and early summer, swarms of termites descended onto any source of light, entering homes through any crack. There were alligators by the side of the road, possum in the trash cans. In New Orleans, colonies of feral cats, products of the aftermath of Hurricane Katrina, were rampant. Vultures picked at dead armadillos.

Everywhere you looked, there was slithering and slinking, waiting and watching. A patience filled with predatory menace.

The way life continues with regularity after a tragedy happens is sometimes the most disturbing part of the whole event. Tragedy happens and then time continues. It was the same for Missy. Wes was gone offshore two weeks after Evangeline died, and so Missy was alone with the house and the kids.

Johnny went to half day Vacation Bible School for the summer months, so most of the day it was just Missy and Sophie. By the time Johnny got home from camp, he was so exhausted they ended up just watching movies or sitting outside and eating popsicles. Then Missy made dinner, gave the kids their baths, called Wes, and tucked the kids into bed. She drank her glass of wine and watched a silly show, finished doing the dishes, and picked up the house. Boring and regular and scheduled. The days were slow.

The unfairness of the regularity was palpable to Missy. Fixing Johnny a bowl of Cheerios. Loading the dishwasher. Helping Sophie use the potty. All the little mundane tasks that made up the day. Each one hurt as she went through the motions, wondering who was loading Evie's dishwasher, who was making Raylynn and the twins' breakfast, who did the twins ask for at night when they were being tucked into their beds?

Missy spent the next few weeks in a fog of trying to cope with how her everyday life had changed, trying to see how Paul and the kids could move forward, and trying to find some reason to what happened.

Everything around her seemed strange and unfamiliar. She felt like she couldn't think. Her children's happy laughter and banter felt jarring, and she found herself snapping at them more often.

Missy yearned for time and space to think, and then she felt guilty for wanting to be away from them. Wes and her parents insisted that the best thing for Missy and the kids was to go and stay with them in Tennessee at least while he was offshore.

But Missy couldn't bring herself to leave. Something nagged at her, pulled at her heart to stay in Stone River. It wasn't just that Evie died. It was how she did.

The whispers and rumors, reaching even Missy, isolated as she was, swirled around her head. The whispers all said the same things The police had botched the investigation, Evie's death wasn't an accident and they knew it, there was to be no justice for Evangeline Nunez.

It clawed at Missy's heart until she thought it would break all over again.

Finally, Missy called her parents and told them she and the kids would be coming to Tennessee as soon as Wes left offshore.

Her parents were set to arrive at her house the day after Wes left in the afternoon. That morning, Missy ignored the untethered feeling and the sadness and the fear she felt and got her children ready to leave that afternoon.

Missy put off telling her mother that she wasn't going to be coming with them until they were in the state.

"Well, we're a few hours north of Baton Rouge so we should be there around 2!"

"Mama, listen," Missy took a deep breath and closed her eyes, "I want you and Dave to take the kids back by yourselves and then I'll drive myself up this weekend."

There was silence on the other end of the phone.

Missy pressed on, "I have some projects I want to do here, and it'll be easier to do it on my own."

Silence again. Then finally her mother said, "But what about everything that's happened Melissa? Won't you be scared staying by yourself?"

"Naw," Missy tried to sound indifferent, "I think it'll be good for me to have some time and space to breath."

"Well, if you think it'll be ok...." Her mother trailed off.

"To be honest Mama, I need some time to myself to process everything."

There was silence on the other end of the phone.

"Mama?"

"You think it's ok to be alone right now, really?"

Missy heaved a sigh.

"Yes Ma, seriously."

"Well ok then. But if you're not here in a few days, we're coming back down to get you."

Missy gripped the phone and grinned. She felt elated and then guilty that she was happily sending her children away. She tried to sound calm and cheerful.

"Deal. I'll be in Tennessee at the beginning of next week. Just in time for burgers by the pool."

Missy circled through the house packing shorts, tee shirts, bathing suits, coloring books, toys, everything she could think of that the kids might need or want. Between the pool at her parents' house and general grandparent spoiling, Missy knew there would be lots for Sophie and Johnny to do.

She worried about being away from them but felt energized by it at the same time. She felt determined and focused, though she refused to acknowledge the idea that was brewing in her heart, the anger she felt at those whispers that rippled through Stone River.

A botched investigation. Justice for Evie.

Her heart hushed the ideas, promising them time and space to breathe when her children were safe with her parents.

By lunch time, the kids' bags were packed and waiting by the front door.

Missy stood looking at the packed bags, vaguely feeling like she was going to cry at the sight of them, and wondered what they would do to pass the time until her parents arrived.

The beginning of the summer had been filled with trips to see Evie and the kids at their house. Johnny and Sophie were met with popsicles, juice boxes, and the gaggle of kids Evie was watching for the day.

Missy had purposely avoided walking down to the street where she would inevitably have to walk past Evie's house, but now with time quickly approaching where she'd have to say goodbye to her children, Missy decided they should take a walk.

Sophie and Johnny happily agreed and skipped in front of Missy without a care in the world.

The neighborhood was silent. No happy laughter or sticky hands.

Johnny walked with his head up looking at the trees and Sophie skipped along, occasionally pointing out a wildflower or bird that she had spotted.

Missy sighed and tried to direct Johnny and Sophie away from the house on the corner, now sitting empty and silent, down Pine View Road instead.

"Maybe Raylynn has her scooter!" Johnny yelled excitedly.

"I told you baby, Raylynn went to stay with their MawMaw for a little while."

"Just like us!" Sophie yelled happily.

"And Ms. Evie too?"

Johnny turned at looked at Missy seriously.

Missy shrugged and looked away. She didn't have the heart to try and explain to Johnny and Sophie what had happened. Johnny had enough trouble understanding the world around him as it was, and Sophie was so young.

The heat was oppressive, and Missy felt an unpleasant trickle of sweat running down her back. The kids ventured ahead of her as she walked with her hands on her hips, head down, thinking.

"Mama, look at that!" Sophie yelled.

Sophie stood in front of Evie's house, pointing at the ground. Missy looked forlornly at the house, closed up and empty, no toys or cars in the driveway.

"What is it? A turtle?" Missy smiled.

There were often box turtles in the drainage ditches that ran alongside the road, and Raylynn had taught Sophie to look for them.

"Nuh uh," Sophie said seriously, shaking her head, "that's a snake."

Missy quickened her step.

"Back up Sophie."

"But where is it, Mama?" Johnny asked, stepped forward.

"Johnny, listen to your mama and back up. Now."

Both children froze. The snake was long but thick like a plump black leech from the stagnant ponds back home in Tennessee.

"Back up both of you!"

The snake hissed and raised its angular head. Missy lunged forward and grabbed both children by the backs of their shirts and jerked them backwards. The snake lunged and struck at the air.

"Mama!!"

Missy hoisted Sophie up and pulled Johnny behind her, backing up as she kept her eyes on the snake.

It coiled back again, hissing and raised its head up. Missy blocked Johnny with her body and pushed him back, pulling Sophie up as high as she could.

Behind the snake, Evie's house sat hulking and dark, shadowed by the trees that surrounded it.

"Mama! Mama, look!"

Missy kept her eyes on the snake as it hissed and struck at the air again. Missy tried to stomp her foot at it, and it struck again, narrowly missing her toe.

Johnny screamed and held onto her leg as she backed up again. The snake advanced on them again, eerily fast, moving its plump body with a speed it didn't seem like it should have.

"Hold still, baby."

Missy froze at the sound of the old woman's voice, her eyes still on the snake.

"What do I do?" she whispered.

"Just stay there, baby, I got to get a good spot on him."

Missy saw the woman's toes appear behind the snake's tail, and lightning fast, the side edge of a shovel slammed down and chopped off the snake's head. The tail writhed and flipped, and Missy lunged to the side, dragging Johnny with her and Sophie, desperate to get as far away from it as possible.

"Jesus," she whispered.

"Cottonmouth," the old lady said, scrunching up her nose, "nasty old things."

Missy looked up at the woman finally and found herself slightly bemused at what she saw: white hair done up in an old fashioned looking French bun, matching blue jogging suit set complete with rhinestone flowers on the chest and down one leg, reading glasses hanging around her neck on a beaded chain.

She didn't look much like a lady who could kill a cottonmouth with a shovel and Missy grinned at her.

"Thank you so much, ma'am." Missy felt herself flush a little, feeling silly that she had panicked.

"Oh, you're welcome, baby. I hope he didn't scare y'all too much."

The woman looked at her, eyes soft with concern and kindness.

Missy sighed and put Sophie down.

"Are you ok?" she asked both kids.

Johnny nodded with wide eyes.

"You got him good old lady!!" Sophie laughed.

"Sophie!"

The old lady laughed too, "I sure enough did get him good, huh baby?"

She looked at Missy, "You all new around here? I know most of the other neighbors."

"Well, kind of ma'am. We moved in about a year ago."

"Oh yeah," the woman nodded slowly, and she put her hand on her forehead, "I do recognize you now. I've seen you around with Evangeline Nunez."

Missy nodded, looking uncomfortably from the woman to Johnny and Sophie.

The woman looked at her kindly.

"I'm sorry, honey. She was a special person."

Missy nodded again, not knowing what to say.

"You know, this neighborhood never was good for young women. Strange area, bad vibes or something," The old woman shrugged, "You say a prayer when you get home, baby."

Missy furrowed her brow.

"What do you mean?"

The woman shook her head and waved her hands at Missy.

"Eh, don't listen to me. To be honest with you, I hate them damn snakes. They give me the creeps."

"Mama, she said a bad word." Johnny said quietly.

"I sure did, huh baby? I'm sorry," she shook her head and smiled, "I'm Ann Marie, honey."

"Well, it's nice to meet you Ms. Ann Marie, I'm Melissa Douglas. Everyone calls me Missy though."

The two women stood for a few more seconds until Johnny pulled on Missy's hand. "Mama, can we still walk to the end of the street?"

"Yeah, baby of course."

Missy turned back to Ann Marie.

"I guess we better head on. Thank you again, Ms. Ann Marie."

"Oh, you're welcome baby."

Ann Marie looked at Missy kindly, and Missy wondered how she wasn't boiling to death in her track suit.

"Do you live around here?" Missy asked hopefully, "Can I stop by tomorrow with some cookies to say thank you?"

Missy felt her heart jump a little at the idea of having an errand to do, someone to talk to.

This neighborhood was never good for young women, Missy's heart whispered, *what did she mean?*

"Me? Live here?" Ann Marie laughed, "Oh no, baby, I live way out on 41. I just come to help Ms. Cindy once in a while. She and I go to the same church."

Missy knew Ms. Cindy lived at the other end of the cul de sac. She looked toward Ms. Cindy's house and saw a beat up green pickup truck parked at the end of the driveway.

"Oh ok," Missy felt slightly crestfallen, "Well maybe sometime when you come back to visit Ms. Cindy, I can stop by and chat?"

Ann Marie smiled kindly and put a hand on Missy's shoulder.

"You bet, baby. It'll get better with time, I promise."

—

Around two o'clock, Missy kissed and hugged Sophie and Johnny, put them in the back seat of her stepfather's truck, warned them both to behave, and tried to choke back tears so the kids wouldn't see and cry too.

Her mother held her hand out the window.

"If I don't hear from you, and you aren't at our house Monday or Tuesday, we're coming back to get you."

Missy nodded. "I'll be there. I promise."

"Come on, Grandpa!" Sophie yelled from the back seat.

"Let's roll!" Johnny yelled.

Missy stood facing the truck, her back to her house, and marveled at the love she felt for her children. Both kids had on their sunglasses and were clutching baggies of goldfish and thermoses of apple juice.

Below that love, Missy felt the heavy pull of something larger than herself, as large as the ocean at night. The pull was coming from behind her, from her house. Whatever worry she might feel about sending her children away, she felt somewhere deep in her heart, where her grief and anger and confusion lurked that her children were safer far away for now.

It wasn't an accident, her heart whispered, *it wasn't an accident at all.*

Missy stood in the driveway in the hot sun as they pulled away. They all waved to her from the open windows, and she waved back until they rounded the corner and turned onto the main road. Then she couldn't see them anymore.

When she was alone in the driveway, Missy put her hands on her hips and turned to face her empty house.

Chapter Four

Unused to any kind of freedom, shocked at how it felt not to have children depending on her, Missy was completely unsure of what to do alone in her house. Her first instinct was to call her mother to turn around and come get her.

She used every ounce of her strength not to.

That place in her heart where she knew that something wasn't right, that there was something very wrong happening around her, pulsed and pounded with a fierceness that surprised her.

Unsure of what to do, Missy decided to put on her pajamas and crawl into bed, letting her grief wrap around her and lull her to sleep.

She woke up once at 8 o'clock when her mother called to tell her they arrived safely in Tennessee and to tell the kids good night. She didn't answer when Wes called. Instead, she laid down and slept until daybreak.

She dreamed of a snake. A thick, black, corpulent thing that waited for her, coiled somewhere in the swamp, waiting and watching and wondering.

—

The next morning, unsure of what to do with herself with no one needing breakfast or needing to be dropped off at camp, Missy decided to treat herself to an iced coffee. She dressed slowly, wondering again who was making breakfast for Evie's kids. Who had tucked them in the night before? The fog around her descended and she felt depressed and lonely without her children.

Missy drove slowly and without really seeing what was around her. She pulled into a strip mall where there was a small locally owned coffee shop and put her car in park. She took a few deep breaths and then covered her eyes with her hand.

It wasn't an accident, her heart insisted.

Missy walked across the small parking lot. The heat pulsed off the pavement already, even though it was still very early. As Missy pushed open the door of the coffee shop, the air conditioning felt heavenly, and the smell of the coffee seemed to jolt her awake and out of her stupor.

"Hey, I'm Alessandra. What can I get for you?"

Missy looked at the young woman named Alessandra and tried to place where she knew her from. Missy took in Alessandra's bright blue hair, nose ring, and dark red lipstick. Alessandra smiled and raised her eyebrows.

"You need a minute?"

"Oh, yeah. Sorry. Just a minute please."

Missy felt herself blush a little.

"No prob. Just call me when you're ready."

The young woman moved like she was going to walk away.

"Oh, I think I'm ready."

Alessandra raised her eyebrows again and shrugged. She lifted her hand as if to say, "And...?"

"Oh, um. I'll take an iced coffee and chicory with just a little cream. And a croissant."

Alessandra nodded and moved away to make the drink.

Missy covered her eyes with her hand again as she realized with a jolt where she recognized Alessandra from.

It was from Evie's front lawn on the day they found the caterpillars.

Months earlier, Missy, Johnny, and Sophie had wandered down the street on a warm afternoon in the late winter. Missy remembered marveling at the puffy clouds in the sky, the warm breeze being carried up the river that ran behind their subdivision from the Gulf of Mexico.

How could a day be so beautiful? Missy had wondered happily, relishing that she lived in a place where winter could be warm.

As they got to the end of their street and could see past the trees to Evie's house, Missy saw Evie, alone, bent over, staring at a tree on her front lawn. It was a strange sight, not just to see her friend staring at a tree, but because there were no children around her. Evie alone.

In the present, sitting in the coffee shop, Missy could smell the strong coffee and felt the cool blast of air from the air conditioning vent.

Allowing herself to drift back to the memory, staring vacantly out of the coffee shop's windows, Missy tried to picture what had happened clearly.

Back then, last spring, in Evie's front yard, did the breeze feel colder then, or was it the cool of the coffee shop? Did a cloud pass in front of the sun? Did the Spanish Moss hanging from the trees move in a way it shouldn't or was it Missy's current grief and confusion and the strange mingling of past and present?

Missy remembered calling out to Evie twice before Evie turned around.

"Hey Evie! Evie?"

When she finally turned around, Evie's small face was curled up in repulsion, and Missy for a split second felt ashamed as though she was interrupting and the look of repulsion was for her.

But Evie's gaze softened and turned desperate when she saw Missy.

"Oh my god, Missy come look at this."

Missy grabbed both Sophie and Johnny by their hands and crossed the street.

"What is it?"

"What is, Ms. Evie?"

Johnny pulled his hand away from Missy's and trotted over to Evie's side, but Evie put a hand out to stop him from going too close to the tree.

"What is, Ms. Evie?" he repeated.

"It's caterpillars," Evie's voice sounded strange as she pointed at the tree.

"Caterpillars?" Missy echoed, laughing a little.

Missy and Sophie stopped about a foot behind Evie and Missy scrutinized the tree, trying to see. Missy stared and saw nothing.

"Mama, look," Sophie whispered.

Missy looked again and let out a disgusted cry. She stepped back from the tree, pulling Johnny and Sophie back by their shirts.

The entire bottom of the huge pine tree was covered with black caterpillars. They writhed and twisted all over each other, making the bottom of the tree seem like it was alive and moving.

The four of them stood staring at the tree, transfixed by the insects.

Missy felt a million miles away as she watched them. They seemed different, unnatural.

"They're eating each other," Evie finally said in the same strange voice.

Missy felt her face pull back in a grimace as she saw the caterpillars climb onto each other in an endless bid to be on top.

"No, Evie, caterpillars don't eat each other."

"But they are, listen."

They all were quiet again, and Missy heard a sickening crunching of bodies and legs and saw Johnny lean in closer, trying to get a better look.

How long did the four of them stay standing there like that, watching the cannibalistic spectacle?

Missy had no idea, now, sitting in the coffee shop. It could have been five, ten, twenty minutes for all she knew. How long had Evie been standing there before Missy and the kids had arrived there? Missy never asked and now she would never know.

What Missy did remember was the sound of the voice that snapped them all out of it.

"Hey, yo! Uhhh what are y'all looking at?" A sharp voice, heavy with a Texas accent, called from the street.

"Caterpillars."

Missy remembered feeling fuzzy-headed and strangely detached.

"Uhhh caterpillars?"

Missy turned her head and saw a young woman with bright orange hair, one hand on her hip, one hand turned up as if to say, "And...?"

Missy turned and walked a step toward the girl.

"This tree is totally covered with caterpillars."

"Wow, gross."

The young woman strode across Evie's lawn, long legs sticking out from cut off jean shorts, a ripped AC/DC tee shirt visible under a worn-out flannel. She stood next to Missy and Sophie with her hands on her hips.

"Sick."

Johnny turned around and echoed, "Sick."

The girl smiled at Johnny, "Yeah, man."

The girl looked from Missy to Evie.

"Y'all are fucking weird," she laughed and shook her head, "Really fucking weird."

"Hey Sandie, watch the mouth in front of the kids," Evie's voice had lost the faraway sound.

The girl laughed again.

"Sorry Ms. Evie, but what the hell. Y'all are standing here looking at some nasty bugs," she did a mock shiver, "I'm outta here, that shit is creepy as hell. "

"Creepy as hell," Johnny echoed again.

"Johnny."

Missy glanced from her son, to Evie, and back to the teenager.

Missy couldn't remember what happened after that, she supposed they drifted away from the tree in conversation, but she still couldn't quite remember. She vaguely remembered that Evie said she was going to tell Paul to come out and kill them.

Missy looked at the girl's back as she made her drink. Sandie. Alessandra. She had different hair, but Evie was pretty sure it was the same girl.

The girl turned back around and handed Missy her coffee. She bent down and grabbed a croissant from a case to the side of the register, and as she did she looked at Missy from under her blue bangs.

"It's Eight twenty. Where do I know you from?"

Missy started a little and passed her hand over her eyes again. She could feel the girl's directness in her gaze.

"You ok?"

"No. Yes."

She looked back at Alessandra.

"I think you knew my friend Evie."

Missy slowly took money out of her purse and held it out.

"Oh," Alessandra nodded and bit her lip on the side that didn't have the piercing, "yeah Ms. Evie was really nice to me."

Missy nodded, "She was a nice person."

The girl nodded her head toward Missy, "Not a lot of people are. You were good friends with her?"

"Yeah, I guess I was."

Alessandra didn't respond but took the money Missy held out.

"You live in Cypress Woods?"

"Yeah, I live right up the street from Evie."

Where Evie used to live, she corrected herself mentally.

"My name is Missy."

"I live in the new section," Alessandra said with mild defiance.

She lifted her chin slightly as though daring Missy to react to the statement.

She means where the trailer park is going.

Missy nodded slowly, "Well, maybe I'll see you around Alessandra."

"Yeah, see you."

Alessandra sounded curt and aloof, and, thinking of Sophie, Missy silently hoped that not all children turned into surly teenagers.

Missy walked slowly back to her car, buckled herself in, and took a slow sip. The memory of the caterpillars brought up a conversation that had happened a few months after Missy and Evie first met. The memories felt fresh and strange. Bright and clear.

Missy started the car and pulled out of the parking lot, deliberately turning the opposite direction from their house. Taking another sip from her coffee, Missy relaxed a little as she drove and let her mind wander back to the new memory.

Wes had been home for a week or so when they all decided to take a walk. Missy and Wes held hands as they walked and Johnny and Sophie Ann skipped around them in circles, Johnny talking up a storm. Wes beamed at him with every new idea he spouted off. Missy looked around happily and smelled the warm spring air.

There had been no alcohol so far that day, and Missy remembered her heart feeling light and hopeful.

In the present, Missy stopped at a red light and marveled at her happiness then. How close it felt now and how different from sorrow she was living with.

The light turned green, and Missy continued, past strip malls, bars, grocery stores. She let her mind wander back again.

"Hey Miss!!" Evie called from up the street.

She was surrounded by her usual pack of children. Missy recognized the twins and Raylynn, and then Evie's niece who everyone called Pumpkin and a few other kids Missy didn't know.

"Raylynn! Pumpkin!" Johnny yelled.

Missy waved.

"Is that your friend?" Wes asked quietly.

Missy looked at him and nodded.

"Come here girl! Is that your man?" Evie laughed.

Wes and Missy made their way to Evie's lawn. The kids happily dispersed into a pack, and Paul came around from behind the house, blowing grass clippings from the mown lawn. Missy watched them as Raylynn and Pumpkin hugged Sophie Ann and a boy who looked to be about eight told Johnny to give him five.

Evie, Missy, Paul, and Wes fell into an easy conversation. At the time, Missy marveled at the naturalness of it: Wes and Paul talking about the Saints' new running back and Missy and Evie talking about the persimmon jelly recipe that Evie had tried that had been an absolute failure.

"Girl. I'm talking sour, bitter, like..." Evie screwed up her face and puckered, "Pinterest fail, for sure."

Missy laughed, "Oh come on, really?"

Paul shook his head sadly, "It was bad. You know me, I'll eat anything. It was bad."

Missy couldn't remember the rest of the conversation, but she did remember the kids playing happily under the pine trees in the front yard (including what would later be the caterpillar tree), the four of them chatting. The conversation lulled when three cars rolled down the street and pulled into the house across from Evie and Paul's house which had been for sale since Missy and Wes had moved in.

"Crazy that house has been up for sale for so long," Missy remarked. "Doesn't it have a pool?"

"Yeah, I always thought it was weird too. It's been for sale since right after we moved in, huh Paul?"

Paul nodded.

"Yeah. I talked to Ms. Cindy a few weeks ago and found out why."

"Yeah, and he didn't tell me about it until a few nights ago."

Evie shook her head and widened her eyes at Missy.

"Well come on man, don't leave us hanging," Wes laughed.

Paul shook his head.

"It freaked her out- I don't want to freak y'all out too."

He looked out of the side of his eye at Wes and Missy and shifted his weight from one foot to another.

Evie sighed and whispered, "There was a murder there."

"Are you serious?" Wes laughed a little when Missy gasped.

Paul nodded his head.

"That's fucking crazy."

Wes shook his head and planted his hands across his chest. Missy remembered seeing the sharp stubble on his cheeks. Neglecting to shave had always been a telltale sign that he had been drinking, but he told Missy he was thinking of growing a beard.

Paul nodded again, "I know."

"What happened?"

"Ms. Cindy said there was a family who lived there; the husband apparently was super controlling. When the two kids went off to college, the wife tried to leave the husband. When the husband found out about it, he threw her off that top balcony."

He turned and pointed to the small balcony attached to the second story window and Missy and Wes followed his finger.

"She died in the driveway."

Evie shook her head, "Poor woman."

A group of people converged in the driveway of the murdered woman's house. They walked across the lawn and into the backyard through a gate in the fence.

"Oh my God, that's so sad," Missy said.

"That don't freak you out having that across the street?" Wes asked.

Paul shrugged.

"Nah man. I mean, I told her," he pointed at Evie with his thumb, "I'm about to cut down a few of these trees and if I do and they start bleeding or something...we're out of here."

They all laughed a little and the conversation shifted away to happier things.

Missy hadn't thought about it at all really until now. The snake, the caterpillars, the murder, Evie's accident.

Not an accident.

Missy shuddered a little and continued up the main road to where she could circle back to her neighborhood.

She drove and thought about it all: snake, caterpillars, the murder, Evie. Missy felt like there was a weight on her chest and her stomach felt jumpy; she felt sweaty but clammy.

Missy stopped at another red light and thought about what the old woman had said yesterday morning. Missy took a sip of coffee and furrowed her eyebrows.

This neighborhood has never been good for young women. What the hell did that even mean?

The weight on her chest felt heavier and she turned the air conditioning down. *Stop being a goose. If you want to know, go ask the woman what she meant.*

When she pulled into the subdivision, Missy took a left to go toward the section where her house was. The section to the right of the entrance used to be all woods but now it was partially cleared. There was a freshly paved road winding off into the distance, and Missy could just see a double wide trailer. There was a new development going in soon, either a trailer park or high-density housing, and it had caused quite the commotion in the neighborhood.

That's where Alessandra must live.

Missy passed through spaced out, smallish Acadian style homes that all looked very similar to her own. If she kept going straight past her own street she would eventually come to a section filled with sprawling mansions in Antebellum style, most complete with lovely Live Oaks hanging with Spanish Moss.

All the way at the end of the subdivision was the largest house of all, surrounded by thick woods and the Stone River itself, owned by Grant Longue. Longue owned most of the land not just in Stone River but in the entire parish. He also owned a Real Estate business. And a lumber yard. And a construction company. Missy guessed he was going to make a serious amount of money when the new section of the neighborhood was developed.

Missy shook her head. None of it had anything to do with Evie.

Instead of turning to go towards her own house, on a whim Missy turned down Evie's street and looked hopefully toward Ms. Cindy's house for the green pickup truck. Her heart leapt when she spied it was in the same spot at the end of Ms. Cindy's driveway.

Missy pulled up in front of Ms. Cindy's house, parked her car, and sat with her hands on the wheel. She stared at Ms. Cindy's house, wondering what to do.

A soft knock on her window made her jump. Missy laughed a little as the old woman who had killed the snake yesterday morning beckoned her out of the car. Feeling a little self-conscious, Missy climbed out of her car. She didn't even know what she wanted to ask Ms. Ann Marie.

Luckily, Ann Marie seemed to want to talk to her, and she spoke first.

"I owe you an apology Missy."

Missy shook her head, "Me? No, you don't Ms. Ann Marie, for what?"

"Well, you're going through a lot, and I probably scared you."

Missy thought briefly about the snake and sending her children away and the voice that whispered to her about Evangeline.

She shrugged and lied, "You didn't."

Ann Marie looked Missy up and down and then looked up at the hot sun.

"It's so hard to lose someone so young. But it's all His plan, isn't it?"

Missy nodded, "I guess so. I guess it is."

"It is, Missy."

Missy looked up at the sky and wondered how to ask what she wanted to ask.

"I was hoping I would bump into you..." she started.

"Aw, come on honey, that snake was nothing, really. I grew up fishing and hunting with my daddy and brothers, killing snakes isn't a big thing."

"No actually, I wanted to ask you about something else that you said yesterday. You said, 'this neighborhood isn't good for young women' and told me to say a prayer. What did you mean?"

Ann Marie looked at Missy and sighed.

"That's what I meant, honey. I shouldn't have said that."

"But what did you mean?"

The bugs whined in the still air, and Missy felt sticky sweat on her back as they stood in the sun.

Ann Marie shook her head.

"Honey, it's the past, I was just feeling spooky because of that damned snake and Evie Nunez..."

"Ms. Ann Marie," Missy closed her eyes and took a deep breath in, "I'm having a hard time right now understanding what happened to Evie. Will you please tell me what you meant?"

"Look, if you really want to know I will tell you. Why don't you come inside with me? I know Cindy would love to have a visitor."

"Oh no!" Missy protested weakly, "I don't want to intrude..."

Ann Marie waved her away, "It's no intrusion, really!"

"Well, thank you then. I think I will come in."

"Morning down there!"

Missy jumped and turned her head towards the voice. A cloud mercifully passed in front of the sun, shading the street for a moment.

Trenise Jones, a teacher who lived in one of the large, expensive houses about a mile away, jogged in place and waved to them.

Missy lifted her hand in response and Ann Marie waggled her fingers. When Trenise was on her way again, Missy followed Ann Marie up Ms. Cindy's lawn toward the house.

Missy found herself wondering again about the woman who was pushed from her balcony and Evie, her wonderful friend, who was found bruised and battered in the woods and died of her injuries unconscious and unaware of her children, her husband, her friends, and family.

Chapter Five

Missy thought if you looked hard enough you could see how beautiful the house used to be: a row of camellias along the driveway, azaleas placed about halfway down the lawn, and two satsuma trees near a fence on the edge of the property.

The azaleas were overgrown and wild and so were the camellias. The satsuma trees stretched over the fence onto the neighbor's lawn. The fence looked like it was one strong thunderstorm away from falling down. The house needed painting and the wood on the wrap around porch sagged in spots. Missy looked sadly at the state of the house and wondered if she could convince Wes to at least come trim back the bushes when he got home.

It had been over a month since Evie died, and Missy realized just how lonely she had been. She loved spending time with her children, but it wasn't like spending time with a friend. Missy found herself excited to visit the two older women, even if she wasn't really sure what she wanted to ask them.

Ann Marie opened the door slowly and stepped aside, waving her in with a smile, "Come on in!"

Missy smiled back and walked past Ann Marie into a bright hallway. Light spilled in from two large windows in what looked like a living room.

In the enclosed space of the hallway, Missy took in Ann Marie. She was wearing a bright yellow tee shirt with small daisies on it and a pair of faded jean shorts. There was a faint smell of bleach about her and the house as a whole.

"I just got done cleaning up the bathrooms and kitchen, so we can sit and have us a nice talk about whatever you want to know. "

"Thank you so much," Missy suddenly felt embarrassed. *What do I want to know, anyway?*

Ask about the woman on the balcony.

"You just wait here one minute, baby, I'm going to tell Ms. Cindy. She doesn't get many visitors aside from me, so she'll be excited to see you."

Missy smiled and chuckled a little, feeling more and more silly. *Well, if nothing else, you brought a lonely old lady some company.*

Ann Marie walked briskly down the hallway, into what looked like the kitchen, and Missy could hear low voices somewhere at the back of the house. She waited in the hall and forced herself not to bolt out the front door out of embarrassment and awkwardness.

Ann Marie poked her head around the corner and waved Missy toward her.

"We were just sitting out back on the porch, straight through here. You go on back, and I'll be out in a minute with some glasses of tea."

Missy smiled and nodded and walked through the hallway and into the kitchen. It gleamed, spotless and sparse, in the sunlight that was filtering through the trees in the backyard. The appliances were old, but they shone brightly in the morning light.

Ann Marie smiled warmly at her, and then turned her back, getting glasses out of a cupboard.

On the other side of the room was an open door, and Missy could see it led out to a screened in porch. Missy craned her head and saw Ms. Cindy sitting in a corner of the porch. In front of her was a small glass topped table.

Missy had only seen Ms. Cindy a few times before when she had walked down to see Evie. Once Ms. Cindy had been walking to her mailbox, slowly, almost painfully, using a cane. Although it had been a hot day, Ms. Cindy had been wearing knit slacks, a button-down long-sleeved shirt, and a sun hat. She was dressed similarly today, even though it was already in the 80s despite the early time of day.

Missy was glad she was in a sundress; the porch was comfortable, but another hour or two and it would be unbearable.

"Ms. Cindy? I'm Missy, I live on the opposite end of the street from you?"

"I know who you are, honey! Come here."

Missy walked across the porch and took Ms. Cindy's outstretched hand. The skin was soft, wrinkled, and smelled lightly of roses. Her face was broad and open, and her thinning gray hair was swept back into a low bun. Her eyes were a bright and lucid blue in her wrinkled face.

"Sit, sit," Ms. Cindy gestured to a wicker chair close to one of the windows of the porch.

Missy wasn't sure what to say next, and she looked up gratefully as Ann Marie walked out onto the porch carrying a tray full of cookies, a pitcher of iced tea, and three glasses filled with ice.

"Well, Ann Marie here tells me you want to ask me some questions about the old stories about Stone River," Missy opened her mouth to speak, but Ms. Cindy continued, "I wonder if this is about your friend Evangeline."

"Well..."

Ms. Cindy nodded, "It's hard to understand it when a young person dies, isn't it? You want to wrap your brain around it, reason it out. There ain't no reasoning though, honey." She reached out and patted Missy's hand.

"Cindy, you got to admit it's strange though," Ann Marie chimed in.

"Of course it's strange. It's always been strange back here and that makes it all make even less sense."

Missy leaned forward, "Ms. Ann Marie, the other day when we saw that snake, you told me this area wasn't good for young women. What did you mean?"

Cindy and Ann Marie exchanged a small glance and Missy waited.

Ann Marie sighed. "There's always been more young women that die in Stone River, under strange circumstances, than should be normal. You understand what I'm saying?"

Missy shook her head, "How do you mean?"

Ms. Cindy pointed behind her shoulder. "You see my neighbors' house over there?"

"The Floyds, yeah." Missy always waved to the Floyds when they were out doing yard work, but they were hardly talkative. All Missy knew about them was that they were in their 60s, had grown children in college, and had bought the house a few years before Missy and Wes purchased their own house.

"Floyds now, but that house sat on the market for five years before they bought it. You know why?"

Dread filling her stomach, Missy shook her head slowly.

"There was a young woman lived there with her two children; bought the house with money from a divorce settlement. Nice enough young woman, first name was Madeline. Well, she started dating a widower who lived up the road a ways. My husband Frank was still alive then."

Missy nodded.

"We saw the woman and her kids, the widower. They looked like a happy group together. They were always outside on the front lawn playing, her and the kids. One day the man came flying down the street in his car, drove up on the lawn, and hit Madeline with the car. Pinned her up against the tree in the front lawn and killed her. Thank God me and Frank were in Mobile and didn't see it. Never saw the kids again, but heard they went to live with their father."

Ann Marie took a sip of her tea.

"Then there was Cheryl Thomasin, she lived in the house across from your friend."

"Paul, that's Evie's husband, I think he told me about her."

Cindy nodded and leaned forward, "That's two strange deaths just on this side of our street."

"Maybe three strange deaths," Missy whispered softly.

Ann Marie and Cindy both looked at Missy.

"But wasn't it an accident, Missy?" Ann Marie asked softly, "Didn't they say it was an accident?"

Missy looked down at the old wooden floor, "The police said it was, but people around town...they're saying it wasn't."

"Who, Missy? Who's saying that?"

Missy felt her cheeks redden.

Me. I'm saying it.

When Missy raised her eyes, both women were looking at her with concern and kindness. Missy thought their silence spoke volumes. They were all silent for a moment, and then finally Missy spoke again, wanting Ms. Cindy to keep talking.

"Nothing happened at my house though- the realtor has to disclose that kind of thing."

"No, you're right, nothing at your house. Not within recent memory anyway."

Missy started and looked at Ms. Cindy, "I never thought of that."

Cindy paused for a moment, lost in thought.

"On Morgan Bluff behind your house there was also the rumor about the house with the double story porch- you know the one that looks like it should be in the French Quarter?"

Missy nodded; she knew exactly what house it was because she loved the wrought iron second story porch and the old-style gas lights.

"They say a woman hung herself from the second story, but I can't tell you for sure if that one is true."

"There was also the one about the woman in the swamp," Ann Marie interjected, "you know way back there behind Trenise Jones's house."

Cindy nodded, "That one is true. Frank told me it happened when he was a little boy. A man took his wife out there in an old pirogue and left her out in the swamp to die. They had search crews and all back there looking for her. The husband eventually felt guilty and confessed- tried to say it was an accident at first- they found her alive, but she died at the hospital."

Like Evie, Missy thought.

Cindy paused and then continued, "This neighborhood is so old, the whole area is old. It was founded right after New Orleans itself was settled and before that it was Indians. They got mounds back there in the swamp all over the place."

"They call them Native Americans now, Cindy," Ann Marie raised her eyebrows.

Ms. Cindy waved her hand, "You know what I mean."

"Well, what are you saying? You think this was an Indian burial ground?" Missy's skin crawled at the idea. She remembered the old movie, Poltergeist, that she'd watched with her brother when she was about ten and shuddered.

Ms. Cindy shrugged her thin shoulders. "Who's to say, is what I'm saying. Who knows what was here before these houses?"

"But you do know about some of what was here, don't you Cindy?" Ann Marie pressed, "Like about the old church and everything. They got people who say they see lights back there in the Honey Island Swamp and all."

Cindy laughed, "Ann Marie Landry, I'm surprised by you. I didn't think you were one to listen to ghost stories. I'm talking the truth here. Do you believe in the Honey Island Swamp Monster too?"

Ann Marie laughed, "Well, everybody used to tell the old stories about that old preacher and the church that burned down. This was back when I was in high school," she explained to Missy. "And I DO NOT believe in the Swamp Monster."

Both women laughed, and Missy looked bewildered.

"They say it's like a Bigfoot," Ann Marie explained, "call it the Rougarou down in New Orleans."

Cindy waved her hands, "Ridiculous, just a bunch of old Cajuns scaring themselves."

Ann Marie stopped laughing and looked carefully at Cindy.

She pressed on, "But it happened didn't it- the stuff with the church and the preacher? The old graveyard is over there back behind the Longue house. And besides, a bunch of old Cajuns or not, what are we talking about here? Ghosts? A neighborhood curse?"

Missy looked from Ann Marie to Cindy and back again.

Cindy looked at Missy, "I doubt any of your friends would've heard about any of this; they're all new people. Didn't grow up here."

Missy thought for a second.

"That's true, I don't think I know anyone actually from Stone River."

Cindy nodded, "Not a lot of locals left. They build up the land to entice people from all over to come since we're so close to New Orleans. Hell, Trenise Jones' husband commuted all the way to Baton Rouge from here because he liked it so much."

"He was local though."

"That's right but not Trenise, she's New Orleans."

Both women paused and Ms. Cindy took a long drink of her tea.

"The only reason I know as much as I do is because my Frank was local. I got involved in the Women's Guild back in the 70's, and so I was involved in preservation, the museum, the Mardi Gras Krewes...." She trailed off and shook her head sadly, "All that's gone now, except the museum of course, since all of us old ladies who were interested are dying off."

Ann Marie patted Cindy's hand.

"I'll tell you how it was told to me, best as I can remember. Ann Marie, you help me if I leave something out."

Missy pulled her chair in closer to the table, folded her arms on the tabletop, and leaned in.

———

"Fairy tales start with 'Once upon a time' but scary stories usually don't. Who wants to think that what happened, happened at all, much less 'once upon a time?'

This story is true, or true enough, so instead of starting 'once upon a time,' it starts, 'In the early 1700s.'"

Cindy drew in a deep breath and continued.

"In the early 1700s, la Nouvelle-Orleans was a port city owned by the French. It was rough, muddy, full of sickness, greed, enslaved people, pirates. It was a place of both immense power and money, and the kind of giddy happiness that comes with those two things, and intense suffering, weighed heavily on the backs of the slaves and Native Americans who must've wondered what kind of horrific world they had been born into.

Perversely interjected into this atmosphere was the ever-present influence of Christianity and Catholicism. While the archbishops and cardinals lined their coffers and pockets with tithes from the wealthy French traders and businessmen, the poor and enslaved died in the streets from yellow fever, dysentery, syphilis, and influenza.

And among all the greed and death and sickness and profit and human misery there were, of course as there always are, those who wished to reform them all. True religious zealots who believed in reforming both the rich and the poor, who believed that the way to salvation was through piety, poverty, and an iron fist.

New Orleans and Louisiana as a whole was a powerful strategic and economic hold. It belonged first to the Native American Houma population, was stolen from them by France, was sold to Spain, was given back to France, and finally was sold to the United States.

Slaves from Africa and Haiti were brought to work in the plantations and businesses, bringing with them their own religions, music, and beliefs.

As a result, the people who lived in Louisiana were influenced, molded, and shaped by Catholicism, Voodoo, mysticism, and fear of the wilderness in which they resided.

Real life monsters in the forms of alligators and deadly snakes loomed from the waterways. The Mississippi River itself was a domineering force; if you worked on a ship delivering goods to or from the city, make a wrong step and the river would drag you into its muddy depths. The swarms of mosquitos and their constant humming carried yellow fever in their tiny bodies."

Cindy paused.

"What I'm trying to make you understand is that the mixture is a strange one. Power, poverty, civilization and wilderness, modernity and deep mysticism, invaders and indigenous."

Missy nodded slowly and Cindy continued.

"Stone River is a direct result of all of it.

The town of Stone River itself was founded late in 1803, early into Louisiana's adoption by the United States. Before it was actually a town, people referred to it as Halloo, and then later Stone, and then finally Stone River, after the river that ran through the back of the town along the Honey Island Swamp. The river itself served to bring logs down from Mississippi to Lake Pontchartrain, where they were then taken to the port in New Orleans. The name "Halloo" is thought to have come about from the loggers yelling "Hello!" to both each other and the inhabitants of the area, who no doubt came to the riverside to watch the boats and loggers as they made their journey to the lake.

"There were people living in the area for much longer than just 1803, however; the area was always populated as it was and still is situated in a crossroads, just as it is now. Even from the time when it was the Houma who lived on the land, there is evidence that crossroads existed for them to use as trade routes among themselves. The fact that there are multiple burial mounds in the swamps along the Stone River points to the fact that the land that is now Stone River was considered culturally important to the Houma.

Back then, there was one trade road (more of a dirt path than what we would consider any kind of "road") that led from east to west and the other from North to South. Now, I-10 leads from Florida to California and I-59 from Hattiesburg, Mississippi to New Orleans.

Being along a trade route from the beginning, Stone River had a general store where people could trade or sell what they had. The trappers came from the swamps and bayous to sell alligator skin and other animal hides. Houmas sold pottery or textiles for what little they could. The area was poor and rural, so there likely weren't many slaves, but any slave traders traveling north would probably pass through with their carts full of degradation and human misery.

Later, taking advantage of Stone River's situation at the crossroads, a railroad was built to deliver goods both east to west and north to south. The population grew in size, and eventually a group of people who lived in the area petitioned the government in Baton Rouge to incorporate into a town. With that came its first church, led by a man named Emmanuel White."

Missy could almost see what Cindy was talking about. The crossroads, the slaves. She could smell the thick swamp and hear the loggers faintly calling, "Haloo."

Emmanuel White, Missy shuddered and didn't know why.

Cindy continued, almost in a trance.

"White was the son of a Scotch-Irish farmer from Mississippi and a Cajun woman from Boutte la Rose. How his parents would have met in those days could be anyone's guess given the distance between where they were from. Although his mother likely was a Catholic given her presumably Acadian Heritage, his father was probably a Protestant.

Emmanuel White, however, was very much influenced by the Second Great Awakening movement in the United States. When he was interviewed by a local newspaper due to his considerable influence both in the area and extending into the neighboring areas, White reflected on the influence the early traveling Baptist preachers on him and the profound experience of being Baptized by one of these preachers in a river nearby the farm where he was raised.

Not much is known about his education or life as a young man until he appeared in Stone River to raise money to build a church. We do know that he was married twice, his first wife likely having died in childbirth. He had three sons from his first marriage and no children that we know of from his second marriage. All three children and his second wife were with him when he set up his church in Stone River.

From the beginning of his tenure at the church, White was a zealous minister who favored the apocalyptic bent of the early Baptists rather than the peace and understanding of the Methodists or Quakers.

A large majority of what we know as comes from a clipping from a Baton Rouge newspaper which described White and his church as "god-fearing, fervent, and shining example of the evangelical movement in the Southern United States."

The rest of what we know comes from legends, myths, and stories passed down and pieced together."

Cindy held up one long finger.

"The first thing that we know is true is that at some point during the mid-1800s, Emmanuel White's church burned to the ground and there is no longer any record of him.

There is no gravestone bearing his name in his church's graveyard, which is the graveyard that backs up to the Longue house in our neighborhood.

Cindy held up another long finger.

"The second thing we know is true is that there is a tombstone for a Dorothea White, aged 30 at death on July 23rd, 1820. The same date and year are shared by a total of six other people in the graveyard, five women and one man, ranging in ages from 18-55.

In local papers, there is a brief mention of White's church burning to the ground on the night of July 23rd, but there is no mention of White or of the cause of the fire. There are some who say the church burned to the ground by some kind of accident, some say it was an angry member of the church, and some say it was Emmanuel White himself, driven by some kind of religious fervor."

Ms. Cindy closed her fingers into her palm, paused, and took a long drink of her iced tea.

Missy thought in silence about everything Ms. Cindy had shared and shifted in her seat. The day was getting hotter already, and Missy could feel her sweaty legs sticking to the chair she was sitting on.

Ms. Cindy continued.

"We don't know much about the truth of what happened in Emmanuel White's church, so the next part of what I'm going to tell you is mostly based on local legend. The story goes that White's religious zeal manifested itself through speaking in tongues, shouting, shaking. Definitely part of the legend but probably based in truth. He ruled his congregation with an iron fist and believed that the fear of God should be first and foremost. Again, this part of the story is part of the legend, but could it be based in truth?"

Cindy shrugged her narrow shoulders.

"Now, from here on the truth of the story gets more and more questionable. There's no evidence to corroborate any of this. But...they say that White had a lust for women that he disguised as a mistrust of them. You understand what I'm saying?

White started his career as a reverend after living in New Orleans, experiencing its pleasures and temptations, and then seeing the error of his ways. The Reverend White was a frequent in the brothels and barrooms that defined the area. He gambled, drank, and sinned. However White made the transition from sinner to saint is anyone's guess.

Did he do it to take advantage of the poor country people? Did he really believe in what he preached? The truth of his motivations are lost and probably don't really matter, if any of this is even true.

"White quickly took advantage of his position of power in the little church he set up in Halloo. He collected donations from his members, preached that piety, hard work, and following the will of God would lead to everlasting Salvation.

Religious dedication aside, White appears to have been a shrewd businessman. He encouraged business and trade, set up a school, provided assistance to those in need. Halloo grew in size both physically and in its population.

Rich folks from New Orleans started to take notice and bought summer houses. Poor folks from New Orleans saw opportunities and fresh beginnings out of the diseased city."

Cindy rested her chin on her folded hands.

She snickered a little, "Now the next part of the story is probably a total fabrication. Just something school kids and old timers told each other to shock one another. My Frank always said it was all bull."

Ann Marie laughed softly, "But he had heard it all, huh, Ms. Cindy?"

Cindy nodded, "Oh yes, heard it all, told me it was all bull. But Frank never would set foot close to the Longue house, not even when we were invited for the big galas Grant Longue's mama and daddy used to throw. He *always* thought of an excuse why we couldn't go."

Cindy shook her head and smiled.

"And let me tell y'all. Those were *some* parties the Longues threw. The ladies would tell tales about them for weeks afterwards. But I trusted Frank. If he didn't want to go, then we wouldn't go."

Missy felt goosebumps on her arms despite the growing heat on the small back porch. "But why wouldn't he, Ms. Cindy?"

Cindy looked up at the ceiling.

"Lots of reasons I suppose but let me tell you the rest of this story first. Frank and the Longues...that's another whole story."

Taking a long breath in, Cindy continued.

"As White's power grew over all members of his Church, he started taking particular notice and interest in the salvation of the female members. At first, his young wife Dorothea led an all-women's prayer group on Sunday afternoons.

White quickly took over these meetings and singled out certain women who he deemed as in need of extra spiritual guidance.

White used his position of spiritual power to take advantage of any of the women and girls in the church that he chose to. He told them that it was God's will, that their father's and husbands were second to him and that they must submit in order to come closer to God.

While White slowly expanded the numbers of women who he victimized through his religious lies, his wife Dorothea became suspicious. On the morning of July 23rd, she confronted him about the adultery she suspected. White berated her for questioning him, for questioning the will of God, and locked her in the church. He called a special meeting for that evening and left Dorothea locked in the church all day.

While Dorothea sweated and cried, White searched the cemetery next to the small church, searching for broken pieces of gravestones. He collected them, piling them up at the entrance to the church.

In the July heat, Dorothea was sweating and feverish by the time White let the other church members in. She begged for water, for fresh air. White dragged her to the empty space just in front of the pulpit and pointed at her, eyes bulging, sweating, pacing back and forth in front of her.

'You see this creature here? She has sinned!' he screamed.

White's congregation stared back at him, all astounded. 'She has accused me, her husband, of sinning. When in truth it is SHE who has sinned. She is GUILTY of pride, of disobedience.'

Dorothea sobbed, red faced and limp with heat exhaustion. Her hair hung out of its usually neat bun in clumps, and her dress stuck to her skin as her chest heaved. She shook her head, 'Emmanuel, I-'

"But White cut her off, 'She has sinned, and I know that other women have sinned.'

He rattled off the names of different women in the church. 'Come forward, you all sinners, to be purified.'"

Cindy paused and stared at Missy, the fervor of her storytelling momentarily broken.

"Some say these were the women who had refused him, the ones who he tried to force himself on and who resisted.

Slowly, the women whose names were called were pushed forward. The women begged and cried, clutching the hands and arms of their families.

'You four, stand here to be judged!'

White called for candles to be lit, for the congregation to bring forward the stones he had piled at the front of the church, and for them to then take their places on the benches that formed rows in the church.

He launched into a sermon, calling down fire and brimstone upon the women, calling them adulteresses, fornicators, liars, thieves, non-believers. His congregation nodded and screamed their agreement.

As White's tirade reached a fever pitch, he reached down and pulled Dorothea up by her hair.

'The Bible tells us!' White howled, 'that he who is without sin can cast the first stone!'

He looked around, 'I AM without sin! Therefore, I CAST THE FIRST STONE!'

White released Dorothea's hair, reached down for a stone, and smashed it into Dorothea's head as she lay below the pulpit.

Dorothea flailed out wildly and knocked over a candle.

White continued his sermon, pulling the unconscious Dorothea by the hair as he gestured to the crowd in their seats. The other women cried and shook their heads as they stood below the pulpit.

White was oblivious as the candle caught the Bibles piled in the rows of the church. Within minutes, the church filled with smoke. As White railed, a blaze started at the front of the church.

Once they realized the building was on fire, all religious fervor was gone, and the congregation could only think about getting out. White screamed to stay in their seats and accept the punishment of the Lord, but he had lost them.

They pushed and shoved each other towards the door. At the back of the crush of people were White and his victims. As the terrified members of his church fled the burning building, White turned back to face the women, driving them back with his fists toward the flames.

White raced to the front of the church and pulled the door closed, leaving the women inside to burn alive. They screamed from behind the closed door, throwing themselves against it, trying to escape."

Cindy's eyes glowed as she spoke and her voice was filled with anger.

'See what this woman has done? Her last act of wickedness is to burn the church!' he screamed.

The fire raged behind him, casting a shadow over his face that distorted his features into a grotesque mask of something that barely looked human.

'Trust in the LORD! Trust in ME! I am the voice of GOD! I am your GOD now!!'

The church began to burn faster, dark black smoke billowing out into the night air. The screams from inside began to slow.

A man pushed past White and attempted to open the door.

'What have we done?' he screamed, 'Honorine! Honorine!'

White tried to grab the man and pull him back, but he wrenched the door open and rushed inside."

Ms. Cindy paused for a moment, letting the story sink in. She nodded slowly and looked out onto her back lawn.

"Here, the stories start to change. In some, the man, trying to save his wife, burns to death along with her. In others, he dies later of grief and guilt."

Ann Marie heaved a sigh, "The version I heard, the man was going in after his sister."

Ms. Cindy nodded, "There's lots of versions of it I'd guess."

Missy took a sip of her tea and held the cool glass up against her forehead. There wasn't a lot of ice left anymore, but she felt almost feverish in the heat.

"One thing is always the same," Cindy continued after finishing the last of her tea, "And that is that White's final words, his words declaring himself to be greater than god, coupled with the horrific murders, created a curse that turned him into something demonic."

Ann Marie clutched a cross around her neck.

"What happened to White?" she asked.

Cindy waved her hands in the air in front of her, "Your guess is as good as mine. But I can tell you this: his name no longer appears in any documents we have that are associated with the town, and he no longer appears in any newspaper articles. We have records that a fire did indeed happen at the church, the ruins of the church and the graveyard are still on the Longue property, but there's no record of White or his family other than that Dorothea and members of the women's group died in a fire."

"So, you do know for sure they died in the fire at the church?"

Cindy nodded.

"Is any of the rest of it true, Ms. Cindy?" Missy asked.

Cindy shrugged, "The pieces I told you about the town, the church itself, some of the names...those are all true. All of that information is in the Tammanend Parish Museum over in Amite Springs. White's Bible is there even. How it all happened, that's just a story."

"It had to have come from somewhere though, right Cindy?" asked Ann Marie.

Cindy shrugged again and looked sadly at her empty glass of tea. She gave Missy a long look.

"What could it have to do with Evangeline?"

Missy didn't know how to answer that and shifted uncomfortably in her chair.

"I don't know" she finally said. "Nothing. How could it have anything to do with her?"

Cindy and Ann Marie both shook their heads and the three sat in silence as the cicadas whined and the heat and humidity pulsed around them.

—-

Missy left shortly after that, promising to come back for another visit next week. There was nothing earth shattering about the story, nothing so out of the ordinary or different compared to any number of other local stories.

Hell, everyone in Little Lake, Tennessee told the story about the White Lady in the Cemetery, who was waiting for her long-lost love to return home from his days in the Civil War.

Missy laughed a little at the memory when, as preteens, she and her friends had waited half the night In Little Lake Cemetery looking for the White Lady and had all gotten raging cases of poison ivy for their trouble.

Still, Missy thought as she pulled away from Ms. Cindy's house, *all of those women dying, strange circumstances, lights in the swamp, Indian burial ground, swamp monsters, and a crazy preacher.*

She shuddered a little in the air-conditioned car and turned on the radio, searching for a happy distraction.

Chapter Six

Trenise Jones was not one to judge anyone. So, when she raised her hand to wave to Missy Douglas as she drove slowly past, Trenise didn't take it personally when Missy gave a slight wave but didn't return her smile. Missy had a faraway look on her face that Trenise knew all too well: grief, confusion, being lost in your own world.

Trenise had moved to Stone River about 20 years ago with her husband John Jones- Big John to everyone who knew him.

Big John had grown up there, went to school there, got a scholarship to play football at LSU (linebacker of course), finished his degree in Criminal Justice, and got a job as a cop in Baton Rouge.

Big John worked his way up to detective and then was transferred to detective for the State Police. Big John, Trenise, and their daughter Jolie (only two at the time) moved back to Stone River so that Jolie and Trenise could experience the quiet country life. Trenise started back to school on the GI Bill to be a physical education teacher, Jolie went to the Methodist preschool, and Big John worked hard for the state.

For a few years, their life was idyllic.

Trenise looked up at the trees over her head as she walked and took a deep breath in, smelling the air heavy with moisture, telling herself to head home soon before it rained.

Trenise moved slowly and deliberately. This walk was her cool down; she had already been for her morning run.

At 55, Trenise had a medium build, wiry muscles from disciplined exercise, hickory skin; she wore her hair in medium length box braids but was seriously considering giving up on braids and letting her hair go natural. Jolie had kept her hair natural for a few years now and encouraged her mother to do the same.

The last time Jolie was home from Howard, she sat on the edge of the kitchen counter, arms crossed under her small chest, new nose ring, hair combed out, and told Trenise, "Natural is beautiful, mama."

Trenise agreed with Jolie and told her so, but thought the box braids were easier to upkeep, kept her hair out of her face when she was running or coaching.

"When I retire, I'll let it go."

Jolie snorted, "You're never going to retire, Mama."

Trenise passed Evie Nunez's closed up house and felt a tug at her heart. She knew how hard it was to lose a loved one when they were young, and her heart hurt for Evie's husband.

Trenise heard a rumble of thunder and quickened her step.

All of her own experiences before Big John died of a heart attack in their backyard couldn't prepare her for the loss she felt after he'd gone.

John loved their house, their neighborhood. He loved how their yard sloped down to the bayou with the cypress trees forming their own fence in the bayou, making a small pool.

Beyond the cypress trees were miles and miles of swamp. John knew the names of every bird and tree and animal and told her about how the roots that stuck up from the ground around the cypresses were called "knees."

"Almost like they could pull up and walk."

He laughed and pretended to be a Frankenstein, chasing after little Jolie.

Trenise grew up in the heart of New Orleans with her mother and grandmother, surrounded by aunts, uncles, cousins. Her grandmother's little shotgun house (so named because if you fired a shotgun at the house, you'd hit every room from front to back) was squished between rows of other shotguns on a pothole riddled street.

Trenise did well in school but knew there was no way she'd get enough scholarship money to go to college. Her mother and grandmother had only been as far from New Orleans as Baton Rouge, and that was only when they were forced to evacuate by a strong enough hurricane.

Trenise smiled and watched her feet as she walked. When she told them she had enlisted in the Army they stared at her like she had started speaking tongues.

"You serious, Nisey?" her mother reached out and grasped her hand.

"I'm serious, Mama."

The three of them stared at each other. Trenise listened to the old clock her grandmother kept in the small kitchen, barely big enough for two people to stand in, which now hung in her own kitchen, big enough to comfortably fit 20 people: tick, tick, tick.

"Mamaw, you're not going to say nothing?"

Her grandmother, small, wiry, built the same as Trenise was now, leaned forward.

"Girl. You can't join no army. They don't take women."

Trenise laughed out loud at the memory and covered her mouth with her hand.

Trenise's mother and grandmother worked hard, both waitresses at the same small café in the French Quarter, but they were dirt poor. Trenise knew she was loved, knew she always had a place with her mother and grandmother, but she had wanted more than that.

She looked around her neighborhood and wished, for the millionth time, that her grandmother could've lived to see it. Trenise would've pushed her around in a wheelchair, let her smell the fresh air, see the birds and wildlife, let her hear the stillness of the world away from the city.

When Trenise was far away on her first station assignment, Trenise's grandmother died of a stroke in her bed.

Trenise sighed and rested her hands on her hips as she walked. She felt the first fat drops of rain start just as she turned onto her street. As she looked up at the blackening sky, she smiled, as she always did, when she saw her house.

Imagine, she thought to herself, as she always did, *Trenise Lafreniere Jones's house.* Her house was painted bright white with plantation style shutters painted dark blue, a wide staircase and railing, and columns along the wide front porch painted the same bright white as the house.

The door was a deep yellow.

The house itself was raised about seven feet above the ground to allow for flooding, so to Trenise, and to most people who visited, her house looked like a piece of the sky itself nestled in the horizon up against the edge of the swamp.

Trenise's yard backed up to an off shoot of the larger Stone River. It was a relatively fast flowing branch of the river at times, but ultimately it fizzled out before reaching Lake Pontchartrain. Frequently, hunters or fishermen would turn up in her backyard wondering where they were and if they were still in the Stone.

Trenise knew and loved every inch of her house. She had meticulously picked out every paint color, every piece of furniture.

Trenise let her mind wander again to Evie Nunez. To the loneliness and hurt her family must be going through. Trenise still missed Big John every day. Some days she managed to hide from it, to save her tears until she was alone where Jolie wouldn't see.

Now, with Jolie off in D.C., Trenise was alone all the time. Close to retirement age. What few cousins she had were in New Orleans- not far, but Trenise hadn't seen many of them in a long time.

The rain started falling heavier now, and Trenise easily quickened from a walk to a jog. She waved to her elderly neighbor, Ms. Rita, who was watching from her window.

Trenise rolled her eyes when Rita nodded but did not return the wave.

Twenty years as her neighbor and Ms. Rita still didn't quite trust that a family of color had moved in next door.

As she ran up the stairs to her house, making sure to stay on the edge of the stairs where she had applied an adhesive strip, Trenise stopped and whipped her head around to the right.

The rain was pouring now, the sound almost deafening. Thunder rumbled. Despite her age, Trenise's vision was still good: good peripheral vision and distance.

She stood there on her steps, feeling her clothes stick to her body, her hair sticking to her neck and stared into her quickly flooding side yard.

The Jones property was about two acres total, with the house situated in about the middle. On the left of her property was Ms. Rita's, which was about the same size. On the right, however, was just the Honey Island Swamp. Cypress trees, rushes, a tangle of green that was slightly overgrown at this time of year.

In the thick of the growth, Trenise had sworn she had seen a man standing facing her house.

She felt her chest rise up and down, heard the rain and thunder, and stood debating what to do. Trenise didn't see any boat from a lost fisherman. There was no outlet from her street, and her house was at the end of the cul de sac.

No, if someone was standing in there, they had walked in or rode a boat up and pulled it aground. Either way they were trespassing on her property.

She stared into the brush, looking for any movement, but the rain made everything move. Trenise wanted to brush it off and tell herself it had been just the rain and wind making strange shapes of the branches.

She wiped her eyes and slowly walked up the rest of the steps to her porch and out of the rain.

Under the porch itself, the rain was still loud but the sound was muffled. Trenise walked slowly around to the section of porch closest to where she had thought she'd seen the man standing. Just waited, motionless.

She scanned the brush back and forth, back and forth until the rain slacked up.

The memory of Evie Nunez's face floated in front of Trenise's eyes.

No one came out and said what exactly had happened to her, but there were rumors. Rumors that her death wasn't an accident and that the police were, for some reason, not investigating.

Trenise didn't know Evie well, but the death had left her rattled and unnerved.

It wasn't an accident, her heart whispered, though it had no business doing so.

Not taking her eyes from the spot, Trenise slowly walked down the steps again. Her shoes sunk deep in the mud when she got to the yard. She walked slowly and carefully, squishing her tennis shoes into the muck, all the while scanning the spot where the brush met the water behind it.

As she got closer, Trenise could tell there was no one there. She could see into the brush at this point and even if anyone was crouching down she'd have seen them.

Besides, the person she thought she'd seen was taller than the brush. At least six feet, she guessed. Not as big as Big John, but big.

Trenise reached out and moved the brush aside with her hand. There, in a clear patch of ground, she saw large footprints, squished down deep in the mud. Bigger than her own shoes by two sizes she guessed.

"What the hell are you doing Trenise Jones?"

Trenise let out a little yelp and swung around.

"Good lord, Ms. Rita, you scared me about half to death." Trenise shook her head at the elderly woman standing in the street.

Ms. Rita was in her rain boots and was clutching a golf umbrella.

"Is something wrong? I seen you come back out in the rain and all, and I thought something was wrong!"

Trenise slowly walked over to where Rita was standing.

"You didn't see anybody come walking back here, did you?"

"Back here? No, just you." Rita looked Trenise up and down.

Trenise looked back at her for a few seconds and decided Old Ms. Nosy would've noticed if anyone had come strolling past her house, especially a big man.

Trenise drew her breath in and looked around, thinking. Rita watched her.

"Listen, Ms. Rita," Trenise finally said, "you got your phone on you?"

"Yeah, I do, why?"

"Ms. Rita, someone's been on my property. I saw him out of the corner of my eye and there are footprints over there."

"A trespasser?" Trenise almost rolled her eyes at the amount of excitement she heard in Rita's voice.

"Yeah, I think so. You think I could take some pictures of the prints with your phone?"

"Aw, I mean, I think if you have to. I mean..."

Trenise eyed Rita and let out a snort, "I'm not going to steal your phone, Rita. You know where I live for Lord's sake."

Rita looked down and stammered, "I- I didn't mean..."

Trenise snorted, "Yeah you did mean. But that's ok. I mean it *ain't* OK, but...Rita can I use the phone or not, mine's all the way up in the house and the prints are probably fading already."

"Of course, Trenise." Rita unlocked her phone and held it out to Trenise. "But don't go dropping it in no mud, now."

Trenise snorted again, "I'm not going to drop it, Rita."

She walked back over to where the tracks were and carefully took pictures. Just past the first two prints, deep in the mud as though the person had been standing there a while, Trenise noticed lighter prints already starting to wash away.

They seemed to come up one side of the bank from the river, make a semi-circle just outside of the brush, then turn and go back into the brush and down to the river again. Trenise stood in the drizzle and looked at the river.

The Stone River was muddy bottomed. Any pirogue or canoe would form ruts when it came up on shore and would've swirled up the mud close to land. Trenise raised the phone and took more pictures of the banks of the river, where there were no ruts and the edge of the water ran clear.

Trenise stood and stared at the tracks. Whatever tracks in the mud the person had made coming towards the house had washed away. But there were footprints clear as day going away from her house. Tracks that went straight into the swamp, like whoever owned them appeared out of nowhere to stare at her house and then descended into the swamp again.

Trenise's mind conjured up an image of a bull alligator pulling itself along the muddy banks back into the swamp to wait and watch. She shuddered.

"Trenise? You ok back there?"

"Yeah Ms. Rita, I'm ok."

Trenise stood with her hands on her hips and looked out into the bayou.

I guess you could swim off, she thought to herself.

From where she'd been standing on her steps, Trenise could see the brush and the trees, but the bank sloped down in a way that she couldn't have seen the edge of the water. *Plus, I wasn't looking at the water.*

"Damn," she whispered out loud.

Trenise stood for another moment or two, looking off into the direction where the muddy bayou snaked its way into the growth. She couldn't see far. It was thick and tangled and deep green.

Everything dripped water as the rain stopped completely. A few more minutes and the sun would probably be out. An hour or so after that and things would start to dry up again. Trenise heard the soft dripping of water hitting leaves. She heard birds start to chirp.

As she walked back to where Ms. Rita was standing, Trenise made her mind up about what she wanted to do.

"Look, Ms. Rita, you mind if I send myself these pictures real quick?"

"Naw, of course I don't mind. My daughter got me the unlimited data plan so I could get pictures of my grandbabies."

"Mmhmm, I did the same for Jolie when she went off to college."

"Where's she's at again? She down at community college in New Orleans?"

Trenise eyed Rita, trying to keep her cool, "No she's not at community college. She's at Howard in D.C."

As you damn well know.

Trenise snorted again and shook her head. She sent herself the pictures she took and waited to make sure they went through.

"You really saw somebody?"

"Yeah, I really did."

"You calling the cops?"

"Yes, I think I am, Ms. Rita."

"You know a bunch of cops still, from when John..."

Trenise nodded, "Maybe not a bunch anymore, lots of John's buddies retired, but I know a few."

Trenise's heart began its whisper again. Slow and steady, over and over, her heart whispered Evie Nunez's name.

—-

Within an hour, Trenise had a young patrolman pull up in front of her house. Ms. Rita had long been home by then, no doubt spreading the word about a trespasser. Trenise was sitting on her porch, feet up on an ottoman, glass of cold iced tea on the small table next to her chair. She had changed out of her soggy clothes and into a dry pair of athletic shorts and a faded Stone River High School Girls Basketball tee shirt.

"Are you Ms. Jones?"

"Yes, I am. And may I ask your name?"

"I'm officer Duane Thompson, ma'am. Lieutenant Bordelon sent me out to talk to you about a possible trespasser. Can I come up?"

Trenise waved him up and tried not to raise an eyebrow at *Lieutenant* Bordelon.

She knew all about Bordelon. About her own age, he had started out in the Stone River Police Department about the same time Big John had started with the State Troopers.

Stone River wasn't *quite* known for being corrupt, but it wasn't *quite* known for being on the up and up either.

Thompson looked like he was barely out of high school.

He took out a small notebook and a pen and asked Trenise to describe what had happened.

As Trenise spoke, Thompson nodded and took notes. Trenise watched him. While she never worked for the police herself, she had been around enough cops to know there were plenty of decent ones and plenty of rotten ones.

She took measure of Duane Thompson and wondered which one he was.

"Would you mind showing me the pictures?"

Trenise scrolled through the pictures on her phone.

"Would it be ok if I sent these to myself?"

"Of course."

Trenise watched the young man as he sent himself the pictures, closed his notebook, and handed her back her phone.

"Well, Ms. Jones, do you have no trespassing signs posted back there?"

"I do."

Thompson nodded, "Unfortunately, there's not a whole lot I can do given you can't give me a description of either the person or a mode of transportation. Probably it was just somebody looking for some shelter during the rain. I'm going to file a report though just so there's a record."

Trenise nodded, "Ok, Officer Thompson, that all sounds fine to me."

Thompson looked at Trenise for a few seconds, "I'd definitely remember to lock your doors Ms. Jones."

Thompson's tone was even. There was no condescension, but not a whole lot of concern either.

Trenise chuckled, "I always do." She followed Thompson down her steps and to the street in front of her house where his car was parked.

"Here's my card Ms. Jones. If you need anything or have questions, just call me."

Perfunctory, Trenise thought and looked at his broad back as he stepped in front of her, into the street to his car. *This guy doesn't give two shits.*

"Thank you, Thompson, I will."

Thompson climbed into his car, nodded to Trenise while he radioed in, and pulled off.

Trenise watched him go and then turned back to face her house. She looked to the right, to the spot where she'd seen the man standing, to where there were footprints that came from nowhere but led back to the water, and where there was no sign of a boat.

Her heart whispered to her again. It whispered over and over throughout the afternoon.

It told her that something wasn't right. That something bad was happening and that it involved Evie Nunez.

Trenise wasn't a woman who was easily spooked. She'd grown up in one of the roughest neighborhoods in New Orleans, had served in the military, was married to a cop, buried a husband as a young woman, raised a child on her own. But something wasn't right, and Trenise Jones couldn't quite put her finger on it.

Chapter Seven

Alessandra Sanchez was waiting for her mother to leave the trailer the trailer so she could be alone. She didn't mind being alone. She was used to it. She closed her eyes and listened to the music playing on her phone, ignoring her mother bustling around the trailer getting ready to leave for work for the night.

Alessandra had spent the majority of her life fending for herself, being alone, or spending time with whatever group of misfit kids would hang around with her. Her father died in a car accident when she was young, and her mother never remarried or dated anyone.

Her mom worked cleaning houses and office buildings. She took whatever extra work she could, leaving Alessandra with various family members all day and sometimes into the evening hours.

The small trailer they moved into when they first came to Stone River was on a short street in what technically was the beginning of trailer park. As of now, the lots were big, and there was a good distance between each trailer.

Their street had one other trailer on it that had been unoccupied since they moved in. Alessandra was glad it was. She didn't like having too many people close to her, and she valued the newfound and unexpected privacy.

When she started her sophomore year at Stone River High School last fall, Alessandra tried to numb herself to being in an unfamiliar place.

She pretended to be tough so people would leave her alone, but she wasn't anywhere near as tough as she pretended to be. Most of the time she felt like a coward, and a lot of the time she felt alone and scared.

They moved from Texas to Louisiana because of what happened to Alessandra a few years ago when her mom, Mariella, was at work. Alessandra hadn't told her mother what her aunt's boyfriend had done until last fall when her little cousin said he did the same thing to her.

Alessandra squeezed her eyes shut, forcing herself to stop thinking about it.

Don't, she thought, *don't go there.*

Alessandra shifted her legs to get more comfortable as she lay on the small couch, eyes closed and tried to focus on the music in her headphones.

She sighed as her brain returned right back to the same thought pattern.

They moved to Stone River because her mother's cousin had a friend who owned a cleaning business and said she could get Mariella a job and fix her up with a place to stay in a good school district for Alessandra.

Mariella didn't involve the police in what had happened to Alessandra. Instead, she let her brother, Alessandra's uncle Berto, take care of her aunt's boyfriend.

"You don't have to worry about him anymore, Miha, your Uncle Berto took care of it. We can make a new start now."

Alessandra was silent, thinking that if the same thing had happened to some of the girls at school, their parents would've gone to the police. Alessandra was young, but she was old enough to know why they couldn't tell the police.

"Your Tio Berto took care of it." Mariella repeated, lips trembling.

Alessandra didn't really mind the move so much. She didn't have many close friends, aside from a few stoners who she occasionally joined behind the gym to smoke before class.

On her first day at Stone River High, no one spoke to her all morning. Alessandra was simultaneously overjoyed at being left alone and devastated by the crushing loneliness.

Finally, halfway through the day, a boy sitting next to her, leaned over and told her, "Anyone warned you about the swamps yet?"

Alessandra laughed and shook her head, "Uh, no, what about them?"

The boy leaned in even closer whispering, "About the bodies people dump out there. The Honey Island Swamp is like, the most haunted place in Louisiana."

Alessandra had arched her eyebrows at him, unsure if he was being serious or just trying to scare the new kid, "I thought New Orleans was the most haunted, you know the LaLaurie Mansion and everything."

The boy arched his eyebrows back, "You know about that? Nah, that's not the most haunted. Out here in the sticks is the worst."

"Stephen what are you telling her?" a girl sitting behind them had chirped.

"About the bodies in the swamp."

"You're such a weirdo." The girl, who Alessandra later found out was named Lexie, laughed and looked Stephen up and down.

Then she turned her gaze to Alessandra and remarked, "Never mind, you look like you would be into bodies in swamps."

A group of girls sitting around Lexie laughed.

Alessandra turned around and leaned closer to her, "You're right. I AM into it. I'm always looking for places to hide bodies."

When Lexie looked horrified, as Alessandra had intended, Alessandra turned back to Steven and said, "Tell me more about it, dude."

Steven told her about people murdering wives and girlfriends and burying them in the swamp, about secret societies of politicians who worshipped the devil, about Indian spirits out for revenge.

Other kids eavesdropped and chimed in with their own versions of the story. The story that was the most consistent was the one about the Preacher who murdered his wife and burned a group of women alive in his church.

"The graves are all still there back in a little cemetery behind that big subdivision," Stephen whispered as he and Alessandra worked on adjacent computers in the computer lab.

Alessandra pushed the memory away. It was summertime now, and she didn't want to think about school.

Alessandra's mother continued to work all day and often into the night when they moved to Stone River. She'd drive into New Orleans to clean people's mansions on St. Charles Avenue and then clean the small offices in nearby Slidell in the evening when the offices were closed. On the weekends she'd drive to Baton Rouge, Biloxi, or back into New Orleans to work with a crew of other women to clean the big office buildings. She offered for Alessandra to go with her to make some extra money, but Alessandra refused.

She didn't judge her mother for cleaning houses and offices, but she just couldn't do it. Her mother seemed to understand and silently accepted Alessandra's refusal just like she accepted everything else from Alessandra:

the hair, the music, the nose ring, the attitude. Her mother accepted it all and said nothing. Sometimes Alessandra wished she would say something, anything, give her any kind of reaction. But never. Only silent acceptance.

Alessandra thought opened her eyes and focused on her phone.

"I might be gone until midnight, miha," Mariella said from the kitchen.

"Ok, Mami," Alessandra responded, her voice bored.

"There's leftover chicken and rice in the fridge, ok? I'm going now. I love you," Mariella stood in the doorway between the kitchen and the small living room, hoping her daughter would look up at her.

"Ok, mami." Alessandra stared at her phone as her mother walked out of the door and closed it behind her. Alessandra turned off the music she had been listening to and instead used her phone to watch an interview on YouTube with her favorite band, Cattle Decapitation, where they talked about their objections to the meat packing industry.

"I'm a vegetarian, Mami," Alessandra said out loud after the front door had closed; she rolled her eyes and took a sip of her Coke.

When she heard her mother's car pull out of the narrow gravel driveway, she sat up on her elbow, then got up to peer out of the window. When she saw the car pull close to the main road, she went to her room, packed a bowl, opened her window a crack. She took a massive pull and blew the smoke out the window, then went back to lay down on the couch.

She watched video after video, a rabbit hole of distraction and escape.

During her second hour of scrolling, above the talking and the music, Alessandra heard a loud bang outside the trailer. The walls were relatively thin, so any falling branch or animal could make a decent amount of noise.

Alessandra paused the interview she was watching, now with the singer of Agoraphobic Nosebleed, and listened. Nothing.

BANG. This time it was loud enough that Alessandra jumped and dropped her phone on the floor. *What the fuck,* she thought, heart hammering in her chest. She sat up on the couch, reached down and picked up her phone, paused it again, listening. Nothing.

She sat for a few minutes, listening. *What if it's fucking Trent.*

Her chest heaved and she clutched her phone in her hand for a few minutes more. She shrugged and pressed play on her video again.

BANG.

This time Alessandra got up off the couch and stood in the middle of the room. From what she could tell, it sounded like it was coming from the front of the trailer close to the front door. *Maybe something fell on the porch?*

Alessandra walked over to the door and pulled back the small curtain that hung over the window in the top portion of the door.

Nothing. The sun was setting behind the trailer casting a long shadow over the porch and small front yard. She squinted and strained to see into the growing darkness past the porch, even reaching over and flicking on the porch light, but she couldn't make anything out.

She pressed her forehead up against the glass and looked to one side and then the other, turning her head to see up and down the small porch that was attached to the trailer. Nothing. Just the two small folding chairs and her mother's potted plants. She titled her head down a little to look at the front steps.

"What the fuck?" she said out loud to herself. There were three large rocks, each bigger than a baseball, resting on each of the three steps leading to the trailer. All in a perfect row like little ducks.

Well someone put them there, she thought rationally. *Dropped them more likely, that's what the bang was. Why would someone do that?*

She stared stupidly at the rocks, beginning to sweat, feeling the hairs on her arm and neck start to raise with goosebumps.

Whoever put them there is probably still there and can see right in at you, you asshole. She let the curtain go and quickly backed away from the door at that thought.

Her mind raced.

Do I call mom? Do I call the cops? Do I go out there and tell whoever it is to fuck off?

Alessandra went to the small closet in the little hallway that connected the kitchen and living room to the two bedrooms.

BANG. Alessandra jumped and then froze. *That sounded like the roof.* She stood frozen, hand on the doorknob of the closet and listened. Nothing.

Then, a quieter *thunk. Thunk. Thunk. Thunk.*

Her eyes darting side to side, Alessandra stood, unable to move, feeling sweat trickling down her back.

They're on the roof.

Bhere was no way to get up on the roof except with a ladder.

"What the fuck." She paused, not wanting to call the cops, not wanting to cave in to whoever was fucking with her. She didn't want whoever it was to know they scared her.

Thunk, Thunk, thunk. Whoever was up there was pacing back and forth across the roof.

Alessandra stood for one more second. *Time to call the pigs.*

She opened her phone and frantically pressed the small circle button at the bottom of the screen.

"No, no, no you piece of shit."

The phone was old and lost its charge if left unplugged and in use for too long. She'd been too stoned to remember to plug it in while she watched YouTube, so of course, it had died. Alessandra paused and listened. Nothing.

She dropped the phone and ran back to the hallway, back to her original plan. Alessandra dug wildly through the closet until she found an old black bag with large shoulder straps.

When she had inherited the car from her grandmother, her Tio Berto had gifted her an updated set of tools to change a tire if she needed to, and those she kept in the trunk of her car.

But he had also given her a different set of tools which were in the bottom of the closet in the black bag.

Right before they moved, Tio Berto had come to visit Alessandra and Mariella. After he checked the car's engine to make sure it was ok to drive it all the way to Stone River, he took the black bag from his truck and handed it to her.

"They were your grandfather's tools. You won't need them, Sandy, but keep them just in case."

Her uncle had explained what each tool was, screwdrivers, wrenches, a hammer, and something called a breaker bar.

"To break off a bolt," her uncle explained.

The breaker bar was a two-foot-long piece of round metal with a socket at the end.

"Or to break a motherfucker's arm if he fucks with you."

Alessandra had laughed at the time, but Berto just shrugged.

"I'm serious, Sandy. Don't let nobody fuck with you. Your Mami and I will help you when we can, but nobody's going to help you but you."

He had hugged her tight and kissed the top of your head, "You call me if you need me."

Standing now in the little hallway, Alessandra wished more than anything that she could call Berto.

Instead, she pulled out the breaker bar.

"Perfect." Alessandra whispered and then stood up listening.

Nothing. She stood listening again.

Chk, chk, chk, chk.

Alessandra could feel the hair on her neck raise at the sound.

Chk, chk, chk, chk.

She stepped out of the short hallway and back into the living room. She squinted toward the front door.

Chk, chk, chk, chk.

The noise was someone turning the locked doorknob on the front door side to side.

Alessandra froze. She felt her chest heave and she heard a different noise coming from down the hallway.

Scrriiittch. Sccrriiiiiitttccchhhhh.

"Oh Jesus." Alessandra's eyes darted back and forth, and she waffled about what to do. *Were there two people?*

Scriiitttcchhhhh. Scccrittttttccchhhhh.

Alessandra tip toed through the living room and back into the hallway.

Scrrriiittttcchhhhhhhhh.

The sound was clearly coming from her room, the sound of something scratching across the glass of her window. The lights in the hallway and her bedroom were both off and her bedroom faced the small backyard which, Alessandra figured, was still relatively illuminated by the setting sun.

If she could peek around the corner into her room, she could see what was making the sound and maybe not be seen.

Somewhere in her mind she still thought this was possibly stoned-out paranoia, that maybe it was just a tree scratching the roof in the window, but that felt like grasping at straws at this point.

If it WAS Trent, she'd be able to see him and then could actually do something about it. Being an asshole at school is one thing, but trespassing on someone's property and trying to terrify them was something else.

Alessandra took a big breath in, held it, and then slowly leaned her right eye into her room.

There, standing in her window, was the shape of a man. The window wasn't big enough to show his whole body, but his forehead was pressed up against the top of the glass. The sun silhouetted him, casting a dark shadow over his face. Alessandra couldn't tell if it was Trent or not, but it was clearly a man. She let her breath out and stood frozen, staring. She couldn't tell where the man was looking, but he slowly turned his forehead in her direction and raised his arms out to his sides.

Alessandra flew down the hallway, snatched her car keys off the kitchen counter, opened the front door, and flung herself toward her car. She immediately tripped over the rock on the top stairs and fell sprawling on her stomach into the gravel path that served as a driveway.

She popped back up onto her feet, but looking at her car, she skidded and lost her footing again, landing on her back.

There, standing on top of her car, was the same man who had been at her window.

She still couldn't quite make his face out in the growing darkness, but he moved his head down as though to look at her. Alessandra scrambled back up and took off at a run down her street toward the main road.

For the first time since moving to Stone River, Alessandra wished desperately that there were more people living close to her.

Her chest pulled as she ran in the darkness of her street toward the streetlight on the corner. She looked over her shoulder, saw the man still standing on her car, arms outstretched again, palms turned up toward the sky, and tried to run faster.

She could see cars passing on the main street and started to scream.

"Help! Help me! Help!!"

She looked behind her again and the man was gone. Her legs pumping wildly as she ran, she also raised her hands above her head waving, hoping to catch someone's eye. She skidded to a stop again as she reached the streetlight that illuminated the main road leading into the large and well-to-do subdivision that was behind the section of trailers.

She looked behind her again.

Nothing.

Alessandra slowed to a jog, moving down the main road toward the nearest house, looking for a car or a person she could ask for help.

She heard a car behind her and snapped her head around and started waving her arms again, and yelled, "Stop! Please I need help!"

The truck was older and black, and Alessandra could see the shape of a man inside.

For a moment, her heart thumped in her chest as she looked around to see if anyone else was driving by.

Wary of both what she had run away from and the man in front of her, Alessandra took a step back off the road into the grass, closer to the drainage ditch that ran along the street.

She could see the man clearly now- late 40s, longish graying hair pulled back in a low ponytail, long graying beard, septum piercing, intricate tattoos on both arms and hands.

The man furrowed his eyebrows, "What's up, kid? Are you ok?"

Alessandra took a ragged breath and spoke as quickly as she could, "No, I'm not. A man was trying to get in my house, and my phone died. I ran outside, and he was on my car."

Her voice sounded far away, small, and broken.

"Shit, seriously?" he reached down, and Alessandra heard the doors unlock.

"Get in, I'll call the cops."

Alessandra shifted her weight from one foot to the other and looked down the street, "I..."

"I'm not going to hurt you, kid. Look," he reached up onto the dashboard where his phone was resting, "I'm calling 911, and I'll put them on speaker. Then you can get in."

The man dialed and pressed speaker, holding the phone up so Alessandra could see.

"9-1-1, what's your emergency?" The man turned and raised his eyebrows.

Alessandra opened her mouth to speak, but nothing would come out.

"A kid just flagged me down and said someone was trying to break into her house, chased her away from her car and everything."

"Can you see anyone, sir?"

"Nah, but she's really scared."

"Is she hurt?"

The man looked at Alessandra, "You hurt, kid?"

Alessandra shook her head no.

"I see you're on Magnolia Loop is that right?"

"Yeah, that's right. Kid, seriously, you should get in the car just in case. I'll keep the operator on the line."

Alessandra thought about the figure standing on top of her car as she had run and decided she'd rather take her chances with the guy in the truck.

"An officer is on the way, sir."

"Look can you stay on the line with us? She's nervous."

"Of course I'm fucking nervous. Some psycho just was jumping all over my trailer like some shit from Scream."

> The man looked taken aback for a second and then burst out laughing, "Sorry, kid, sorry." He stopped laughing when Alessandra scowled at him.

"Are you still there sir?" the voice of the operator barked through the phone.

"Yeah, we're still here." The man turned back to look at Alessandra again and raised his eyebrows, "Do you know the guy? Like a kid from school being an asshole or something?"

Alessandra thought for a second.

Did she know him? She assumed it was Trent but didn't consider that it could be someone else she recognized.

She hadn't really gotten a good look at the guy's face, so she couldn't say either way if she knew him or not. She let out a long sigh and covered her face with her hands.

"I don't know." She rubbed her eyes and looked at the man.

He looked concerned and opened his mouth to say something, then seemed to think better of it and shook his head.

Alessandra studied the man sitting next to her. She didn't know about the creep who had harassed her, but *this* guy did look familiar.

"Hey, do I know you from somewhere?" she blurted out.

"I don't know, kid. Maybe." He turned his head and looked in his rearview mirror, "Here's comes our friends."

The operator chirped, "The officer is arriving at the scene, so I'm going to hang up now."

Alessandra looked in the mirror on her side of the car and saw the blue and red lights flashing but didn't hear a siren. The cop pulled up behind them as Alessandra and the man were both climbing out of the truck.

"Get back in the truck!" the cop yelled.

"What? We're the ones who called!" The man yelled back, throwing his hands up.

Alessandra put her hands up to about her shoulders and climbed back into the cab of the truck. The man climbed back in also, shaking his head and looking in the rearview mirror.

"Fucking pigs, man."

Alessandra grinned, in spite of her fear, and pointed a finger at the man.

"I do fucking know you." She said grinning even more at him.

The man next to her laughed and threw his hands up just as the cop came and knocked on his window. The man in the driver's seat looked at him and scoffed.

"Oh man not this fucking asshole."

"You know the cop?" Alessandra asked.

"Unfortunately," the man responded as he rolled down the window, "Took you long enough, man. Some psycho was trying to break into this girl's house."

"You back getting into trouble? Someone told me you had cleaned up." The cop leaned against the door and peered in, "I didn't know you were into underaged girls."

"I was just driving by, and she waved me down for help."

The cop chuckled, "Mike DiCostanza to the rescue, huh?"

Alessandra's mouth fell open. *This is the weirdest night of my life.*

"Mike DiCostanza," she whispered.

The man next to her looked at her and smiled a little.

"And who are you?" the cop asked, peering in through the window at her.

"Alessandra Sanchez."

"Ok can you step out of the car young lady?" he gestured back to his cruiser and then turned to Mike, pointing at him.

"You stay here."

Mike nodded, and Alessandra climbed out of the truck, not believing what was happening. She was coming down from the adrenaline rush after her run from the trailer and felt weak and strange. Meeting Mike DiCostanza, a New Orleans heavy metal icon, the way that she just did was compounding the weirdness.

The cop beckoned her towards his car and motioned for her to sit on the hood. He stood over her looking down, arms folded.

"What happened now?" he said grimacing.

Alessandra stared up at him. *What was his problem?*

Alessandra started with sitting on the couch watching YouTube after her mom left for work, skipping the massive hit of weed for obvious reasons, and stopped at the point when she flagged down, of all people, *Mike DiCostanza.*

She noticed as she spoke that the cop didn't write anything down, but nodded, said, "Mmhmm" in a few spots, and continued to grimace.

Alessandra also noticed cars passing, slowing down to look at them. She stopped speaking and waited for the cop to say something. He stood staring at her, arms folded across his chest.

"What, you don't believe me?"

The cop laughed and put his face close to hers, "Now I didn't say that. But when you walked over to my car...honey, you REEK of marijuana."

Alessandra stared at him.

"You have any on you?"

"No, I don't."

The cop nodded and pursed his lips. "You're not under arrest, but I'm going to put you in the back of my car."

"What?? Are you fucking serious?"

The cop nodded again, "Oh yes, young lady. Until I figure out what's going on here."

"You gotta be kidding me! I didn't do anything and some asshole was trying to break into my house. You're not even going to go look for him? Don't you want to know what he looks like?"

"Lower your voice, young lady. You said you can't give me a description because it was too dark. Besides, you told me you live in a trailer, not a house."

The cop chuckled and Alessandra ignored the insult, trying to reason with him.

"But I think I might know who it was. There's this idiot I go to school with who's been following me around. His name is Trent Longue."

The cop burst out laughing, "Girlie, if you think Trent Longue would fool with a girl like you, you MUST still be stoned."

Alessandra stared at him and sputtered, trying to find a different line of reasoning, "But...but...look at the scratches on my arms from where I fell..."

"I'm not saying you didn't fall...."

"Hey you ok, kid?"

Alessandra and the cop both turned to look at Mike, who had gotten out of his truck and was standing next to his door.

Mike threw his hands up and bobbed his head, "You not going to look for this guy?"

The cop pointed at him again, "I told you stay in your truck."

"You're not even going to call her mama?"

"I'll deal with you in a minute," the cop raised his voice and turned an ugly shade of red.

He turned back to Alessandra, "Stand up, I'm going to pat you down."

Alessandra stood up, holding her arms out in a T shape, shaking her head. "This is un-fucking-real."

The cop laughed, "I can see you've been patted down before."

Alessandra didn't respond and the cop laughed again as he patted.

"Ok, I'm not arresting you, but go ahead and take a seat in the back." He took her by the elbow and led her to the back seat of the cruiser.

"What the fuck are you doing, dude! What are you arresting her for?" Alessandra heard Mike yell as the cop closed the door.

The cop walked back to Mike's truck and Alessandra couldn't hear anything else. She peered through the bars separating the back seat from the front and could see the two of them talking.

She could see that they were going back and forth and finally Mike opened his car door, turned and waved to her. Alessandra waved back glumly as Mike got in his truck and drove off, flipping the cop off behind his back as he drove past.

The cop came back to the car and opened the front door.

"I'm guessing your parents aren't home?"

Alessandra shook her head, "My dad's dead. My mom's at work."

The cop nodded, "Give me her number so I can call her."

Alessandra knew better than to argue and rattled off Mariella's number. Her chest heaved with anger as she listened to the cop tell Mariella that he had "picked up Alessandra for causing a disturbance" and that he was holding her in his car because she smelled like marijuana.

Mid-conversation with Mariella, a voice came over the cop's radio.

Alessandra didn't know what all the codes were that the dispatcher used, but the cop quickly cut the conversation with Mariella short, telling her he'd call back shortly.

He turned on his sirens and flew off into the subdivision causing Alessandra to fly back into the seat.

"What the fuck is going on?" she yelled.

"Shut up, kid." The cop said calmly.

Alessandra looked out her window as they passed Evangeline Nunez's house and turned down the opposite side of the street. The cop pulled in behind another cop car.

"Stay here," here he told Alessandra and quickly exited his car.

"Where the fuck am I going to go?!" she screamed after him.

Chapter Eight

Earlier that evening, four streets away from where Trenise Jones stood in her kitchen feeling that things weren't right, and about two miles from where Alessandra Sanchez laid on her couch, Missy Douglas stood in *her* kitchen cooking a hotdog in a pan while she chatted on the phone first with Sophie and Johnny and then with Wes.

After both phone calls, as she sat alone at the kitchen table to eat, Missy felt as though her heart would break.

When Evie was alive, on nights like this when Wes was gone, she would walk down to Missy's house after Johnny and Sophie Ann went to bed and the two of them would sit on the porch and eat cheese and crackers and gossip. It helped Missy through the day and the evening knowing that she wasn't totally alone; even if Evie couldn't make the short walk to Missy's house, Missy knew Evie was down on her side of the street if she needed anything.

The feeling of being alone was crushing.

Missy and Wes had neighbors on both sides of them. On the left were the Gilligans- retirees who spent most of the summer touring the country's National Parks in their RV. On the right was a house that had been for sale for about six months.

The Gilligans were very nice and Missy and Wes both liked them very much, but they kept to themselves for the most part. On the other side of the Gilligans were the Marquises, who stuck their noses up at Missy and Wes when they learned Wes worked on an oil rig. The Marquises also didn't like the Gilligans and so didn't like Missy and Wes because they DID like the Gilligans.

Evie and Missy had laughed about the little neighborhood drama, and it was Evie who made Missy feel better when the Marquises' grandson marched up to Missy and said, "My grandma says your house looks like you're always having a garage sale." Missy had been mortified; Sophie Ann's playhouse, Johnny's basketball hoop, and bikes, scooters, big wheels, and strollers were lined up at the end of the driveway closest to the house.

"My mom and stepdad buy it all for them!" Missy had moaned, laughing.

Evie had laughed and laughed, "Oh yeah, imagine that....kids having toys? Grandparents buying presents?" She had rolled her eyes, "Stuck up assholes! Just ignore them. I can't even imagine what they say about all of Paul's lawn equipment."

Hot dogs eaten, Missy washed her face and put on her pajamas. She sat with a glass of wine half watching a silly reality tv show and half remembering the conversation about the Marquis grandson.

The spot on the couch where she was sitting faced the tv, which was mounted above a small fireplace; next to the fireplace was a sliding glass door that led out to the small concrete patio and the half acre or so that made up their backyard.

Missy smiled a little to herself, *what was the grandson's name anyway? Mitchell? Marcus?* She turned her head slightly, away from the tv, and looked out the sliding glass door trying to remember the Marquis boy's name.

The sun was setting and most of the backyard was dark except for a few spots that shone in the reddish glow. She was pretty sure it was Mitchell.

The sunlight faded by the second, and as the light shifted, Missy clearly saw the figure of a man standing about five feet away from the edge of the patio, close to where there was a huge azalea bush.

Missy felt her stomach drop and heart hammer simultaneously as she jumped up, dropping her glass of wine on the carpet. She stared at the spot where she'd seen the man, but the sun was down enough now that the whole backyard was black except for a few spots that had only a little dim light left.

Her heart beat against her chest so badly it hurt. Whoever was out there could definitely see her since the living room light was on. Her eyes flitted to the lock on the door, which, thankfully, was in the down, locked position.

Darting to the kitchen, Missy grabbed her phone, unlocked it, and pulled up the phone icon.

Missy paused and sidestepped back to the living room.

I DID see someone, she thought, trying to calm herself down, *or was it the light?*

She bit her lip and thought about what an idiot she'd feel like if she called the cops about a shadow. She took a deep breath and stepped forward to flick on the light switch for the patio light.

Her mind didn't process at first that there was still a man standing there, clear in the porch light, right at the edge of the patio. Missy backed up as she stared at him, trying to process what she was seeing. He was youngish, about her own age, wearing dark pants and shirt.

She couldn't see his face as the light cast by the patio light wasn't strong. His arms were at his side, but as Missy backed up, mouth open, he raised his hands and arms open wide, as if to say, *Come here to me.*

The gesture was enough to force Missy to move. She bolted out of the living room, wildly shaking hands dialing 911 as she went.

"911 What's your emergency."

"There's a man standing in my backyard right by my window. I have no idea who it is."

"Ok. Ma'am are the doors to the house locked?"

"Yes, but it's a sliding glass door he's next to, he could break in relatively easily."

"Ok ma'am, stay on the line with me, an officer is on the way."

"Ok," Missy positioned herself in the middle of the hallway where the bedrooms were, directly between Johnny and Sophie Ann's rooms.

It was silent except for her own breath. Missy assumed the man was still in the back, but there was no reason to think he couldn't walk around to the front. Missy's chest tightened at the thought. Wildly, she thought of Evangeline.

You know it wasn't an accident, Missy's heart screamed, *you know it wasn't.*

"Are you there?" The 911 operator sounded calm and cool.

"Yes, I'm here."

Missy stood frozen, trying to listen. She pressed her back up against the wall of the hallway and stifled a scream as she heard scraping on the window in Sophie Ann's room.

"Are you still there?" The operator asked.

"I'm here," Missy whispered as she opened the door to Sophie's room, "I think he's trying to get in a window."

Missy felt like her head was moving in slow motion as she turned toward the window on the opposite wall.

Why the fuck are the curtains open she thought stupidly, *I know I closed them.*

There in the window, silhouetted by the streetlight in front of the house, was the same man. Dark pants, dark shirt. Missy couldn't see his face because of the shadow from the streetlight, but as Missy stood there frozen in the doorway, he raised his arms again in the same gesture: open arms, fingers spread wide.

Missy screamed until the hair on the back of her arms stood up. She lunged backwards out of the room.

"I called the cops!" Missy shrieked.

"MA'AM? MA'AM?" from far away, Missy heard the operator's voice and realized she'd dropped her phone. She scooped it up and sprinted down the hallway toward the kitchen, which led out to the garage.

Get the bat, the thought was as cool and calm as the 911 operator's voice, cutting through her panic, *get the bat out of the trunk.*

Missy darted through the kitchen, not daring to look to her right toward the windows. She pulled open the door to the garage.

"Ma'am are you hurt?" She heard the operator yell.

"No, I'm not but please hurry!" Missy yelled back. She flung herself towards the plastic trunk where she knew the baseball bat was and threw out old life jackets, balls, extension cords, until she finally found it.

Missy snatched the bat from where it was resting at the bottom of the trunk and raised it over her shoulder, spinning around wildly. The overhead light had switched itself on automatically and Missy kept her eyes on the small windows that faced the street.

"MA'AM?" she heard the operator say again.

Her chest hurt with adrenaline as she faced the small window in the garage.

Where the fuck are the cops, she thought.

There was a small window in the garage that faced the front yard. It was small and high up, just enough to let in a little sunlight during the daytime.

Now, all Missy could see was blackness. She strained to listen but could only hear her own rattling breath.

Finally, she saw blue lights flashing through the tiny window and heard a man's voice yell, "Tammanend Sherrif's Department!"

"I'm in the garage!" she screamed.

"Stay where you are!" the voice yelled back.

Missy tucked the baseball bat under her arm and reached down for the phone.

"Hello?" she said.

"Ma'am, the officer just radioed that he's there at your house. His name is Officer Thompson. Stay where you are."

"Ok." Missy breathed.

"I'm going to stay on the line with you until the officer is with you."

"Ok." Missy said again.

"Ma'am? This is Officer Thompson ma'am," Missy heard the officer's voice outside the garage door, "Can you open the door?"

Missy reached behind her shoulder and pressed the button to open the door. She saw the officer's black shoes and dark pants first as the door opened and brought the bat back in front of her body for a moment thinking it was the same man who she had seen through the windows.

The officer bent down and ducked under the opening door.

Missy heaved a sigh of relief at the sight of the Stone River Police Department logo emblazoned on his shirt.

Officer Thompson was sweating and out of breath. He held up a hand and pressed the button on the radio attached to his shoulder. "I had a visual on a possible suspect. Fled on foot, but I lost him around the house. Send backup."

"You saw him?" Missy asked.

The officer nodded.

"Fast son of a gun," he breathed out heavily, "I was right on top of him, but he must've cut into those woods."

Thompson shook his head and looked bewildered. "I lost him."

Missy shook her head, "What the hell..."

As they were talking, Missy saw what she assumed were headlights light up the driveway. She saw blue and red lights reflecting off of Sophie Ann's playhouse and heard a car door slam and a muffled voice over a radio. Missy leaned the baseball bat up against the wall.

"You can go inside if you're ok," the cop said, "I'll be in to talk to you in a few minutes."

Before Missy could turn and go inside, another police officer came around the corner of her garage. He was at least twice Thompson's age, balding, out of shape, and looked somewhere between completely unconcerned and annoyed.

"This guy's having a busy day, huh?" he said loudly.

He looked Missy up and down, "You the homeowner?"

"Yes, I am," she responded, "I'm going to go inside and sit down. Officer Thompson said he'd talk to me in a few minutes."

"Oh, I bet he did, ma'am," The older cop laughed, looked at Thompson, and clapped Thompson on the back.

"What're you doing here, Bordelon?" the young cop asked.

Missy heard the annoyance in the young cop's voice and decided to ignore the older cop's comment and go inside.

As she walked into her kitchen, Missy started at the lights flashing around in her backyard. She realized it was probably the police looking around with flashlights. She walked over to the sliding glass door and drew the curtains over the window.

Missy walked down the hallway to Sophie Ann's bedroom. As she flicked on the lights, Missy stepped into the room and stood facing the window with her hands on her hips.

I know I closed the blinds. Positive.

She always closed the blinds after lunch, when the day got really hot, to keep the house from warming up too much. In the summer months, sometimes the central air had a hard time keeping up with the high temperatures outside.

Missy walked over to the window and looked at the string that raised and lowered the blinds.

Could Sophie have reached up and opened them? Could she have opened them before they left?

Missy furrowed her eyebrows together and shook her head to herself.

The thought of the man looking into Sophie's room, a man who was a peeping Tom or pervert, or burglar or whatever his intentions were, made Missy feel like she was going to vomit.

She turned around and left the room.

Missy walked to the kitchen and filled herself a glass of water from the tap. She drank all of it and filled herself another. She stood looking out of her kitchen window at the two police cars.

What the hell had the guy been doing? What did he want?

She thought of Evie and how she died. The Stone River police department was small. Were these the same cops who had found Evie? Were they the same ones who refused to investigate what had happened?

The door to the garage opened, and Missy jumped, spilling water down her arm and in the sink.

The younger police officer waited in the doorway for a moment, looking at Missy and then walked into the kitchen.

"Do you want something to drink?" Missy asked, "Coffee or water?"

Thomspon shook his head and held a hand up, "No thank you."

Missy nodded and leaned up against the countertop. Thompson looked at her and took a small notebook and pen out of his back pocket. "Can you tell me what happened?"

Missy recounted what happened, pausing every now and then so Thompson could catch up writing.

"I mean what did the guy want?" she asked when she was finished.

Thompson wrote a little more and then asked, "So you didn't recognize him?"

Missy shook her head, "No. I mean...I couldn't really see much of his face because it was dark."

Thompson paused in his writing and asked, "Could you give me a physical description of him at all?"

Missy thought for a second, "Well he was standing by the azalea. It comes up to about my husband's chest and he's 5'10...this guy was definitely taller than that. Maybe a lot taller. Dark clothes. White. That's really all I can say."

Thompson nodded as he wrote, "Yeah, that's the same as what I saw too."

Missy waited as Thompson finished writing.

"You say he was bigger than your husband. Is your husband living here too?"

"Yes, but he works offshore. He's there now."

"No way he came home early?"

"No definitely not. I just talked to him about an hour ago and he was on the rig. I could hear it. Besides why would he scare me like that?"

Thomspon didn't answer and wrote again.

The older cop opened the door from the garage and stood at Thompson's shoulder, reading his notes. Missy read that his name tag said Bordelon.

Thompson finished writing and looked at the older cop.

"What do you think?" he asked.

"Oh, it's definitely the same guy." Bordelon said.

He looked at Missy, "Any angry boyfriends, anything like that?"

Missy stared at him, "No. I'm married."

Bordelon stared at her, "Doesn't mean you don't have any angry boyfriends."

Missy felt her cheeks go red with anger, "I don't like what you're implying. I told you the answer was no."

Bordelon shrugged, "No reason to get angry. I have to ask those kinds of things so we can figure out what's going on."

Missy ignored him and turned slightly to look at Thompson instead. "What do you mean 'its's the same guy'?"

"This is the third report of the night of some creep looking in people's windows. Well...one the guy was trespassing in someone's backyard staring at the house. But the description is the same."

Missy folded her arms over her chest.

"What do you think he was doing?" she shuddered a little.

"No idea, honestly." Thompson sounded curt and irritated and Missy felt her face grow red again.

Bordelon chuckled a little, "Don't mind him Mrs. Douglas. He's just mad he let the guy get away."

Thompson shot Bordelon an irritated look, making him laugh even harder.

"Hey, Duane," Bordelon said, pointing a finger at Missy, "You know who she looks just like?"

Thompson shook his head no, even though he knew exactly who Missy Douglas looked like.

Elise.

"She looks just like that ex of yours, Elise," Bordelon rested an elbow on the door frame and looked Missy up and down.

Thompson shook his head.

"She was a nice girl, Duane, what happened to her, anyway?"

Thompson shook his head and glared at Bordelon. Missy looked from one cop to the other, feeling extremely uncomfortable. She wanted both of them out of her house.

"Can I tell you something else?"

"Anything you think might help, Ms. Douglas," Bordelon interjected.

Missy ignored him, "This is going to sound crazy, but I'm sure I closed my daughter's blinds this afternoon. But when I went in there, the blinds were wide open."

Thompson and Bordelon both stared at her.

"I'm the only one home, my kids are visiting my parents in Tennessee..."

Bordelon had a bemused expression on his face and motioned for her to continue.

Missy sighed, feeling annoyed and silly, hating the sound of her own voice getting high pitched with frustration, "How could the blinds be open? I'm the only one here."

"If there's no sign of a break-in, either you forgot to close the blinds or your daughter opened them," Thompson said, closing his small notebook in annoyance.

Missy closed her eyes and rubbed her forehead, feeling silly. Thompson looked at his watch and then at the door. Bordelon nodded.

"No, you're right," she glanced in the living room again, "she must have."

The three of them stood in silence for a moment and then Missy dared to ask what she had been thinking.

"Do you- do you think this could be the same person who hurt Evie Nunez?"

Both officers stared at her and Missy looked back and forth between them.

"Evangeline Nunez's death was an accident," Bordelon said slowly.

Missy spoke slowly and carefully, trying to read to read both men's faces, "Are you sure?"

Thompson stared at her and Bordelon's wide face clouded. He sneered at her and shook his head.

"Unbelievable. I'm going back out to my cruiser, Thompson. I think you got all you can from her...for now anyway," Bordelon growled, "I got the other one in the back, still waiting on the mama to call from Baton Rouge."

"You mean there's another guy? You got him?"

Bordelon looked at her, "No. I mean I have one of the other complainants. Some teenage girl- the guy was peeping in her windows too. Must've been right before he came to your house."

"Who is it?" Missy asked breathlessly.

"Can't tell you that, Ms. Douglas. She's a minor." Bordelon turned and walked back out through the garage door.

Missy watched him walk out of the door from the kitchen to the garage and then looked back at Thompson.

"So, what now?" Missy asked him.

"I fill out my report, and then you sign it. Then we see if we can find him..." Thompson was curt and refused to look at her.

Missy sighed and shook her head, "I wasn't trying to insult you. I was just asking the question."

"Just lock your doors. And if anything else happens, call 911 again." Thompson smiled slightly and walked out.

"Thanks, Officer Thompson," Missy followed him out of the kitchen into the garage.

Bordelon stood in front of his car, talking loudly on the phone. Thompson walked up the driveway to his car without a backwards glance.

Missy closed the garage door and then checked to make sure all of the doors and windows were locked.

She went back to the living room and called Wes, trying not to cry. She knew there was no way he could come home tonight or even tomorrow or at all. He'd have to call for a special helicopter to come home early, and he'd probably lose his job if he did. Leaving the rig early was reserved for extreme emergencies only.

Missy forced herself to avoid looking outside. She slumped onto the couch, crying softly while the phone rang.

Chapter Nine

Alessandra sat in the back of the cop car and laughed.

"Oh, what's up now, huh? Now you believe me?" she asked when the cop came back and asked to repeat her story. This time he wrote things down occasionally in a small notebook he pulled from his back pocket.

Her mother arrived about an hour later and frantically asked if Alessandra was in trouble.

"Oh no, Ma'am. Someone just gave her a good scare. Probably just a prank."

The cop looked from Alessandra to her mother and back again.

"Yeah ok, whatever," Alessandra sneered at him.

Alessandra was tall for her age and for a girl, but the cop towered over her. He bent down and put his face close to hers.

"You better button up that attitude, *Sandy*," He sneered back at her, "Make sure you stay out of trouble now."

Alessandra glared back at him, "Back at you, *Bordelon*."

Mariella glared at Alessandra and pulled her into her car. She nodded at Bordelon, "Thank you, Officer."

Mariella pulled away and demanded in Spanish that Alessandra tell her exactly what had happened. Alessandra was shocked that her mother didn't chastise her for getting an attitude with the cop, and she told her mother what had happened.

"Eso no es una broma."

"Yeah, no shit, Mami. But that fucking pig didn't give a shit. He didn't even come look at the trailer or my car or anything."

When they got home, her mother used her phone to take pictures of the rocks still sitting on the steps. They looked around at the trailer and the car, but nothing was wrong with either.

As Alessandra lay in bed, trying not to look at her window, her mother knocked softly on the door.

"Mami?" she whispered softly.

"I'm awake."

"Listen miha, I have to go back early tomorrow. Are you going to go to work still tomorrow?"

"Yeah."

"Ok, I will be gone before you wake up. Is that ok?"

"Yeah, I'm ok."

"Ok we talk more tomorrow night. I think we should go to police station to ask more questions."

"Ok, Mami."

—-

Alessandra woke up the next morning with an aching head. She rolled over and checked her phone to see what time it was.

Are you kidding me? She rolled back over and groaned. Still another twenty minutes before she had to get up to get ready for work at the coffee shop.

She groaned again and kicked off her covers. Her head was absolutely pounding, like a terrible hangover, and she put both hands over her eyes. She got up and wandered into the small kitchen, looking for ibuprofen.

She pulled a glass of water from the tap, popped off the top of the bottle, shook two pills into her hand, shook out one more, and then swallowed all three in one gulp. She grabbed a box of cheerios from the cabinet and headed to the small kitchen table.

Slumped down at one of the two chairs at the tiny table, Alessandra grabbed Cheerios by the handful and scrolled through her phone, looking at her social media profiles like they were a news outlet.

In some ways they were- she was looking for something in particular. There were lots of posts about some party Lexi had thrown, lots of peace signs, duck faces, tits and asses barely covered, biceps uncovered and flexing.

She scanned every picture she could for Trent to see if he was there at Lexie's party.

There, she stopped at a group picture of kids from Stone River High around a fire and zoomed in. It was definitely Trent. She'd recognize his stupid face anywhere. He had one arm around Lexie and one arm around a girl who she worked with at the coffee shop named April.

Alessandra curled her lip and mimed gagging.

The picture was definitely taken at night, so technically he could've been at her house in the evening then gone to the party.

But you don't have any way to prove that. Plus, that asshole cop doesn't believe you that someone was here. Forget about believing that the Golden Child could've done it.

Alessandra shoved another handful of Cheerios in her mouth and covered her eyes again with her hands as she crunched them.

Ok. So clearly the cops weren't going to help.

She thought about what Berto had said, slowly nodding to herself. Maybe she could help herself, find some way to prove it was Trent last night.

Although she knew who Trent Longue was almost as soon as she started at Stone River High, Alessandra had no interaction with him until this past spring. Trent played football, had tons of friends, a brand new truck. He had money. He wasn't funny as far as Alessandra could tell, except for in a mean bullying sort of way.

Her first time talking to him was the Monday after the date of the spring dance was announced. Alessandra scoffed when other kids in her class happily talked about who they were going with. Deep down, though, she knew no one would ask her and there was no one she could imagine wanting to go with.

She was daydreaming about finding a partner in crime who would ask her to the dance and then make fun of it with her. Alessandra was lost in thought, changing out her books at her locker. Trent walked up behind her, smashed his body into hers from behind, pinning her up against her open locker.

"Get the fuck off me." She had said turning her head slightly so she could see who it was.

"Go to the dance with me."

"What the fuck? Fuck you." She had been totally bewildered. The only interaction she'd ever had with Trent before was him making fun of her hair in front of a group of people. And now he was asking her to the dance?

He had pressed her harder into the locker and she used her arms to try and brace herself so she didn't go face first all the way in it. She was tall but was very slimly built. She was pretty sure she would fit all the way inside the locker if Trent decided to push hard enough.

"Go to the dance with me so I can fuck you after."

"Oh, that's lovely. Really romantic. Get the fuck off me." The hall was full of people, but no one said anything or did anything. No one even stopped to watch. Everyone was scared of Trent because of who he was, who his family was.

"Longue get your body off of her," Alessandra had felt Trent let up at the voice.

"I'm just playing around, Mrs. Jones."

"That's not playing, Mr. Longue, and you know it. Come with me." Mrs. Jones, the gym teacher, had led Trent away, after asking if she was ok.

Alessandra shook her head as she moved from the kitchen to the bathroom, turned on the shower to warm up, and undressed. She wasn't sure if it was a good thing or a bad thing that Mrs. Jones had intervened. Mrs. Jones had taken Trent to the principal, but rather than giving him any kind of punishment, the principal called Alessandra down to his office so that Trent could "apologize."

She stepped into the hot shower and let it run over her face and hair. As he had "apologized," Alessandra stood awkwardly in the doorway, while Trent sat and stared at her like he wanted to kill her. The principal stood behind him, hand on his shoulder.

"Now, we can put this misunderstanding behind us, can't we Ms. Sanchez?" as the principal spoke, Trent licked his lips suggestively.

"Yeah sure," she had said, her voice robotic.

Trent grinned and stood up, towering over her as he walked past her and into the hallway. He stood just outside the door, smiling at her.

"You both can go," the principal said and turned quickly back to his desk.

Alessandra just about ran out of the principal's office and into the crowded hall, wondering if Trent was following her. She turned to look behind her and he was huddled with two of his friends laughing. She made eye contact with him, and he laughed even harder.

Although Trent didn't do anything physical to her after that, people treated her differently. Even more differently than normal.

Lexie whispered, "pathetic" under her breath every time she saw Alessandra. She noticed people staring and laughing. And then as they were in the locker room changing for gym, one of Lexie's friends loudly and pointedly stared at her saying, "Don't worry about it, Lex. She thinks Trent would ever be interested in HER? She's just an UGLY SPIC."

Used to holding in tears, Alessandra had finished putting on her gym clothes, turned to the now snickering girls and told her, "Trent Longue is a piece of shit. Whatever he told y'all he's lying. Oh, and your ass looks fat in those pants."

Alessandra had grinned at the looks on their faces and walked past them out into the gym.

Mrs. Jones gave her a measured look then looked at the group of girls just emerging from the locker room, "You alright, Ms. Sanchez?"

"I'm wonderful, Mrs. Jones!" she had responded, laughing. Inside she wanted to curl up and die, but she'd never give Lexie the satisfaction.

Alessandra mulled this all over as she slowly lathered shampoo into her hair. She felt angry. Not small or scared, or embarrassed or ashamed. She just felt angry. Scowling as she rinsed the shampoo from her hair, she mulled over her situation.

Alessandra had inherited an ageing Oldsmobile from her grandmother which is why she was able to have her after school job and enjoy some freedom. She shuddered to think what she would have spent her time doing if she hadn't gotten the car. Hanging around the trailer, walking everywhere, no money.

Alessandra rinsed the shampoo from her hair and thought more about Trent.

Toward the end of the school year, Trent started waiting for her in the parking lot. Sitting on the edge of the bed of his brand new truck, swinging his legs. Then he started following her to work. He'd sit in the parking lot for a while, sometimes he'd come in for a coffee. Then he started following her home. Alessandra told her mother about it and her mother brushed it off.

"He likes you, Sandy. Maybe be nice to him?"

Alessandra rolled her eyes as she used the special conditioner she used to protect the color in her hair.

Then, abruptly, about two weeks ago, he had stopped. She didn't see him at the coffee shop, or on the main road outside her trailer. She had been so relieved, and just assumed that he'd found someone else to be a creep to.

But after what happened last night, Alessandra wondered if that was true. Stepping out of the shower in the small bathroom, she wiped the fogged-up mirror and looked at her reflection.

An idea was starting to bloom. If she was going to help herself, her first step was to see when the party Trent was at last night started. If he could have been at her house, then gone to the party afterwards.

April, she thought, *if April is at work, I can try to get information from her.*

Alessandra looked at her latte-colored skin glistening with water and her bright blue hair hanging limp and clinging to her face. She nodded to herself in determination and studied her own face. Her eyes were round and wide and made her look like a little girl. She reached out and fixed the silver hoop that threaded through one nostril.

> She bared her teeth at herself in a scowl, then dropped it and shrugged. Tough enough. *Definitely not white girl pretty.* She laughed a little.

She blew her short hair dry, threw on some black eyeliner, thick and even, and dressed in ripped jean shorts and a black tee shirt. Her work apron was in her car.

As she stepped out of the front door, her phone rang.

"Hola, Mami," she tried not to sound exasperated.

Alessandra said "si" or "uh huh" or "I know" when it was appropriate during the conversation that followed with her mother. "Be careful, miha," "lock the doors," "call the cops again if you need to."

Fat lot of good calling the cops did, Alessandra thought as she hung up with her mother.

Alessandra took the anger she felt and willed herself to turn it back into determination. She'd talk to April. Find out where Trent was. Go from there.

Alessandra locked the front door behind her, then stood on the small, swept porch of the trailer looking around. The next closest trailer was about a half mile away, but the highway was relatively close. Alessandra could hear the drone of cars and trucks.

There was nothing there to give any hint about who might have been there the night before, except for the three large rocks. They weren't on the stairs anymore- now they were lined up at the bottom of the stairs to one side. Alessandra guessed her mother must have moved them.

Alessandra bent down and looked at them. Each was jagged, about the size of a bowling ball. Alessandra furrowed her brow, straightened to standing, and put her hands on her hips.

Where did they come from?

Louisiana was muddy and filled with swamps, but it definitely wasn't rocky- not in Stone River anyway. Alessandra looked around the yard- she didn't see any rocks anywhere that looked like these.

Why the fuck would he carry rocks here?

Alessandra felt sick to her stomach at the strangeness of it. She looked up at the roof of the trailer.

How did he get up there?

She supposed he could've pulled himself up to the roof from the porch.

That's the only way. And you were too fucking stoned to notice. He was probably looking right in the front window at you.

She shuddered despite the already hot day, walked the few steps to her car, got in, and locked the doors. As she backed down the driveway and turned onto her street, she felt her cheeks burn red with embarrassment and anger with herself.

Sitting at a red light she stared at the scratches all over her left hand. Behind her, a car blew its horn, and she realized the light had turned green. She flipped the person off and pushed down on the gas.

By the time she pulled into the coffee shop Alessandra had decided on two things: the first was that the cops definitely weren't going to believe her that Trent was following her around and the second was that she absolutely HAD to get information about where Trent was the night before.

She opened the door of her car, ruffled her bright blue hair, and smiled a little. Her headache was finally gone, and she felt a little more in control with a plan.

Alessandra smiled to herself as she walked into the crowded coffee shop, remembering who she had met the night before, making the whole experience even more bizarre. She marveled that she had almost forgotten about sitting in a car with a New Orleans music legend.

"Mike fucking DiCostanza," She said out loud to her coworker Claire, who was frothing milk for someone in the drive through.

"Who?" Claire asked quizzically.

"Mike fucking DiCostanza, dude. You know, the lead singer and guitar player from Sistern?"

"Never heard of them."

"It's METAL DUDE!" Alessandra said loudly, looking around and laughing.

"Hey, Alessandra, you're in a good mood."

Andy, another coworker who was a few years older than her came out of the back tying his apron.

Alessandra smiled, "I guess I am. Hey, do you know if April is on today?"

"Uh," Andy paused and looked at Alessandra quizzically, "Yeah, I think so? I was at a party last night and she was there for a little while. I think she said she was on today."

Alessandra smiled even more.

"You were at that party last night?"

"Yeah, why?"

Alessandra nodded to herself. She felt giddy, elated. Finally, she might get some answers.

Before she could ask any more questions, though, Andy motioned to a group of women who walked in.

"I'll talk to you about it later," Alessandra said glumly, feeling some of her giddiness evaporate.

As she took orders and made drinks, Alessandra decided that one of her musical icons saving her from her harasser *had* to be a good sign. She felt in her heart that she was on the right track, that

Chapter Ten

Missy woke up feeling energized, despite being awake half the night. Wes's reaction the night before was immediate: anger and then decisiveness. She needed to go and stay with her mom and stepdad in Tennessee for a few weeks until they figured out what was going on.

Missy felt her stomach knot up at the suggestion, but Wes was insistent when she said she didn't want to leave their house.

"With everything that's happened...with Evie gone, now this, me off on the rig. It's too much Miss."

Missy sat on the couch for a long time after their conversation feeling her stomach clench and unclench, feeling her jaw tighten and her head pound. In the end, she had flat out refused to leave. She could feel Wes's anger when they ended their conversation but didn't care.

Missy felt better this morning only because, like Alessandra, her fear and sadness had been replaced with anger. Missy was mad about Evie, mad that the cop last night hadn't taken her seriously, mad that the cops and doctors hadn't taken what happened to Evie seriously, mad that she had married a drunk, mad that she wasn't working, mad that she wasn't appreciating the privilege of being able to stay home with her kids; everything she could think of made her angry.

But Missy was happy with the anger. It felt better to be angry than to be sad, confused, and scared.

Why are you even doing this?

She asked herself the question at least a hundred times this morning but still didn't have an answer.

She had no idea where to start, no idea what she was looking for, but she knew in her heart there was some connection between what had happened to Evie and what had happened to her last night.

Missy spent an hour walking around her house, wondering where she should go and what she should do. Finally, she remembered that she hadn't told Johnny's camp that he wouldn't be there for a few days.

Missy dialed the number for the camp's office and heaved a sigh when the camp director, Ms. Judy, answered instead of the answering machine.

Johnny liked Ms. Judy, but Missy found her simpering and fake. Her pink manicured hands and bleached blonde hair, to Missy, belied the unkindness that lurked below the surface of her demeanor.

"Good morning, Ms. Judy, this is Missy Douglas, John Douglas's mom?"

"Oh honey, are y'all alright?"

"What?"

"Oh, everybody heard, honey. Creepy peeping Tom is what it is! They said the same guy was at Trenise Jones's house AND a little girl who goes to Stone River High with my Lexie!"

"Trenise Jones's house?" Missy felt her mouth drop open.

"Mmhmm," Judy sounded breathless, and Missy realized it was excitement, "Are you all alright, really?"

Wouldn't you love it if I said no, Missy thought grimly and rolled her eyes.

"I'm ok. The kids weren't home, thankfully. They're in Tennessee visiting my parents. I called to tell you John won't be at camp for the next two weeks."

"Oh, so the kids weren't home? That's a good thing..."

"Mmhmm," Missy agreed.

"And you stayed all by yourself? I'd be scared to be home all alone, and look what happened to you! I guess you'll be going up to Tennessee too now?"

Missy shook her head, "Yes, I will as soon as I'm ready."

"Oh, hold on Ms. Douglas, Lexie just walked in. Now you tell us both what happened," Judy exclaimed, "Hold on I'm going to put you on speaker!"

"Are you ok, Ms. Douglas?"

Judy's daughter Lexie was a carbon copy of her mother. Missy felt every inch of her body recoil from them.

They don't give a shit, the anger in Missy stomach insisted, *they just want to be the first with the story to spread.*

"I'm ok, Lexie." Missy took a deep breath, hoping they couldn't hear the revulsion in her voice,

Lexie's voice sped up a little with excitement, "Well, you're lucky! Apparently, some guy chased the new girl at my school up the street! Her name is Alessandra and, listen, between us, I can't *stand* her. *And,* whatever happened to you and Mrs. Jones, I'm guessing Alessandra was involved because she got hauled off in a police car!"

Lexie laughed a little.

"Alessandra? She has dyed blue hair?"

"Yeah, that's her. She's kind of a trouble maker...you know what I mean."

"Oh really?" Missy asked, her mind racing, desperate to hear more information.

"Jesus loves us all, Lexie" Judy admonished.

"I know, Mama."

Neither mother nor daughter sounded genuine.

Judy dropped her voice to a whisper, "But she *is* a trouble maker though. Lexie told me she was going after Trent Longue at school. Tried to get him in all kinds of trouble."

Lexie's voice turned petulant, "Like Trent would have anything to do with a piece of trash like her."

Now, Missy was itching to get off the phone with them, her heart raced and she knew she had to talk to both Alessandra and Trenise Jones.

"Well, thank you both. And I'll let you know when John will be back."

"Listen, honey, really," Judy continued, ignoring her, "You let me know if you need anything. These sure are scary times."

"They sure are," Missy agreed.

—

Missy pulled into the coffee shop half an hour later and wondered what the hell she was doing. She had told herself the whole way from her house to the coffee shop that she was just getting a coffee, but sitting here now staring around at the few cars in the parking lot, she couldn't deny what she was *really* doing.

She looked around at the cars, looking for something specific. A teenager's car. More specifically, a quirky, rebellious teenager's car. An aging Oldsmobile caught her eye, and her heart jumped a little.

There was a Stone River High school parking sticker on the back along with a few stickers showing what Missy assumed were names of different bands.

Could that be the car driven by a certain blue haired, slightly mouthy teenager? One who had seen the caterpillars on Evie's tree and who was chased from her home by a man the night before?

Missy put her hand over her mouth and closed her eyes.

What the hell am I doing? What am I even thinking right now? Am I really playing detective?

Missy couldn't think of any answer except for a vague feeling in the pit of her stomach that it all was connected. Evie, the other women in the neighborhood, the stories, all of it.

"This is crazy," she whispered out loud.

Her stomach had a horrible tight feeling and her legs felt strange; it was a familiarly unpleasant feeling that she specifically recalled feeling one other time in her life.

When she had graduated from high school ten years earlier, Missy's parents had taken her on a cruise around the Bahamas to celebrate. At night, after dinner, they had wandered out onto the deck, into the pitch black. There was no horizon visible. There was just blackness. The crashing sounds of the waves below and the air above.

Missy had felt a pulling sensation toward the edge of the railing, toward the rushing sea and air below and above and all around her. She had felt terrified that her feet would start moving of their own accord and would pull her out into the blackness.

It was exhilarating and horrifying at the same time. She had clutched the wall behind her, not trusting herself. Her parents asked her over and over if she was ok and eventually forced her back inside away from the blackness, telling her not to go near the edge.

Now, walking toward the coffee shop's entrance, in the broad daylight and sweltering heat, Missy felt the same sensation. Her feet pulled her toward the gleaming glass door of the coffee shop, toward some crashing blackness that she wanted to run both from and toward.

Every fiber of her body told her to get back in the car, drive straight home to pack her bags and head to Tennessee away from this craziness.

Every fiber of her being told her that wasn't an option and that nothing mattered but going inside and finding the teenager with the blue hair.

Missy pulled the door open and looked around, almost marveling at how normal it all looked.

What did you expect? Ghosts and thunderbolts and fortune tellers?

Missy saw only a male employee washing dishes at a sink behind the counter. As she walked toward him, she felt herself blush a little and felt stupid and silly.

"Excuse me," Missy said to the teenager's back, "Is Alessandra working today by any chance?"

The teenager turned around and looked at Missy, "Yeah, she's in the back. You want me to get her?"

Missy felt her mouth hang open stupidly, "Uh..."

The boy widened his eyes at her and tucked his head forward, "I mean...I can go get her? Or do you want something to drink?"

"No, I mean...don't get her if she's busy, it's ok."

"No, it's ok, we just slowed down from the morning rush, I think she's just restocking."

He walked a few steps to a door behind the counter and leaned his head around, "Hey Alessandra! Someone's asking for you out here."

"Is it the policccee??" Missy heard Alessandra's voice float out, "Because if it is please tell them Alessandra is unavailable!"

"No, it's some lady."

"Uh ok...tell her I'll be out in a second."

Missy shifted her weight from one foot to the other and vaguely wondered again what she was doing and what exactly she was planning on asking.

Missy turned to the teenager, "Can I have a small coffee with just a little milk please?"

Missy paid, took her coffee, and sat as far from the counter as she could.

Alessandra sauntered out from behind the counter, a few minutes later, talked briefly to her coworker and then walked over to where Missy was sitting.

"Andy said you were looking for me?"

"Uh...do you remember me?"

Alessandra nodded, "Yeah, you're Ms. Evie's friend."

"Missy."

"Right Missy. So, what did you want?"

Missy smiled a little at the roughness in Alessandra's voice, wondering where it came from.

"Well, my son goes to day camp and his counselor is a girl named Lexie-she said she goes to school with you?"

"Yeah, I know who she is." Alessandra rolled her eyes.

"Well," Missy pressed on, smiling internally that apparently she wasn't the only one who disliked Lexie, "she said something happened to you last night. That someone tried to break into your trailer?"

Alessandra let out an exasperated puff of air and looked over her shoulder at Andy, who was eyeing both of them, clearly trying to eavesdrop.

"What did she say?"

"She said some guy was looking in your windows, chased you up the street..."

Alessandra shook her head and scoffed, "Goddamn small towns."

"I'm sorry if it's not my place, but someone was...I don't know what he was doing. Harassing me? Trying to break in? I don't know WHAT he was doing, but somebody was trespassing outside my house last night too. I thought maybe it was the same person that was bothering you."

Alessandra stared at Missy. Her eyes were bright and her cheeks flushed a little. Alessandra leaned in toward Missy and studied her. Alessandra didn't want the whole world knowing that she was trying to get information about Trent. She tried to read the woman in front of her and if she was someone who she could trust.

Ms. Evie was always nice to Alessandra, had asked her how who she was, how she was, wanted to hear about school. This woman was Ms. Evie's friend.

Alessandra lowered her voice and looked Missy straight in the eyes, "Listen. Someone was trying to break in, or scare me, or something last night. And I'm pretty sure I know who it was, but the cops wouldn't listen to me."

Whatever answer Missy was expecting, this wasn't it. Missy looked around at the empty coffee shop.

"What do you mean they wouldn't listen?"

"I mean they wouldn't listen." Alessandra said in exasperation.

"Well tell me what happened," Missy squared her shoulders and held Alessandra's gaze, "I'll listen."

Alessandra looked Missy up and down and told her exactly what had happened the night before, but this time, unlike with the cop, she included the weed, the suspicion that it was Trent because of Trent's behavior toward her at school, and the bizarre encounter with Mike DiCostanza.

She also included what the cop had done and said as well.

When she was done, Missy sat back in her chair and looked at Alessandra.

"Two cops came to my house. The first one was ok, the second was a complete dick. Bordelon was the name."

Alessandra laughed, "Yeah, that's him. Definitely a dick."

Missy felt the nasty knot in her stomach begin to untie. Instead of that awful nauseating feeling she had before entering the coffee shop she now felt anger instead.

"So that was you he had in the back of his car?"

Alessandra nodded.

"I mean, what the hell is this? A shitty movie from the 90s where the cops protect the football players?" Missy shook her head angrily.

Alessandra grinned and then slumped back into her chair, "I don't think it's just about football though."

Missy gave her a quizzical look.

"You know...the LONGUES." Alessandra waved her hand, "They own like...everything."

Missy paused a moment and looked at Alessandra, "Well, so what? You're saying the cops won't do anything because of this kid's family?"

Alessandra shrugged, "Maybe."

They sat in silence, looking at each other.

"So, I told you what happened, now what?"

Now what. Missy furrowed her eyebrows and took a sip of her coffee.

"It was obviously the same person, right?" Missy asked.

"Yeah, it had to be."

"The cops wouldn't listen to you, but maybe they'll listen to me."

Alessandra shrugged again, "Maybe. But why would you suddenly be like, 'Oh, yeah, I think it was this kid I've never seen-Trent Longue? You know- Trent Longue- big dumb asshole whose dad pretty much everyone either owes rent to or works for?'"

Alessandra shook her head, "It doesn't make any sense."

Missy nodded in agreement, "True."

"You didn't get a good look at him?"

Missy shook her head glumly, "No, he was silhouetted the whole time."

"Same."

They looked at each other, out of ideas.

The knot in Missy's stomach loosened again, "Trenise Jones."

"What? Ms. Jones the P.E. teacher?"

"Yes. Lexie's mom told me someone was trespassing at her house last night too."

Alessandra perked up, "You think it was Trent too?"

Missy widened her eyes and cocked her head to the side, "I mean? What a crazy coincidence if it was a different person, right? Trenise lives about a mile from me to the West, and you live about a mile from me to the East. It makes sense if he went from her house, to mine, to yours."

Missy didn't dare speak aloud what else she was thinking: that maybe this Trent kid had had something to do with Evie's death also. She couldn't explain why she felt it so strongly, but the voice in her heart that whispered that Evie's death wasn't an accident also whispered that Trent Longue was somehow involved.

A part of her wanted to believe it was paranoia, that of course the police had investigated thoroughly, but the doubt she'd felt all along bubbled to the surface after hearing Alessandra's story.

Alessandra slowly nodded, her blue hair bobbing around her face, "So what do you think we should do?"

"Let's go talk to Trenise and see what she thinks."

"I get off at 3, but I might be able to sneak off a little earlier. Would that work for you?"

"Yeah, that sounds fine. Do you want me to come pick you up?"

"Nah, I know you live on Ms. Evie's street. I can just come by you."

"Ok," Missy said, pulling herself up to standing, "I'll see you around 3."

"What are we going to say to Ms. Jones? I mean...it feels kind of weird just knocking on her door and being like..." Alessandra made her voice rise a few octaves, "Hello, Ms. Jones, we think Trent Longue is stalking us, what do you think?"

Missy laughed a little, "Yep. I think that's exactly what we'll say."

"Ok, lady. See you around 3."

Alessandra nodded to Missy curtly, turned, and walked back behind the counter.

—

Missy pulled into her driveway, got out of the car, and tried not to look at the kids' bikes and toys as she walked through the garage. The feeling of purpose, anger, and determination she'd felt all morning faltered, and Missy felt her lower lip tremble. She stood in the garage looking around, wondering what the hell she was doing, and her eyes fell on the baseball bat from last night.

Her brother Jim's baseball bat.

Missy's mouth fell open as she stared at it.

Why did I run for the bat last night? Why of all things in the house had I gone for the baseball bat?

Missy looked around the garage again, skin crawling. She saw Wes's hedge trimmers: sharp and jagged. She saw a crowbar, a hack saw. There were knives in the kitchen. There was an unloaded shot gun in the hall closet. Out of all the things she could've used last night as a weapon, why had she thought only of Jim's baseball bat?

The automatic light popped on as soon as she stepped into the garage and now it reflected off the silver metal of the bat. The worn black grips were facing up, the wide end down, and Missy reached out and grabbed it from where it was resting up against the wall.

Her skin stood out in goosebumps and the sweat that had covered her body while she stood in the driveway under the sun now felt clammy.

Jim had been five years old than Missy, and Missy had looked up to him with a reverence that was closer to that of a father. Their real father had left their mother shortly after Missy was born.

Jim never treated her like a normal annoying little sister (which she was sure she had been). He had always included her, looked after her, had taken her for walks in the woods, let her tag along with his friends while they rode their bikes. When he was older, Jim excelled both in school and at baseball. He had lots of friends and girlfriends, and all of them were kind to Missy because they loved Jim so much.

After he graduated high school, Jim wanted to go to school at the University of Tennessee so he could stay relatively close to Missy and their mom.

Jim got a scholarship to play baseball and their mom threw a party to celebrate. Missy was proud of him and wanted to do something special. She had some money saved up from babysitting and asked her mother to take her to the local Walmart to buy Jim a gift. As she walked through the store, she gravitated to the sports section and her eyes landed on a gleaming silver bat. It wasn't the most expensive, nor was it the least, but Missy decided on the spot that that's what she would buy Jim for a present.

The night of the graduation party was one that stayed in Missy's memory as one of the greatest nights of her life. Friends and family mingled and mixed. By that point, Missy and Jim's mom had put up an inexpensive above ground pool (not as big as the one that Sophie and Johnny were on their way to swim in, but a decent size).

Happy shouts and laughter came from the pool, from the lawn, from the back porch which was filled with folding chairs, from the kitchen where every square inch of counter space was covered with food.

Missy remembered standing in the middle of the kitchen in her bathing suit munching on a plate of potato chips and feeling like there could be no place happier on the whole planet than her house right at that moment.

There was a small table set up in the living room where people deposited gifts as they entered through the front door. Front and center was the baseball bat Missy had purchased, tied up with an orange bow (University of Tennessee color, of course).

As she chomped on her chips and felt the cold from the air conditioning blow on her wet hair, Missy felt a quick wave of shame and doubt. Was her present good enough? Jim was *almost* a professional baseball player (in her mind anyway)- was a Walmart bat good enough?

No, she decided, *not good enough at all. What had I been thinking?*

Missy put her plate of chips down and walked over to the table. There were huge presents, small ones, and hers seemed to stick out. She picked it up, turning it over in her hands.

I'll take it back to Walmart, Missy decided, *I'll buy something else.*

"What are you doing? Trying to steal my presents?"

Missy jumped at Jim's voice, and froze, baseball bat in her hands.

Jim had obviously just gotten out of the pool too and was dripping water all over the floor. Missy put her hands on her hips.

"You're dripping water all over, Jim. Mama's going to whip your butt!"

Jim laughed and looked at the bat in Missy's hands.

"What're you doing? Practicing your swing?" Jim had tried to teach Missy to play, but she was hopeless. She never could hit the ball right, didn't like to run, couldn't catch very well, and always closed her eyes when someone threw her the ball.

Jim teased her whenever she was doing something she wasn't supposed to be doing that she was "practicing her swing."

"No...I..." Missy shifted her weight from one foot to the other.

"What?"

"I bought you this bat, but I don't think it's good enough Jim. You're a real baseball player now, and this is just from Walmart. It was stupid of me to buy."

Missy remembered feeling a tear roll down her cheek and wiping it away angrily, feeling stupid and not wanting to ruin Jim's party by crying like a baby.

Jim walked over and bent down, "Hey. It's not stupid at all. Let me see it."

Missy handed him the bat reluctantly. Jim hoisted it above his shoulder.

"Feels pretty good to me."

Missy perked up, "really?"

Jim laughed, "Yeah. Come on, let's go outside, and I'll hit a few. See how far they go."

Missy laughed, grabbed her chips, and followed Jim out the front door. He walked over to the garage and pulled out a bag of baseballs that he used to practice. No one was in the front yard, and Missy could hear muffled talking and laughter coming from the back yard.

"You sit there!" Jim yelled from the driveway and pointed at the small front porch.

Missy plopped down and balanced her plate of chips on her bare knees. Standing now in her hot garage, Missy remembered how her damp bathing suit still felt cool from the air conditioning.

Jim walked out to the street where cars lined up and down in both directions and to the empty field that was across from their house.

"Ok let's see how she does!" he shouted.

Missy gave him two thumbs up and held her breath.

Jim threw a ball up in the air, and swung expertly, twisting his hips. Missy heard the bat crack up against the ball. She stood, spilling some of her chips, shaded her eyes, and watched the ball soar up the street and out of the field.

"YEAH!" she shouted, jumping up and down, "That was a home run for sure!!"

Jim laughed and yelled back, "Oh yeah! Let me see if I can get another!"

They stayed like that for another 15 minutes or so, Missy standing on the porch cheering like crazy and Jim cracking ball after ball with the bat she had bought him. Eventually, Jim wandered back over with the bat hoisted over his shoulder.

"I can't wait to use it in my first game, Miss!"

Now, standing in her garage, Missy held the bat tight in her hands until the bones in her fingers hurt. She could almost taste the salty chips, almost smell the pine trees and chlorine from the pool, almost hear the laughter from a party that had happened almost 20 years ago.

Missy closed her eyes and held the bat to her chest. A few days before his twentieth birthday, when he was coming home from a game, Jim was killed in a car crash by a drunk driver. The driver was given a light sentence since it was their first offence and Missy and her mother and the world was left without Jim.

Wiping tears from her face, Missy gripped the bat and stepped back out into the hot sun. She raised the bat above her shoulder, planted her feet, crouched slightly. She swung from the hip like Jim had shown her. She raised the bat again and swung again. Letting her heavy breath come out in one long grunt, Missy swung again and again.

She swung into the air in front of her, hitting nothing and everything.

Chapter Eleven

When Alessandra arrived at Missy's house, Missy was still working on her swing. She had gotten Johnny's t-ball stand and a random baseball that she supposed was either Wes's or Jim's and was hitting the ball as hard as she could, then running off into the woods behind her house to chase it down.

A few times she managed to hit the ball all the way to the service path that ran behind her house. It was a narrow strip of cleared land that ran behind the houses in her neighborhood that allowed any meter-readers or parish workers to freely move from house to house without walking in the street.

Sweaty and red-faced, Missy crossed the tree line at the back of her property and entered the access alley again. She paused for a moment in the cool clearing, peering up and down the path for the ball. She spotted it rolled to the edge of her back neighbor's yard, scooped it up, and returned to the t-ball stand.

Alessandra pulled up, watched Missy for a few minutes, then turned off her car and got out. Missy didn't turn around when Alessandra pulled in, and she didn't turn around even when Alessandra closed her car door.

"Hey," Alessandra said, "Uh...hey?!" again when Missy didn't turn around.

Missy smashed the ball again and then followed it at a jog toward the edge of her backyard. She stooped down to pick up the ball, unhappy that it hadn't gone further. Missy turned and saw Alessandra.

Alessandra lifted a hand in a wave, "You trying out for softball this year Mrs. Douglas?"

Missy stopped for a second, heart hammering at the scare Alessandra had given her, then laughed a little and started walking back toward the t-ball stand, where Alessandra waited for her.

"You can call me Missy, Alessandra."

"Are you ok?" Alessandra looked at Missy's sweaty face and at the bat in her hand. She tucked her own hands into the pockets of her jean shorts and looked down at the ground.

"Yeah, I'm ok. Just working through everything I guess."

Alessandra nodded.

Missy put the ball on the tee but didn't hoist the bat to hit it again. Instead, she rested the bat on the ground and looked at Alessandra, trying to read her face.

"You really think it might've been this kid from your school?

Alessandra shrugged, "Could have been. Could've been one of his douche bag friends."

Missy watched her silently and Alessandra took a deep inhale before she spoke again, "Let me put it to you this way. I can't wrap my brain around who else it could've been, and I don't really want to try."

Missy stared at her and frowned, "What do you mean?"

Alessandra lifted the oversized, mirrored sunglasses she was wearing and put them on top of her head.

"I don't know *what* I mean. All I know is that some creep bothered both of us last night, maybe Ms. Jones too, and I know that Trent is a creep."

"There's a lot of creepy shit around here."

Alessandra shrugged and nodded.

"Are you saying you think it might've been something like that?" Missy asked quietly.

Alessandra shrugged, "It's just weird. All of it."

Missy nodded and started walking to the garage, "Let me go change my clothes."

"Take your time, I got nothing going on this afternoon or tonight."

When Missy went into her house through the garage, Alessandra wandered back to her car, turned on the engine, and let the cool air from the air conditioner blow in her face. Her Ipod kicked back on, and Sistine blared out of the speakers.

"*I can't see you/I can't see you/I can't see you. Rocks in your pockets and down, down, down to the deep/Sleep baby, sleep/Rocks in your pockets and down in the deep.*"

Alessandra sang along, bobbing her head with her eyes closed, and thought more about how incredibly strange the past 24 hours had been. She had told herself over the course of her dealings with Trent that she wasn't bothered by it, that he was just an asshole, but after last night she realized just how scared she'd been of him.

"Rocks, rocks, rocks, in your pockets/Pockets full of rocks, and you're down in the deep."

Alessandra squeezed her hands into fists. She wasn't scared anymore, though. She only felt anger. Anger at what had happened to her at her aunt's house, angry that she felt ashamed of it, angry that no one could help her, angry at her mother for always being gone. She felt it in her stomach, and it thrummed through her fingers. She squeezed them tight into fists. Strangely, she was aware that she felt better angry now than she had in months, maybe years.

"DOWN IN THE DEEP!" Mike DiCostanza howled through her speakers and Alessandra howled right along with him, smiling. She opened her eyes as the guitars hammered the outro and looked over on her passenger seat to wear Berto's breaker bar sat, glittering in the sunlight.

Alessandra jumped at the sound of a knock on the window. She looked up at Missy's smiling face, turned down the music and unlocked the door for her.

Missy had changed into a different pair of workout shorts and a University of Tennessee tee shirt. Her hair was now pulled up into a ponytail and she looked like she had rinsed her face and the edges of her hair with water. She was still a little flushed, but Alessandra thought she didn't look as crazy as she had when Alessandra had first pulled up.

Alessandra pressed the button to unlock the doors and Missy climbed in, moving the breaker bar to the center console as she did.

Missy sat in the passenger side seat and buckled her seatbelt. Alessandra grinned at her and wondered if she was going to comment on the music.

"Sistine isn't it?"

Alessandra was taken aback, "Yeah you like them?"

Missy scrunched up her nose in distaste.

"Honestly, no, not really, but my husband does. He dragged me to see them at their reunion show in the French Quarter this spring."

"Aww what? Are you serious?" Alessandra banged her hand on the steering wheel, "I was dying to go but it was 21+ only."

Missy shrugged, "It was really loud."

Alessandra laughed and shook her head, "They're supposed to be loud."

Missy laughed, "So are we going or what?"

Alessandra put the car in reverse and backed down the driveway, "Just tell me where to go."

As they pulled off Missy's street, Missy again felt the sense of doubt and uncertainty but pushed it away. She looked at Alessandra's face, which was tensed up, eyebrows stitched together.

"You ok?" she asked.

"Me?" Alessandra put her hand to her chest, "Fine."

Missy continued to look at her and Alessandra glanced back, "I mean...I'm *not*. This feels totally weird. But it feels right too, you know?"

Missy nodded, "Turn here."

Missy guided Alessandra down the different short streets to the cul-de-sac where she knew Trenise Jones lived. She knew which one it was because she and Evie had taken the kids down to look at the flooded river that spring, and Trenise had ushered them all to her backyard to look.

"Right here." She pointed to the large house with the columns, marveling at the beauty of the house and the landscape.

A large live oak was to one side of the house and the rushes and reeds that led back to the bayou swayed gently in the light wind. Missy had lived in Louisiana long enough to know that there would be thunderstorms soon. The day had been humid and the air thrummed with the built up pressure. She rolled down her window and, sure enough, she could hear thunder rolling in the distance.

"You don't think she'll be pissed that a student is at her house?" Alessandra asked uneasily, "Maybe you should've just come by yourself."

Missy shrugged but before she could answer, she saw Trenise herself come from around the back of the house. Her back was to the street, so she didn't see them. She was wearing an outfit similar to Missy's, but her shirt read Louisiana State University instead of University of Tennessee. In one hand she had a pair of electric trimmers and in the other she had a huge pair of hedge trimmers. She put both down next to a small table and picked up an ax that had been laying on the ground.

Alessandra and Missy both watched with their mouths hanging open as Trenise flung the ax over her shoulder, walked to the edge of her property where it backed up to the bayou, and hacked wildly at the overgrowth there.

Missy thought she didn't seem to be making much progress until she noticed that there were cut branches all along the edge of the property that bordered the bayou behind it. She wasn't cutting the brush down, which probably would've been easier in Missy's opinion, just thinning it out.

If she was cutting the brush down, she wasn't doing a very efficient job at it. Missy didn't know Trenise very well, but she knew her and her reputation well enough to know that "half-assed" probably wasn't in her vocabulary.

"So, she can see the river?" Alessandra finally asked.

Missy shrugged and gave Alessandra a bewildered look.

Alessandra looked from Missy, whose mouth was hanging open as she watched Trenise hack away at the growth, to Trenise, and back.

"Well, are we going to go talk to her?" she finally asked.

"Oh...yeah," Missy opened the car door and stepped out. The humidity made her catch her breath. It felt like it would rain any minute, and the sky to the West was darkening rapidly.

Alessandra closed her car door and started across the lawn as Missy looked up at the sky.

"Ms. Jones!"

Trenise jumped about a mile and dropped the shears she was holding. She bent down and pressed one hand over her heart, the other on one knee as she bent forward.

"Good-NESS, Alessandra Sanchez. Don't you know not to sneak up on someone when they're holding something that sharp? I could've poked my own eye out."

"Sorry Ms. Jones!" Alessandra yelled back and then smiled sheepishly at Missy.

"Missy Douglas is that you?"

"Hi Trenise!"

Trenise stared at the two younger women, her hands on her hips, not quite knowing what to say. Even though Alessandra had scared her, Trenise wasn't particularly surprised to see either one of them. She was surprised that they had showed up like this, together, but she figured she'd be seeing one or both of them at some point.

Stone River was a small town with very little crime. To have three women in the same neighborhood who all vaguely knew each other victimized in the same night seemed like more than a coincidence.

It did to Trenise anyway. Her neighbor Rita had made sure to run over and tell her that morning that a young girl with blue hair and the young woman from the North who was friends with Evie Nunez had also had an intruder.

"*And*," Rita told Trenise breathlessly, "They said the guy chased the blue haired girl up the road! *And* the guy was chasing that Missy Douglas all around her house."

After Rita had told her this, Trenise had immediately gone inside and called Detective Thompson.

"What can I help you with, Ms. Jones?"

"Well, Detective Thompson, I know that you're probably handling all three of the cases from last night?"

Thompson answered slowly, and Trenise could hear the exasperation in his voice, "Yes. Well....it's a team effort now."

"I see." She paused, "Are you aware that Missy Douglas, Alessandra Sanchez, and I all know each other? I'm Alessandra's gym teacher and Ms. Douglas and I were mutually acquainted with Evangline Nunez."

Thompson was silent.

"I feel like this may be significant, Thompson."

"Ms. Jones, it might be, but I don't know what it has to do with Evangeline Nunez."

Trenise tried not to let anger creep into her voice, "Evangeline Nunez was probably attacked and died because of her injuries. Now three other women are stalked at their homes. Y'all don't think it might be related?"

"Ms. Jones, all I can say that as of now Ms. Nunez's death was ruled an accident. AND that I can't comment on any open investigations."

Trenise laughed, "Even mine?"

Thompson sighed, "Yes, I can't comment on yours Ms. Jones. The thing is that," Thompson paused, "the thing is that I'm not handling the other cases."

Trenise sighed. "Right, of course, Officer Thompson. Just do me a favor, and pass that along to whoever is handling the other cases? Can I ask you who's handling the other cases?"

"Yes, I'll pass it along. And his name is Bordelon."

Trenise snorted through her nose, "Bordelon? You're kidding?"

"No ma'am." Thomspon sounded like he was gritting his teeth as he spoke. *Your foot is out the door,* Thompson told himself, *don't get involved in this.*

"I can't believe they're letting him handle cases again."

"The new sheriff decided that his demotion was unfair and reinstated him as a detective."

Trenise snorted again, "Well, alright, Thompson. Thank you for your help."

As far as Trenise was concerned, Bordelon was everything a bad cop could be. And *he* was handling what happened to Evie Nunez, Missy Douglas, and Alessandra Sanchez.

After the conversation with Thompson, Trenise had felt angry and helpless and she didn't like feeling either one of those feelings. Trenise Jones didn't get angry; she used her brain. She didn't feel helpless; she helped herself.

So, she did the only thing she could think of to help herself and that was to grab her lawn cleaning equipment and start working on clearing out the brush behind her property. She didn't want it gone; she just wanted it cut back enough that no one could sneak up on her again.

Trenise grabbed her hedge trimmer again, opened them as wide as she could, and then snipped off a few of the larger branches. She pulled them off and threw them at her feet and then looked down the line of brush she had made. She'd made it about halfway down the part of her property that bordered the bayou, and she could see clearly down to the bank and then to water.

Now, Trenise stared at both Missy and Alessandra, and found she was genuinely happy to see them both. She wiped the sweat off her forehead. The humidity was almost unbearable, but Trenise figured they were about to get a good downpour sooner rather than later. She looked up the length of her yard to her house.

Her house was elevated about ten feet, so that under the house was a sort of covered patio. One side of the patio, the side facing the street, was closed off with a concrete wall. The wall had holes along the bottom to let any flood waters through, but it helped give the house extra support- and helped give some privacy from nosy neighbors out at the street.

Before Alessandra had startled her, Trenise reckoned she'd bring her tools under the house, grab herself an iced tea from the fridge upstairs, and then park herself in one of the lounge chairs under the house to watch the rain, admire her hard work, and figure out what her next steps were going to be.

Now it seemed she'd have some company.

"Y'all best come under the house on the patio, it's fixing to rain!" Trenise called as she gathered up her tools and motioned Missy and Alessandra toward the patio.

"Y'all want something to drink? Tea or water?"

"Either Trenise, thank you!"

"Thanks Ms. Jones."

Alessandra and Missy walked across the large yard toward the patio as Trenise put her tools down and continued to the front staircase and up to the front door.

Missy, who had been in Trenise's backyard before with Evie and the kids, was again impressed by Trenise's style and tidiness. The patio under the house looked like an outdoor room: potted plants hung from hooks in the ceiling, the cement floor was swept spotless, and there was striped yellow and gray area rug and artfully mismatched patio furniture in different bright colors: teals, pinks, and oranges.

Alessandra looked around with her mouth hanging open. Coach Jones was stern but fair and Alessandra always liked her (and not just for taking up for her with Trent). Her admiration grew as she looked at Ms. Jones's yard, house, and furniture.

Missy watched Alessandra admire the patio under the house and smiled.

"It's really beautiful, isn't it?"

Alessandra nodded and ran her fingers through her hair. She plopped down in a solitary teal armchair, unwittingly matching hair to chair. Missy sat in a hot pink chair across from her, leaving Trenise either a bright orange loveseat or a teal and pink striped chair to sit in.

Looking out over the large backyard that sloped down to the bayou, Missy took in the beautiful view with its rushes, Spanish moss-covered cypress trees and their knobby roots rising out of the ground. A heron soared overhead, and red winged blackbirds called from the trees.

"Did you know they're called knees?" Missy asked Alessandra.

"What?" Alessandra looked bewildered and looked off to where Missy was pointing.

"The roots of the cypress tree. They're called knees. I always thought that was funny. They look like they could pull themselves up from the ground, don't they?"

Alessandra scrunched up her nose, "Yeah they do."

She got up out of her chair and walked across the backyard and down to the edge of the water. Missy stayed in her armchair and watched, tilting her head toward the breeze that was circulating now.

"Watch out for snakes, Alessandra!"

Missy and Alessandra both turned at the sound of Trenise's voice, and Missy rose to help her with the full tray she was carrying. Alessandra lifted a hand in acknowledgement and stood by the edge of the water, looking out through one of the spots Trenise had cleared.

"I got it, Missy. Just clear a spot on that table if you would."

Missy pulled a placemat and vase of flowers that was in the center of the small glass patio table off to one side so that Trenise could fit the tray. Trenise poured iced tea from a pitcher into the three ice filled glasses that were on the tray. Next to the pitcher was a bowl of potato chips and some napkins.

"I try not to keep cookies in the house, because I'll eat them. But I always keep some Zapp's to crunch on in the afternoon with my tea. They're spicy, now."

Missy smiled, "I love the spicy ones. Thank you, Trenise, this is very nice of you. I hope we aren't interrupting you?"

"Nah, I was just getting ready to take a break and come up here." As if on cue, the dark clouds that were overhead let out a few drips of rain.

Alessandra was halfway back up the lawn now, and she broke out into a jog as the rain quickly turned from a few drops to a steady downpour.

"Shoot," she muttered as she came under the porch and shook the rain out of her hair.

"You want a towel or you just going to shake it off like a dog?" Trenise laughed.

Alessandra gave a soft bark and grinned, "I'm good, Ms. Jones."

"Well, y'all help yourselves," Trenise responded, gesturing to the tray. Missy and Alessandra both took a glass, Alessandra took a handful of chips and wrapped them in a napkin.

All sitting in their chairs now and sipping their drinks, the three women were silent, each listening to the sound of the rain falling.

"I can guess, I think, why you two are here." Trenise said finally.

Missy and Alessandra exchanged a glance.

Trenise looked at them both and laughed. "I know you both and neither one of you is stupid. And I'm sure as hell not stupid. All three of us had an intruder, trespasser, whatever you want to call it, or whatever the cops want to call it," Trenise rolled her eyes, "on the same day."

Missy nodded her head, and Alessandra stared at Trenise, trying to gauge what she was saying.

Trenise nodded and continued, "You think it's the same person, same as me."

Missy nodded again and looked at Alessandra, "We do. And Alessandra thinks she might know who it is."

Trenise raised her eyebrows and looked at Alessandra.

"I think it's Trent Longue...him or one of his asshole friends." She looked down at her hands as she spoke.

"That's a serious accusation, Alessandra." Trenise's face was stern as she looked at Alessandra. There was no reproach in her voice, but her statement was as hard as steel.

"I know it is," Alessandra said looking down, "But I really think it was him."

"Do you have any proof other than his treatment of you at school?"

Alessandra's head snapped up, "You know it was more than just that time you caught him?"

Trenise laughed, "Oh yes, trust me, teachers gossip just as much as students."

"What do you think Trenise? You must know what this Trent kid looks like..." Missy leaned forward in her chair and sipped her tea. The rain was thundering now, so she had to raise her voice a little to be heard.

"I know what he looks like, and it could've been him."

Alessandra brightened in her chair, sitting up and gripping the arm rests, about to speak.

Trenise held her hand up, "I'm not saying it was for SURE though. Could've been anybody, y'all."

"But Ms. Jones...I thought your husband was a cop. That's what the kids at school said."

Trenise nodded and laughed a little "Yeah, he was. So what? Doesn't make me a cop, Ms. Sanchez."

"So don't you have some kind of like...influence or whatever with the cops? Won't they listen to you?"

Trenise snorted and grabbed a handful of chips from the bowl, "They listen because I'm old and don't mind being loud, if you know what I mean. It doesn't have anything to do with Big John. And just because they listened doesn't mean they *believe me* or will *do* anything."

Alessandra slumped back into her chair shaking her head.

Missy reached over and lightly squeezed her arm, "Trenise are you saying you tried to talk to them already?"

Trenise nodded, "Yeah, I did. A young cop over there at the police department named Thompson. He said both of your cases were taken from him and given to someone else. Wouldn't tell me anything else about it."

"So, Trenise you do think they're connected?" Missy asked.

Trenise nodded, "Like I said, I'm not stupid, and neither are you. Do you think they are?"

Missy nodded, "Yeah."

Trenise leaned forward, "And...?"

Missy looked at the older woman, seemingly opposite her in everyway: dark skinned where Missy was pale as milk, wiry and strongly built where Missy was full in the hips and chest, confident where Missy felt unsure. Trenise was silhouetted by the rain coming down behind her, running in sheets down the side of the house and filling up the stone drains that lined the outside of the patio under the house.

Missy straightened in her chair, "And I think maybe it has to do with Evie too."

Trenise nodded again and leaned back in her chair. She ate a chip from her hand and looked down to the water behind her property.

"Me too," Trenise said softly.

Alessandra looked at Missy, "Ms. Nunez? I thought that was an accident?"

Missy looked down at her hands. Whatever strength she'd found to verbalize that she thought her friend had been murdered, vanished.

Trenise continued to look at the water, "They're saying it was an accident. That Evangaline hit her head on a rock when she slipped down the river bank. First of all, that bank isn't sloped enough to fall down hard enough to hit your head, and second of all there aren't any rocks. None. No. Someone threw that rock at her or used it to hit her with."

Missy nodded, "Someone hit her in the head so hard it caused a hemorrhage. The hemorrhage caused sepsis. The sepsis killed her. Turned her hands black. They amputated them, did you know that?" She felt her lower lip tremble.

Trenise shook her head that she didn't and looked down at her hands.

The three of them sat in silence. Missy finished all of her tea, trying to regain some composure.

Trenise finally spoke, "So what we have here is a vague idea that four crimes might be connected, but a damn good idea that three of them definitely are."

Missy and Alessandra both looked at her nodding.

"We also think we might know who committed a crime against Alessandra only. Trent has little motive to try and do anything to me and no clear motive to do anything to Missy."

"Except being a creepy pervert." Alessandra barked, "AND being angry at you that you took up for me."

Trenise pointed at her and then touched the finger to her own chin, "But you have no proof of that."

"The hell I do! You reported him to the principal."

"But he didn't do anything. And neither one of use reported his assault to the police."

Alessandra snorted, "You think the fucking police care about what happens to some little brown girl?"

Trenise stared at Alessandra, "No. I don't think all of them do. But some of them might. And don't forget I was a little brown girl once too, Alessandra. And I have a little brown girl of my own away at college."

"Sorry, Ms. Jones."

"Don't be sorry, Alessandra." Trenise waved her hand and stood up, arms folded.

"Do you know anyone with the police department thought Trenise? Anyone you think might listen?" Missy asked.

Trenise sighed, "No, not in Stone River. I know people with the state, which I don't mind calling if I have to, but I don't want to do that yet. I don't want to step on too many toes if I don't have to."

Missy stood up too and walked to where Trenise was standing by the edge of the patio.

"Trenise, I have to do something about this. It's driving me crazy." Missy looked at Trenise desperately, and then lowered her voice, "And I think Alessandra might be in real trouble. I sent my kids away with my parents, your daughter is at school for the summer...Alessandra needs our help."

Trenise looked over her shoulder at Alessandra, who was brushing her hair back over her head with one hand and eyeing them both.

"I'm going to call Thompson. Tell him we want to come and talk to him. Alessandra, you'll tell him about Trent harassing you." Trenise shrugged, "Who knows if he'll listen, but it's a start."

Missy nodded, "He was at my house last night too. Before the Bordelon guy."

"Bordelon was at your house?" Trenise scoffed, "Now that is strange. Why would a Lieutenant both with a call of a trespasser?"

Trenise folded her arms across her chest, trying to reason out why Bordelon would have done such a thing. Her mind ran in circles.

"Is that ok with you Alessandra? Would your mom be ok with it?" Missy looked at Alessandra with concern.

"I'm not going to tell her. She'll worry too much."

Missy felt her heart break as she looked at Alessandra. Her exuberant, loud exterior was clearly a front. Missy saw it, and she guessed Trenise probably did too.

—

Within fifteen minutes, Trenise had arranged for Alessandra, Missy, and herself to meet with Thompson the next morning at 8 am. She wasn't specific with him on the phone but told him they may have some important information to share.

"That way he'll come in with an open mind," she told Missy and Alessandra afterwards.

Alessandra quickly called her manager to tell her she was feeling sick and needed to swap shifts so that she'd have the next day off.

While Trenise and Alessandra made their phone calls, Missy put their glasses back onto the tray and tried to tidy up. She thought of her children, far away in Tennessee and was happy. They were safe there.

The rain had stopped, the sun was out, and the steam coming off the back lawn hovered around the water below. Only the cypress trees were visible above it, rising like ghosts out of the mist.

"Y'all come over here tomorrow morning at 7:30, and we'll all ride together." Trenise nodded to both younger women.

Missy and Alessandra walked out from underneath the patio under the house and started walking to the car.

"Do you feel any better?" Missy asked Alessandra.

Alessandra grinned, "Yeah, I do actually. Not, like, super thrilled about going to talk to the cops at fucking 8 am, but it feels like a start." She laughed, "Ms. Jones is bad ass."

Missy laughed, "She really is."

"Hey, y'all! Wait a sec!"

Alessandra and Missy turned at the sound of Trenise's voice. Trenise jogged down the cement path from the house to catch up to them.

She grabbed them both by the elbow. "When y'all get home, lock all the doors. Lock all the windows."

Missy nodded, "Way ahead of you Trenise. My house is locked up like Fort Knox."

Trenise nodded, "Just double check everything. Alessandra is your mother working tonight?"

"Nah, she took off. She's cooking and then we're supposed to watch that dumb Jennifer Lopez movie where she's the maid." She rolled her eyes and grinned.

Trenise nodded, "Ok good. Lock up anyway. And call the cops if you have to."

Alessandra nodded.

"I'll see y'all tomorrow."

Missy and Alessandra both said goodbye and walked back to Alessandra's car.

Alessandra glanced in the back seat at Berto's breaker bar, reached back, and pulled it into her lap. Missy watched her but didn't say anything. She was thinking of the baseball bat in her garage.

Chapter Twelve

Alessandra dropped Missy off at her house, waited until she was inside, and then pulled out of the driveway. As she did, her phone rang.

"Shit," she swore when she saw it was her mother.

"Where are you, Alessandra?"

"Just heading home from work" Alessandra lied, gritting her teeth, "Someone asked me to pick up their shift."

"Ah ok. Come straight home, don't forget I'm cooking."

"I know, Mami, I'll be there in a few."

Alessandra hung up and drove down past the medium-sized houses like Missy's and Ms. Evie's, and to where the houses and lots got smaller, then turned down the off-shoot road, past the empty trailer lots, to where there were just trees and trees and the trailer she lived in with her mother.

Marietta Sanchez's car sat in the small driveway. She had pulled far enough over so that Alessandra could fit her car next to hers. Alessandra looked around before she got out of her car, then opened the door and ran up the steps.

As soon as she opened the door, she could smell chicken, rice, beans cooking.

"Hola, Mami." Alessandra called.

"Hola, come and see." Marietta was around the same height as Alessandra, almost 5'8, but fuller in the hips and chest and had a rounder face. Alessandra was lanky in the body and long in the face, but the two still had similar looks, especially around the eyes and nose. Marietta had already changed out of her Merry Maids uniform and was standing at the small stove in grey sweats and an old tee-shirt from a radio station back in Houston.

Alessandra walked into the kitchen and pulled a coke out of the fridge.

Marietta turned from the stove and eyed her, "Are you ok?"

Alessandra shrugged, trying to act nonchalant, "Yeah, I'm ok. Two other women had trespassers last night too. Both of them up the street."

"Really?" Marietta furrowed her eyebrows together.

Alessandra nodded, "One was Ms. Jones. She's the gym teacher from school."

Marietta shook her head, "Well at least you weren't the only one. Probably some jerk trying to scare people."

Alessandra nodded again, "Did, uh, did the police call you or anything? Like with information or something?"

"They called but didn't say much," Marietta deepened her voice and imitated a Louisiana drawl making Alessandra laugh, "We workin' on it, ma'am."

"Pfftt," Marietta put the spoon she was using to stir the food down and flapped her hands at the air, "Sounded like a pendejo to me."

Alessandra laughed again, "Mami!"

"What? He did. Go take shower and put on your pjs. We will watch Jennifer and eat. And look at this!" Marietta reached in the fridge and pulled out a white box, "Tres leches!"

Alessandra groaned happily.

Marietta stopped and raised an eyebrow, "You're not too cool for Jennifer, are you?"

Alessandra smiled at her mother and suddenly was struck by how old she looked. She'd spent her life cleaning other people's houses, and Alessandra had never heard her complain once.

She was so excited about a cake, and Alessandra felt a crushing guilt at the amount of grief she'd caused over the years, both intentionally and unintentionally. She felt guilty not telling her about going to see Trenise and Missy, guilty about not telling her about Trent, about meeting with the police tomorrow. Seeing her excitement, her gray hair noticeable against the black hair pulled back into a bun, Alessandra thought she might cry.

I'll tell her as soon as I know if it's true or not, Alessandra promised herself, *for tonight I'll spare her the heartache.*

Alessandra forced a grin, "I can't wait, Mami, and I'm not too cool for Jennifer."

—

As soon as Missy got into her garage and closed the door behind her, she grabbed the baseball bat and went from room to room making sure every door and window was locked.

She left the baseball bat next to the kitchen door that led to the garage and went into the living room. She sat on the couch to call first her kids and then Wes.

To her delight, both Johnny and Sophie Ann sounded as though they were having a wonderful time. Her mother put them on speaker phone and they spent the better part of 15 minutes yelling over each other about what they were doing.

"We're swimming in the pool!!"

"Grandpa's making hot dogs for dinner AND we get to have smores for dessert AND we get to stay up late and watch a movie!"

Missy laughed and *oohed* and *ahhed* over their excitement.

"I miss you, Mama," Johnny finally said.

"Yeah, Mama, when are you coming here?"

"Soon, guys, I just have to deal with some things here first."

"Ok let me talk to Mommy, now," her mother finally said.

Missy spent another fifteen minutes filling her mother in about her conversation with Trenise and Alessandra.

"I'm just going to stay until we talk to the police. Then I'll come up."

"Ok, Missy," her mother's voice was tight with worry, "but if you think this person might've hurt Evie, that means they could hurt you too."

"We don't know that for sure, yet, it's just an idea. I won't know anything until we go and talk to the police, though."

"Are you sure you don't want me to come down?"

"No," Missy said firmly, then, not wanting to hurt her mother's feelings, "I just feel like I have to deal with this on my own."

After another fifteen minutes of goodbyes from the kids, Missy called Wes next and went through the whole conversation again. This time, however, she left out the part where she thought there might be a connection to Evie's death.

"So, you think it's some punk high school kid?"

"Yup. It sounds like it."

"Little asshole."

Missy laughed.

"Yeah, it sounds like it," she said again.

Wes seemed relieved at the idea that it was just a kid pulling a prank, and after making sure that she felt safe in the house and didn't want him to come home, he told her he was exhausted. They said their goodbyes, and Missy was finally alone.

It was about 7 o'clock now, the sun was still out, but it would be down soon. Missy stood up and closed every curtain and blind in the house and made herself a peanut butter and jelly sandwich for dinner.

The house was quiet, so Missy turned on an old Friends rerun while she ate. She left it on while she took a shower and put out clothes to wear the next day. She wanted to look respectable, *believable,* so she laid out a pair of khaki capri pants, a sleeveless blue blouse, and bronze gladiator sandals. She set the alarm on her phone for 5 am.

Returning to the kitchen, Missy grabbed the baseball bat from next to the door, checked the doors and windows again as she moved from the kitchen down to the opposite end of the house where the master bedroom was. She'd turned off Friends in the living room and turned it on in the bedroom instead.

As she washed her hair, she tried to keep her mind blank and not to think about her first night alone in the house and who or what might be walking around outside.

The day had exhausted her, and she hadn't realized it. As she climbed out of the shower and put on her pajamas, it was only 9 o'clock, but she climbed in bed. By 9:30 she was asleep sitting up with the remote in her hand and the next episode of Friends playing on Netflix.

She startled herself awake, not knowing what time it was. The tv screen was asking her if she was still watching Friends. *I guess I'm not,* she thought as she reached for her watch to see what time it was. 3 a.m.

Well that's good, at least I slept most of the night.

Missy rolled over and closed her eyes again. The house was silent.

But that wasn't right. It wasn't *totally* silent. Missy's eyes shot open and she froze, gripping the pillow, listening. Her heart hammered.

A low almost rustling noise.

The wind?

Missy slowly sat up in bed and turned her head in what felt like slow motion toward the slightly open bathroom door. She had left the light on in the bathroom so a wedge of light stretched across the floor. Missy leaned over and grabbed the bat from where it was leaning up against her nightstand. She slowly got out of bed, stood still, and listened. The air conditioning was running, and she strained to hear over its hum.

It was still there. A rustling, wet sound.

Did I leave the faucet running? Maybe it's hitting a washcloth?

Missy crept toward the bathroom door, bat raised. The air conditioning kicked off, and Missy froze again. The sound was louder now. It was a wet sound and a familiar sound.

Sweat standing out across her forehead, Missy pushed the bathroom door open with the bat. The sinks were empty, so Missy turned her head to the right to look at where the toilet and bathtub stood.

After processing what she was seeing, Missy backed out of the bathroom on stiff legs, screamed, and fell backwards over a laundry basket. The baseball bat clanged against the floor as she dropped it. The wet sound was louder with the bathroom door open.

Hundreds of black caterpillars were crawling out of the bathtub drain. They climbed over each other and were filling the tub. They looked slimy, huge, moving unrelentingly. They looked like the ones that were on Evie's tree that day, so long ago, and Missy realized as she sat frozen on the floor of her bedroom, the sound that she recognized was the sound of them eating one another.

Missy felt herself retch in her throat, looked around for the baseball bat, grabbed it and stood up.

As she did, she noticed one of the caterpillars coming out of the bathroom door and into the bedroom. The thought of one of them in her bed filled her with a loathing she couldn't control, and Missy vomited all over the floor.

Anger filling her, she stepped toward the slimy black creature and smashed it with the end of the baseball bat. It squelched and writhed as she crushed it and when she saw it was still moving, she twisted the bat.

Missy reached forward and closed the bathroom door. She pulled towels from the laundry basket she'd tripped over and stuffed them underneath the door, filling the crack.

When she'd crushed the caterpillar, it let out a putrid smell of rot. Between that and the smell of her own vomit, Missy was sure she was going to vomit again. Gagging, she ran down the hall, just like the night before. She ran to the garage, again with a weapon in mind.

When they had first moved to Louisiana, their yard was overrun with red ants. They made huge ant piles that looked like sand, making their yard look like a mine field. Wes had gone to Home Depot and bought a huge container of poison, specifically for the ants. It was higher strength than other poisons and the clerk warned Wes specifically that it could kill small children or pets when it was first used on the ant piles.

It turned out a small amount of the poison went a long way, so locked away in a cabinet was the giant container of poison, almost completely full still.

Missy unlocked the cabinet using the key that hung on a little hook next to it and hoisted the poison out. Wes had put a pair of safety glasses next to the container, she assumed to protect his eyes when he'd put the poison down, so she grabbed those too. She put on the glasses, tucked the bat under her arm, and walked carefully but quickly back down the hall.

The sound was louder now as she stepped back into her bedroom. She wondered how many more had come out while she was gone.

The stench of vomit and rot was almost unbearable, so Missy leaned the bat against the wall, grabbed one of Wes's tee-shirts from his dresser drawer and wrapped it around her mouth and nose. She took a pair of Wes's old boots from his closet and slipped them on her bare feet.

The noise was almost as unbearable as the smell, so Missy quickly took the top of the poison container and filled the scoop inside with the white powdered poison. She skirted around the crushed caterpillar and vomit and opened the bathroom door, scooting the towels to the side.

The caterpillars were about two inches thick in the bathtub now, writhing all over one another. The smell was foul, and the wet sound was now punctuated with sickening crunches as some of the bigger caterpillars appeared to be eating the smaller ones with more enthusiasm.

Missy thought the caterpillars seemed contained in the tub, but she could see a few that had crawled over the side like the one she had crushed in her bedroom. She'd deal with them next.

Stepping toward the tub, Missy lifted the scoop and in a sweeping motion spread the white powder across the tub. The effect was instant. The bugs writhed even faster and then after a few seconds they stopped. Missy scooped up another full scoop of the poison and swept her arm again across the tub. She continued until she couldn't see any more movement and then sprinkled more just to be sure.

Turning now, she saw a few more coming out of the drains of each sink. She dumped poison on them and closed the drains. The tub was filled with the dead caterpillars and poison.

A few more caterpillars were on the floor, so Missy smashed them with Wes's boots. She turned a circle, scanning the small bathroom, but couldn't see any more.

Walking out of the carnage filled bathroom, Missy went down the hall to the kids' bathroom and checked the drains. Nothing. She checked the kitchen sink. Nothing.

Missy looked at the kitchen clock and saw it was 4 am. She felt exhausted and sick. The thought of the caterpillars in the house was nauseating. She was supposed to be at Trenise's house by 7:30, that gave her three and half hours to clean up the mess in the bedroom and get dressed.

Going back out into the garage, Missy gathered the think black contractor's garbage bags Wes kept on hand, a pair of elbow high kitchen gloves, and a shovel. It took her until 5:30 to get rid of all the dead caterpillars and until 6:30 to wipe out the last traces of guts and vomit.

As she took a shower in the guest bathroom in the hallway, trying to scrub off her feeling of repulsion, Missy tried not to think about the sound the caterpillars made, slimy and then crunching as they ate each other. She tried not to wonder why it was all happening to her.

She went back into her bedroom, wrapped in a towel, and grabbed the clothes she had laid out the night before from the dresser. She quickly went back into the master bathroom and grabbed the toiletries and makeup she needed, wondering if she'd ever be able to go back in there without wanting to vomit.

By 7:15, Missy was forcing herself to eat a granola bar in her car and driving to Trenise's house, wondering what else the day would bring. By lunchtime, Missy would look back and marvel at the caterpillars and the fact that they were by far the least revolting and disturbing thing to happen to her that day.

—

Trenise Jones was showered, dressed, and eating toast and drinking coffee on her front porch by 6 am. She hadn't slept well the night before. Normally she was the type of person to fall asleep as soon as her head hit the pillow and sleep for eight hours without waking up. Trenise knew she was lucky in this regard and had heard from many women she knew that after menopause they had trouble sleeping.

Rocking now in her chair and relishing her hot coffee, watching the sun come up over the trees at the end of her street, Trenise wondered how people who had sleep problems regularly made it through their days.

Trenise went to bed at her normal time, 10:00 p.m., after making sure her house was locked, and fell asleep immediately. But she was plagued by nightmares. In one, the trees in the backyard creaked and groaned like they were alive. In another, a woman made of mud crawled up her lawn toward the house as she stood frozen on the back patio wondering if she could see her, but knowing deep in her heart the mud woman knew EXACTLY where she was and was looking right at her.

Trenise woke up every two hours, covered in sweat.

In the last dream, the one that woke her up for good at 4 am, was the most vivid. In the dream, Trenise had been standing by the banks of the water in her backyard. She heard Jolie calling her from off in the distance in the water, but Jolie sounded younger. Trenise waded in up to her waist as Jolie's voice became more frantic; in the dream, she suddenly was sure there was someone waiting for her under the murky water. A hand closed around her ankle, and Trenise screamed herself awake.

When Trenise sat up in bed, panting, she was again covered in sweat, but this time only from the waist down. Waist to toe, Trenise was wet.

Shuddering, Trenise had gotten up and went straight to the shower, wondering vaguely if she had been so terrified that she'd wet herself. Once in the bathroom, she stripped off her wet underwear and pajama pants and held them up in front of her face. They didn't smell like urine or sweat, though. They smelled like water from the bayou in her backyard.

Impossible, she told herself as she threw the soiled clothes in the washing machine.

Trenise blocked out every explanation as to how she'd woken up with pants wet from the bayou. She sat on her porch, trying not to think, and waited for Alessandra and Missy to arrive.

—

Alessandra fell asleep around 11 pm, without the aid of marijuana for the first time in over a year. She was wrapped up in an Afghan her grandmother had made her, her feet on her mother's lap. They had finished watching Jennifer nab the cute guy and had moved on to old reruns of a telenovela.

Marietta Sanchez, used to working overnight, stayed awake until 2 am, keeping watch over her daughter. She slept sitting up on the couch from around 2 am until 5 am. She dreamed about a snake under the trailer, one that knew her daughter's name.

When she woke up at 5, she showered, dressed, and left for her job cleaning houses.

Marietta checked to make sure Alessandra's alarm was set so that she wouldn't be late for work, kissed her sleeping daughter's face, and left.

Alessandra woke up two hours after her mother left, hurriedly dressed, skipped breakfast, and left her driveway by 7:15.

By lunchtime, she would be dry heaving the breakfast she'd skipped behind a gravestone and wishing she was back on the couch in her trailer under her grandmother's afghan.

Chapter Thirteen

A week earlier, Alicia Ann Briggs, who had left home when she was 16, also wished that she was anywhere other than where she was.

Alicia was 19 now and had spent the majority of the last three years hitch hiking and traveling with other gutter punks (what most of the street kids called themselves) and so was used to being in difficult situations, especially involving men.

Walking through the woods looking at this kid Trent's back, Alicia cursed herself for getting into this mess. When the kid stopped his truck next to where Alicia was hitching on an on-ramp in some town called Stone River, he told her he'd take her as far as the edge of New Orleans.

Usually when men picked you up, in Alicia's experience, they expected something. Alicia wasn't necessarily against a transaction of that sort and certainly had done many of them in the past to get where she needed to go. However, she hadn't done it in over a year. Not since she had met Baby.

When Alicia met Baby a year ago, she had immediately fallen head over heels for her.

Baby's features were delicate and small and she was tall and thin. On the night they met, Baby's blonde hair was shaved off and she had piercings in her eyebrows, lips, nose, and ears. She had a tattoo of a rose with thorns over her right eyebrow.

Baby swore more and with more vehemence than anyone Alicia had ever met, and Alicia had personally witnessed her fight with a violence that her thin body wouldn't have hinted at.

Baby was tough as hell, and Alicia thought she was the most beautiful person she'd ever seen.

The night they met, Baby had been playing an ancient-looking acoustic guitar, and Alicia sang along with her, in a sweet, high voice. It was like electricity.

Baby gave Alicia a stick and poke tattoo of a rose, simple and beautiful, to match her own. Alicia had given Baby a ring with a dolphin on it; it was a cheap ring, but Alicia loved dolphins and loved that Baby had put it directly on her own finger with solemnity.

They talked about the ocean until dawn and were together ever since.

The week before finding herself in her current situation, Alicia was with Baby and a group of punks headed to New Orleans for some fun- the cops were lenient with them, and drunk people were always more willing to be generous.

Plus, Baby could play guitar and Alicia could sing and maybe they could earn a little extra money. Baby had a friend who worked in a kitchen in New Orleans and last summer the friend had told her he could get her a job.

To Alica, working in a kitchen alongside Baby, busking when they could, sharing whatever room they could find to rent sounded like heaven.

Finally, some peace.

The night before they were supposed to leave, Alicia and Baby had a fight over Baby talking to some other girl. Not one for jealousy or possessiveness, Baby told Alicia she could fuck off and leave, so Alicia had.

The next morning, after sleeping by herself in the woods, Alicia had returned to where the punks were camped out the night before. They were gone. Next to the burnt campfire on top of a pile of empty beer cans was a note scrawled on a torn piece of paper: "I'm sorry. I looked for you all night. I love you. If you get this and forgive me, come to New Orleans."

Now, walking through a different set of woods with this kid, Alicia felt like slapping herself. She sighed heavily. She could be in New Orleans right now, singing, drinking, having fun with Baby.

Why had I been so stupid?

Instead, she'd probably have to fuck this stupid kid in the woods behind his house before she'd be able to get back to the highway.

May as well get it over with.

"So, hey dude!" Alicia called, "What's the deal? I thought you said you had to grab something from your shed or whatever before you took me to New Orleans?"

Alica was average height, but this kid, Trent, he had told her his name was, was huge.

At least six foot three, she thought.

The woods were shaded and relatively cool compared to the paved highways she had been on for the last week, but Alicia broke into a sweat.

She had a small knife in her bag, but if this kid wanted to hurt her, he could with relative ease.

Trent turned and grinned at her.

Alicia wasn't particularly attracted to men, but she could appreciate his conventional good looks: blue eyes, straight teeth, dark hair, tanned skin.

"Girl, don't you *listen?* I didn't say I had to get something, I said I had to *show* you something near a *building* in my yard."

"Oh," Alicia tried to gauge his tone of voice, "Well are we close?"

Trent grinned even wider, "Yeah, we're close. I can't *wait* to show you this."

With that, he turned and kept walking.

Alicia sighed and rolled her eyes.

I bet you can't wait to show me. "Ooooo aren't you big!"

Alicia rolled her eyes again, balled up her fists. She looked back the way they had come, back toward the road. They were far from the interstate now, but she debated taking her chances and just walking away.

She wanted so desperately to be in New Orleans, to find Baby, and she couldn't stand the idea of prolonging her search by being lost in some backwater town.

He's definitely off, Alicia thought to herself, *but he's a kid.*

She shrugged and kept following Trent deeper into the woods.

Trent passed into a clearing a few minutes later, stopped and pointed.

"There!"

Alicia stepped up beside him and looked, puzzled, into the clearing, trying to see what he was pointing at.

Trent sucked his teeth and gestured.

Alicia could just make out what looked like the ruins of an old building.

"Uhh ok, what is it?"

"Come and see," Trent grabbed her hand and pulled her closer.

Alicia laughed a little at how child-like the gesture seemed.

Maybe this kid is just lonely.

Trent let go of her hand, and Alicia looked at the large square of old stones that had made up the building.

Alicia bent down and looked at the blackened, mossy stones, then up at Trent who was smiling at her with his arms folded.

Alicia smiled a little, "Ok what is it?" she asked again, "An old building?"

"It *was* a church. Over there is the old graveyard, but it's kind of grown over."

Trent pointed to his right and Alicia could make out the unmistakable shape of gravestones below the tree line.

Alicia nodded her head and smiled at Trent.

"Wow, so you just wanted to show me some old ruins?"

She felt a small relief bubble in her chest. As soon as he picked her up, Alicia had thought there was something strange about this kid- not many teenagers in expensive trucks pick up homeless people and offer them rides.

She had thought he was looking for sex, but maybe he was just trying to share something with someone who he thought would care.

Alicia smiled gently at him.

"Have you...have you brought anyone else out here?"

"Well, I brought some friends here to party and they listened to the story," Trent looked slightly crestfallen, "but I don't think they really cared."

Alicia nodded, gently, "Well, I think it's cool. You can tell me the story."

Trent perked up again, "It's a cool story! Like a ghost story!"

Alicia smiled, "Sure Trent."

Alicia sat down on one of the piles of stones that she guessed had been a corner of the old church. Trent walked along the jagged edge of one of the walls and came toward Alicia, holding his arms out like he was walking the tight rope as he talked.

"Well see there was this preacher, and he controlled all of Stone River, that's the town we're in, like all of it. And everyone was scared of him and would do anything he said."

Trent let his voice trail off dramatically. Alicia smiled and laughed a little.

"So what he did was, he started fucking all of the women in town. Like all of them. Even the little girls. And he made them do whatever he wanted. Like real orgies and stuff where the women had to fuck each other and then fuck him."

Alicia's smile faltered and she felt her heart drop.

Don't panic she told herself, *don't panic, you know what this is. It's ok.*

Trent stopped walking and crouched down about ten feet from her and bent his head to the side. He laughed and then dropped his voice to a whisper.

"Then his stupid bitch wife found out and wanted him to stop. So you know what he did? The preacher locked her in the church and gathered all of the people in town. Then he told them she was a lying bitch, and they burned her to death."

Alica sat frozen and watching, wondering where the knife was in her backpack and if she could get to it before he got to her.

Trent jumped off the pile he was crouched on and walked toward the gravestones.

"They burned her up. Her and some other bitches. And then his OWN CONGREGATION turned against him. Don't they know to do as they're told? Someone got scared, ran out, and the church burned up with some women in it. Isn't that a shame? A beautiful church burned up just because some stupid bitch didn't want to suck dick anymore."

Trent shook his head sadly. His back was to her and Alicia slowly stood up.

She slowly backed away, looking toward the direction they had come from. She wasn't stupid. They were out in the middle of the woods in Louisiana. If this kid didn't hurt her, the alligators or snakes would. Trent still had his back to her as she backed toward the small path she spotted and assumed it must be the way they had come from.

She backed up more and decided as soon as she reached the path, she'd run. She'd take her chances with the alligators. She pulled her bag to her stomach and slowly undid the zipper, easing a hand in to feel for the knife.

"You want to know the best part?" Alicia could barely hear him now, his voice had gotten softer, and she was getting further and further away, "Everyone says the preacher was never heard from again, that he ran away, but that's not true."

Alicia was about five feet from the path now.

"He did leave, but he came back here afterwards. After he died, he sent his sons back here and they stayed. They brought his ashes with him and buried them over there in the churchyard."

Alicia felt her hand close around the knife's bottom and she wrenched it out, putting her bag back on her back.

Trent turned and looked at her. He didn't seem shocked or perturbed that she was so far away. Alicia took the knife out of its hilt and held it to her side. She wiped the sweat out of her eyes and blinked, thinking wildly about everything Baby had taught her to do during a fight. Go for the eyes, the ears, the balls.

"I'm his great great, great, great grandson," Trent laughed, "Or however many greats. My dad told me so."

Alicia looked over her shoulder at the path again and back at Trent.

"I'll catch you." Trent said simply, as though reading her mind.

Alicia decided she'd take her chances. She turned and sprinted toward the path. Within a few seconds, Trent tackled her, knocking her body to the ground and crushing her. Alicia's nose smashed into the ground and she could taste blood as it broke. Her hand holding the knife was out to her side and she swung it behind her hoping to connect.

Trent knocked it out of Alicia's hand and grabbed her by her chin length hair. Alicia howled and kicked, scratching at his hand.

Trent dragged her back toward the ruins of the church by her hair, adjusting his grip as he ripped out pieces as he pulled. He dragged her into the center of the square ruins and sat on top of her hips.

"Please," Alicia said, breathlessly, "Please don't." Her eyes burned with blood from her nose as she looked up at Trent looming over her.

He furrowed his eyebrows and moved his hands all over her body, pulling and ripping her clothing as he went.

Alicia squeezed her eyes shut and remembered a conversation she had had with Baby as they held each other, camped out in the woods somewhere in Virginia.

"I just used to close my eyes and go somewhere else," Baby had said. "I grew up near the ocean, so I just closed my eyes and thought of the waves and the wind."

“Have you seen the ocean?” Baby had asked. Alicia whispered no, shaking her head where it lay between Baby’s small naked breasts.

Alicia squeezed her eyes shut now, thinking about that conversation. She thought about the wind, the crash of waves, about Baby’s face and arms. She thought about the dolphin ring she had given to Baby. She thought about Baby’s gentle fingers. None of it distracted her from the current pain below her waist, but Alicia thought she could bear it until she could figure out a way to get away.

She heard his grunting noises and felt it as he flipped her over on her stomach, but she was far away. She was with Baby at a beach she conjured up from pictures she’d seen. Baby had on her dolphin ring and was playing her guitar.

When Trent began smashing the back of Alicia’s head with his fist as he thrusted, she cried out in agony when her front teeth broke against the rocks below her. When Trent reached out and grabbed a rock from the wall of the ruined church and smashed her once below the nape of the neck, Alicia lost consciousness.

She didn’t hear or feel it as Trent cried out as he finished, smashing the back of her head once more with the rock. Alicia was gone. She drifted away to a place where the hands of men couldn’t touch her, a place where she could find peace among the endless waves of eternity.

—

On the morning of Missy, Trenise and Alessandra’s visit to Officer Thompson, Trent lay on his bed thinking about Evangeline. For a long time, Trent had been angry at her. Angry for what she had done to him, angry for what she made him do to her.

But now, lying on his bed and thinking about her, and the girl in the woods, and Alessandra, Trent felt grateful. Evangaline is the one who opened the door.

He had heard the stories about the preacher growing up just like every kid in Stone River had. His dad had told him the stories trying to scare him, but they never had. Trent remembered being on hunting or fishing trips and his friends' eyes, wide and spooky, telling about how the preacher had controlled the town, had hurt people, and had finally killed some of them.

But Trent knew the truth in his heart about what the preacher was trying to do. He was trying to help. He was trying to show people how to do things. In his way, the preacher was the same as his own father and grandfather. They knew that sometimes when you were trying to help people, you had to hurt them to make them understand.

He had learned that lesson from both his father and brother both at a young age. He had seen it in how his father controlled his mother and made her do as he wanted.

Trent rolled over on his side. He knew he should probably get up and take a shower since he was expected to be at the lumber yard in a few hours. His father had forced him to get a job this summer and arranged for him to haul lumber. Trent didn't mind since the foreman, the father of a friend from the football team, was in absolute awe of Trent's dad (Grant Sr. -who also just happened to be owner of the lumber yard).

Trent earned a decent amount of money to simply goof off and smoke weed. The fact that it also kept his father off his back was an added bonus.

Reaching over to the bedside table, Trent looked at the clock on his phone. Eight thirty. Just enough time for a quick visit, then a shower, then work. And if he was late, so what? It's not like his boss was going to rat on him to Grant.

And besides, Trent thought to himself happily, *old Grant is far away on vacation in Mexico with his new piece of ass. Well, new to Grant. In reality, she was an OLD piece of ass with too much Botox.*

Trent sat up and grinned at himself in the full length mirror he had propped on the wall opposite his bed. He looked at his shirtless body, admired his pecs and squeezed his arms into muscles. Whenever Trent brought girls home to have sex with, he always admired the way his arms looked in the mirror as he held them down and moved his hips against theirs.

He hadn't brought anyone home last night, even though Lexie had been nearly begging him to. Last night when he had seen her, Lexie had been in rare form- squealing about how some guy had tried to break into Coach Jones's house and some other bitch's house.

Trent knit his eyebrows together when he remembered that Lexie said whoever it was had also tried to break into Alessandra's house. Coach Jones getting scared was funny. Some punk going after Alessandra was most certainly NOT funny. Alessandra was his. He just hadn't quite figured out how to get her yet.

Trent could've brought Lexie home, but with her in a *squealing* mood, he just couldn't bring himself to. Not that he was worried about his father hearing. His father encouraged him to bring home whoever he liked and even occasionally bragged to certain business associates about the quality of girls his son was able to bring home.

"My lord, you should've seen the one he was with the other night. Blonde, 120 pounds, huge tits."

Trent laughed. He wondered what his dad would think about the tail he had stashed in the woods. No, he definitely wasn't into squealing girls anymore. Not after the silence he'd grown used to.

He grinned again and pulled on a pair of dirty jeans and a Stone River High School Football tee-shirt. A trip out to the woods would be just the thing to fix him up and get both Evangaline and Alessandra off his mind.

Plus, he didn't know how much longer the one out there would last. Even in the shade of the trees, she was starting to smell.

Trent went to the bathroom attached to his room to take a piss (no point in brushing his teeth until after), and then down the large staircase to the kitchen. He grabbed a water and a protein bar and walked out the back door and across the lawn. It was hot already so Trent took a swig from the water bottle, making sure to save some since he knew he'd be thirsty when he was done.

Evangaline swam back into his head as he walked. He thought about her small breasts and hips, her long black hair. He thought about how she felt, limp and lifeless, as he dragged her into the woods by the side of the road. His heart raced at the thought, and he felt himself swell with excitement.

As he walked across his back lawn, Trent told himself the story again. The story of Trent and Evangeline.

Trent first saw Evangaline in church. She'd been with her fat husband and shitty little kids, but Trent couldn't stop staring at her. He'd watched her as she talked to Lexie's bitch mother and a bunch of old women.

She laughed loudly when she talked. She laughed like she didn't give a shit that she was in church. She'd tossed her head back and stuck her breasts out.

She had been wearing a thin blouse, modest, but thin, and tight blue jeans.

It wasn't hard to track her down. A quick internet search turned up her Facebook profile and there he had found that she belonged to her neighborhood's Homeowner's Association. The neighborhood was close to his own house, separated by his large property. Plus, not only did he know kids from football in that neighborhood, but his dad rented small houses and trailers on the outskirts of it.

It wouldn't be weird at all for him to make a trip through. Technically the main road through the subdivision led to his house if you took it all the way to the end.

Trent drove past her house in his truck with the windows down and the music loud so that she'd turn and look at him when she was outside playing with her kids. The first few times, she turned and looked and waved.

He had slowed way down so she could see in the window, see his face and arms and chest. He'd tighten his arms so she could see how hard he'd worked to keep them chiseled.

Then she stopped looking. She just kept playing with her kids and waved at him with barely a glance. The first time she'd done that, Trent had smashed his dashboard with his fist, screaming with rage. The second time she ignored him, she had been talking to a blonde woman with big tits. Trent refused to believe that a woman like Evangaline was a dyke, but jealousy burned hot in his face as he drove.

Trent wanted to smash something again but decided not to. Instead, he decided that the next time he went past her house, he'd be on foot. He carefully picked tightish gym shorts and a sleeveless shirt with wide arm holes. His wavy brown hair was short on the sides and longer on top and he was tanned from summer and fall football practice.

This time when he jogged by, music blasting through his headphones, Evangaline and the blond woman again had looked at him as he jogged past. He gave them his best smile and waved.

Both women waved and then said something to each other. He couldn't hear what they said, but he could guess what it was.

He jogged by two more times, but she ignored him again. Just a wave and then back to her kids or her husband. The second time she'd ignored him, he broke into a run, turned around and went back home.

What he was doing wasn't getting her attention, so he decided to change his tactic. He didn't particularly enjoy being around the bush. No, Trent had always preferred a direct approach, especially with the opposite sex.

Thinking about Evangeline like this, as he walked to the edge of the cleared lawn and to where the wooded part of the Longue property began, Trent could feel his pants bulge so uncomfortably he could barely walk. His hands shook as he ran them through his hair and on his neck.

As he wound his way down the familiar path, he let his mind wander back again as he massaged his crotch and walked.

The two guys on the football team who he knew who lived in Evangaline's neighborhood, Terry Fawer and Wyatt Prittini, were perfect for what he needed: morons who were younger than him, looked up to him, would laugh when he wanted them to, look tough, and be loud.

Plus, both of Fawer's parents worked long hours in New Orleans. Trent told a few other friends to come meet him at Fawer's house so they could drink one Friday afternoon, then casually suggested going for a walk down to *his* house.

Just as he'd hoped, as he walked at the head of a pack of six guys, Evangaline was outside of her house. Trent remembered his heart beating fast, and his stomach lurching. Not only had she been outside, but she was outside *alone.* No husband, and no kids.

"Hey gorgeous!" Trent had yelled. Evangaline looked up puzzled and incredulous and the guys with him laughed. "You dropped something back there!"

Evangaline tipped her head to the side, "Really? What"

Trent grinned, "My jaw, gorgeous! Want to come bend over and pick it up?"

Evangaline's face turned from amused to angry, "Oh that's real nice."

She turned and walked back to her house as Trent and his friends continued walking, the other boys howling with laughter.

He snapped back to the present as a walked heavily along the narrow path that wound its way through the wooded section of his father's property. Off to his right, to the east about a half mile or so, the Stone River would be lazily flowing (lazy at this time of year, but wild in the spring) to Lake Pontchartrain. He was walking north to the old ruins on autopilot and almost missed the small fork in the path that he needed to take to get there.

Trent thought about Evangaline again, trying to bring his memory back, but instead he thought of Alessandra from school. Alessandra didn't look like Evangaline, really, but she had the same attitude, the same way of carrying herself. They both were dark and slim, too, but Alessandra was much taller.

Trent hadn't meant to go out looking for someone to bring to the ruins with him, but he had spotted the girl by the side of the road, hitch hiking, and was struck by how much she looked like Alessandra. Trent sighed to himself, trying to think clearly.

Evangeline. Alessandra. The girl in the woods.

Even in the shade, the heat was starting to get oppressive, and Trent could feel his shirt clinging to his back as he started to sweat. He felt his face turn red with anger and shame as he thought about Alessandra.

Trent was used to being able to fuck pretty much anyone he wanted. Hell, he was sure even some of the guys he played football with would suck his dick if he asked them to, if he was into that. He thought Alessandra would be a sure thing. But not only had she turned him down, but she turned him *in.* And, oh boy, had he gotten his from his father for that one.

Grant Sr. might encourage Trent's behavior with the girls from church, but he made it very clear to Trent how he felt about being called by the school principal and told that a teacher had witnessed Trent physically assaulting a girl in the hallway. Not that Grant Sr. particularly cared about Trent assaulting a girl. He cared that it was *careless.*

Grant forced Trent to explain who the girl was and why he was after her; he made Trent explain what would happen to the family businesses if they had to deal with a lawsuit.

Trent reached down and started to undo the fly of his pants, still walking. He shook his head to get rid of thoughts about the beating he had taken after Principal Pitre's phone call to Grant Sr. Even though he was in his fifties, Grant Sr. took pride in his appearance and worked out daily. He was strong and vicious.

Trent's eyes filled with tears as he thought about Grant twisting his balls in one hand, how he had held in his screams as Grant laughed and twisted, telling him to be smarter or face the consequences.

Trent wiped the tears from his face and thought again about Evangaline.

The next Friday after his first conversation (conversation in his mind anyway) with Evangline, Trent suggested the same thing to his pack of friends. Drinking, and then a walk down to his house to shoot pool or ride four wheelers.

This time, Evangaline was out in her yard with her kids, the blond woman he had seen her with before, and who he assumed were the blond woman's kids.

"Hey gorgeous!" Trent yelled again, making Evangaline look up from where she was playing with her twins. The blond woman looked too, which Trent also enjoyed. She wasn't really his type, but she reminded him of an older, bustier version of Lexi.

> Evangaline said something in a low voice to the blond, who shook her head slightly. Evangaline laughed.

Trent did not like that she was laughing at him, but he forced himself to keep smiling.

He pointed at her daughter, "Does she have a daddy? If not you and her both can call me Daddy!"

His friends absolutely howled with laughter and one or two slapped him on the back.

The blond woman looked repulsed, and Evangaline turned bright red. Trent grinned even more at her embarrassment and, what he assumed was, shame. Trent kept walking with his friends, Evangaline now behind him.

She must've jogged to catch up with them since her front yard stretched about 20 feet to the road, so she made Trent jump a little when she yelled, "Hey wait a minute!"

Pleased, Trent had wheeled around, "Coming to take Daddy up on it, gorgeous?"

To his absolute horror, Evangline threw her head back and laughed, "The fuck would I want to fool with a little baby dick like you for?"

She may as well have slapped Trent and he stood there, stupidly, with his mouth hanging open.

"Oh, nothing to say now, Daddy?" she laughed again, "You listen to me, son, I know who you are, and I know who *your* Daddy is. You say any more of that bullshit to me again, and you can bet your ass I'll march straight over to your house and let him know."

Evangaline had looked at all the boys, "And that goes for all of you, too. Terry, I've got your mama's number in my phone."

None of the boys spoke now, and Evangaline nodded her head, "Yeah, that's what I thought. Now get the hell away from my house."

His heart pounding, Trent had walked to his house with his friends like a whipped dog.

"Forget that bitch" Terry had said, and Trent felt like pounding his face in with both hands. Pounding his face until it looked like raw meat.

They had spent the rest of the afternoon riding four wheelers and getting wasted, but Trent could feel that they all knew he had been bested. That Evangaline had made fun of him, mocked him, called him "baby dick."

Now in the woods, Trent was getting near to the clearing where the old ruins and the graveyard was. His pants were all the way down in front and he was so hard it hurt.

He grabbed himself with one hand and yelled, "Baby dick this, you fucking cunt!"

Walking around to the small gravestones, half jerking off with anticipation, he spotted the two fallen gravestones where he had lazily stashed the homeless girl.

When he got close to her, Trent took his hand off himself to hold his nose, "Whooo goddamn, girl, you gotta wash that pussy!"

He laughed loudly, then reached down to grasp her ankles and pull her out to where he could get to her body like he wanted to.

She was stiff now and he wondered if he would even be able to spread her legs apart again. With some force, he found he could. He let his mind wander to Evangline, to Alessandra, to them both looking at him with anger, to them both telling him off. Now though, he was telling *them* off, he was telling *them* what to do, and they did it.

In his mind they did everything he told them to.

It didn't take him long to finish (he had, after all, spent the better part of the fifteen minute walk here with a raging hard on). Then he dragged the girl's body back between the two gravestones, zipped up his pants, and stood wondering what to do.

He really didn't think she'd last too much longer out here before stinking so bad she might attract attention. A road ran behind the property, the same road he'd used to drive the girl here instead of bringing her to his house.

That would have been careless.

Grant rented the land out during hunting season, and there was a small inlet Grant had cleared for parking that opened on to a path that led straight here. Signs reading "No Trespassing" were posted all over and most people were scared enough of his father to heed them.

But most people didn't mean everyone.

Trent didn't really *want* to get rid of her, he had been enjoying her company *very* much after all, but didn't think he had much choice.

He pulled out his phone to check the time: only half an hour had passed. He looked longingly at the body stashed behind the gravestones but didn't think he'd be ready for another go so quickly. Deciding unhappily that this couldn't wait any longer, Trent started walking back.

As he walked back toward the house, toward the shed where he knew there was a shovel, Trent thought about the girl and Evangaline.

When he had hit Evangaline in the head with the rock, it was spur of the moment, it had come from anger and shame when she ignored him again and then laughed at him again. But when he had hit the homeless girl with the rock, it felt calculated, strong, wild, but he felt totally in control.

He thought about hitting Evangaline, and what had happened after, as he walked. When he had been with Evangaline, he felt totally out of control, like an animal. He let his mind drift again, telling himself their story. His and Evangeline's.

After she had chastised him in front of his friends, Trent started walking all the way to her house using the service alleys. Narrow and cool, Trent could take his time to think about her as he walked. He'd go at night when her house was all lit up so he could see in, or in the afternoon when she'd be outside. He'd stand in shadows of the trees behind her house and just watch.

He didn't speak to her again for about a month.

Really, he thought now, it was almost like serendipity. He shook his head, bemused, as he walked through the woods, listening to the whine of the bugs and feeling the sweat drip off his forehead and back.

The night before he spoke to her the last time, he and a group of friends (guys and girls this time) had been out by the old ruins. They had been partying close to the Longue house when Lexie had left her group of friends, sauntered up to Trent, and grabbed his arm.

She pressed her body against his, "Trent is it really true the ruins to that old church from the story are out there on your property?"

Trent grinned at her, "Yeah, it's true."

Lexie looked at him, doe eyed, "Will you take me and Monica out there to look at it?"

Trent leaned over Lexie's head to eye Monica. She was currently dating one of the other guys on the football team, but judging on how much she'd had to drink, Trent didn't think she would take very much convincing.

The whole group of them ended up walking out to the ruins, Trent in the lead and telling them the version of the story that he knew, the one that his older brother, Grant Jr., had told him.

"So, everyone knows different versions of The Preacher story, but the one I know is the TRUTH. This is the one my dad told me, and his dad told him, and all the way back. My family was here during the time the preacher lived."

Someone had laughed at that.

"Shut the fuck up," Trent yelled, "It's fucking true. Now let me fucking talk."

They all fell silent as they walked.

"So this guy, Emmanuel White, he lived in Stone River back when it was called something else. He was the most powerful guy in town and everyone went to him with, like, questions and problems and stuff so he knew everybody and everybody's business. Everyone respected him."

"Kinda like your dad, Trent."

"Yeah kinda," Trent continued, "So he tried to help everyone out but he had his, you know, stuff that he liked to do."

"You mean like he liked to fuckkkkkk!" his buddy Joel yelled.

Trent laughed and nodded, "Well, that's what some people say, but my dad said that's not the truth. But like even if he did...is that a crime?"

Joel laughed, "Not by me, dude!"

Trent shone the flashlight he was carrying in his own face and winked at Lexie.

He continued again, "All right now shut the fuck up and let me finish. So, the real story is that his wife and some of her friends were the ones who were having sex with a bunch of the dudes in town, like fucking them in the church and stuff, and Emmanuel found out about it. They were witches; they worshipped Satan and used voodoo to hurt people. He locked her in the church so he could figure out what to do with her and gathered a council of church members to help him. He brought the other women too and locked them all in. When they all got to the church, his wife had gone crazy and was trying to burn it down."

Trent lowered his voice, feeling their waiting silence heavy on his back. He knew no one had heard this version of the story before, this was the Longue family version.

"Emmanuel White tried to rush into the burning church to save her, but the members held him back. Because of what his wife did, all those women burned alive in the church."

Trent paused. All he could hear were the bugs in the woods, the crunch of footsteps, and some ragged breathing. The lights from their flashlights swung back and forth through the dark woods and finally shone into the clearing.

"Is that it?" Lexie whispered.

Trent nodded, "That's it. She's buried in the graveyard over there. And my dad says Emmanuel White's sons buried him here too, so he could be with her even after they had died."

He pointed off to the side of the clearing. They broke into little clumps and looked around, some goofing off and laughing, some looking solemnly at the gravestones and the ruins.

Trent thought about Evangaline as he walked with his arm around Lexie. He thought about what she was probably doing with her husband right then and felt his stomach clench at the idea.

He bent down and picked up a blackened, jagged rock that just fit into his hand and put it in the pocket of his cargo shorts.

He had gotten so wasted that night he didn't really remember anything, and when he woke up he felt nauseated and his head was pounding. He rolled over on his bed, away from Lexie, and felt for his shorts where his phone would tell him the time. Instead, he pulled out the rock from the graveyard.

When he had held it in his hand, his head had cleared instantly. And suddenly, he knew what he had to do, knew with the surety as if his own father had whispered it in his ear. Calm, firm.

He had to put the fear of God in Evangeline Nunez. He, Trent Longue, would be her god now.

—

Musing over all of this, Trent reached the shed in the backyard, checked the time, and decided to buy himself an extra hour. He called his boss, put on his best, "Aw shucks" voice, and told him he'd had a late night. Would it be a problem if he came in an hour late, sir?

"Aw hell, kid. That's no big deal. Happens to the best of us when we're young. Take some ibuprofen and drink some water. See you after lunch."

Trent hung up, grabbed the shovel, and started walking back to the church, thinking about the day he had become Evangeline's god.

He felt a deep loss that he would have to give up the girl in the woods, so he turned his thoughts to Alessandra. To her long legs and wide eyes. He thought about what he could do with *her* out here in the woods. About how much he had learned and how he could stop being careless.

He felt himself swell again below the waist, felt his pants tighten, and reached down again with the hand that wasn't holding the shovel.

Maybe he'd get one more round in before he buried her after all.

Trent grinned, slung the shovel over his shoulder, and whistled to himself as he walked.

Chapter Fourteen

All three women were silent as they walked out of the police station and back to Trenise's SUV. Trenise unlocked the car door remotely and all three climbed in, closing their respective doors behind them.

"You think he believes me?"

Alessandra was in the back seat and she shifted the backpack she'd brought with her and quietly unzipped it. There wasn't much in it: a sweatshirt, her phone charger, and Tio Berto's breaker bar. She wrapped her hand around it and then let it go, feeling calmer at its weight.

She leaned forward gripping both Missy and Trenise's seats.

Trenise sighed heavily and glanced at Missy, who was watching her evenly, "I don't know, Alessandra."

Alessandra slumped back in her seat, "Yeah."

Thompson had listened closely to everything Alessandra said. He took notes, asked all the right questions. At the end of her story, he asked if any of them could positively identify Trent Longue as the person who was at their houses. There was a definite look of exasperation when he asked it.

In the car now, Missy couldn't help feeling crestfallen and defeated.

"Do you trust him, Trenise?"

Trenise laughed a little, "Nope. I don't think I do. I think Thompson is out for himself."

Missy had fully believed that Thompson would tell them he would go talk to this kid Trent at least. She thought about her kids in Tennessee, her husband in the Gulf of Mexico, and the black worms in her bathroom. She thought about her brother's baseball bat that she brought with her into Trenise's car with her that morning, the one that Trenise and Alessandra had both glanced at but hadn't questioned.

Missy reached next to her leg where it was leaning and touched its cool metal.

"Do y'all mind if I take the long way back?" Trenise's voice broke the silence in the car, "I need to think."

"You're driving Ms. Jones, wherever you want to go is fine with me."

Trenise glanced at Missy, "That ok with you?"

Missy nodded and avoided Trenise's eyes. She was thinking about the sound, the squelching, crunching, slimy sound as the caterpillars writhed all over each other, and about the smell of rot that had filled her bathroom and bedroom.

"Missy? Are you ok?"

Missy nodded and closed her eyes, "Just a little overwhelmed."

"You want me to head straight home or you ok with a little drive?"

"No, I'm good with a drive. Can I open the window a little?"

Trenise opened the passenger side window and turned off Highway 60, otherwise called Military Road, that led back from the main part of Stone River where the police station was to their subdivision. There was an old road back here that led to different hunting camps and that ran along the river for more than ten miles before it looped around behind the edges of Cypress Forest.

It rounded behind the expansive Longue property and then connected to Morgan Bluff on end of the subdivision that was furthest away from Alessandra's trailer.

"Where are we?" Alessandra finally asked after about ten minutes.

Trenise looked at Alessandra in the rearview mirror, "We're behind our little friend's house."

Alessandra looked out the window to her left at the thick of trees and shook her head to herself. She knew that Trent lived in a huge house with a huge lawn, pool, and a huge piece of property behind it.

She knew because she had overheard Lexie talking about it at school. She thought about her small trailer on the land that she and her mother didn't own.

Imagine. Alessandra felt a small bubble of envy but pushed it away. She'd take her little trailer with her mother over all Trent Longue's bullshit.

"Trenise?"

"What's wrong Missy?"

"Pull over, Trenise, I'm going to be sick."

Trenise looked to her left and saw a small clearing, probably where hunters parked when it was the season, and pulled in quickly.

As soon as she stopped, Missy jumped out, breathing deeply.

I'm ok, she thought, *I'm ok.*

She stood with her hands on her hips and the memory of stepping on one of the caterpillars ripped through her. She imagined a rotten boil popping.

Leaning over, Missy gagged three times, but nothing would come out.

She didn't hear Trenise approach, but felt her gentle hand on her shoulder as she squeezed her eyes shut. When she opened them, she saw that Trenise was crouched down next to her, a bottle of water in her hand, eyes large with concern.

Alessandra was standing a few feet off shifting her weight from one foot to the other, shading her eyes with her hand.

"I'm ok." Missy muttered and then slumped down onto a fallen log that was near her. It looked like it had been placed there intentionally to delineate where cars should pull up when they parked there.

Trenise sat on one side of her, opened the water bottle, then handed it to her.

Alessandra sat down heavily on her other side.

"I kinda want to barf too," Alessandra said glumly.

Missy laughed a little and shook her head, "It's not...it's not just the stuff with the..." she burped a little and waved her hand, "excuse me, sorry, y'all."

Trenise waved her manners away and Alessandra laughed, "Nice one."

"...not just the stuff with the cops," Missy continued, "It's something that happened before we left."

As they sat on the log and Missy took small sips of the water Trenise gave her, and she told them not only about the caterpillars that morning in her bathroom, but also about the day she had seen them on the tree in front of Evie's house.

When she was done, she felt marginally better and looked at Trenise and Alessandra. The two of them were as different as could be, but they had the exact same looks of disgust on their faces. Missy laughed a little.

"Sick." Alessandra whispered.

"You should really call an exterminator, Missy." Trenise said seriously, "I know a good one, he could be over this afternoon probably."

"Really?" Missy perked up at the idea of complete annihilation of any and all bugs in her house.

Trenise stood up and offered Missy a hand, "Yeah, I'll call him in the car."

Alessandra stood up too, "Ok good, because, y'all I didn't want to say anything but it's hot as shit out here."

Missy laughed a little and wiped the sweat off her forehead.

Trenise reached the car first and was opening her mouth to say something when a howl ripped through the woods behind them.

Trenise froze, hand on the door. Missy turned toward the dark woods behind her and, despite the heat, felt cold sweat on her back and the hair on her arms stand up.

"What the actual fuck was that?" Alessandra reached out and grabbed Missy's arm, turning toward the woods in the same direction as Missy.

Trenise stepped away from the car and stood on Missy's other side. She reached an open hand up and pressed it against Missy's other arm in a gesture of "wait."

She cocked her head to one side, her braids brushing Missy's bare shoulder.

The three of them stood there together, frozen, for what felt to Missy like an eternity. The bugs whined, a crow called.

Alessandra could hear her own breathing heavy in her ears and tried to quiet it as she strained to hear.

"Was it an animal?" Missy finally whispered.

Trenise shook her head no and held one finger to her lips.

Alessandra took a hesitant step toward the woods. As she did, the howl came again. Missy gasped, and Trenise closed her hand around Missy's arm and brought her other

hand to her chest. Alessandra took a step back and looked at Trenise with wide eyes.

"FUCK!" whoever it was screamed, "FUCK! FUCK!" The voice sounded like it was in agony.

"You think someone is hurt?" Missy whispered.

"God, it sounds like it doesn't it?" Trenise and Missy locked eyes.

"Or it's some fucking weirdo." Alessandra nodded her head at the woods.

Trenise spoke slowly, "Look, you two stay here. I'll go in a little and see if I can see or hear anything, then we'll call the police if we have to."

"Um have you never seen a horror movie, Ms. Jones? Get real."

Trenise walked over to the car, reached in, and grabbed her phone from her purse.

"Either one of you have yours?"

Alessandra nodded and pulled her phone from her back pocket.

Another howl echoed through the woods making all three of them jump again.

Trenise pointed to what looked like a small path that led into the woods.

"I'll go down and see what I can see or hear. You two wait here."

"You sure, Trenise?"

"Yes, absolutely. One person makes less noise than three."

Missy looked doubtful. She didn't like the idea of Trenise going off on her own. She didn't know Trenise Jones well, but she knew her enough to trust her judgment.

"If you're not back in five minutes," Missy said resolutely, "I'm coming looking for you."

Trenise nodded and walked to the path, quickly disappearing into the thick woods.

—

Trenise walked for less than a minute before she turned around to look back, making sure she could see the path she had come down. Walking off into the woods without knowing how to get back out again wasn't a good idea. The path was clear though, both in front of and behind her, so Trenise tried to walk as quietly as she could, pausing every now and then to listen.

The ambient noise of the woods around her was vaguely comforting. The bugs droned, lizards or squirrels scuttled through the brush, birds darted to and fro, rustling in the full leaves on the trees. It was still hot, but the shade given by the trees felt refreshing.

Trenise paused again, listening.

Another howl echoed around her. Trenise jumped and then darted off the path, crouching behind a tree. It seemed like it came from just up ahead of her. Keeping close to the ground and off the path, but making sure she could still *see* the path, Trenise crept forward. It was difficult work with the brush being so thick.

What are you doing? Big John's voice floated through her mind, *Don't get involved in this. Be smart. Get in your car and drive away.*

Trenise paused and looked behind her, then in front of her. Just up ahead, it looked like the woods cleared and there was some kind of large open space. She couldn't see a house, but it was definitely a clearing. Almost on her stomach, Trenise crept forward and paused again.

She could hear that someone was talking, but she couldn't quite make out what they were saying. She stayed frozen and listened. It was a male voice. Whoever it was seemed to be speaking normally, not screaming like the voice they had heard by the car. Trenise debated turning back around, but she felt she couldn't.

Crouched down, fingers half buried in the wealth of leaves, grass, dirt, and branches in the underbrush, Trenise felt drawn forward.

As she did, a memory surfaced, strong and sharp.

The houses in the ninth ward where she had grown up were so close together, they may as well have been apartments. "Spittin' distance" is what her grandmother had called it. She knew all of her neighbors and they all knew her. She knew which people were safe and which to stay away from. Oh yes.

At the end of her street there had been a "funny man" as her grandmother called him.

"You stay away from there, you hear me?" Her grandmother admonished her one day, waving a wooden spoon she was using to cook in her general direction. Trenise was sitting at the small kitchen table and looked at her grandmother's scrawny figure, strong and tough, built the same way as Trenise was now.

"Why Mamaw?" Trenise had asked.

"He's funny in the head. Dangerous to little girls. He comes near you, you scream as loud as you can and you run on home as fast as you can."

From the day of her grandmother's warning, Trenise felt compelled to walk past the man's house. He often sat on the front porch and stared with wide unblinking eyes at her as she walked past. The house was dingy and looked dirty. There were never any lights on. The small side yard was overgrown. And yet Trenise walked past, feeling his eyes on her. And she stared right back.

Today, in the woods, only 50 miles from the neighborhood where she grew up but for all intents and purposes on another planet, Trenise felt the same pull. The same desire to look at something she wasn't supposed to. She felt the same desire to defy, to challenge.

So, Trenise crept forward, toward the clearing. She felt the same pull as when, as a child, she walked past the Funny Man's house even though her grandmother had told her not to go near.

As she inched forward, Trenise could hear what sounded like groaning. She stopped and listened again.

She froze, hearing something behind her and turned slowly, eyes wide. Missy and Alessandra were about three feet from her, crouched down and creeping along the slim path, holding onto one another like Hansel and Gretel.

Trenise sucked her teeth and made her way through the brush from her hiding place to the spot in the path where the two were slowly walking, trying not to scare them.

Missy saw her first and gasped quietly, putting her hand over her mouth.

"Someone's up there up ahead, " Alessandra whispered.

"I know that." Trenise whispered back, "come on over here"

She pulled them both into the woods to a crouch, "What are y'all doing?"

"Ten minutes, Trenise." Missy said.

"Look, y'all go on ba-"

Another howl interrupted Trenise and the three of them froze, silent, listening.

Missy craned her head up and over the brush and could just make out the clearing up ahead.

"Someone's moving up there." She mouthed.

Trenise nodded and Alessandra sat motionless, eyes wide.

"Fucking BITCH!" the voice was close, loud but not screaming.

Alessandra whipped her head around at the sound of the voice.

"That's Trent," she whispered frantically.

"Are you sure?" Missy whispered back.

Trenise held up a hand to silence them both and looked toward the clearing. She inched forward to see if she could get a better viewpoint. After poking her head around a large tree, she had an unobstructed view into the clearing.

Just behind her, she felt Missy and Alessandra both creep up and peer out into the clearing as well.

Missy could just make out what looked like the foundation to an old building that had fallen to ruin. She also saw a man, or a teenager, if Alessandra was right, with his back to her, digging.

He was placing the dirt into a relatively neat pile, but he seemed to struggle now and then. When he did, he let out a stream of curse words which echoed through the clearing.

Alessandra knew exactly what the ruins in the clearing were. In the stories she'd heard at school, the kids always said that the old ruins were still out there, somewhere on the huge property that Trent's family owned. They all said that the ruins of the church and the graveyard showed that the stories about the preacher were true.

Alessandra tried to swallow and heard a click in her throat as her mouth went dry.

She felt with certainty that they shouldn't be here, shouldn't be seeing this, that they needed to leave. She felt that whatever they were about to see would pull them further into something way beyond any of their control. This wasn't somebody trespassing, or someone trying to scare her; this was something else.

She reached out and grabbed Missy's elbow, but Missy didn't look away from the clearing.

The man lifted the handle end of the shovel and then reached down to pick something up off the ground. The shovel had broken and now the person in the clearing held the two pieces in his hands.

As he did, he turned to face them, still looking down at the broken shovel.

Missy, Trenise, and Alessandra all ducked back into the underbrush.

"Was that Trent?" Missy asked.

Both Trenise and Alessandra nodded that it was.

"We need to go." Alessandra whispered urgently.

Trenise held up a hand and nodded her head, "Just wait."

As if on cue, Trent threw the broken shovel down, all the while muttering under his breath. He pulled his phone out of his pocket, looked at it, and then walked out of the clearing onto a small path opposite the one that Trenise, Alessandra, and Missy had taken.

After a minute or two where the three women had sat motionless and silent, looking at one another, Alessandra finally broke the silence.

"We need to leave," she whispered again urgently.

"Yeah," Trenise agreed, "I saw a few No Trespassing signs back there and don't really fancy having a student call the cops on me for being where I'm not supposed to be."

"It's not just that," Alessandra whispered, "Something is wrong here."

Missy nodded her head in agreement, "No, she's right, Trenise. Something isn't right."

> Alessandra stood up, shifting her weight from one foot to the other nervously. "Something's not right." She said again.

Trenise paused and thought of the Funny Man and then finally nodded in agreement.

"The path is right over there, let's cut through and get the hell out of here before he comes back."

Missy stood up last but didn't walk in the direction the other two were.

"Trenise," she called raising her voice slightly.

Trenise and Alessandra both turned and looked at her.

The buzz of the insects was deafening and the heat baked through the trees. The air felt heavy with humidity.

"Come on Missy." Trenise gestured to the path.

"Trenise," Missy paused and looked from Trenise back to the clearing, "what's he burying?"

Trenise heaved a sigh and looked up, hands on hips.

"I don't know, Missy," she said almost pleading, "But if he comes back and we're here...we're going to be in a heap of trouble. We just accused him of harassing us to the police and now we're trespassing on his property? Come on."

"I'll be quick," Missy said resolutely and cut through the few feet of woods that stood between her and the clearing.

"No," she heard Alessandra say behind her, "Ms. Jones, don't let her."

"Stay here." Missy heard Trenise say.

Trenise was on the path and moved parallel to Missy. They ended up entering the clearing at the same time, emerging from the woods suddenly, about six feet away from each other.

They moved in tandem toward the spot where Trent had been standing, and Missy could see clearly now that he had been standing in an unkept graveyard where the stones were broken, sagging, and covered with moss.

The trees cast a shadow over the edge of the graveyard, so that it was darker than the sunlit clearing through which they were moving. Missy strained, trying to see what Trent had been doing with the shovel.

Trenise saw the hole in the ground first, on the edge of the graveyard. Long, about 6 feet, and deep, about three. There was a pile of dirt at the edge of the hole.

She pointed, and Missy squinted, then nodded. She saw it.

They kept moving forward, unconsciously inching closer to one another until they were shoulder to shoulder. They were picking their way through the ruins of the church now, cutting across the longest part. Missy cast a glance over her shoulder and saw that Alessandra had entered the clearing too and was moving quickly to try and catch up with them.

When she turned back, she saw it.

Her body froze, tense and stiff. Her stomach turned. Missy felt her heart hammer in her throat. Trenise made a groaning noise and Missy heard her choke and breath raggedly.

"Is that..." Missy trailed off.

Trenise nodded, "There's someone over there."

In between two of the graves, they could clearly see that someone was lying on their back. The person's shoes were just barely visible.

"What the fuck is that?" Alessandra whispered from behind them.

Trenise and Missy both shook their heads.

"We have to go check now, Trenise." Missy said.

Trenise nodded, heart hammering.

She thought wildly of her basic training when she had entered the army. Her first week they ran drills, running miles, completing obstacle courses. Trenise completed all of it easily until she got to the climbing wall. She pulled herself up easily the first six feet and then she froze.

She thought of the drill sergeant screaming at her to get her scrawny black ass over the wall. He himself was a huge, intimidating, dark skinned man, who would've dwarfed even Big John. She thought of how she had hauled herself up, scraping the skin off her fingers as she did.

Her heart had hammered, full of anger and shame, as she reached the top and looked back down at him, where he was standing eating an orange, peel and all, smirking at her. She swung her leg over the top and shimmied down the rope on the other side to her waiting squad.

Trenise felt like she was swinging her leg over the top again as she looked from Alessandra to Missy, to whoever's feet those were sticking out from between two graves, to the large hole beside the graveyard.

Moving in tandem again, Missy and Trenise started forward, with Alessandra close on their heels.

—

Trent stomped through the woods, down the small path that led back to the house. He was dirty, sweaty, and pissed off. He was happy to have had one last go at the homeless bitch, but right as he was about to finish, a huge black caterpillar had crawled from the bitch's body and onto his hand.

The fucking thing was disgusting, slimy. Trent had never seen one like it before, but he guessed it had been attracted by the now rotting corpse.

Trent stopped, leaned over, and retched over and over until his stomach felt like it was about to come out of his mouth. He didn't mind that the bitch was getting rotten, but the fucking caterpillar. Trent retched one more time, stood up, and shuddered.

The caterpillar was bad enough, but when the shovel broke, Trent didn't think he could take much more.

He was sick from the caterpillar and sick at the thought of losing the graveyard girl and Evangeline. He had found them both all on his own, taken them, tried to keep them. They had both been his only briefly and then he had to give them both up. There definitely was no way around it though with the graveyard girl. He just couldn't risk her being found.

He had lost Evangaline and now he was going to lose the homeless girl too. Not that the homeless girl was any comparison to Evangaline. He rested with his hands on his knees and remembered his thoughts of Alessandra when he was riding the dead girl and felt his heart flutter with excitement.

Trent pulled his phone out of his back pocket and stared at the screen. He was supposed to be to work in an hour, but there was no way he could finish his little chore and get cleaned up in time. He didn't want to miss work and then hear it from his father, but now having a dead girl who was filled with his semen and a half-dug grave in his back yard was making him a little nervous.

Fuck it.

He dialed his boss again and fed him a sob story about the stomach virus.

A free afternoon now stretched out in front of him, after he finished with his little friend in the woods of course.

Trent grinned and thought about taking a swim in the pool, drinking a few beers, ordering takeout.

The thought of it made him feel a little better. He happily turned his thoughts back to Alessandra.

—

As they wound their way through the old ruins, careful of the loose rocks and overgrown roots, each noticed a change in the atmosphere around them.

The air in the woods was humid, oppressive. It made it hard to breathe, like trying to breathe through a damp cloth. But that was normal in Southeastern Louisiana in July, even in mid-morning hours. The sun beating down was unrelenting, even in the shade of the trees. The insects, a background noise that didn't stop during the summer months, seemed to die away and was replaced by an awful silence. A silence that seemed to come from everywhere at once, rushing out from the trees at them.

"Stop," Missy said as they approached the pit that Trent was digging.

She clutched her throat.

"I can't breathe." Alessandra said, panting.

She put her hands on her bent knees and dipped her head down.

Trenise nodded and put her hand to her chest. The clearing offered no relief from the sun, and the heat was unbearable. She felt sweat standing out all over her face and wiped at her brow with the back of her hand.

Missy, still clutching her throat and breathing slowly and deeply, forced herself to step forward. One more step or two and she would be able to move beyond the shadow cast by the trees and into the small graveyard itself.

She felt like her feet weighed twenty pounds as she lifted her legs to take the next step. Next to her, Trenise staggered forward. Missy glanced back at Alessandra, just behind her, who was pale as a sheet and bent almost in half, but moving toward the graveyard with them all the same.

The silence was deafening, the sun an inferno, as the three of them moved forward.

I can almost see, Missy thought and strained her eyes. She lifted a leaden hand to shade out the sun and saw it.

Missy heard Trenise gasp, and she clutched Missy's arm.

"Is she alive?" Alessandra whispered.

Trenise covered her mouth and nose and gagged silently, "No, Alessandra. You stay where you are."

Missy leaned forward and took another two steps forward, hoping she wasn't seeing correctly.

It's a mannequin, Missy told herself, *it can't be real.*

She heaved herself around what was clearly a half-dug grave.

Behind the gravestone was a young woman, laying on her stomach, her face turned to the left. Her limbs stuck out straight in what Missy assumed was rigor mortis.

There was crusted blood on what was left of her face. There was no way to tell how old she was. She was completely nude except for a pair of jean shorts that were pulled down around her ankles, exposing her entire bare backside. Her legs were bent up and out in a way that suggested whoever killed her had been using her for another purpose after the fact.

The smell was unbearable.

Missy stood, stock still, gaping. She was vaguely aware of both Trenise and Alessandra close to her, could hear Trenise's ragged breathing, could hear her repeating the same phrase over and over again.

"Oh no, Jesus, no."

Alessandra sobbed and clutched her elbows.

Trenise suddenly reached over and clamped her hand over Alessandra's mouth. She looked desperately at Missy's back.

"We have to leave, Missy. Someone is here."

—

Trent strode across the large back lawn toward the gardener's shed, whistling as he went. He felt better about having to give up the girl in the woods, because as he walked, another brilliant idea, an idea for a replacement, was just dancing across his brain.

He couldn't quite work out how to do it, but he figured he had time to think about it.

Trent grinned to himself as he dug around in the shed, looking for another shovel. The shed was like an oven and sweat dripped into his eyes.

Behind a pile of old plastic storage containers, Trent found a shovel, smaller than the one he had broken, but it would work.

Walking out of the shed and back into the sunlight, Trent lifted the shovel over his head caveman style. He laughed to himself and walked toward the woods again, turning the shovel over in his hands.

When he looked up, he saw a man standing in the center of the narrow path that he needed to take to get back to the clearing. The sun was in his eyes, and Trent squinted.

"Dad?" he called, his heart stopping for a moment at the idea that his father had come home early for some reason.

The person standing in the path didn't respond. Trent lifted his hand to shield his eyes from the sun and stepped forward a few feet.

"Whoever you are this is private property!"

Closer now, Trent could see the man clearly. He was tall, about the same as Trent, but thinner and older. He was wearing a black jacket and black pants over a white shirt. A black hat tipped back on his head. His hair was long and blond, tucked behind each ear. There was a few days' worth of a beard on his face, and his blue eyes were bright and cold.

"Hey, do you fucking hear me?"

The man didn't move, but stared at Trent, smiling slightly.

Trent opened his mouth to yell again and then remembered the story Lexie had been on about the night before. Hadn't she said all three women had said the guy had been dressed all in black?

"Hey motherfucker, I don't have a fucking pussy! Why don't you fuck off to someone's house who does, huh?"

Trent gripped the shovel with one hand and made a "shoo" gesture with the other.

The man didn't move, but his smile widened.

"Trent." His voice was soft and indulgent, like a parent talking to an overtired child.

Trent covered his ears and fell to his knees at the sound of it.

It was soft, but, like the silence in the clearing where Missy, Alessandra, and Trenise stumbled upon the old church, seemed to come from everywhere and nowhere. The man spoke, but the trees spoke too. The air spoke, the sun spoke.

Trent.

His voice was coming from inside Trent's own head as well. Trent howled and covered his ears.

"What do you want?" Trent whispered, squeezing his eyes shut.

He started as he felt the man's heavy hand on his shoulder.

"I can help you, Trent." He whispered, "But I need you to help me first."

Trent moaned and covered his ears tighter, squeezed his eyes shut so hard that tears rolled down his cheeks.

The hand squeezed his shoulder even tighter, "Listen to me, Trent. Don't be afraid. I am the voice of God."

Trent let his eyes slowly open, took his hands off his ears, and he looked up at the man. Trent listened, hanging on his every word.

—

Alessandra raised her hand and slowly pointed. Trenise's released her grip on Alessandra's mouth, and her eyes followed Alessandra's pointed finger.

Missy, a few feet ahead of them, was looking down, transfixed by the half-naked corpse wedged between the two gravestones.

There was a man standing at the opposite end of the graveyard. To Trenise he looked like a preacher she had seen while visiting the Amish country with Big John right after they had gotten married.

He smiled at them.

"Missy," Trenise hissed.

Alessandra snaked her hand into the back pocket of her jean shorts and pulled out her phone.

Trenise registered that Alessandra was moving but didn't take her eyes off the man. He shifted slightly to his right and leaned against a tree, folding his arms.

"Dial 911, Alessandra." Trenise said calmly.

The man smiled more widely.

"Who are you?" Trenise finally asked.

"I am the Lord God."

Missy felt her knees buckle at the sound of his voice. She hit the ground hard, staring in disbelief.

His lips were moving, but the sound of his voice came directly from the corpse in front of her. She was sure the body would start to move. She was sure it would slither towards her and drag her down into the shallow grave.

Missy scooted herself backwards and grabbed Trenise's leg.

"Dial Alessandra."

Alessandra sputtered, tapping the circle button at the bottom of her phone, but it wouldn't turn on.

"Motherfucker. No, no, no."

The man smiled. His black clothes seemed to blend in and out with the shadowy trees behind him.

The shadows themselves loomed out of the woods like wolves.

Trenise took a ragged breath again.

"You're not God. Now who are you?"

"Who are you?" Missy echoed.

Again, the corpse said, "You may call me Reverend. In time, you *will* call me your Lord God. For you will bend your knees to me."

Missy pulled herself to her feet with the help of Trenise's outstretched hand, and the three of them began to back away.

The man laughed, and the corpse laughed.

Alessandra turned to try and run and felt the earth move beneath her. It heaved and threw her away from Trenise and Missy. She felt herself land hard on the ground, and she rolled, trying to soften her fall.

She propped herself up on one elbow and wiped her sweaty hair out of her eyes. She looked wildly around the clearing and saw Missy directly across from her, not moving.

She looked to her right and saw Trenise trying to stand up, using the ruined stones of the church to claw her way up.

They were separated across the clearing, but as far as Alessandra could reason, they were separated across eternity.

Her eyes snapped back to the graveyard as she sensed movement in her peripherals. She gasped and scuttled backwards, flinging her legs wildly at the dirt and sticks and rocks she was sitting on.

The man was gone. In his place was David. Her Aunt's boyfriend. The one who had hurt her.

"I want some more, Sandy." He said licking his lips. "It was so sweet, I want some more."

He walked towards her, grabbing his crotch the way he had that night in her aunt's house.

"No!" Alessandra wailed, "Nooo!"

Across the clearing, Missy popped her head up at the sound of Alessandra's voice. She was dizzy and wasn't sure where she was.

"Alessandra!"

Alessandra watched as David whirled to face Missy.

Missy didn't see David. She saw Wes. But he was different. He was sweaty, and she could smell the rotten beer and whiskey coming off his body even though she was more than 20 feet away.

His smile was terrible, and his eyes didn't make sense. They saw her, but there was none of Wes's kindness or humor. There was only the meanness. The meanness they got when he drank. It was Wes, but it wasn't.

"Wes?" Missy whispered.

The Wes-thing, advanced on her, pounding a closed fist onto its chest as it went.

"Why don't you *listen*? *I told you to LISTEN.*" It closed in on her, thumping its chest and grinning.

"Where are the children?"

"No!" Missy shook her head, "No Wes, you wouldn't hurt them."

Wes smiled and raised a fist as if to strike her.

"Missy!"

Missy stumbled to her feet and watched as Wes rounded on Trenise.

Trenise didn't see Wes. She saw the Funny Man. His bathrobe was open over his dirty pajama pants and bare chest. His eyes were insane, and Trenise knew that if she looked at those eyes for too long, she'd go insane right along with him.

"Look here, little girl, you should've listened to your grandmamma."

He shuffled toward her, rubbing his stomach. "Imma get you this time, little girl. Bring you in my house. You wanna come in my house, little girl? I got some candy for you."

Trenise gripped the stones behind her with both hands. She couldn't run home to her cozy shotgun now. Her Grandma wasn't home waiting for her because her grandmother was dead. There wasn't a fence between her and the Funny Man. He was right there, and he was going to bring her into his house to do what Funny Men did to little girls.

"Trenise!" Missy yelled.

Alessandra, keeping an eye on David's back, scrambled to her feet and dashed in a straight line across the clearing to where Missy stood.

Missy's hands curled into fists, and she rushed forward her eyes on Wes's back.

"You leave her ALONE, Wes!!"

When Alessandra reached her, Missy held out her hand and together they charged toward David/Wes/Funny Man as he bore down on Trenise.

"Trenise!" Missy yelled again.

Trenise cowered against the stones, watching the Funny Man advance.

"Coach Jones!" Alessandra shrieked.

Trenise's eyes snapped to the side, to where Missy and Alessandra charged toward her, coming up behind the Funny Man.

Lifting herself up with both hands on the ground, Trenise raised one leg up and landed a kick square in the Funny Man's chest. He grabbed her leg easily and flipped her onto her stomach.

Not shuffling anymore, the Funny Man dragged Trenise by one foot across the clearing toward the graveyard.

"Now you can come see my house, little girl," he snarled.

Trenise screamed and kicked her leg, trying to shake him off. She grabbed at the rocks and each around her, trying to stop him from dragging her back, but she may as well have tried to stop the tide from coming in.

She felt her skin tear as she tried to grip anything, anything that might halt the Funny Man's progress.

Missy and Alessandra rounded and sprinted toward her. Trenise held her hands out to them as the Funny Man pulled her.

Missy dove forward and grabbed Trenise's outstretched hand.

"Wes! Leave her alone!" Missy sobbed as she inhaled again the rank smell baking off his body.

Wes stopped for a moment, turned to smile at her, and tightened his grasp on Trenise's leg. Missy pulled on Trenise's hand to try and free her, but Wes pulled even harder.

They were close to the open grave now, the one that Trent had prepared, and Missy knew with certainty that Wes was going to put them in and bury them.

Seeing that he meant to pull Trenise and Missy both into the grave, Alessandra flung herself on David's back. She beat at him with her fists, shrieking and crying.

"Let them GO, you motherfucker! Let them GO!" She squeezed her arms together as tightly as she could around his neck.

David flung her over his shoulder like she was a rag doll and threw her backward so that she landed in the dirt next to Trenise.

Missy grabbed Alessandra's arm as Wes pulled Trenise closer to the grave. Trenise writhed, twisting her body back and forth, trying to roll out of the Funny Man's grasp.

Alessandra dug her heels in the dirt and grabbed Trenise's other outstretched arm. Together, she and Missy pulled backwards. The Funny Man/David/Wes paused, turned to smile at them as they struggled beneath him, then tightened his grasp and started to pull them forward again.

To Missy, it looked like it was more difficult for him now. She watched as the thing pretending to be Wes panted and strained. The smell of old alcohol was nauseating. Missy reached forward and grabbed Trenise under her armpit and wrapped her arm around her shoulder, pulling backwards.

Alessandra leaned over to do the same and peered into the wide mouth of the grave Trent dug. Now though, it wasn't just a deep dirt hole.

Instead, the air inside of the hole was swirling downwards, pulling dirt and debris down with it. She couldn't see the bottom of the hole anymore, just a current of air pulling down.

Alessandra screamed and wrapped her arm around Trenise, the same as Missy. She heaved backwards at the same time as Missy, and miraculously, Trenise felt her foot slip out of the Funny Man's grasp.

Trenise was up in a flash, hauling Missy and Alessandra with her.

The three of them scrambled over the rocks that made up the old walls of the church.

"Head to the path!" Missy screamed, grabbing Alessandra by the arm as she started to veer off wildly toward the other end of the clearing.

Trenise, however, stopped and grabbed Missy's elbow.

"Look," she whispered breathlessly, "Look at it."

The three of them stood there, holding onto one another and looked to where Trenise was pointing.

About halfway through the churchyard, the thing that was pretending to be David, Wes, and the Funny Man had stopped.

Trenise watched as the Funny Man lifted one foot as though to take another step forward and then put it back down.

"Leave us alone, Wes!" Missy shouted desperately.

She watched as Wes staggered, but couldn't move forward, his eyes narrow and mean.

Alessandra watched as David took one hesitant step and then his whole body started to quiver.

"Let's go" Missy whispered.

Alessandra whimpered and grabbed Missy's arm.

The thing in the clearing stopped and cocked its head to the side as though listening to something. To Trenise, it was the Funny Man, scratching his crotch and smiling broadly. To Missy, it was Wes, rubbing his eyes and forehead, sweating and swaying. To Alessandra, it was David, and he was slowly unbuckling his belt.

"He's coming." The thing said in all three voices.

Alessandra whimpered and her long body crumpled to the ground.

Missy grabbed Alessandra under her armpit, feeling her sweaty, limp body press up against her.

"Trenise, help me."

Trenise's eyes snapped away from the Funny Man to Alessandra. She whipped Alessandra's quivering body around, grabbed underneath her other armpit. Together she and Missy dragged her forward.

"He's coming," the voice was a soft song.

Trenise and Missy both looked back and saw the man in black clothes again, the Preacher. He was smiling again.

"Go Missy," Trenise heard her voice crack as she pulled Alessandra forward, Missy lock step with her as they dragged Alessandra back up the path toward the car.

—-

What snapped Trent back to reality was the feeling of sweat dripping down both sides of his face, down his back, down his legs.

He felt woozy, the sun was too bright. He sucked in a deep breath and staggered toward the shade of the trees at the edge of the woods.

Holding his chest, and then his head, he doubled over.

What the fuck just happened.

He straightened up and flexed his fingers, forcing himself to breathe in and out slowly.

He remembered the man, God, speaking to him. He thought of all the wonderful things he said, how he could help Trent come to his potential, how he could show Trent the way.

He remembered that God told him he would make him stronger. He flexed his hands again and could feel that strength.

He could feel the power of God coursing through him. And in that moment, God spoke to him again from inside his head.

Come to the clearing. They have seen what you've done.

Trent saw in his mind the faces of three women. Three women who he knew.

"Fuck" he whispered.

Come. And I will tell you what to do.

Trent bounded to the entrance of the path and ran toward the spot where he knew God was waiting for him.

Chapter Fifteen

Trenise desperately tried not to panic. She couldn't get her brain around what had just happened, so she detached herself from it, focusing only on getting to her car.

Missy glanced over her shoulder every now and then as she ran, sure that each time she would see the man in black clothes, who she was sure was one in the same as the Wes who had dragged her toward the grave, looming toward her.

Alessandra's mind was elsewhere. Her eyes were open, and her legs made her run, but later, when she tried to recall how they got away from the clearing, she couldn't remember any of it. Her last memory was of the grave, of the swirling air leading down into darkness for what she knew in her heart was forever.

"There's the car!" Missy finally yelled.

"I see," Trenise whispered breathlessly.

Missy started to sob as they finally came up next to the side of the dark SUV.

Trenise let Missy bear the bulk of Alessandra's weight and fumbled, trying to get the keys out of her pocket.

Missy danced on the spot at the rear passenger door.

"Trenise please. Trenise hurry."

She felt herself choking on each word as she struggled to hold Alessandra up.

Trenise finally pressed the unlock button, and Missy pushed Alessandra in, pulling herself in after. Trenise climbed behind the wheel and backed out, spraying gravel as she did.

She pulled on to the main road and sped toward the highway, locking the doors as she went.

"Is she alright?" Trenise heard her voice on the edge of panic.

"I don't know, I don't know." Missy moaned.

Missy reached into the case of water that was on the floor of the back seat, pulled out a bottle, and splashed some into her hand and onto Alessandra's face.

Alessandra's eyes were open, wide and unseeing. She muttered indistinguishably.

"Alessandra, can you hear me?" Missy shook her and held water to her lips. It drippled down her neck and pooled on the seat below her.

"Is she coming to?" Trenise asked.

"No, she isn't. Alessandra, can you hear me?" Missy slapped lightly on each side of her face, and Alessandra flinched.

"Does she need a hospital?" Trenise asked.

"Trenise, what the fuck was that?" Missy asked, ignoring Trenise's question, "I mean what in the hell was that?"

Trenise shook her head. She couldn't go there yet. She couldn't look for answers to that yet. Her focus now was Alessandra.

"I don't know yet. Does Alessandra need a hospital?"

"What's a hospital going to do?" Missy yelled, "I think she needs a goddamn priest!"

Trenise turned onto the main road that led through Stone River and toward the entrance to I-59. I-59 ran from north to south, connected to I-10, which led south straight to New Orleans.

"I'm sorry Trenise I didn't mean to yell." Missy sobbed, "Alessandra, please, baby."

Trenise looked at Missy in the rearview mirror. She was cradling Alessandra in her lap, rocking gently.

"Don't apologize Missy." Trenise said firmly.

Trenise used her signal to show she was turning left onto 59.

Missy looked out the window as they turned, "New Orleans? Are you taking her to Children's Hospital?"

Trenise nodded, "No, not Children's. I know a priest who might be able to help."

Trenise brushed her hand across her sweaty forehead and then turned down the air conditioning, relishing the cool air on her face.

"Are you serious, Trenise?"

Trenise nodded and took a deep breath in.

"I'll explain to you in a second, but I have to make a phone call first. My purse is in the back seat, Missy, will you hand it to me."

Missy shifted and handed Trenise her purse. Trenise dug around and pulled out her cell phone. She looked through her recent calls and found the number she was looking for.

She put the phone on the front seat next to her.

"Missy there are two things we need to deal with, and I want to run both by you before I do anything. I'm trying not to lose my mind here."

Trenise felt her lip tremble.

"Ok," Missy looked down at Alessandra's half-open eyes.

Trenise took a deep breath.

"I don't know who killed that girl, but I'm guessing it was Trent. That's the first thing that we need to deal with."

Missy felt her face crumple as she remembered the naked girl, bent and twisted by the gravestones.

"Yes."

Trenise felt tears running down her face, and she continued.

"The second thing is whatever we saw. That.... thing. That was not...that was not..."

"Natural," Missy finished.

Trenise nodded, "Right."

"What was it, Trenise?"

Trenise shook her head, "I don't know."

"Was it a ghost?"

Trenise shook her head, "I don't know. But I'm hoping to find some help in New Orleans. Both for Alessandra and for us."

"So, what do we do about the girl?"

"I'm going to call Officer Thompson. Tell him what we saw and ask him to go out there and look."

"But Trenise, won't they want to talk to us, make us come into the police station?"

"Maybe. But it'll just be me. I'm going to tell him I was going for a walk and thought I saw the same man I saw at my house. Then I'm going to tell him I was technically trespassing and to please not log that I told him, because it could affect my job."

Missy nodded, "He'll go out there to look, and he'll find the body or the...the grave."

"Right," Trenise nodded.

"Ok," Missy said, "Now what about the other problem?"

Trenise shook her head, "I'm hoping Rainbow can help us."

Missy looked up from Alessandra's pale face, "Rainbow?"

Trenise shook her head, "I'll explain after I call Thompson. You agree I should call him, right?"

"Right," Missy repeated, looking down again at Alessandra, "Make the phone call to Thompson. And then tell me about Rainbow."

—

Rainbow Rhodes lived in the same small shotgun house in Arabi, a town in St Bernard Parish, just next door to the Ninth Ward in New Orleans, for going on 20 years. She kept the house a bright, cheerful orange with green shutters.

Along the path that ran from the house to the street were all types of plants and bushes, all of which bloomed brightly at different times of the year. The house was raised enough so that the water from different floods passed underneath it.

Her steady stream of clients, both old and new, native New Orleanians who trusted the old magic and newcomers who were looking for alternative medicine, allowed her to stay in the neighborhood even as it got increasingly gentrified around her.

Rainbow watched as her elderly neighbors died, and their children sold their houses for hefty prices to people who wanted to live closer to New Orleans to shorten their commutes.

St Bernard Parish, much like New Orleans, had its own history of violence, magic, sadness, and evil. The corrupt police and politicians frequently helped their own at the expense of the poor and working class. The Battle of New Orleans was fought coming up the river and on the grounds of a plantation worked by slaves.

Rainbow felt all of the sadness and injustice- it was palpable to her, a living and breathing thing sharing her space. She let it be and gave it room.

The ground was fertile, moist, filled with life. People kept small greenhouses to grow tomatoes, green beans, lettuce, and herbs. Rainbow grew herbs and spices to make tinctures, teas, and powders which she sold both to the different herbal and metaphysical shops around New Orleans and through her own small but growing online business.

The knowledge and magic Rainbow knew used herbs and charms and was passed down to her from her mother and grandmother. Rainbow expanded on it by learning Reiki, tarot, and hypnosis. She felt the magic in everything she touched, in the air she breathed. She saw the magic in the face of every child, in the gait of a dog running down the street. She heard it from the mouth of every bird.

When a change happened, Rainbow felt it, felt the *wrong*, in every bone of her body. At first, she thought she was getting sick and used her Thieves Oil on her temples and wrists and the bottoms of her feet. She drank chamomile tea and rested.

Her head felt like it was floating, and she saw dark clouds over the river even though the days were clear. She heard coyotes outside her door yipping a warning to her at dawn and at dusk.

She looked at her Tarot cards and pulled The Tower, The Devil, the Wheel of Fortune, and the Three of Swords. Rainbow shuddered and wrapped her cards in silk and placed them in a bowl of clear quart fragments. The next day, she shuffled and pulled three cards again. The Tower, The Devil, The Wheel of Fortune, the Three of Swords.

Every morning for a week, Rainbow wrapped herself in a blanket and sat on her front porch in her rocker. Even though the morning heat was well into the 80s at this time in the summer, Rainbow shivered with a cold sweat.

She rocked and she waited.

—

Thompson hung up the phone and rubbed his eyes.

What the fuck.

He put his hands on the back of his head, elbows out. He looked up at the ceiling of his cruiser, trying to process what Trenise Jones had told him and how to proceed.

He shifted his gaze out the front window at the empty storefronts across from him, at the parking lot overrun with grass and garbage.

More than anything he could think of, Thompson hated Stone River. When he had gotten accepted into a private high school to play basketball, Thompson thought that he'd gotten his ticket out.

But lackluster grades and poor test scores meant no college. Then his mother had gotten sick and had no one to care for her.

As angry as he was, Thompson couldn't abandon her.

He'd been offered a job as a police officer from a friend's father and worked his way up the ranks by keeping his mouth shut, turning a blind eye to corruption, and hoping against hope that this would help him be accepted into the academy to become a state trooper.

If he could make it to Baton Rouge, it would be his ticket out of Stone River.

He knew damn well that Ms. Jones knew people with the State. He knew damn well he didn't want to stay in this shit town forever and that helping someone who knows people could be a ticket to the State Police Academy.

Thompson logged the call from Jones indicating that she was driving down Pump Slough Road on her way to visit a sick relative in New Orleans and saw a group of kids trespassing on a designated No Trespassing property.

That is *not* quite what she told him on the phone, but close enough.

He radioed in that he was going to check out possible trespassers and was informed by the dispatcher that the property he was describing belonged to none other than Grant Longue.

Thompson laughed and shook his head. He pressed the button on the side of the radio, let go again.

"What the fuck, Ms. Jones," he said out loud to himself. "Of course it's the Longue property."

He pressed the button again on his radio.

"Ok don't let the homeowner know just yet, it might be nothing."

Thompson didn't wait for her response, hung the radio back up in its spot, and pulled out of the vacant lot where he had been sitting and doing paperwork.

He had a strong feeling that Trenise Jones wasn't being honest with him and that she was sending him on a wild goose chase. Thompson sighed and shook his head to himself as he headed toward the Longue property.

—

Rainbow pulled herself out of bed, feeling better than she had in days. Her bones still ached, she still felt a heavy dread, but something felt different. She showered and then dressed in a loose white cotton dress.

Rainbow took her cards from their spot on the window and sat at her kitchen table. She took three deep breaths in and out, shuffled the cards and drew.

The Queen of Cups, the Queen of Wands, The Queen of Swords, The Queen of Pentacles.

Rainbow's hand trembled as she felt called to pull another two cards. The Devil. The Tower. She heaved her breath in and stood up, leaving the cards where they were.

She went into the kitchen and made a pot of coffee. She added chicory to the grinds. Next, she pulled out flour, baking soda, butter, and milk and set to making biscuits.

She forced herself to be steady and methodical in each thing she did, focusing on each step in turn. If her thoughts pulled away, if they pulled to questions, she stopped and refocused on her work at hand.

In the pit of her stomach, Rainbow knew that she would be having visitors today. As she put her biscuits in the oven to bake, she poured herself a cup of the strong coffee and chicory and took it onto the front porch to wait.

—

Trent could feel the Preacher with him now. He could feel another heartbeat, another set of eyes, another voice in his head. When he breathed in, it was with two sets of lungs. When Trent threw the dead girl's body in the pit he had dug, it was with the strength of two men.

He shoveled the dirt over her in no time, covered the disturbed ground with old rocks and bricks, trying to make them look haphazard. When he was done, he sat in the shade, waiting to be told what he should do next.

The bugs droned and thunder rumbled in the distance despite the hot sun.

No voice came. He heard nothing. Trent could feel the Preacher with him, but he didn't speak.

"What do I do?" Trent asked out loud.

Be still, the voice finally came, *be still and listen.*

Trent felt something tug at his neck, felt his neck and head turn, back toward the clearing.

He watched as a man walked out from the path and into the clearing. Watched as the man put his hands on his hips as he looked around.

Trent froze.

Be still, the voice came again.

The man looked around and finally shook his head and threw up his hands. Trent could see clearly that he was a cop but not one who he recognized.

Go talk to him, the voice came, *he could be an ally.*

What do I say? Trent thought wildly.

Don't worry. I'll tell you what to do.

Trent relaxed his body, and felt it stand up of its own volition and walk forward.

"Excuse me officer! Can I help you?" Trent's body walked forward, one hand to his side and the other held up in a greeting.

The cop jumped and his hand flitted to his weapon on his hip.

"Woah," Trent's voice laughed, "Didn't mean to startle you."

> Trent could feel that his voice was light and friendly, but on the inside, he was burning.

The cop was about the same height as him, good looking, honey colored skin. He looked athletic. Trent seethed with jealousy. He didn't want an ally.

"Just stay right there. Who are you?"

Trent's body stopped where it was, "I'm Trent Longue."

The cop nodded, "Yeah I recognize you, now."

Trent smiled, "Is everything ok?"

The cop nodded in return.

"Yeah, we got a call from a passerby who thought she saw some kids trespassing," the cop paused, "Guess she probably saw you."

Trent's mouth grinned sheepishly.

"Yessir, probably. I was supposed to go to work today but.... Well, sir, I broke up with my girlfriend and just...I just needed some alone time."

The cop eyes him and nodded, "I get it. So, you haven't seen anyone back here I take it?"

Trent's head nodded, "No, sir. Just me."

"Alright then. I'll be on my way."

The cop turned and headed back down the path.

Trent felt himself regain control of his body, marveling at how wonderful it felt to let the Preacher take over.

"That was amazing." He whispered out loud.

Follow, but stay back. Listen.

Trent crept forward, straining to hear anything.

"Yeah, copy." He heard the cop's voice say from far off.

Trent moved forward again, trying to move quickly and silently.

"No, no. Tell Bordelon Ms. Jones won't be able to come in for a follow up today, I just talked to her, and she told me she's on her way to New Orleans to visit a sick relative."

Trent stopped and allowed the cop to pull ahead of him. He heard the muffled static of the radio again.

"I mean, I guess he can try and call her, but like I said, she said she's visiting a sick relative. I mean it took him long enough to realize the two might be connected, fucking dumbass."

Trent guessed he hadn't said that last part to the dispatcher and grinned.

Trent froze again and turned his head to the side like a dog that heard its master calling in the distance. He turned around and started heading back to the house. He would take a shower, change his clothes, gas up his truck.

He would take money from his father's safe, just in case. He didn't give a shit about what his father would do when he found out. That didn't matter anymore.

The Preacher had shown Trent what he could do to his father, to nosey ass Ms. Jones, to beautiful Evangeline's dumpy friend, and especially what he could do to Alessandra. The Preacher could fix all of his problems, he just needed Trent to help *him* first.

Trent wasn't sure where to go once they got to New Orleans, but he had faith the answer would appear to him. He had God on his side.

—

Just before lunchtime, Rainbow leaned forward in her chair and peered down her street toward the highway. A dark SUV had turned onto her street and was headed toward her.

Rainbow's breath caught in her throat. She stood and prepared herself for whoever might get out of the SUV. She watched as it slowed, as if the driver was looking for something.

Rainbow half raised her hand in a greeting, then lowered it uncertainly. She took a deep breath and walked down the steps of her house, just as the SUV started to pull slowly in front of her yard. She raised a hand to shield her eyes from the sun as she peered into the driver's seat.

"Trenise?"

Rainbow's eyes watered and her mouth felt dry. She stepped forward and put her hand on the driver's side door as Trenise put the car into park. Rainbow pulled the door open and pulled her cousin into a hug.

"Hi Rainbow," Trenise whispered softly.

"I didn't know it was you, Trenise. What happened?"

"I'll tell you everything, but first I need your help with a young woman in my back seat. She's in some sort of shock."

Trenise opened the back door to the car and Rainbow peered around at a young white woman cradling a sleeping teenaged Hispanic girl in her lap.

Rainbow looked back at Trenise. "If you want me to help her, I need to know what happened."

—

When Thompson got back to his cruiser, he stopped, hand on the door and listened. Sweat ran down his neck, and he looked longingly in the window thinking about the ice-cold water in his small cooler and the feel of the air conditioning.

Thompson felt his skin crawl in annoyance.

Trenise Jones hadn't succeeded in making him listen at their meeting earlier that morning, so now she phoned in a bogus call to get him to come talk to Trent.

And he'd bought it.

Thompson looked back in the direction he came from. He knew that the Longue family ruled Stone River and much of the surrounding areas, and they ruled it with an iron fist. The older son was some high-powered lawyer in New Orleans but, from what he had heard, the younger one, this kid Trent, was something of a fuck up.

He had also overheard whispered conversations that Trent Longue had something of a crush on Evangeline Nunez before she died. Apparently, some of Trent's friends had told their parents, who in turn told police, who in turn told them to keep their mouths shut about it.

Because Trent was a Longue, and he was a good boy.

Thompson wondered vaguely how true that was.

Thompson blinked the sweat away from his eyes and thought about his own upbringing in a small trailer in the undeveloped, wooded section of the northernmost edge of Stone River.

It couldn't have been more different from what he imagined a kid like Trent Longue had grown up with.

Thompson's mother did what she could, but they were beyond poor. She worked during the day at McDonald's and a few nights a week at a gas station. She was bent and broken by the time she was 30. Thompson had very few memories of his father except for that when he showed up at their trailer, Thompson and his mother would receive a beating.

Thompson saw his father for the last time when he was a senior in high school. At 18, Thompson worked out regularly and was right around

6 feet. His father came home one night looking for money, and when he threatened his wife, Thompson hit him with a chair.

Thompson's deep love and feelings of protection for his mother were starkly overshadowed by the feelings of deep disgust for weakness that his father imbued in him.

Thompson put a hand over his face at the recollection of how it felt when the chair connected with his father's face, breaking his nose and spraying blood all over the small dingy kitchen.

Thompson stared into the woods. While deep in his gut, he knew Trenise Jones was lying to him, he was overwhelmed by his desire to get out of Stone River. His service to the Stone River Police Department didn't seem to be getting him any closer to that goal.

He was at a crossroads. Thompson could either help Trenise Jones and hope that she could help get him to in with the State Police, or he could ignore her and in effect pledge allegiance to Stone River.

Thompson thought for a moment and then reached up and pressed the call button on his radio.

"Tessa, it's Thompson, I made contact with the relative of the homeowner at the Longue property, all is well. But I dropped my wallet. I'm headed back to look for it."

"10-4."

Still thinking about his father's smashed face and his mother's strained and wrinkled eyes as she mopped up the blood in her McDonald's uniform, Thompson headed back down the narrow path into the woods.

—

Missy finally stopped talking and looked down at her empty coffee cup. She played with a crumb from one of Rainbow's biscuits.

She had told them everything she could think of. Everything she knew about how Evangeline had died, about the worms in Evie's tree, about what Ms. Cindy and Ms. LeeAnn told her about the neighborhood, about the night she saw someone at her house, the worms in her bathroom, and finally about what she had seen back at the clearing. The dead girl and the boy who killed her and the thing that had morphed itself into Wes.

She shuddered.

Rainbow looked from Missy to Trenise, "So whatever he was appeared different to all three of you."

Missy and Trenise both nodded and Alessandra muttered a quiet, "Yeah."

Missy looked at Alessandra and smiled. She looked much better, and she was talking at least.

To Alessandra, he was David, the man who raped her. To Trenise, he was the Funny Man, the child molester who lived in her neighborhood when she was a child. To Missy, he was Wes when he was at his violent alcoholic worst.

Alessandra took a deep breath in and took a bite of her biscuit.

"That's good, honey. You eat that all up."

Rainbow smiled gently at Alessandra. Rather than giving the poor child the coffee and chicory she served to Trenise and Missy, Rainbow made her a tea of cane sugar, hibiscus, High John the Conqueror Root, and lavender.

Missy marveled when the tea roused Alessandra from her stupor. She marveled more as Trenise and Alessandra both recounted their versions of what had happened over the last 48 hours to Rainbow.

She chimed in in agreement when Alessandra recounted what the kids at school had told her about the legends and stories about the preacher. She cried softly when Alessandra told briefly of her assault in Texas and of how Trent had gotten away with harassing her at school.

The four of them sat without speaking, until Trenise finally broke the silence.

"Rainbow what is this? What do we do?"

Rainbow shook her head.

"I'm honestly not sure, Trenise. This is a little beyond me," She paused, "What I can say, is this is some kind of spirit who has been awoken."

Missy felt her breath catch in her throat.

"It sounds like the land where you all live is holding the trauma of that event. And something has awoken it."

Trenise shook her head, "No, no, no. Y'all. Are we really saying this is the spirit of some dead Reverend?"

Rainbow shrugged, "Maybe, Trenise."

"I don't believe that Rainbow."

"But do you believe what you saw? Do you believe these two women sitting with you?"

Trenise looked from Alessandra's wide brown eyes to Missy's almond blue eyes, both looking to her silently.

"I believe them."

Rainbow threw her hands up, "There you go. Just because it sounds crazy, doesn't mean it always is."

She paused again, "Or maybe I should say just because it's crazy doesn't mean it's not true."

Missy leaned forward, "So what do we do Rainbow? If you can't help us, what do we do?"

"I can help you some, that's for sure. And I know someone who can help you get rid of this spirit."

"What about Trent?" Alessandra asked.

Rainbow shook her head, "Spiritual stuff I can help. What that boy did...all I can say is that his evil will be revisited on him three-fold."

Alessandra's shoulders slumped and Trenise reached out for her hand, "One problem at a time, ok?"

Alessandra nodded reluctantly.

"Now," Rainbow put her hands palm down on the table, "I'm going to make each of you a protection bag to wear around your necks. Do not remove them. Then you're going to go see a woman who can help you. She's powerful, and she knows the old magic. She is the most respected practitioner in New Orleans."

Missy nodded, "Where is she Rainbow?"

"You'll find her at Razoo this evening, that's where she always is on Friday night."

Trenise burst out laughing, "You're telling me there's a High Priestess who hangs out at that crappy tourist bar on Bourbon Street?"

Rainbow shrugged her shoulders, "Two for one beers."

Trenise rolled her eyes, "Jesus Christ, Rainbow."

Rainbow stood up.

"You'd do well not to doubt Trenise Jones," she pointed a long finger at Trenise, "And don't blaspheme in this house."

Trenise rolled her eyes again and threw her hands up, "Ok, Rainbow I'm sorry."

Rainbow looked down at Trenise and sat again.

"Why did you bring Alessandra here, Trenise? Why didn't you bring her to a hospital?" she asked quietly.

Trenise looked at Rainbow and shook her head. She looked down at her hands on the table. Trenise had asked herself the same two questions since they had left Stone River.

"I don't know Rainbow," she said finally.

"You do know," Rainbow said calmly, "You felt it. You felt it, and you listened. I don't know what exactly is happening here, but my first piece of advice to you is this," She paused and held up one finger, "If you feel that again. Listen."

Trenise looked up at Rainbow and nodded.

Rainbow bowed her head slightly, "Now. I have work to do to prepare your talismans. My home is your home in the meantime. Trenise, the store on the corner sells po'boys. You and Missy walked down there and buy a few."

She looked at Alessandra, "You are to drink two more cups of tea and then eat a po'boy. You are not to move from the spot you're in."

Alessandra nodded meekly.

Rainbow moved away from the table to her spare room where mason jars filled with dried herbs stood on tall shelves. She grabbed a wicker basket, and moved deftly through the room, carefully choosing different jars and gently placing them into the basket. Dill. Lavender. Oregano. Parsley.

She listened and heard the front door close gently as Trenise and Missy left on their errand and heard quiet liquid pouring from the teapot and into Alessandra's mug.

Rainbow focused her energy and set to work.

—

With a sense of clarity, calm, and strength, Trent went through the motions of cleaning himself up from his busy morning. He showered, brushed his teeth. He went downstairs into the large, empty kitchen and made himself four sandwiches. He ate an entire bag of chips with them and drank two cokes.

He felt a sense of purpose. He felt pride in what he knew he would accomplish.

The Preacher didn't speak to him, but Trent could feel him there. Trent knew he had to drive to New Orleans, but he didn't feel any sense of worry about where he should go or how he would find Alessandra and the other two women. The Preacher wasn't worried, so Trent wasn't either.

Trent thought about Evangaline and how it had all just...worked out. He thought about her as he sat at the kitchen table and ate in silence.

He had been out driving around in the evening, hoping to get a glimpse of Evangaline through her lighted window. Instead, he saw her walking, in workout clothes, headphones in her ears. She was smiling slightly and with the soft light of the setting sun, Trent thought she was the most beautiful woman he had ever seen. He passed her, then watched as she cut down the gravel path called Log Cabin Road that led back to a few camps.

He knew the road, knew that it ran along a branch of the West Stone River. It was a beautiful spot and Trent decided it was time to let Evangaline know how special she was to him.

He pulled his car into the driveway of a house that had a For Sale sign in front, turned off his headlights, and pulled all the way up under the house's car port.

Making his way back up the street on foot, jogging slightly, he turned right onto Log Cabin, and could see Evangaline about a half mile ahead of him.

He felt the rock in his pocket, the one he had taken from the old Churchyard the night before with Lexi digging into his leg.

Enough of this.

Trent stopped his reverie, stopped chewing the ham sandwich he had in his mouth, and listened.

Go now. Someone is interfering.

Trent put his hands down on the table and pushed his chair back. He grabbed two more cans of coke and the keys to his truck.

New Orleans was about an hour drive from the Longue estate. Looking at his watch, Trent estimated he would be there by the early afternoon if there was no traffic.

Although he felt calm and collected still, Trent couldn't help but also feel excitement. The preacher knew what he wanted and promised to help him get it. All Trent had to do was to get the three women and bring them back to the clearing by the churchyard.

He didn't know who was interfering, but he knew that he could stop them. It would be easy.

"Easy," Trent said to himself out loud as he drove down the long driveway and onto the main road toward the highway.

He looked over at the ropes, shovel, gloves, and garbage bags the Preacher had told him to put in his truck and smiled.

Chapter Sixteen

Slowly but surely, Alessandra started to feel more and more like herself. She sat at Rainbow's table and tried not to think about David and the thing in the woods and the black pit in the grave.

Instead, she concentrated on the dried flowers hanging in Rainbow's bright, clean kitchen. Some were yellow, some pink. Some looked like herbs rather than flowers.

She drank her tea. When Missy and Trenise returned with sandwiches, Alessandra felt her stomach give an expectant rumble.

"So, Ms. Jones, how do you know Rainbow?" Alessandra asked between mouthfuls of roast beef po'boy.

Missy and Trenise looked at each other, happily surprised to hear Alessandra speaking.

"She's my cousin."

Alessandra scrunched her face up, "Seriously?"

Trenise laughed, "Yeah, seriously."

"Wow, y'all are really...different."

Trenise laughed again.

"Yeah, I know," she eyed Alessandra, "I'm glad you're feeling a little better Sanchez."

Alessandra nodded, "So what's the plan?"

Missy and Trenise looked at each other again.

"What?"

"We have to go into the French Quarter."

Alessandra looked from Missy to Trenise and raised her eyebrows.

"But we think you should stay here with Rainbow, Alessandra," Missy finished gently.

"What?? No way!" Alessandra put her sandwich down and shook her head.

"Alessandra," Trenise said calmly, as though she were talking to a toddler, "You just went through something traumatic."

"Well so did you both! Don't," Alessandra stood up, sputtering, and leaned over both women, "don't treat me like I'm some dumb kid. I'm part of this as much as you both are."

Missy held her hands out to Alessandra, "We know that, we do...we just think that..."

"She has to go too."

Rainbow was standing in the doorway holding three small muslin pouches in her hand. There was a brown leather cord attached to each pouch.

Alessandra looked at Rainbow's kind face and thought she saw sadness and worry there as well.

Turning back to Missy and Trenise, triumphantly, she sat back down with a smirk.

Rainbow shook her head sadly, "Don't be excited, Alessandra. This is going to be difficult."

"Then Rainbow, why does she need to come with us?" Trenise asked, trying to keep the exasperation out of her voice.

"Because three is a powerful number. The Trinity. The Maiden,"

She pointed to Alessandra.

"The Mother," she pointed to Missy.

"And the Crone."

Rainbow rested her finger on Trenise and then lowered her hand.

Trenise snorted, "Jeez thanks, Rainbow."

Rainbow gave Trenise her own look of exasperation.

"Think about what happened in the woods. You only were able to free yourself when you were all together. When you were all touching."

Missy nodded her head and Trenise sighed.

"Stay together." Rainbow said firmly. "I will come with you to help guide you to Ms. Sarah the Priestess, then after you meet with her, and she gives you guidance, the three of you will have to continue alone."

All three nodded.

Rainbow smiled gently, "And here. These will protect you too."

Trenise made as though she were going to stand up and Rainbow motioned her to sit. She put her finger to her lips.

Rainbow focused all her energy on the bags. In her mind's eye, she saw them glowing with white light. The white light went up each side of the leather cord until it touched in the middle. Rainbow closed her eyes and asked for protection for each woman.

She started with Alessandra and gently placed the necklace with the sachet on the end around her neck. Then she moved to Missy, and finally Trenise. All three women watched her silently as she moved around her circular kitchen table.

"Join hands," she told them in a quiet voice.

When the three women's hands were clasped to form a circle, Rainbow said, "I ask you, the Being, the Creator, the Good in the World, protect these women on their journey. Their journey will face a great evil, and they need the power of the Light."

Missy looked from Trenise to Alessandra and met both of their eyes. She saw the same fear and resolution she felt.

Missy didn't know exactly what had happened to them or to Evangaline or to the women in her neighborhood or to the women of the Stone River church all those years ago. But sitting at Rainbow's table in Arabi, Missy felt the weight of it and decided then and there she wouldn't stop until she put an end to it.

—

Trent made it to New Orleans in record time. No traffic. Thunder clouds, but no rain. Huge Lake Pontchartrain, over which the long Twin Span Bridge passed, was like a mirror, flat and calm. Trent felt calm too but excited. He forced himself to drive the speed limit.

How will I know where to go?

Trust. I will listen for them.

Trent took the exit off I-10 that said "Vieux Carre" and grinned.

It was late Friday afternoon and, despite the heat, even the edge of the French Quarter was already bustling. Trent tried to turn down a street that led into the heart of the Quarter and found it blocked by the barriers the cops put up on the weekend to keep certain streets pedestrian only. Tourists swarmed in front of him.

Trent wanted desperately to park, to get out and look, to see all of it. As he turned around, he passed a group of young women wearing matching hot pink tank tops and short jean shorts, one of whom was wearing a sash that said, "Bride to Be." He licked his lips. They were followed closely by family groups, middle aged couples, of all walks of life.

On the next corner, a group of serious young adults climbed out of a van that said, "Grace Baptist Church." They were carrying signs that read, "Repent," "God is Nigh," and "Get the devil out of New Orleans."

Trent stopped at the light next to the group and caught the eye of a young woman who was carrying a sign that said, "Repent. Jesus is your savior." He nodded somberly to her, and she nodded back.

Trent laughed as the light turned green. He wondered if that girl had any clue that God really was in the French Quarter tonight and was ready to roust the devils who were hiding there.

—

Trenise deftly navigated the traffic through the lower ninth ward and along the levee that held the Mississippi River back from flooding the Marigny.

Rainbow sat silently in the front seat next to her, arms wrapped tightly around herself.

Alessandra and Missy sat in the back seat, each looking out of their respective windows. Missy had been living in the area for over a year but still marveled at New Orleans.

Young men and women in trendy, off the wall clothes rode bikes toward the French Quarter. Tourists lined up outside a small restaurant called "Elizabeth's," laughing and smiling and sweating, waiting to eat. The houses in the Marigny and the Bywater were close together, filled with plants and wrought iron, small shotguns that resembled Rainbow's. The houses were in various states of disrepair still from Hurricane Katrina. One house was blighted, the next was renovated smartly and expensively.

While walking to the corner store with Trenise earlier, Missy had called her mother and spoke to Johnny and Sophie. They were happy, just coming in from the pool and getting ready to watch a movie. They wanted to know when she was coming, and Missy had assured them it would be soon. When her mother pressed her for a definite day, Missy skirted the answer as best as she could. She was resting, she assured her mother, fixing up the house, coming to terms with Evie's passing.

As they passed a house painted hot pink, Missy smiled and thought about how much Sophie would love it.

Alessandra didn't speak but watched each house and person they passed, searching each face and brick and plant for clues as to what she should do moving forward.

"Pull in here, Trenise."

Rainbow motioned to an open spot along a wall that blocked the street from a set of train tracks. Trenise parallel parked between a brand-new Audi and, judging from the curtains in the windows, what looked like a van that someone lived in. Across from their parking spot was a ratty playground and across from that were rows of the expensively renovated shotguns.

Alessandra hoisted her backpack out and slung it over her back.

"You think someone's living in there?" Missy asked quietly, gesturing toward the van.

Rainbow shrugged.

"Probably. Gutter punks come from all over to New Orleans since you can sleep outside and tourists might give them money."

Missy nodded and thought she heard low voices coming from the van.

"It's a little bit of a walk to Razoo," Rainbow said almost apologetically, turning toward Trenise and Alessandra, "But, since it's Friday night, it's going to be crowded and some of the streets are pedestrian only."

"That's ok," Missy said, "I feel like a walk might do us some good." She smiled at Alessandra.

"Have you been to the Quarter before, Alessandra?" Trenise asked.

Alessandra shook her head no slowly.

Trenise sighed, "Stay by me. Don't talk to anyone."

Alessandra grinned, "Missy can bring her baseball bat with her, Ms. Jones, I got Tio Berto's breaker bar...we can take care of any assholes."

She made a swinging motion, laughed and then looked serious.

"You both brought those with you?" Rainbow asked, "The same ones you told me you felt compelled to find the night before last?"

Missy nodded.

"It's up there next to you."

Rainbow reached over and touched the bat where it had squashed itself between the seat and the center console. As she did, Alessandra pulled the dented breaker bar from her bag and held it up.

"Hm," Rainbow said, touching both.

Trenise stared at her, "I don't think it's a good idea to be walking around the Quarter with those, Rainbow."

Rainbow nodded reluctantly, "No, you're right."

Alessandra put the bar back into her bag where it was resting on the floor of the car, the end of it sticking out slightly. Missy eyed the bat wishing she *could* take it with her.

The four of them walked silently, in sharp contrast to the increasing number of people around them, all of whom were laughing, talking loudly, drinking, and looking around.

"If we get separated, head back to the car. Remember we're on North Peters, by the railroad tracks."

"And the scuzzy van!" Alessandra added laughing.

Missy and Trenise walked together and pulled slightly ahead of Alessandra and Rainbow.

"Stay focused," Rainbow admonished looking at Alessandra who was smiling and watching the people they passed.

"Ms. Rainbow, you really think we could be in danger all the way down here?"

Rainbow shrugged, "Did you really think this morning that some kind of evil spirit would drag you into an open grave leading to God knows where? Or that the boy who harassed you at school had murdered a girl and was raping her corpse?"

Alessandra shook her head no silently and her lips curved down.

Rainbow touched her elbow gently, "Just be careful is all I'm saying. Stay close to me."

—

At the opposite edge of the French Quarter from where Trenise parked her small SUV, Trent circled the cramped blocks of the Central Business District looking for a spot to park. He had driven all along the edge of the Quarter that was farthest from the Mississippi River and hadn't been able to park.

Here, although the parking spaces along the street were smaller and harder to come by, Trent felt more comfortable and off the beaten path. He passed bums and gutter punks. Garbage littered the street under the I-10 overpass that led to the bridge that would take you across the Mississippi River to the Westbank of New Orleans. Trent turned his truck around illegally in the middle of Tchoupitoulas Street and waved merrily as people blew their horns at him.

He headed back down St. Peter Street looking for a spot.

In front of an abandoned building, Trent noticed a spot large enough to accommodate his truck. He parked, got out, and locked the truck, looking around.

What am I here for? he asked silently.

Ahead of him, he could see Canal Street, marking the edge of the French Quarter. He could hear talking, cars, music.

Someone is interfering.

In his head, Trent saw an image flash quickly. A middle-aged black woman, very pretty. Long braided hair, white dress. He couldn't see her face, but next to her was a face he would recognize anywhere: Alessandra.

Trent squeezed his fists into balls.

She is feeding the girl the Devil's lies. She is setting things into motion with her. Find them.

Trent took a shaky breath in and started walking forward toward the French Quarter.

—

"You know what I just realized..."

Trenise stopped walking as the four of them turned onto the cobblestone walkway that formed Jackson Square. She motioned them over to the wrought iron fence that boxed in the small park in front of St. Louis Cathedral.

There were street musicians performing at the amphitheater across from them, and the hum of talking and laughter and music from the bars and stores around them made it hard to hear.

"What Trenise?" Missy asked.

"Alessandra isn't going to be able to come in with us."

Rainbow, Trenise, and Missy all looked at Alessandra, "Razoo is a bar."

"Well," Rainbow said slowly, "You and Missy can go in and Alessandra and I can wait outside for you. Or if there's a restaurant close, we can wait there."

"But Rainbow," Missy said shaking her head, "You said to stay together."

"I know, but" Rainbow shrugged, "What choice do we have? You have to go see Ms. Sarah."

"Wouldn't she come out of the bar to meet us, Rainbow?"

Rainbow paused and tilted her head to the side, "Maybe, maybe not. Sarah is incredible, powerful. But she's..."

Rainbow trailed off and waved her hand in a circular motion.

Trenise put her hands on her hips, "She's what, Rainbow?"

"She's a little...hesitant to interfere in other people's affairs more than she has to."

"Oh," Trenise threw her hands up, "great."

"So, you're saying we have to tread a little lightly around her to get her to help?" Missy asked.

Rainbow nodded reluctantly, "Maybe. It's best to meet her on her terms. At Razoo."

Trenise and Missy exchanged a glance, and Missy shrugged.

Rainbow gestured toward the church. "Bourbon Street is that way, just past the church. We can take Pirate's Alley around it, it's less busy."

—

Canal street was filled with cars coming and going in both directions. People meandered toward the river and toward Bourbon Street. The music from the souvenir shops and Daquiri bars blared pop music from some and Cajun music from others. Anything to lure in the tourists.

Trent emerged from St. Peters into the crowded street. He looked to his right and saw the sun just beginning to dip down over the river. He could see the Natchez Steamboat and hear its distant calliope music echo over the buzz of the crowd.

He moved toward a souvenir shop and waited, just a young man standing on the sidewalk looking around, marveling at the sight of the French Quarter. How many other young men before him had done the same? Wondering where to go, what to see, what to do first.

Trent tilted his head to the side and listened.

Walk forward.

Looking toward the River, then toward Bourbon Street, and then behind him down St. Peter from the way he had come, Trent decided forward meant down St. Peter across Canal Street and into the French Quarter.

He didn't feel any rush, although he knew what he was doing was important. Trent looked again to his right toward the setting sun. He welcomed the anonymity of dusk and darkness.

He wasn't sure what he was going to have to do, but he didn't want to be seen, didn't want anyone to know what he was doing.

Trent smiled to himself as he thought about how far the day had taken him. With every step forward, he felt more in awe of where he might be by the end of the day tomorrow.

—

As they entered the space in front of St. Louis Cathedral, Missy took a moment to stop again to look back at the statue of Andrew Jackson on his horse. The sun was setting under the horse's raised forelegs, silhouetting the former president. Tourists sat on the edge of the fountain around him or milled around taking pictures. Fortune tellers were set up with chairs and tables, beckoning the curious toward them in the fading light.

Missy's hand snaked up to touch the sachet around her neck that was hanging under her shirt. The skin on her chest felt damp with sweat. The heat and humidity were still powerful even in the evening and would continue to be into the night.

Alessandra smiled at her as she and Rainbow walked by her. Missy wondered what her children were doing. If they were safe.

Missy squeezed the sachet tighter and jogged slightly to catch up with the others.

—

Even during the daytime, Decatur Street was known for being the scummy rathole end of the French Quarter. Bars like Molly's at the Market, Turtle Bay, and small restaurants were slim beacons of light and sanctity next to places like The Abbey and The Dervish.

If you wanted to drink alone, to get lost in the darkness, the Abbey was the place to go. But you needed money to buy drinks in the Abbey. Taking what she could get in the way of getting lost in darkness, Baby sat on the ground in front The Abbey. She knew the bartender from riding trains years ago, and he didn't bother her or the other gutter punks she was with as long as they didn't bother the tourists too much.

Baby's guitar was in her lap, and she played softly and sang low, hoping to get enough money to buy either a forty ounce from the liquor store down Decatur Street or, if she really lucked out, a few glasses of beer from inside the Abbey. Maybe even enough to put a few songs on the jukebox.

She stopped and looked up and down the street, hoping, as she had been for the past two weeks, that she would see Alicia's slight frame come around the corner.

I'm sorry, Baby would say, *I'm sorry, I'm stupid, I love you.*

Alicia didn't come, but an older woman stopped and put a few dollar bills in Baby's guitar case, smiling kindly.

Baby nodded to the woman and continued to play her guitar, soft and low.

—

Alessandra had never been to Bourbon Street. So, like everyone who comes to Bourbon Street for the first time, her senses were assaulted at every front.

The music from the bars was loud, and raucous drunken laughter spilled from the open doors and windows. The gutters that lined the streets were filled with liquid that smelled all at once like sour beer, vomit, rotten cheese, and piss.

Tourists laughed and drank hand grenades. Strippers wearing expensive lingerie beckoned in customers at the doors of their clubs. The street was blocked at both ends somewhere down further, so people walked slowly, taking their time as they strolled.

The four women bumped and jostled and maneuvered their way onto the crowded street.

"Stay close, Alessandra," Missy said anxiously over her shoulder.

Tripping over an empty cup, Alessandra bumped into a large man's back. He wheeled on her.

"Hey sweetheart, I can bump you back if you want."

"Sorry," she muttered.

The man laughed and kept walking.

Trenise grabbed Alessandra's arm and jerked her closer while Missy gave the man the most withering look she could muster.

"It's just up there!" Rainbow pointed and yelled over her shoulder, weaving in and out of the crowd.

"Rainbow, hold up!" Trenise shouted, pulling Alessandra along.

The street was too busy, there were too many people. A deep unease settled into Trenise's stomach.

Missy looked around over each shoulder, trying to both keep up with her group and watch those around her. She felt dizzy and overwhelmed by all of the noise and electric lights from the bars and shops. She scurried after Trenise and Alessandra and tried to stay focused.

"Here!"

Rainbow stood next to the door to a bar and waved at them.

"This is it?" Alessandra yelled over the loud music that throbbed from the building.

The entire front of it was an open window. Alessandra could see where they would close the windows after hours almost like a garage door. Inside, there was a stage with musicians belting out a song from the 90s and crowds of people dancing.

Rainbow nodded and yelled, "She'll be somewhere upstairs! Usually at the end of the bar by herself!"

Trenise and Missy both nodded.

"The stairs are all the way at the back!" Rainbow pointed toward the back corner, "Tell her I sent you, and tell her everything!"

"Where will you two be?"

Rainbow pointed across the street, "There's a coffee shop down the side street there, we'll go there. We'll be able to see the entrance!"

"I should be going in there with you two!" Alessandra yelled over the music.

"Stay with Rainbow, Alessandra." Trenise shook her head now. Missy reached out and squeezed Alessandra's hand.

"This is such bullshit."

> Alessandra turned and crossed the street, and Rainbow jogged to catch up with her. Trenise and Missy stepped to the door of the bar where a bouncer waved them in.

"Should we have tried to sneak her in?" Missy yelled.

"Too late now! Let's just get this over with!"

Missy nodded and pointed to the back of the large room, beckoning Trenise to follow her as she tried to move through the crowd of dancing people to the darkened staircase.

—

Trent moved through the edge of the French Quarter along Canal Street as quickly as he could manage. He sidestepped slow moving families and middle-aged bikers. He crossed the street in front of a horsedrawn carriage.

He saw all of it and none of it.

The closer he got to Jackson Square, the more Trent felt a pull as though he was moving in the right direction. He looked at the fortune tellers with disdain and spit on the ground in front of them. He cut to the side of the church and headed toward Royal Street.

Not sure where to go now that he was on the back side of the Cathedral, Trent paused and listened. He let himself be jostled by the people around him. He looked to his left and to his right.

The preacher was there with him, in him, but he did not speak.

He moved to the right and took a left onto Orleans Street. There, ahead of him on the corner of Orleans and Bourbon, was the group of protestors he had seen earlier holding up their signs and placards.

Trent smiled to himself and walked toward them.

"REPENT NOW!" a man yelled into the crowd, "JESUS SAVES!"

The tourists around the protestors ignored them, laughed at them, and Trent watched as a group of young men posed in front of them while one of their friends took a picture.

Trent smiled as he walked past them, and the young woman he had seen earlier held out a brochure to him.

"Jesus saves," she whispered.

Trent smiled at her, "I know."

Trent stopped again, looked left and then right, and looked at each bar and shop in his eyeline. They all were loud and bright.

Alessandra was underaged. She wouldn't be let into any of these places. Trent stopped to listen again but heard nothing.

Instead, he saw a dazzling refracted light emanate from the street itself to his left. The music stopped, the people around him slowed.

Trent gasped.

The light thrummed once more, brighter, and then stopped. Trent turned to his left toward where the light had come from.

As he walked, he looked from side to side, hoping for another sign that he was headed in the right direction.

—

Missy made her way up the deserted staircase with Trenise close behind her. The stairway smelled like old beer and grease and sweat. The music faded the further they walked.

When they reached the small landing, Missy saw far fewer people were in the upstairs section of the bar. A few couples sat around high tables, and she could see that the outside balcony was much more crowded. The people outside laughed and yelled to the tourists below.

"Missy," Trenise said her name softly and gestured with her head toward the bar.

The bar was large and shaped like a U in the middle of the room. At the end of it sat an elderly woman wearing a bright purple tee shirt with a Louisiana State University logo on it. Her gray hair was wrapped up in a yellow headscarf and she was watching a TV play what Missy knew had to be a rerun of an old LSU football game. She had two bottles of Coors Lights in front of her.

The woman took a sip from one of the bottles and slowly turned her head toward Trenise and Missy.

"Are you going to come talk to me or not?" she laughed.

The bartender looked from the old woman to Missy and Trenise.

"You ok, Ms. Sarah?" the bartender asked.

The woman, Ms. Sarah, held up a hand, "You know I'm fine, Pumpkin. Get my friends here a glass of cold water, each."

Trenise and Missy walked toward the woman and sat down on either side of her. Ms. Sarah picked up a beer and scooched her stool back so she could see them both.

"Now let me look at you," she said as she surveyed them, "And where's the other one?"

Missy and Trenise exchanged a look, both shocked and not shocked at the question.

"She's outside with Rainbow, Ms. Sarah," Missy finally responded, "she's underaged and couldn't come in."

"Hm. Ok well better make this quick then."

Missy and Trenise looked at each other again.

"You first," Trenise finally said.

Missy nodded and started with Evangeline.

—

Rainbow picked a set of squashy, forlorn looking armchairs by the window and settled herself down.

Alessandra knew it wasn't Rainbow's fault that she couldn't go with Missy and Trenise to speak to this Ms. Sarah person, but she was still pissed off about it anyway. She glared out the window of the coffee shop at the bar across the street.

"I'm sorry Rainbow."

Rainbow looked startled, "For what?"

"For being rude before."

Rainbow smiled kindly and took Alessandra's hand, "You had a difficult day, Alessandra. And more difficulties are ahead of you."

Alessandra nodded and shrugged, unsure of what to say.

Rainbow turned back to the window. She wasn't sure what she was looking for, but she hoped Missy and Trenise would hurry. She felt nervous and unsettled as she looked out of the window and into the crowded street.

Hurry Trenise, she thought as she watched the surreal pantomime of Bourbon Street play out in front of her eyes.

—

Trenise finished speaking, having told her own part of the story and, with Missy's help, Alessandra's part of the story. Ms. Sarah sat motionless the whole time Trenise and Missy spoke, and Trenise wondered if she was even listening.

Ms. Sarah took a long, slow drink from her bottle of Coors light. She smacked her lips together.

"There's nothing I can do to help you with the boy's actions *before* he came under the influence of this spirit. That's up to the police. The spirit, or the preacher, as you're calling him, that I might be able to help."

Missy leaned forward eagerly.

"What do we do Ms. Sarah?"

Ms. Sarah looked from Trenise to Missy, "The first thing is to follow Rainbow's advice and stay together. Three is a powerful number and it will give you strength. The next thing is to find the spirit's physical link to the corporeal world and destroy it."

Trenise made a face and threw up her hands, "What in the world does that mean?"

Ms. Sarah gave Trenise a long look.

"Your time with me is limited, so listen. There is something physical that once belonged to the spirit. There's also a place that he draws his power from. That's how he's able to stay on this plane. Find his possession, take it to his place of power, destroy it, and you will destroy his grip. I can't help you more than that."

Missy looked out onto the balcony and into the darkening street. The inside of the bar was suddenly too loud, too bright.

"Can't help or won't help, Ms. Sarah?" Missy asked, feeling like her voice sounded strange and muffled.

Ms. Sarah laughed, "This isn't my fight, young woman. This thing didn't show up at my door. You two did."

Missy felt a knot bloom in her stomach.

"Come on Trenise, let's go find Alessandra and Rainbow."

Trenise nodded, "Well thank you, I guess."

Ms. Sarah nodded an acknowledgement as they stood up to leave, "One more thing."

Missy held onto the back of her chair and looked out at the street again, "Trenise..."

"Whatever this spirit is...it's strong. To get that strong it had to have done many unnatural things. Be careful of what or who it may control. It may use the natural world to be as unnatural as *it* is. It may guard itself in ways that feel unnatural to you."

"Like the worms in Missy's bathroom or on Evangaline's tree you mean." Trenise said.

Ms. Sarah nodded.

"Go on now. Missy's looking like she's got the heebie jeebies," she laughed.

Missy nodded and quickly moved toward the stairs.

"Missy what's wrong?" Trenise yelled over the music.

"Something isn't right!" she shouted over the music, "We need to find Alessandra!"

—

Alessandra jumped as her cell phone buzzed in her pocket.

"Shit. It's my mom," she held the phone up to show Rainbow, "If I don't answer she'll freak."

Rainbow made a face and gestured for her to answer.

"Hola, Mami!"

Alessandra tried to sound cheery as she moved away from Rainbow and closer to the coffee shop door.

"Hola, where are you?"

"Oh, I'm at work! I was just about to call you- they asked me to do overnight inventory."

"Ok..."

Alessandra tried to sound casual, "I told them I could do it, Mami, is that ok?"

"I don't know Sandi..."

"Come on mami, I'm safe here. There are other people...plus I want the money."

Mariella hesitated, "Your manager is there?"

"Yeah, all night!" Alessandra hated the forced cheeriness in her voice and wondered if her mother would buy it.

"Ok then. I was going to come home tonight but they offered me to work tonight too. If you're at work too, I'll stay."

"Ok Mami." Alessandra felt her mother's exhaustion through the phone, and her heart twisted knowing she was lying to mother.

"Next weekend, we both take off and do something fun, ok?"

Alessandra smiled, "Ok Mami."

"Call me when you get home in the morning, ok?"

"Ok I will," Alessandra paused, "Mami?"

"Yes? I'm still here."

"I love you," Alessandra bit her lip.

Marietta paused again, "I love you too, Sandi, more than anything."

Alessandra said goodbye and pressed the red button to hang up. She looked out the window of the café and sighed, wondering how much longer Missy and Trenise would be. She didn't know if it was her conversation with her mother leaving her feeling sad and alone, but she had the strongest feeling that they needed to leave New Orleans and get back to Stone River.

Tourists passed the front of the coffee shop, and as Missy watched, a bright white light pulsed and buzzed on the street corner to her left, close to Razoo.

"Rainbow what was that?" Alessandra yelled as she rushed out onto the street.

People in the coffee shop stared after her as the door slammed shut behind her.

"Alessandra come back!" Rainbow called desperately as she watched Alessandra run by the window she was sitting by.

Rainbow jumped to her feet and rushed out onto the street.

—

Trent walked down Bourbon Street with his eyes down, doing his best to sidestep the puddles of spilled beer and vomit. He forced himself to think of the clean crisp late May air when he followed Evie down the gravel path that led to the river instead of the rank air and electric lights of Bourbon Street.

He let it play out in his mind, as he always did.

Evie was far ahead of him and clearly couldn't hear his feet crunching behind her over the music she was listening to. The wind blew gently in the green leaves and the branches called him forward in soft, sweeping motions.

He could see her back up ahead, and he could smell the softest trace of her perfume. He wanted to bury his hands in her hair and squeeze her small body against his. He felt his heart quicken and thought of all the beautiful things he would tell her.

When Trent looked up, there she was.

Not Evangaline in the woods, but Alessandra on Bourbon Street. Her blue hair seemed to glow in the neon lights. Her ripped denim shorts clung to her long legs and a loose black tank top hung off her shoulders, showing her lithe arms and the swell of her breasts.

Trent froze, watching her as she looked around. She finally seemed to see what she was looking for and dashed across the street, stopping in front of a loud bar with a high balcony.

Behind her, a middle-aged woman in a white dress dashed out from the crowd, calling Alessandra's name. It was the same woman the preacher had shown Trent, the one who was interfering.

Stop her.

Without thinking, Trent plowed through the crowd, using every muscle in his body to knock tourists out of his way. He ignored the squawks and protests and mowed through the crowd toward the woman in white.

—

"No, you don't understand!" Alessandra screamed over the music to the bouncer, "It's an emergency! I need to find two women in there!"

The bouncer laughed and shook his head, "No way, kid."

Rainbow appeared at Alessandra's shoulder, panting, "Alessandra...what are you doing?"

"Something's wrong!" she yelled, "I feel it! I need to find Missy and Ms. Jones!"

Rainbow grabbed Alessandra's arm to pull her back to the coffee shop when she felt what she assumed was someone on a bike slam into her left side. As she felt her body smash against the pavement and roll to the side, she felt another body crush on top of hers.

As she fell, Rainbow half-pulled Alessandra with her, finally releasing her as she was midway to the ground. Alessandra stumbled and rolled to the side, off the sidewalk and into the street.

Trent followed through on his tackle and smashed Rainbow into the pavement with his body as hard as he could. Rainbow's head struck the hard ground, and she lost consciousness.

People screamed and the bouncer standing at Razoo barreled toward Trent.

"Hey, you fucking asshole!"

The bouncer picked Trent up by the neck and the back of the pants. Trent whirled on him, screamed, and smashed the bouncer's nose, driving him backwards into the outside of the souvenir shop behind them.

Trent grinned and felt like an electric current ran through his body. He picked up the bouncer and held him over his head, then threw him into the crowd that circled them.

Women screamed and people ran like herds of cattle down each end of Bourbon Street.

Alessandra ran with them, glancing over her shoulder to see where Trent was. She watched as he took a step over Rainbow's body and into the street behind her.

People shoved and pushed her from every side. Stumbling, Alessandra knew the terrified crowd would crush her if she fell. Cutting to the left, Alessandra ran down Toulouse Street, trying to stay in the thick of the crowd. She tried not to panic as she looked around for somewhere to hide.

—

Baby could not believe her good luck. Not only had she managed to scrape together enough money for a beer in the Abbey, but she ran into someone else she knew from traveling the country who was now permanently in New Orleans.

Baby couldn't for the life of her remember his name, but he remembered her. The guy and his boyfriend both worked as bartenders at Checkpoint Charlie, a club on the corner of Esplanade and Decatur that had live music, cheap drinks, cheap food, and a laundromat in the back.

Baby wandered down Decatur with the guy, listening on and off as he droned about how wonderful New Orleans was, about the Japanese noise rock band playing at Checkpoint's tonight, how she should stay and get a job.

"What the fuck I'm going to do with a job, Dude?" Baby laughed.

"That's it! Same old Baby!"

Baby laughed again and followed the guy into Checkpoint's, right past the bouncer who was taking a cover charge from everyone else.

"Sit over here, Baby, I'll get you a bowl of red beans and a PBR," the guy yelled over the noisy punk band on stage.

Baby nodded her appreciation and slumped down in the booth the guy had pointed to. Her grin faded and she fell back into wondering where Alicia was, if she had something to eat, if she was ok. The guy plopped a watery bowl of red beans with a plastic spoon stuck in it in front of her and sloshed a beer in a plastic cup next to it.

Picking up the spoon, Baby looked at the ring on her pinky. She looked at the dolphin on it and thought her heart might break. Baby had told Alicia all about the ocean and Alica had found the dolphin ring somewhere and given it to her. Baby touched the ring with her other hand and said the closest thing to a prayer she had said in years.

Please just let me find her.

When she opened them, she picked the spoon up again and began shoveling the red beans in her mouth. Her eyes shifted around the room, unconsciously looking for any sign of Alicia.

—

Alessandra allowed herself to stop and catch her breath when she reached the back of the Cathedral. The crowd had thinned, and now her running was only garnering strange looks from the people around her. She stood in the covered entrance to what looked like a closed art gallery to try and collect herself.

A throbbing guilt pounded in her stomach. She had left Rainbow lying on the ground to save herself, to get away from Trent even though he could be doing God knows what to Rainbow right now. Peeking out from around the corner of the entrance way, a million questions raced through her mind.

Where do I go? Where are Trenise and Missy? Why is Trent in New Orleans? Did he follow us? I need to get back to Rainbow.

Alessandra drew a shaky breath in and figured that, yes, he probably had followed them there.

And he clearly isn't here to relax and have a fucking drink.

Alessandra decided she'd head back up to Bourbon Street, where someone had surely called the police by now. Trenise and Missy had probably noticed the commotion and would be there helping Rainbow.

Plus, Alessandra thought, *they'll probably have arrested Trent. Problem fucking solved.*

Alessandra poked her head around the corner again and looked both ways. She had very little idea of where she was and needed to get to a street corner to see which direction Bourbon Street was.

Seeing no sign of Trent, she cautiously stepped out onto Royal Street and crossed.

"Hey! Hey, Alessandra, there you are!"

Alessandra froze stupidly and looked ahead of her. Trent was standing on the corner talking to two police officers. He wiggled his fingers at her and smiled.

"Don't worry! I told them about how that woman was trying to mug you! They're here to help!"

Alessandra took a deep breath in and turned and ran back toward the Cathedral. She ran down the alley way, then ran on the side of the church and looked around the crowded area in front of the Cathedral wondering where to go next.

She knocked people out of her way as she darted through the throng toward Decatur Street.

She had no plan. She didn't know where she was going. She thought to duck into a storefront again but glanced over her shoulder and saw Trent burst into the area in front of the Cathedral about 500 feet behind her.

"Shit," she said breathlessly, and rounded the corner onto Decatur Street. She knew Decatur was less well lit, there were less tourists; it had a reputation for being the alternative fringe of the French Quarter.

She had always wanted to go to see different shows at the different clubs, but her mother wouldn't allow it.

I'm sure as hell seeing it now.

Running as fast as she could through the heavy crowd, Alessandra looked for opportunities to blend in, to hide, and found none. Instead, she ran on adrenaline.

"Alessandra!"

Alessandra recognized Trent's voice and glanced behind her to get a handle on where he was. She couldn't see him, so she pushed forward again, past store after store, bar after bar. She wove between people as quickly as she could, trying not to attract attention, trying to blend in.

She passed a golden statue of Joan of Arc, passed a bar called Molly's at the Market that was bright and welcoming. Alessandra paused, glancing over her shoulder for a sign of Trent, and saw him across the street a little way down from her, jogging in and around tourists.

Alessandra set off at a run again.

She passed by gutter punks sitting on the sidewalk, groups of metal heads drinking beer in front of bars where she could hear heavy metal music being played both live and on jukeboxes.

On the next block, she saw a bar on the corner with a huge crowd of people in front. She darted across Esplanade Avenue and heard her name called again.

"Alessandraaaaa!"

Trent jogged behind her. Watching how slowly he was going, Alessandra realized he was playing with her. He was grinning, not out of breath like she was.

He'd chased her away from Missy and Ms. Jones and Rainbow. He had gotten her alone.

She stopped and her stomach clenched as she realized, of course, Trent was faster than her and probably could have caught her at any time.

"Just come here, Alessandra," he said calmly, and then he paused and tilted his head to the side, "I just had to get you away from them!"

Alessandra turned to face him and backed away not knowing what to do or where to go next.

—

This is unbelievable Baby thought to herself, grinning. *I must've done something really great to have impressed old What's-His-Name this much.*

After she had finished her red beans, What's-His-Name (as Baby was now referring to him in her head) appeared at her shoulder with a group of kids all dressed in what were clearly expensive and highly curated punk style clothes.

She guessed they were all a little younger than her own 23 years.

"Baby, these are some friends of mine! I told them all about you, and they wanted to meet you!"

Baby suddenly found herself rattling off tales from her past to the delight of what she found out to be a group of Tulane students. Wealthy, sheltered, trying to rebel, they relished each story and provided her with both beers and cigarettes. One even offered her a couch to crash on.

Maybe I should stay in New Orleans after all, she thought happily through her buzz.

For the first time in two weeks, she was able to think of something other than Alicia.

"Brian told us you were awesome!" one young woman laughed.

Baby looked the young blond up and down, admiring her slim build, "Who the fuck is Brian?"

They all laughed, "You know, Brian! Your friend!"

"Aww yeah, *Brian*. I gotta go thank him!"

Baby sauntered toward the door where she had seen Brian (no longer What's His Name) talking to the bouncer. She was jostled by people dancing and moshing in front of the band and gleefully pushed a man twice her size back into the undulating bodies.

Baby stopped and looked around the bar. She could just see it: she and Alicia could get jobs here, washing dishes or whatever, listen to music, maybe even play music themselves.

Whenever Alicia showed up, that was.

Baby twisted the dolphin ring around and around on her finger, suddenly feeling like the bar was too loud, like she'd had too much beer. She longed for open space, for trees, for the wind. She pushed her way through the crowd and toward the door.

—

A tall bouncer perched on a barstool held his hand out to her.

"ID, kid."

Alessandra shook her head, "I don't have an ID, but I need help."

The bouncer shrugged his shoulders, "What the fuck do I look like? A cop?"

A man standing next to him tittered and leered at Alessandra, "Get the fuck outta here, kid."

Alessandra looked over her should toward where Trent was standing, watching her from across the street.

"Please, that guy over there is going to hurt me."

The bouncer rolled his eyes, "Jesus Christ. Go over to one of the restaurants and have them call the cops. I don't want any fucking pigs around here."

"Who's fucking pigs?"

Baby lurched out of the doorway, feeling better as soon as she hit the evening air. The crowd had all moved inside, and Baby felt calmer not being around so many people.

Alessandra looked from the bouncer to the young woman who had emerged from inside the bar. Shaved head, tattoos on her hands, ragged, dirty clothes.

The bouncer and the other man laughed.

"I think this chick might be."

"Brian says, you're fucking pigs. Are you?" Baby laughed and looked at the blue-haired teenager in front of her.

> "Listen to me. That guy over there is going to hurt me. He already hurt one girl. Please." Alessandra was near tears and her chest felt tight from running.

When she looked back at where Trent had been standing, he was gone. Alessandra looked wildly up and down the street.

"Look at that!" Baby yelled, "I chased him off for ya!"

"Please," Alessandra said, directly to Baby, "He's not gone, I promise. Please help me."

Baby eyed Alessandra, "Look at me, how the fuck am I going to help you?"

"Please, I'm looking for two people I came here with. I got separated from them, and I'm in trouble."

Baby looked at the terrified girl in front of her and thought of Alicia.

"I'm looking for someone too."

Baby stepped closer to Alessandra. The dolphin ring on her finger felt warm as she took a cigarette she had been saving from behind her ear and held it out to Alessandra.

Alessandra shook her head no but stepped closer to Baby.

"Please," Alessandra said again, "I just need somewhere where he won't find me until I can find my friends."

Baby was silent as she took a book of matches from her pocket and lit her cigarette. She sighed and looked Alessandra up and down, feeling her heart wrench.

The kid was clearly scared.

Baby reflected briefly on the times she'd felt scared and alone. Most of all, she thought about the fact that Alicia might be somewhere right now scared and alone. Hoping someone would help her.

Baby touched the warm dolphin ring and took a long pull from the cigarette.

"I have a spot you can hide."

Chapter Seventeen

Trent's stomach was in knots as he gripped the wrought iron fence around the old New Orleans Mint. He could sense the preacher was angry and couldn't understand why.

All he knew was that things felt different once Alessandra started talking to the bitch with the shaved head.

When he had slowly pursued Alessandra though the Quarter, separating her from Bitch Jones and her Chunky Friend, as the Preacher whispered for him to do, he felt powerful and in control. He could have taken her at any time, whenever he felt like it.

Alessandra had been scared and out of breath. She wasn't fast. Trent was patient, just as he had been with Evie and the girl in the woods when they had fought against him, he knew the further he got Alessandra from the other two, the better off he'd be.

The Preacher had howled with rage when he saw the girl with the shaved head. The pain of it sent Trent reeling and he staggered down the street, finally gripping the fence as he was now, losing sight of Alessandra in the process. It was a bright electric pain, and Trent squeezed his eyes shut, panting.

Now, as minute after minute passed, Trent could feel the anger and pain subsiding.

"What do I do?" he whispered, "Who is she?"

It's not a powerful connection, the voice finally said. *You can still overpower them.*

Trent didn't know what that meant, but he testily straightened up looking around. He felt shaky but began walking toward the spot he'd last seen Alessandra and the new bitch. They were nowhere to be seen.

There were very few people outside the bar, and Trent jogged straight up to the bouncer at the door.

"Hey dude, that was my girlfriend y'all were talking to. She's really pissed at me and took off. I'll be in a shitload of trouble with her parents if I come home without her."

Trent tried to look sheepish.

The bouncer and the man next to him said nothing.

Trent looked them both up and down.

"Did y'all see which way she went?"

"Yeah, I saw her," the man next to the bouncer finally said.

Trent perked up.

"She left with some chick. Guess that dick isn't that good, dude. Baby's probably face down in that shit right now."

The bouncer roared with laughter.

Trent looked at the beer bottle that was sitting on a small table next to the bouncer, calmly picked it up, and smashed it across the bouncer's face. The bouncer called out in surprise and swung at Trent but missed. Trent stabbed the broken bottle as hard as he could into the bouncer's cheek.

He picked the man who had disrespected Alessandra up by the throat.

"She's *mine*. She was promised to *me*," Trent said calmly as the man's legs dangled in the air, "Now tell me where she went."

"She went with Baby," the man sputtered, turning a deep red.

"Where?"

"I don't know," the man sputtered again going from deep red to purple.

Trent eased up to let the man speak, "I think she said she came in on North Peters with her friends."

He lifted an arm and pointed down the street.

Trent gave the man's throat one last squeeze and dropped him next to where the bouncer lay moaning and bleeding on the sidewalk. The music was so loud that no one in the bar even knew what had happened.

Trent put his hands in his pockets and calmly walked in the direction the man had pointed. When he got to the corner, where there were no streetlights, Trent broke into a run.

—

Rainbow groaned and tried to pick her head up.

"Don't do that," a woman's voice said, "You were assaulted. Just stay where you are."

Rainbow ignored the voice and sat up.

"I'm a nurse," the voice came again, this time more firmly.

Rainbow opened her eyes and looked around- she was on the ground, and an older woman peered over her. A small crowd was gathered around her.

"Alessandra," Rainbow muttered weakly.

"Help is coming. You probably have a concussion."

Rainbow pressed the heel of her hands to her eyes and tried to think.

"Rainbow!!"

Missy and Trenise burst from the door of Razoo where they had been held back by a crowd of people, unable to come out onto the street. A huge crowd had gathered to watch what Trenise assumed was a fight, stopping Missy and Trenise from leaving.

Rainbow watched as the two women ran frantically toward the coffee shop across the street where they had left her and Alessandra.

"Here!" Rainbow called out as loud as she could.

Missy and Trenise both whipped around, saw her on the ground, and darted to her.

Trenise bent down next to Rainbow, "What happened?"

"Where's Alessandra?" Missy asked breathlessly.

Rainbow moaned, "I don't know. I think it was...that boy. That...that boy showed up. He tackled me."

"Shit," Missy swore and looked around desperately.

"The girl with the blue hair?" the nurse looked around at the three of them with growing concern.

"Yes," Trenise said, "Did you see her?"

"She went that way," the nurse pointed toward the street where Alessandra had run away, "Is she in trouble?"

Trenise didn't respond to the woman, and Missy leapt to her feet.

"Rainbow, we're going to leave you here."

Trenise grabbed Missy's arm and backed toward the street.

"No," Rainbow pulled herself to her feet, "I'm coming too."

"Well, come on then."

"No wait! The police and EMTs are on their way!" the nurse squawked.

The three women had already set off on a run toward the direction of the church where the nurse had pointed.

Used to running from her daily jogs, Trenise easily pulled ahead of the other two.

"Where would she go?" Missy yelled wildly, "Back to the car?"

"If she's got any sense, that's where she'd head!" Trenise yelled back over her shoulder.

"How did he find us here?" Missy yelled again as she pulled out her cellphone and dialed Alessandra's number. She growled with frustration as the call failed over and over again.

This time, Trenise didn't answer. She both didn't know and feared the answer.

—

Alessandra trailed slightly behind Baby, suddenly wary of the fact that she was following a stranger through a dark section of New Orleans. She looked around her and other than the occasional group of people walking toward the loud sounds of Frenchman Street, they were alone.

No one was in sight, including Trent.

"Is your name really Baby?" she asked, trying to sound at ease.

The girl laughed, "That's what the call me. Baby Rosebud if you want to get formal about it."

"Baby Rosebud?" Alessandra asked and wrinkled up her nose.

Baby laughed.

"It's a long story."

Alessandra thought that the name "Baby Rosebud" was about as incongruous of a name for this person as she could get. With her shaved head, tattoos, grungy clothes, and guitar slung over her back, she looked more like someone out of a Mad Max movie than a tiny flower.

"I'm Alessandra."

Baby nodded, "Who's the guy?"

Before Alessandra could answer, Baby stopped and threw her hands up. She turned to face Alessandra.

"You can walk next to me. I'm not going to fucking hurt you."

They started walking again, Alessandra next to Baby now.

"I don't know how to tell you. But like I said, he hurt one girl already," she paused, "Probably two girls. I just need to find my friends, and I'll be ok."

Baby nodded and Alessandra was grateful that she didn't ask any more questions.

"Where are we going?" Alessandra finally asked as Baby made turns down different streets, "To your apartment or something?"

Baby laughed, "Kinda."

Alessandra tried again desperately to sound casual, "Is it safe?"

Baby laughed again, "What in the world about me, tonight, or whatever situation you're in is in any way 'safe?'"

Alessandra shrugged and silently followed as Baby made another turn.

For her part, Baby was hoping all the turns she was making would throw anyone who was following them off from where they were going. She didn't see anyone when she glanced behind them, but they didn't mean they weren't there.

Baby didn't believe in God, or karma, or anything but herself. She knew from her adventures around the country that there was a good chance if you did right by someone, they might do right by you.

Just like old Brian back there, Baby thought.

As brash as she was, Baby didn't like to do harm to others unless they deserved it. She tried to help when she could, ease the horrible burden of life. She stole a glance over at Alessandra: younger than Alicia, taller, slimmer build. But Baby recognized the same guard, the same woundedness.

Maybe stupidly, Baby had a grim conviction that maybe if she helped this girl, somewhere out there someone would be helping Alicia. Maybe someone was giving her a ride right now, bringing her closer to Baby.

Baby and Alessandra turned another corner and Alessandra stared.

Ms. Jones's car.

"That's my friend's car!" she yelled excitedly, pointing at the SUV.

Baby looked at her with disbelief, "Really? That's my friend's van right there. That's where we're going."

Alessandra saw that Baby pointed to the van she had noticed when the first arrived in the French Quarter.

The two young women looked at each other quizzically, speechless at the coincidence. For her part, Alessandra started to think that there were no coincidences in life. For hers, Baby started to have a gnawing dread that something was wrong here. More wrong than just some asshole chasing his girlfriend around the French Quarter.

"We can hide from your boyfriend in the van." Baby said, eyeing Alessandra.

"He's not my fucking boyfriend," Alessandra snapped, almost spitting with rage.

"Ok, Alessandra, got it."

The two crossed the empty street, and Alessandra felt the hair on her neck stand on end as she heard her name screamed somewhere off in the distance.

"Alesssannndddraaaa!"

"No..." Alessandra whispered, eyes wide with fear.

"Is that him?" Baby whispered.

Again, Alessandra heard her name echo down one of the streets behind them.

"Alessssannnnddddraaaaaaa!"

Without waiting for an answer, Baby grabbed Alessandra by the arm and dragged her the rest of the way across the street.

—

The pain from the Preacher's anger coursed through every muscle and nerve in Trent's body. The streets turned and twisted with no seeming reason or pattern.

Trent knew from coming to the French Quarter with his dad on business trips that North Peters Street, the street the asshole at the bar had said the shaved head bitch was going to, was by the river. Trying his best to run in the direction of the river, Trent made twists and turns down different narrow streets. He was well out of the French Quarter now. It was dark and residential.

Trent felt himself panic as the thought of Alessandra and the bitch with the shaved head *together* rose in his mind. His muscles were strained and achy but, in spite of that, he felt the pleasant hardening below his belt again at the thought.

You can have the other one now, came the voice of the Preacher, *but save your blue- haired darling for when we get home.*

Trent made a right again and pressed forward, dreaming of stripping Alessandra down and doing what he wanted.

"Alessandra!"

Her name came out of his lips like a howl, like the sound a wounded animal makes. It echoed down the dark street and Trent thought he could see the street ripple back in response.

He thought for a second he could hear her voice, small and quiet, say, "No.."

Like a bloodhound, sniffing the air as he went, Trent sprinted toward where he had seen the ripple, heard the whisper.

He howled her name again.

This time the ripple was stronger, like a wave.

"Is that him?"

It was a voice Trent didn't recognize.

Trent sped up, relishing how good it would feel to maul the girl with the shaved head. Alessandra would watch, and she would know just how strong he was. He wouldn't have to take her like he did the others. She would give herself to him.

As he burst out onto North Peters Street, he saw a row of cars parallel parked along a sidewalk opposite him. There was a small, sad-looking park between him and the cars. Trent grinned, as he made his way through a dilapidated set of swings, scanning up and down the street for a sign of them.

He knew they were here. He could almost hear their hearts beating, feel their ragged breath. They were scared, and that was good.

—

Alessandra lay motionless except for her heaving chest under a pile of mildewed blankets. She tried desperately to calm her breathing. It sounded like tidal waves crashing out of her mouth.

After hiding Alessandra in a corner of the van behind a pile of broken music equipment, Baby piled the blankets on top of her and warned her not to move.

"I'll be back," she whispered.

Alessandra heard the door of the van slam shut.

Now, Alessandra strained to hear anything: Trent, Baby, a passerby. All she could hear was her own breathing and then, close to her head but outside the van, she heard a small knock.

"I'm outside. Don't come out."

Alessandra desperately wished for the breaker bar she knew was in Trenise's car. As they ran past the SUV and into the van, she tried to tell Baby to break the window and get it, but Baby wouldn't listen.

Alessandra fumed with herself.

Hiding again, she thought, *leaving Baby to fight alone.*

"Baby, I'm coming out."

"Shut the fuck up, Alessandra. I see him."

Alessandra froze, sweating under the blankets.

"Hey," she heard Baby yell, "hey fuckwad!"

Alessandra strained to hear if Trent answered.

"Yeah, that's right!" Baby yelled, "It is that bitch! Alessandra's gone you fucking idiot!"

Baby's voice drifted away, and Alessandra threw the blankets off herself as she heard Trent yell something she couldn't quite make out.

She sat up and peeked out one of the van's dingy windows.

She could just make out Baby's tall figure moving across the street toward the junk yard playground and heard her laughing derisively. Alessandra scanned the playground and saw Trent leaning casually against a set of monkey bars.

"Yeah, come on bitch! Come on over and get some of this!" He grabbed his crotch.

"I know she's in there!" he pointed at the van with his other hand.

"Fuck," Alessandra whispered.

"That ain't nothing!" Baby yelled, "Why don't you take your baby dick out of here, asshole?"

Baby advanced on him and Alessandra wondered what the hell she was doing. Baby was tall, but Trent was three times as wide as her.

Alessandra left her perch at the window and rushed to the door of the van jerking it open and falling out onto the street.

—

Baby felt cool and calm. She let trash talk come out of her mouth, hoping to lull him into thinking she was angry, that she was not thinking clearly.

Everything felt like it was in sharp focus around her. She felt the ground under her feet, felt the stagnant humid air in her lungs.

She remembered one of her mother's boyfriends, the only nice one, the only one who didn't touch Baby or hit her or scream at her. She hadn't been Baby Rosebud then, she was just Tanya.

The boyfriend didn't last long, and Baby only knew him as Rooster, the nickname her mother had called him. At ten, Baby was already as tall as Rooster. He was fun and always smelled like weed.

One night in her mother's trailer, Rooster reached past Baby to grab a beer from the fridge, and she noticed his hands and knuckles were bruised and scabbed over.

"What happened, Rooster?" she asked, timidly. Back then Tanya was always timid, always scared of being in the way.

Rooster shrugged, "Bar fight."

"Did...did you win?"

Tanya jumped as her mother laughed raucously, drunkenly, at the question. Tall, and thin with a pile of blond hair and shockingly bright pink fingernails, her mother planted one hand on her hip.

"Rooster always wins."

Rooster laughed.

"Why?" Tanya had asked, looking at Rooster evenly.

"'Cause I don't fight fair. Gouging eyes, fingers in the ears, squeezing balls. That's how you win a fight."

Rooster laughed and cracked his beer, "Life ain't no goddamn Golden Gloves, kid."

Rooster vanished not long after that, one in a long line of men, but Tanya, who later came to be known as Baby, always remembered it.

Any time she had to fight, Baby clawed, bit, tore, and squeezed, going first for the most tender spots on her opponents' bodies that she could. She ripped off clothing, tore out earrings.

She'd been in lots of fights over the years- many of them with men bigger than her. Every one of them, she fought dirty like Rooster said.

No fight scared her. No opponent scared her. Because life wasn't a fucking Golden Gloves boxing match.

Life was mean and unfair and Baby knew that through and through.

Baby Rosebud, once a scared little trailer park girl named Tanya, crossed the decrepit playground on North Peters Street. She balled up her fist and felt the warmth of Alicia's dolphin ring. She stepped into the grass, faded black boots crunching through garbage.

Across from her, Trent stood up and laughed. Baby advanced and circled around to her left so that she was closer to the metal chain of the broken swing.

Trent gave her a patronizing look and folded his arms across his chest.

"I'll break you, little girl."

Trent smiled wider. "I'll break you like I broke the one you're looking for. The other one with the rose tattoo."

Baby paused, mouth dry and open wide.

"What did you say?"

Trent stared at her, smiling and unblinking.

"You heard me. The one you're looking for. The one with the rose tattoo. The girl who loved the ocean. I fucked her in the ass while I smashed her face in with a rock."

Baby stared dumbly as Trent walked closer to her.

"Do you miss her? Because I do. I kept her for a little while after, to use when I wanted. To use like I'm going to use you."

Baby stood frozen next to the broken swing not wanting to believe it.

"If you hurt Alicia, for real...I'll fucking kill you."

Baby's voice sounded small and ragged and unsure.

Trent laughed condescendingly, he was almost within arm's reach of Baby as she stood rooted to the ground, face open and shocked.

Trent took another step forward and reached out, fingertips almost on Baby's face, "It'll be over soon if you don't fight."

Baby stared dumbly as Trent's face relaxed into complacence. He reached down and unzipped his pants.

"Close your eyes and you'll be with her soon."

Baby looked down and back up again, not moving.

Trent nodded to her calmly.

Looking at his expectant face, Baby watched as his eyes half closed in expectation as she reached down toward his exposed and bulging genitals.

Instead of the pleasure Trent was expecting, Baby latched onto one of his testicles with her hand and squeezed as hard as she could. She used her other hand to grab the chain of the broken swing behind her.

As Trent bellowed in pain and hit her arm that was squeezing him with a fist like a hammer, Baby swung back and whipped the chain of the broken swing across his face. The chain connected with one ear and swiped his nose, leaving both bloody. Baby was forced to let go and fell backwards.

Trent stumbled too, retching and holding his crotch.

Baby jumped up and kicked him in the face as hard as she could, sending him reeling backwards, moaning. She heaved a deep breath and moved towards him to kick him again in the face, one more blow to knock him out, she guessed.

Before her foot could connect, Trent reached out, grabbed her ankle, and pulled her leg out from under her. He was on top of her in a flash, faster than she thought possible, pinning down both of her arms. He grinned at her, showing bloody teeth.

Baby struggled to get up. She bucked her hips, tried to use her knees to kick him off, but the more she moved, the tighter he held her.

On her finger, Alicia's ring grew hot and pulsed. As Trent loomed over her, watching her, holding her down, Baby closed her eyes and saw Alicia walking through the woods somewhere, saw her sitting on a pile of stones. She saw Alicia talking but no sound was coming out of her mouth. She saw Alicia lying on the ground with her mouth open wide in a silent scream.

In her mind, Baby reached out to her. Alicia turned toward Baby and her voice sounded muffled and watery, "Stop him."

"How?" Baby asked out loud, eyes closed.

"How what?" Trent asked amused, rubbing his body against her. "Do you need me to explain to you how this works?"

Baby squeezed her eyes shut blocking out the sound of Trent's voice and asked, "How?" again.

"The ring," Alicia reached a hand out to touch Baby's face and then she faded away.

The vision was gone. The ring burned and Baby clenched her fist around it.

—

Missy clutched her side and desperately tried to keep running forward. With every step they took, she felt more and more like they were running out of time.

"Trenise!" Missy yelled, "We have to hurry!"

"I know, Missy!" Trenise yelled back as she ran in and out of the crowd.

Rainbow limped along behind Missy, trying her best to keep her eyes on her back.

"Here Trenise!" Rainbow yelled, "Trenise turn down Esplanade, it's faster!"

Not waiting for Missy and Rainbow, Trenise crossed Esplanade at a run, dodging cars and ignoring the people blowing their horns at her.

When Trenise got to the corner of Elysian Fields and North Peters, she heard the first scream.

"Missy!" Trenise yelled, "Hurry!"

Ignoring her burning side, Missy pushed herself so that she was only a few steps behind Trenise. She knew Trenise's SUV was down the street they were on, but she couldn't see it in the dark.

Another scream echoed from the direction of where Trenise's car was parked.

"Is it Alessandra?" Missy yelled as they heard the screaming again.

"I can't tell!"

Trenise, breath heaving, burst from her jog to a sprint, pushing her legs to go faster, arms pumping in stride. She thanked God for every day she had forced herself to get out on her morning jog.

"Open the car, Trenise! Open the door!" Missy yelled.

Trenise fumbled in her pocket, slowing slightly, and pushed the button. Ahead, the lights on her car flashed.

—

Trent let go of one of Baby's hands and quickly moved it to her throat. She beat at him with her free hand, and he ignored it. He squeezed, hard, and Baby choked and sputtered. He let go a little and then squeezed again, watching as Baby turned red and purple.

Baby closed her fist that Trent still had trapped around Alicia's ring, waiting. She began to lose consciousness and fought to drag in even the smallest breath.

"Hey Trent!"

Baby registered that it was Alessandra's voice.

Her eyes shot open as Trent turned to look at Alessandra. When he did, Baby took her free hand and shoved her thumb in his eye.

Trent howled and let go of her left hand. When he did, Baby swung up in a fist connecting with him in the fleshy section under his chin and above his neck.

For a moment, Baby thought she had punched straight through his windpipe and that her hand was somehow lodged in his throat.

As Trent howled and flopped to the side of her, he pulled her arm with him and Baby could see that Alicia's ring shone a blinding blue. Her fist wasn't inside Trent's neck. The ring itself appeared to be burning its way through his skin.

Baby screamed and jerked her hand back trying to free herself.

Trent howled in pain and flung his arm out trying to disconnect himself from Baby.

"Alessandra help!" Baby screamed, panicked, watching as steam rose from the ring as it smoldered with blue heat.

Blood from Trent's neck oozed and sputtered as it hit the scorched area around where her ring was lodged.

"Lean back!" Baby turned and saw, not Alessandra, but a middle aged blonde woman, sweating and wielding a baseball bat appear on the playground to her right.

Baby leaned back, arm stretched as far as she could, hand still connected to Trent's neck.

The blond woman swung the bat down hard like she was playing golf and connected to the side of Trent's head.

Baby watched, mouth open as midway through the swing the bat glowed a ferocious blue, like her ring. When it connected with Trent's head, it knocked Baby's hand loose, freeing her.

Baby scrambled away and landed at another person's feet. She looked up at another middle-aged woman, this time one with ebony skin, long braided hair, and a white dress. The woman helped Baby to her feet and pulled her to the sidewalk where Baby collapsed down next to Alessandra.

"Baby are you ok?" Alessandra grabbed Baby around the torso and held her half laying in her lap.

Baby nodded and gasped for air. She watched as the blond woman and an older black woman darted to one edge of the playground.

"Where is he Trenise?"

"There!" Trenise raised her hand and pointed down one of the side streets.

Missy took off after him, bat raised over her shoulder. When she got across the street, to the spot where she had seen Trent run, clutching his throat, Missy yelled in frustration.

Trenise appeared at her elbow, "What is it?"

"Trenise, he's gone," Missy gestured down the empty street, "How is that possible?"

Trenise looked at the stoops and high fenced yards of the small houses around them.

"Shit," she swore, "Missy he could've jumped the fences, ducked into any of these yards. We need to get the hell out of here."

Missy looked one more time down the street.

"Come on, Missy," Trenise tugged her arm back toward the playground.

—

Baby heaved herself up from the sidewalk and away from Alessandra, back toward the van.

"Wait, Baby!" Alessandra called, "You're hurt!"

Baby waved her away.

"Go on," she squeezed out through her burning throat.

"We can help you," Rainbow called gently.

Baby wanted to tell her that no she fucking couldn't. That no one could fucking help her, but her throat burned and ached as she breathed.

Instead, Baby shook her head no and waved the two of them away again.

Trenise and Missy crossed the playground, both watching and listening as Alessandra and Rainbow followed the young woman who Missy had helped.

"Alessandra," Rainbow finally said. "Respect her wishes and leave her be."

Alessandra looked desperately from Rainbow to Baby and back again.

"She saved me, Rainbow."

Rainbow nodded gently, "Then thank her and respect what she's asking you."

"Y'all, we need to go!" Trenise called as she and Missy crossed the street.

"We don't know where he went."

Trenise turned the car on, letting the cold air blast on her overheated face.

"I can't leave her here alone, Rainbow, what if Trent comes back?"

Rainbow shook her head, "I don't think he will."

Baby stumbled to the van and yanked the door open.

Rainbow turned and headed to Trenise's SUV and plopped down into the interior, welcoming the air conditioning.

Missy stood, car door open, and watched Alessandra as she approached the van door.

Baby stood in the door of the van, sipping water from a bottle. Her eyes were red, and her throat was already starting to turn black and blue.

"Thank you, Baby."

Baby nodded and chuckled, "Happy to help."

Her voice was raspy and barely more than a whisper.

"I hope you find who you're looking for," Alessandra said quietly.

Baby nodded sadly, thinking of what she had seen as Trent had tried to choke the life from her.

Alessandra turned and walked to Trenise's car, head down.

Baby watched as the four women sat in the car for a moment, briefly talking to each other. The lady in white said something and the older woman at the wheel nodded to Baby.

Baby nodded back.

She waited until the SUV made a U-turn in the middle of the road and pulled away. Then, Baby wrapped her arms around her stomach, doubled over in pain. She wanted to howl as an indescribable grief raced through her body.

She knew for certain that Alicia was gone and that she would never find her. Her beautiful girl was gone, and Baby was really and truly alone.

Chapter Eighteen

Alessandra sat with her head pressed up against the window, peering out at nothing as they drove through the ninth ward.

"Rainbow, shit, you're bleeding." Trenise said, looking at her cousin out of the corner of her eye.

"What? Where?" Rainbow looked at herself in the mirror and saw there was blood on her dress.

"I don't know, looks like the back of your head where you fell. You need to go to the hospital, Rainbow."

Rainbow put a hand to the front of her head and nodded, "Yeah probably. The lady back there on Bourbon Street said I was unconscious. Drive me to Baptist, Trenise."

Rainbow leaned back in her seat, forcing herself to keep her eyes open. She felt woozy and sick.

"On the way," she said as calmly as she could, "We need to share what happened."

"Y'all start," Trenise said, "So Missy and I know before we drop you."

When Rainbow and Alessandra finished telling them what had happened, Trenise and Missy recounted what Ms. Sarah had told them.

"Well, that makes sense," Alessandra said sarcastically.

"It does make sense, Alessandra." Rainbow said softly, "There's something supernatural here."

"Trent's not fucking supernatural" Alessandra countered.

"No," Missy said, "But something else is. Something else that's attracted to what Trent is."

"Right," said Trenise, "As much as every fiber of my being doesn't want to admit it and hates the idea of it, there's something else going on here beyond just Trent"

Rainbow nodded.

"So, what do we do?" Alessandra asked.

"Well, it's obvious," Rainbow said as they pulled in front of Baptist Hospital, "Find the entity's connection to this world and destroy it. Sarah told you that."

"Oh yeah, Rainbow," Trenise rolled her eyes, "You make that sound really easy."

"How are we supposed to know who or what this entity is?" Missy asked quietly from the back seat.

Alessandra picked her head up from the window and turned slowly toward the front seat.

"The Preacher," she said softly.

"What?" Missy said.

"When we saw that guy in the woods before he...changed. We all said he looked like a preacher, right?"

The other three were silent, listening.

Rainbow's head pounded and ached, and she felt dizzy again.

"That story, you know Ms. Jones, the ones all the kids tell, the one about the preacher stoning his wife to death and burning down the church..." Alessandra trailed off.

Missy's mouth hung open thunderstruck, "The clearing, the graveyard. My neighbor told me that the ruins of the old church are still back there."

Alessandra slammed her fist into her other hand, "It's him."

"Trenise?" Missy turned and looked at Trenise.

Trenise nodded, "It's worth a try at least."

Rainbow smiled grimly, her hand on the door handle.

"I'm going to go now," she said, "I think I've helped you all I can for now."

Trenise looked her up and down, "You want me to come with you, Rainbow? At least walk you in?"

Rainbow took a long look at Trenise, "No, Trenise. You need to go."

Trenise nodded, "Ok Rainbow, but you call me, ok?"

Rainbow nodded and stepped out of the car.

"Thank you, Rainbow," Missy said softly.

"Thanks Rainbow," Alessandra echoed.

Rainbow nodded to both of them, "I'm sorry I can't help you more. Remember to stay together."

Rainbow turned and closed the car door.

"I'm going to watch you walk in Rainbow!" Trenise rolled down the window and called.

Rainbow waved, paused, then turned back to them. Missy had rolled down the back window too, and she and Alessandra peered out at her.

"One other thing I thought of after what happened back there with Trent," Rainbow called, "You know there's always an opposite. Dark has light, light has dark. If there's this darkness at work, there may be light at work as well. Look for it."

"Ok, Rainbow," Trenise called, "You go on in now."

Rainbow nodded and slowly made her way through the automatic doors that led into the emergency room.

Rainbow shone brightly for a moment as the light silhouetted her, and then she was gone.

Trenise rolled up the car windows and looked at Missy and Alessandra in the back seat.

"You said your neighbor told you the story, Missy," Trenise said slowly, "Who was it?"

"Ms. Cindy," Missy answered, "she was really involved in local historical preservations."

Trenise nodded slowly and tightened her grip on the steering wheel, "Of course Cindy would know."

Alessandra grinned, "Got him!"

—

Trent didn't dare feel his wounds until he was back in his truck. He could feel the warm, sticky blood on his cheek and neck. He reached up and gingerly touched his neck where the bald-headed bitch had punched him. It felt hot and bumpy like there were blisters there.

He felt the side of his head where the blond bitch had hit him with the baseball bat. It felt like his hair was crunchy and singed, and he thought he could feel blisters forming there too.

He barely remembered how he made it back to his truck.

He was alone.

Totally alone.

Trent sat in his truck and strained to hear anything, either from inside of his head or out. All he heard were distant noises from cars driving to the French Quarter. He didn't hear the Preacher, and he didn't feel him.

He remembered pulling himself up and over the fence that he was hiding behind and walking down the railroad tracks to get back to where his truck was parked.

Trent felt his lower lip quiver. He no longer felt powerful, or sure of himself. He was scared and alone.

Trent realized that after his fights on both Bourbon Street and Decatur that the police would be out looking for him. True, he had given two cops a bullshit story that the woman he hit was trying to mug his girlfriend, but would they buy it after talking to witnesses?

He heard sirens in the distance and shakily started his truck. How many people had seen him? Could they give a description of him?

Where is He?

Still not daring to look at himself in the mirror, Trent pulled out of his spot, carefully obeying the Speed Limit. When he made it out of the French Quarter and into New Orleans East, headed back to Stone River, he was able to relax a little. He stopped looking in his rearview mirror as much.

When he hit the foot of the Twin Span Bridge that would bring him over Lake Pontchartrain, he allowed himself to glance at his face in the mirror.

Blisters filled with fluid and blood were clustered on his already bruising neck. The hair on the side of his head was indeed burned and there were blood blisters there too, but nowhere near as bad as his neck.

His fear was replaced with rage.

As he crossed the Parish line, midway across the bridge, he felt a small pulse in the back of his head. He felt a small whisper of a voice, almost like a sleeping person's soft breathing.

Trent's chest swelled with hope.

Trent pulled his truck back into the driveway to his house and bounded up the stairs of the porch, through the living room and up the stairs to his room. There, on his dresser, was another rock he had taken from the clearing, a rock from the stone of the church building. One that looked just like the rock he'd used on Evie.

His lip quivered again as he reached out his hand and touched it.

I'm here.

Trent felt hot tears on his face as he cried with relief.

Don't be frightened. The Witch has helped them. But that doesn't matter. We have the power of God on our side.

"Yes," Trent whispered, "The power of God."

Trent felt scared again at how weak the voice sounded.

Don't worry, the voice came, *you can make me strong again. Listen. Listen to the voice of God.*

—

"You're sure your mother isn't going to mind?" Trenise asked again.

Missy laughed in spite of herself at the expression on Alessandra's face.

"I told you Ms. Jones," Alessandra said from the spot where she was curled on Trenise's bright orange couch, "I told her I was doing inventory at work overnight, and *she's* working overnight in Baton Rouge. I already checked in with her again- I got it covered."

After dropping Rainbow at the hospital, Alessandra, Missy, and Trenise formed a plan. They discussed and made changes and had a decently worked idea ironed out by the time they pulled into Trenise's driveway.

Missy called and told her mother she'd be late because she was helping Trenise with a project at her house. She talked to Sophie and Johnny and tried not to cry at the sounds of their happy little voices. She wanted to be with them more than anything in the world, but she knew in her heart that she couldn't leave Stone River yet.

Alessandra called her mother and told her again that she was doing inventory, that she would be with her manager all night.

While they made their phone calls, Trenise gathered pillows and blankets and brought them to her living room.

While they were driving, the first decision they made was that they should not split up again. Trenise's large, worm-free house seemed like the best choice. They decided they would all sleep in the same room for safety and so that they could take turns standing guard if they felt it was necessary.

In the morning, they would go to Ms. Cindy's house to ask her where they might find something that belonged to the Preacher. Together, they agreed that the entity's "place of power" as Ms. Sarah had called it, was the clearing where the old church had once stood.

When they found something that belonged to the Preacher, they would take it back to the clearing behind Trent's house and destroy whatever it was either by smashing it or burning it or both.

Alessandra reclined on the couch and thought about the girl's body out in the woods by the old graveyard. Missy made up a bed for herself on the other, larger couch, and tried not to think about the feeling when her baseball bat had connected with Trent's head.

The living room was large and open, connected to the kitchen by an archway. Trenise was slowly walking around the room, watering her many potted plants, forcing herself to walk slowly to check that the front door was locked. She had checked three times already, but she knew that the act of checking to see that the door was locked was her way of coping with what was happening.

Missy watched Trenise out of the corner of her eye.

"How are we going to tell the cops she's out there?" Alessandra said out loud finally.

Missy straightened and shook her head.

"We'll figure it out, Alessandra," Trenise said from somewhere behind her.

Missy's hair was wet from the scalding shower she'd taken in Trenise's guest bathroom and she sported an old Stone River Girls Basketball sweat suit. She plopped herself down onto her makeshift bed.

"I guess the most important thing is getting rid of...whatever's helping Trent."

Trenise stood by the front door and peered out the window into the dark around her house. She told herself this was the last time she'd check the lock on the door, then she carefully put her small watering can in its spot on the shelf.

Trenise turned on a light in the hallway that led to the bathroom and turned off the overhead light, throwing the room into darkness.

"Is that ok?" she said quietly.

Alessandra's eyes gleamed in the light from the hallway, and she muttered yes. Missy nodded as Trenise walked by and settled into a recliner.

The night was quiet and all three tried desperately to sleep in spite of what they had seen that day.

—

All Trent needed to do was make one phone call. He marveled at the wisdom of the Preacher, how he really was speaking with the voice of God. Because how else could it be this easy?

Lexie was excited to meet Trent in the woods behind his house. Trent knew she never told her mother when she came to meet him, since her mother wouldn't let her come. Usually they met at his house, but he could almost feel the excitement in her voice when he told her he had something special planned, something *different.*

"Different how, Trent?" Lexie breathed.

He smiled and toyed with her, "You'll see, babe."

Now, Trent waited in the clearing for her, standing on the fresh dirt of the grave he had dug earlier in the day. He rubbed his groin in anticipation for what he'd get to do to Lexie. The preacher had whispered to Trent what needed to be done to bring his strength back.

It was your first sacrifice that began my awakening. The second made me strong. Now the third will give me the strength to overcome our foes, to vanquish our enemies.

"Trent?"

"Here," he said, voice husky. He waved his flashlight toward the path he told Lexie to take- the same path that he used to bring the other girl here.

He watched as Lexie picked her way carefully through the rocks and bricks from the old church, moving toward him. He wondered what it would feel like to be inside her while he ripped her hair out. He wondered if he could bite through the tender flesh on her neck.

As Lexie got closer to him, she glanced down at his erection and grinned, pulling her dress over her head and revealing her naked breasts and a pair of lacy panties.

"What's the surprise?" she said and slowly walked toward him.

Trent grinned and shoved her to the ground, pinning her to the dirt with his foot as she squawked.

Lexie tried to squirm away from him, hit his leg with her fist, but Trent just pushed harder.

He bent down and put his face close to hers, pinning her shoulders now with both hands as he sat on top of her.

Trent waited until the look in her eyes turned from confusion to panic to terror and then he went to work.

—

Trenise held her arm up to her face, straining in the dark to read her watch. She could just make out that it was a little after 3 am.

She lifted her head slightly and could see the still outlines of both Missy and Alessandra, One of them snored softly.

Trenise tried to roll over on her side, but the angle of the recliner made it almost impossible. She flopped over onto her back, staring up at the ceiling fan.

Trenise glanced over at the front door to her right and then to the dark kitchen on her left. She didn't dare get up to get a bottle of water from the fridge for fear of waking Missy and Alessandra. Instead, she slowly and carefully swung her legs over to one side of the recliner and stood up, knees creaking. Despite her daily physical training, she felt tired and sore.

You feel your age, girl.

Her mother's voice came so clearly Trenise jumped, looking over her shoulder. She stared into the blackness for a moment, wishing more than anything that she could talk to her mother.

Missy's head was just visible where it rested on the arm of the couch. Trenise walked as quickly and as carefully as she could past her and into the dimly lit hallway. She went into the guest bathroom and closed the door behind her.

Trenise sighed and looked at her haggard reflection in the mirror. There were dark circles under her eyes, and her skin looked flaky and dry.

Trenise reached into the cabinet under the sink and pulled out a paper cup from the package she kept there. She drank three of the small cups and then bent forward to look more closely at herself in the mirror.

A light, quick tapping made her snap her head back.

"Just one sec!" she whispered and opened the door, expecting to find either Missy or Alessandra standing there waiting to use the restroom.

When she opened the door, the apology she was going to say for waking one of the girls up died before it was spoken. The hallway was empty.

Trenise felt ice cold, and her skin crawled with goosebumps. She stood in the doorway of the bathroom and looked to the left into the dark living room where both Missy and Alessandra still were sleeping. She looked slowly to the right down the short hallway that led to her and Jolie's bedrooms and heard the tapping again.

Trenise took two slow breaths, clutched Rainbow's bag hanging around her neck, and stepped out into the hallway. Trenise usually kept the air conditioning down at night to a cool 68 degrees, but the air in the hallway felt muggy and hot. Trenise tried to remember if it had felt that way before she'd gone into the bathroom.

She heard the tapping again, louder.

She stopped at Jolie's open door and peered in, waiting and listening. She could feel the cool air pouring out of Jolie's room in stark contrast to the heat of the hallway. The tapping came again, and Trenise knew it was coming from her own bedroom.

She took another breath and watched the door to her room carefully, trying to make as little sound as possible with her bare feet. When she got to the bedroom door and looked in, straining to see through the darkness, the tapping became a steady rattle and scrape.

Trenise reached to the side of the door and flicked on the overhead light.

Her eyes winced as the light came on and she looked around the room trying to find the source of the sound. Movement next to her dresser caught her eye. She furrowed her eyebrows and took a step closer.

Her dog tags and Big John's dog tags hung where they always did from the corner of the mirror above the dresser. Now, however, they swung back and forth and hit the wall as though someone was pushing and pulling them.

The heat and humidity pulsed, and Trenise looked at the dripping condensation on the walls around where the dog tags swung. She took another step toward them and reached out a shaky hand.

The dog tags stopped. Trenise stopped also, then took them in her hand.

They felt warm, like they did when she had worn them close to her skin. She closed her fist around them and then closed her eyes.

At her ceremony when she graduated basic training, Trenise's mother had taken her dog tags in her hand just as Trenise was doing now.

"Girl, you listen to me."

Her mother pulled firmly on the tags so that Trenise had to move closer to her. Standing in her bedroom now, Trenise could inexplicably smell fresh cut grass, the mix of sweat and perfume. She could feel the pulsing heat on what had been an uncharacteristically hot day Illinois.

Her mother said nothing, and Trenise had stared at her with wide eyes, "I'm listening, Mama."

"You keep these tags together, always. I don't never want one without the other, you understand me, girl?"

Trenise looked at her mother and nodded slowly, "I understand, Mama."

Her mother nodded and let go of the tags. She'd pulled Trenise close to her, and Trenise breathed in her soft smell of baby oil and baby powder and rosewater.

When Trenise left the military, she never put the tags on again; instead, she hung the pair first on the small vanity she'd had in her apartment, then on the large heirloom dresser she shared with John after they got married.

When she and John built the house she lived in now, Trenise solemnly hung both her tags and thought of her mother. When John had died, Trenise hung his tags next to hers, stringing them on the same chain.

Trenise had made it out of the Ninth Ward. She'd made it through military service during a time when not a lot of women did; her tags never separated.

She thought of her mother and her mother's worry and her eyes pricked with tears.

No more worries, Trenise had promised when she left the military, *no more fighting.*

Trenise released the tags and opened her eyes. The tags hung and swayed gently in their spot.

Trenise reckoned she had something to be worried about now. Something bigger than school, and work, and basketball and trespassers. Trenise Jones reckoned she had a fight on her hands again.

She reached out and took the tags off their spot and put them around her neck. They nestled with familiarity between her breasts, and she patted their warmth.

As Trenise left her bedroom, she could already feel the cool air of the air conditioning cutting through the steamy remnants of whatever or whoever had directed her to her dog tags.

Her eyes pricked with tears as she thought of her mother.

Although it was early still, and she felt calm for the first time since yesterday morning, Trenise knew she wouldn't be able to go back to sleep. Instead, she made her way to the linen closet and pulled out a soft white washcloth and headed to the hall bathroom to take her morning shower.

Trenise undressed, except for her tags, and let the hot water run over her face and back. The vague plan that the three of them had made the night before seemed crisper and clearer.

By the time she left the shower and went back to her bedroom to dress, the heat and humidity were gone and the walls were no longer running with condensation.

Trenise could hear Missy and Alessandra in hushed conversation in the living room and, gripping her tags in her fist again, Trenise left her bedroom and walked down the hall, ready to face whatever would come that day.

When Trent was done, Lexie was unrecognizable. Her face and hair were a squashed mess of gore. Trent licked his lips and could taste her still, he reached down and rubbed between her legs, then licked the slick blood from his fingers.

When he looked up, the Preacher was standing over him. He reached down and took Trent's face in both of his hands, smiling.

"Come," the Preacher said in a voice that sounded solid, one that came from his body and not Trent's own mind, "There is much to do."

—

Cynthia Devaunt, born Cynthia Shea, lay in bed in her too-big, too-empty house. She rolled over creakily and looked at the picture of Frank that she always kept on her bedside table.

She felt lucky that she had found him. He respected her, loved her. He didn't gamble or cheat like some of her friends' husbands had.

The worst things he had done was that he was what's now called a workaholic and occasionally got too drunk at parties.

That and he had left this world without her.

Cynthia, now known as the crazy old lady at the end of the street, she supposed, marveled that her old eyes could still muster up tears. The small box fan that she used more for noise than cooling effect since the blood thinners she took made her perpetually cold, whirred softly.

She rolled over again and looked at the alarm clock which she still kept on Frank's side of the bed, even though Frank was dead five years now.

Three a.m.

Five years had passed and that she was still here. How could it be so?

Sadness settled into her narrow chest. Cynthia and Frank had never been able to have children. Although she hadn't spent her life miserable about it, since she and Frank enjoyed each other's company and had enough money to do as they pleased, she wondered now if she would feel less lonely if she had children or grandchildren to take care of her.

Didn't bother you much when you were showing off your childless figure on the beach in Hawaii in 1980, though did it?

Cindy laughed gently at the thought.

Not one to feel sorry for herself for too long, and knowing that worry and sadness was always worse in the dark, Cindy sat up and reached for her cane where it was resting on the nightstand.

Today was Saturday which meant Ann Marie would not be coming by. It meant no gossip or happy chatter: a day alone. Tomorrow was church at First United Methodist Church in the neighboring city of Slidell, of which

Cynthia had been a member since she was married in 1950. The church would send the van it used to collect the elderly church members to fetch her. She looked forward to the service, to the coffee hour, to talking to friends.

But today, she was on her own.

Cynthia sighed as she sat on the edge of the bed. She mentally made a list of how she would pass the time.

Get up, make coffee and eat one of the muffins Ann Marie had brought the day before, pick out her church outfit, sit on the back porch and read her library book, work on the hats she was crocheting for the babies in the NICU at Slidell Memorial Hospital, take a nap, and, hell, maybe she'd even go crazy and order a delivery pizza for herself.

Cynthia nodded to herself and thought it might just be enough to keep the loneliness at bay. As she hoisted herself up with her cane and made her way to the top of the stairs where her lift chair was waiting to take her down to the kitchen in style, Cynthia had no clue the direction in which her day was heading.

—

Trent worked hard all night to follow the Preacher's exact instructions. He retrieved all the tools he needed from the shed. His phone rang once, and he told his father he was busy with Lexie. His father laughed and told him not to stay up too late.

Other than that, Trent worked uninterrupted and with an urgency he had never known before. He had never done anything this important before.

The Preacher listened and watched silently. He occasionally urged Trent to move faster.

By 3 am, Trent's work was done, and the Preacher placed a gentle hand on his shoulder and squeezed. His touch was firm.

He nodded solemnly, "You need to rest now."

Trent made his way back to his dark house, showered to rid himself of the dirt and sweat which covered him, and fell into a deep sleep.

Emmanuel White, stronger now, feeling Lexie's spirit course through him, stood watch.

Chapter Nineteen

Alessandra unbuckled her seatbelt and leaned her right elbow on the front seat where Missy was sitting and her left elbow on the driver's seat where Trenise was sitting. Alessandra watched as both older women looked out into the yard where they were parked.

"So...." Alessandra finally said, breaking the silence, "Are we going to knock on the door or what?"

The engine of Trenise's car hummed softly, and the air conditioning pumped cool air into the car, trying desperately to keep up with the heat outside.

Missy made a face, "I don't know...it's still kind of early."

"She's old though, you said. Old people get up early."

Trenise turned her neck slightly and gave Alessandra a scathing look.

"What?" Alessandra laughed.

"I wish Ann Marie was here," Missy said, ignoring Trenise and Alessandra's exchange, "I'd feel more comfortable knowing Ms. Cindy was up."

Trenise pointed to the clock on the car, "It's 7 now. If we're going to try and locate some kind of artifact or family member or...whatever the hell it is we're looking for by tonight, we need as much time as possible."

Missy nodded, "Ok. Let's go then."

The three women climbed out of the car, and Missy looked behind her all the way down to the other cul de sac where her house sat, looking completely unremarkable. Before they arrived at Cindy's house, the three of them had stopped first at Alessandra's house so she could change her clothes and then at Missy's house so she could change hers.

Missy hadn't dared to look in the bathroom but now wondered if any more of the worms were crawling through her bathtub drain. She shuddered at the thought.

She had spoken to Johnny and Sophie Ann that morning, so she knew that they were going to swim in the morning and then go see a movie after lunch, but she still wondered what they were doing right now.

Missy let her hand brush across the bag that Rainbow had given her, which she had checked and rechecked was still hanging there all morning.

Missy walked up the steps slowly, Trenise at her side and Alessandra slightly behind. The door had a large window covered with slightly sheer fabric, but Missy could see there was no one in the hallway. She strained her ears and listened for noise from a tv or radio.

She knocked loudly and waited. The last time she was here, Ms. Cindy had a walker next to her.

"She uses a walker," Missy said out loud, "Oh God, I feel terrible making her get up."

"It's ok," Trenise said in a gentle voice, "Hopefully she can help us."

"Maybe you should knock again?" Alessandra asked quietly.

Missy raised her fist to knock but caught movement through the window and saw Ms. Cindy slowly making her way up the hallway. Missy waved, hoping Ms. Cindy would recognize her.

"Hold on!" Ms. Cindy yelled, "I'm coming!"

"Take your time!" Trenise yelled back.

Missy and Trenise stepped back as Ms. Cindy fumbled with the locks and finally opened the door.

"Well, what a surprise!"

Cindy's heart leapt at the sight of the three women on her doorstep. She couldn't remember the last time she'd had an unexpected visitor. Cindy looked from Missy to Trenise and then craned around to look at Alessandra behind them.

"Trenise Jones?" she said, looking at Trenise again, "Your husband John knew my Frank. Frank did the accounting for the state police fundraiser."

Trenise smiled, "Well yes, ma'am I suppose they did know each other then."

Ms. Cindy looked back at Missy, "And it's so nice to see you again so soon, Missy! Oh! Excuse my manners, would y'all like to come in?"

"Yes, Ms. Cindy, we would," Trenise answered, "If it's no trouble."

Cindy took a hand off the walker she was using and waved it at Trenise, "Oh course, not."

"We want to ask you a few questions, Ms. Cindy," Missy said as they followed Cindy slowly down the hallway.

Rather than going back through the kitchen to the sunroom as they had done last time Missy visited, Cindy pivoted to the right and into a large, old-fashioned sitting room.

Alessandra looked around in amazement. The furniture was obviously expensive, maybe antiques. There were black and white photos and a painting of an elegant couple in evening attire above the fireplace. There was no television.

"Is that you?" Alessandra asked pointing to the painting.

Cindy laughed, "Yes, it is! I had an artist friend years ago, was in some financial trouble, so I commissioned him to paint it for us."

Missy and Trenise sat next to each other on a striped love seat, while Ms. Cindy settled into an armchair closer to the fireplace. Alessandra looked around desperately, feeling completely out of place in her workout shorts and ripped tee shirt, and finally perched herself on the edge of a long sofa that matched the loveseat.

Ms. Cindy looked at her kindly, "And, young woman, I don't know your name."

"Oh, I'm Alessandra. Alessandra Sanchez."

"And I'm Cynthia Devaunt. You can call me Ms. Cindy."

Alessandra nodded and smiled.

Cindy looked from Alessandra to Missy to Trenise and felt her heart flutter a little with excitement. Even if they wanted nothing more than a cake recipe from her, it still felt lovely to have visitors in her formal room again.

"What can I help you with?" she asked.

—

Trent felt himself being shaken awake.

"You need to get up," a firm voice whispered, "Another woman is interfering. We don't want another incident like we had last night."

—

Their request was simple enough and required little to no effort or thought from Cindy. Within fifteen minutes of their arrival, the three women were gone, each with a promise that they would come back soon to visit.

Cindy was on her own again.

She no longer felt lonely. Nor did she feel happy as she had when she had first opened the door and seen Missy's smiling, slightly sheepish face.

Cindy felt uneasy. She felt tired and confused as to why they had come. Their questions felt strange.

Right before they left, Cindy asked Missy if their visit today had anything to do with the story she had told her during their last visit. If it had anything to do with the neighborhood women and Missy's dead friend.

The young woman, Alessandra, sucked in her breath at this question and looked down at the floor. The elder women shared a look with each other.

"I think so," Missy finally said.

Cindy replayed the visit in her mind as she sat on her back porch staring out into her yard. The yard was large, slightly overgrown, and shaded by live oaks, tall pines, and magnolias. Birds twittered and darted among the leaves.

"Ms. Cindy," Missy had asked, "You told me that the story about the Preacher in Stone River was based on something true. That the legend was based on something that actually happened to a person who had actually lived."

What she had said next sounded full of emotion to Cindy, more emotion than it should have had.

"Is there anyone that you know of who could be related to this person? Anyone who might have any of his belongings?"

"Now, any relations" Cindy had said slowly, "that I can't tell you. But I can tell you that Reverend Emmanuel White's Family Bible is on display over in the Amite Springs Museum."

"The Family Bible?" Trenise had asked.

"You know," Cindy explained, growing more perplexed, "It shows the family names, names of towns where people were born, that kind of thing."

Cindy had explained that the Bible was never completed, that most of the spaces left for names were left blank, so it wouldn't be of any genealogical help.

She stared out of the large back windows of her sunroom, letting the silence of the house wash over her as she recalled the conversation.

As the three women left, Trenise turned back to her and asked, "Ms. Cindy, is the Bible the *only* thing that there is in the museum that belonged to Emmanuel White?"

"Yes, Trenise, that's it. There are some newspaper clippings about him and the fire and the deaths, but the Bible is the only thing that belonged to him- at least that I know of anyway."

Cindy sat on her porch and felt strange. Telling historical facts, even the legends and ghost stories like the one about the preacher had always fascinated her. Gossip did not.

Cindy's eyes unfocused as she stared out into her yard. When she first started volunteering at the St Tammanend Historical Society, a group of women in the Society were interested in creating a more specific Town of Stone River Historical Society with accompanying museum. Cindy was asked to join in their research for important historical information since she lived in Stone River as well.

Most of the information Cindy relayed to both Missy came from that time period, when she was helping to research for the Stone River Museum.

Everyone knew that the Longues owned the property where Emmanuel White's church was. Grant inherited it from his father, who had inherited it from his. How Grant Longue's grandfather acquired that land, however, was something of a mystery. After the First World War, the ruins of the church and the accompanying church yard were property of the town of Stone River.

When Cindy and the other ladies of the St Tammany Historical Society looked back through the property transfers to find records of the old church due to its historical significance, they found the rather vague note, "reclaimed by descendent of previous owner."

"Reclaimed?" Annette LaBord, long dead now, but at the time a curvy bleach blond who was ten times smarter than she looked had asked Cindy, "What in the world? Why didn't they sell it?"

"Well I don't know, Annie. Was it a seized property?"

Annette flipped back and forth between multiple pages of records and wrinkled her nose, "I can't see a darn *thing* in here."

"Aw, just leave it, Annie. What's it matter? We can ask the Longues if they'll let us have a look at the church, maybe take some pictures?"

"Because it doesn't make any *sense*, Cindy."

Cindy had shrugged and laughed at the perplexed look on Annette's face.

"Come on Annie, let's finish up and go get lunch."

Cindy, old, wrinkled, and alone on her porch, forty years later, finally agreed with Annie and wished she hadn't brushed her off.

It really *didn't* make any sense. The property transferred to the Longues didn't just include where the church was, it included the huge swath of land that ran along the length of the Stone River, into Slidell, and down to Lake Pontchartrain.

It was the land that Grant Longue's father had eventually developed into the subdivision where she was now sitting. He developed the land into a shipping facility, a lumber yard, rented out hunting leases, owned every strip mall, gas station, and grocery store. That land was worth a fortune.

Aw hell, Cindy thought to herself, *really what the hell does it matter? So, some crooked politicians long ago made some underhanded deal, and the Longues came out on the top of it. What does it have to do with anything?*

Cindy thought of Annette's wrinkled up button nose, her insistence that it didn't make sense.

Cindy tried to mentally wave the whole thing away, tried to think about Church tomorrow, about takeout pizza. But she couldn't. The whole thing was a fly in her ointment.

Because how would the town or the parish have benefitted from letting the land go? What profit could they have made? Maybe one of them owned the construction company that built the houses?

Cindy shook her head. That seemed too much of a short term financial benefit to let that amount of buildable land go.

There was something else too. Not just Annie in the long-ago basement and the Longue's property. Something that Trenise had asked her.

Cindy shook her head again and threw her hands up.

She reached out for her walker, stood, and slowly walked to the kitchen. Halfway down the hall it dawned on her. Trenise had asked if the Bible was the only thing she knew of that had belonged to Emmanuel White.

Cindy had told her no, but that wasn't the truth.

And that's what had made her think of Annie.

Annie LaBord and the deed she had found.

Ms. Cindy felt her flesh crawl, and she moved as quickly as she could to the kitchen. She picked up the landline phone and dialed Ann Marie's cell phone number.

When her back was turned, a figure moved slowly through her backyard towards her house.

When Ann Marie's voicemail picked up, Cindy sucked her teeth.

"Listen, Ann Marie, it's Cindy. I don't know Missy Douglas's or Trenise Jones's phone numbers, but I need to talk to them. If you have them, would you call them for me please and pass along my phone number? Tell them it's about one of their questions they asked me this morning. Thank you honey, and I'll see you tomorrow!"

Cindy hung up the phone and stood for a moment or two in her kitchen. She felt uneasy again and looked toward her chair in the sunroom. Her house suddenly felt too big. The effort of having to pick somewhere to sit down was overwhelming.

Ms. Cindy had the terrible feeling that she was now, and had always been, a part of some strange story from the moment she and her husband had bought this house. All of her life, she was just a cog in the wheel leading up to this moment. She had an important part to play, and she hoped that she wasn't too late.

Less than a half an hour ago she had told Trenise that the Bible was the only thing she knew of that belonged to Emmanuel White. Now, she knew that wasn't true. Now she knew that the *other* thing belonging to him was right here in her house.

When Annie LaBord passed away, Cindy was given a box full of notes and records from the Historical Society that Annie had been working on.

Cindy remembered clearly now that one file was marked "Longue" and she knew in her heart of hearts that that deed was in there. That Annie

LaBord, all those years ago, had known something was wrong and had been trying to sniff it out like a bloodhound.

Cindy went into the small family room that had an old squashy couch, some crocheted blankets, and an ancient television. Standing in the doorway with her walker, Cindy thought it looked terribly old-ladyish. She felt small and old and scared.

She looked down at her wrinkled hands and sighed. She made her way to the couch, grabbed a blanket and the remote. She hoped Ann Marie would call her back soon, put her in touch with Trenise.

As Cindy sat down, she sighed with relief, turned on the tv, and didn't bother searching the channels. She just let whatever was on wash over her as she covered herself with the blanket, closed her eyes, and went to sleep.

—

Cindy woke with a start, heart pounding. She sat up slowly and looked at the television.

The same old rerun of MASH was playing as when she first laid down, so she hadn't been asleep very long, less than 15 minutes.

Cindy again felt that something wasn't right. She reached over for the remote, turned off the television, and then she froze and listened. The house was as silent as it always was.

The gnawing feeling that she missed something important in her conversation that morning started again. Cindy remembered the deed, Annie LaBord, the box upstairs. She couldn't rest until she saw if it was there.

She swung her legs down off the recliner and, using her walker, made for the lift chair that would take her upstairs to where her upstairs walker would be waiting for her.

Her old notes and clippings and minutes from her time as the St. Tammany Historical Society Secretary were stored in some old boxes in the spare room upstairs. Right along with the box she had inherited from Annette LaBord.

After Frank died, Cindy wanted to go through them all, maybe see if there was anything worth donating to the Amite Spring Museum. She never did get around to it.

She could curse herself for not getting to it before now.

As she buckled herself into the lift chair, leaving her downstairs walker at the foot of the stairs like she always did, Cindy wondered if that old deed was even in there. As she rose in her lift chair, Ms. Cindy caught herself thinking of Annie's words that day long ago: *something isn't right.*

She smiled in spite of herself.

Cynthia Devaunt amateur P.I. On the case with her walker and musty old meeting minutes.

She chuckled a little as she reached the top of the stairs.

And you thought today would be boring.

As the electronic lift chair slowed to a stop, Cindy stared, dumbfounded, at the empty hallway.

It shouldn't have been empty. Her upstairs walker should be right there at the top of the stairs, next to the lift chair where she'd left it this morning.

Cindy sat in the lift chair and tried to remember the morning. She knew she had brought the walker from the bedroom to the lift with her. She always did. She had to.

Trenise, Missy, and their young companion, Alessandra, hadn't left the sitting room, so none of them had moved it.

As she debated what to do, Cindy heard footsteps walking from the spare room and out into the hallway.

Her thin chest heaved beneath her cotton sweater as she realized that someone was in her house.

Quickly, Cindy pushed the button to lower the chair again, silently cursing how loud it was. As the chair started to move, Cindy watched, terrified, as a young man stepped out of the spare room and held her walker out in one hand.

An older man, dressed all in black stepped out behind him, smiling.

Cindy moaned softly, tears seeping from her eyes as she realized the trouble she was in. Both men looked deranged, the young one laughing silently as the older man gestured calmly in her direction.

The lift chair stopped in the middle of the stairway.

Cindy furiously pushed the down button again and again, but the chair wouldn't budge.

The young man placed her walker down next to the top of the stairs and slowly descended toward her.

"Leave me alone!" Cindy croaked, "What kind of men are you? To terrorize an old lady?"

"You have something of mine," the older man whispered.

Cindy sputtered and stared, "Something of yours? Who are you?"

The man in black stared and smiled serenely.

"There were three women here this morning. What did they want?"

"They were just here for a visit," Cindy choked.

The younger man laughed out loud and looked over his shoulder at the older man again. The older man nodded to him.

The young man reached out and placed his hands on the arms of the lift chair. As Cindy screamed, he pulled the entire chair from its metal track along the wall, holding both Cindy and the chair in front of him.

"See your new strength?" the older man whispered.

The younger man lifted Cindy's chair up so that she was eye level with him. He smiled and breathed heavily in her face. Cindy recoiled from the smell of rot that came from him.

"Don't," she whispered, "Please, don't."

"What did they want?" the man in black asked again.

Cindy looked wildly down the stairs, at the deranged child in front of her, and back to the man on the landing.

"They wanted Emmanuel White's Bible."

The man in black's face crumpled with rage for a moment and then resumed its serene expression.

"I am Emmanuel White. The Bible is mine."

"That's not possible," Cindy whispered as she squeezed her eyes shut, not wanting to see the man in front of her.

"Do you have my Bible here?" White snapped.

"I don't have anything here."

"Don't lie to ME," White growled, "What were you coming up here for?"

Cindy looked again down the stairs, feeling sweat pour from her body, her hands shaking with the effort from gripping the chair.

"A deed. An old deed."

Emmanuel White nodded softly and gestured to Trent with a small wave. Then, he turned and disappeared back into Cindy's guest room. Cindy watched him go and thought wistfully about how the room had been intended to be for children, the children she was never able to have.

She felt angry with herself for telling them, for betraying Trenise and Melissa and Alessandra.

Cynthia Devaunt, former debutante, card carrying Methodist, proud volunteer for so many charities over the years, felt a rage bubble up in her that she had never felt before.

"You little piece of shit coward," she defiantly spat into the young man's face.

The young man smiled, reached his arms forward, and dropped both Cindy and the chair the remaining six feet down the stairs.

Cynthia Devaunt lay at the bottom of the stairs, crushed between the weight of the heavy metal lift chair and the floor. Her head hit the bottom of the landing with the same sound a pumpkin makes when it's thrown against pavement.

Trent stood in the middle of the stairs and knew if she wasn't dead yet, she would be soon.

He walked back up the stairs to find Emmanuel White standing in front of an open closet door looking in at a pile of old junk.

Trent stood next to him, relishing his calm presence.

"What am I looking for?"

"A deed. With my signature on it. An unexpected bonus for my family."

White rested his hand on Trent's arm and looked at him hungrily.

"My family. Who owes me so much."

Chapter Twenty

"Well, stealing a Bible from a museum with my gym teacher was definitely not on my list of things I thought I'd be doing this weekend," Alessandra said from the back seat with a laugh.

The ride from Stone River to Amite Springs took about 45 minutes on a back highway that cut through a swath of hunting properties. There wasn't much to look at, and Alessandra, Trenise, and Missy spent the first half of the drive talking in circles about what they would do once they located the Bible Ms. Cindy told them about.

Trenise chuckled in spite of herself at Alessandra's comment, but Missy stared silently out the window.

"Did you hear me, Missy? I said..."

"I heard you, Alessandra, I'm just thinking."

Alessandra stopped smiling and nodded.

"If it's in some kind of glass case or something, I don't know what we're going to do."

"We just have to go and see, Missy, and go from there." Trenise said calmly.

Missy nodded and turned in her seat to look at Alessandra. "I don't think you should be the one to take it Alessandra. I think you should wait in the car."

Alessandra snorted, "Uh, do you not remember what happened last time y'all left me out?"

Trenise had to agree with her, even though she didn't want to.

"No," she said reluctantly, "I think you should come."

"Besides," Alessandra laughed, "have either of you two ever stolen anything? I mean...you both don't seem like the 'grand theft' type."

Missy laughed, "I stole a candy bar from the dollar store one time as a kid and felt so bad I went back in and snuck it back on the shelf."

Trenise laughed at Missy and shook her head. She looked at Alessandra in the rearview mirror.

"I never stole anything, but I've *caught* enough students stealing over the years that I know what *not* to do."

"Let's just see what they have and what we might be able to do," Missy said, trying not to let her nervousness creep into her voice.

Trenise nodded, "Right, exactly."

Missy had never been to the Amite Springs Museum, but she knew where it was. The small town of Amite Springs was founded around a natural spring. Some of the large estates that ran along the bayou there boasted natural spring pools and antebellum roots.

In the small downtown area, there was a bike path, a brewery and restaurant, a splash pad, and a playground. On Saturdays there was a farmer's market and art market filled with middle class yuppies drinking craft beer and buying locally grown produce.

The museum itself was in the downtown area, close to playground. Missy had taken Johnny and Sophie to the splash pad a few times and remembered it being crowded and hot.

"Trenise," Missy said suddenly, "It's Saturday. The farmer's market. It's going to be crowded."

"I forgot about that," Trenise bit her lip, then shrugged, "Maybe that's a good thing. We'll blend in a little better."

The road they were on led directly into downtown Amite Springs, and Missy could see already that it was indeed crowded. Cars were parallel parked on every side street she looked down and people were slowly walking toward the farmer's market, with kids, wagons, chairs, and ice chests in tow.

"I'm going to try and park at the First Baptist Church," Trenise said turning off the main road and onto a side street.

Trenise pulled into the large church's parking lot and found a shady spot all the way at the back of the almost full lot. She turned off the car and paused.

"We stay together," She said calmly. "No one does anything crazy. We don't want to get caught. There's no way we'll be able to sneak in a baseball bat or a mechanic's bar, so we'll be flying on our own."

Missy and Alessandra both nodded.

"We go in and scope it out. We find the Bible. Once we figure out a way, we take it. Then we go outside and get back to the car as soon as possible. Then we go from there."

"Got it," Alessandra said looking pale.

"Got it," Missy echoed.

The walk to the center of town to the museum was less than a mile. Alessandra walked behind Trenise and Missy once again, looking around at the large houses whose wrought iron fences alone probably cost more than what her mother made in a year.

Smiling children played in the small front yards and their parents sat on the porches watching them.

As they approached the farmer's market, which they would have to go through to get to the museum, the crowd thickened substantially. Alessandra stuck close behind Missy as they wove through the people.

It felt the same as weaving through the French Quarter the night before, despite all the stark differences. The day was bright, there were families with small children, it was early enough that few people were drinking. But Alessandra still felt uneasy.

The buzz felt the same as it had yesterday in the clearing, the feeling that the light was too bright, that it was too loud, that they shouldn't be there. That something was wrong.

Alessandra reached out and grabbed Missy's arm. She felt dizzy and sick.

Trenise stopped and put her hand over her chest. Missy closed her hand over Alessandra's, grabbed Trenise's upper arm, and pulled them both into the shade of a nearby tree.

"What is it?" Trenise said breathlessly.

Alessandra's eyes darted toward the museum, "Something feels wrong."

Missy leaned against the tree and wiped away the beads of sweat that had popped up on her forehead.

"Ms. Sarah said whatever this thing is would try and keep us away. Maybe that's what this is."

"Yeah," Trenise said breathlessly, " maybe you're right."

Alessandra nodded and clutched the sachet from Rainbow.

"Can you make it?" Missy asked Alessandra.

Alessandra shoved her chin out and tilted her head back defiantly.

"Of course I can."

The three women started again toward the museum, trying to block out the drone of laughter, shielding their eyes from the sun, pushing themselves through whatever force was trying to keep them away.

—

Using both hands, Trent threw aside boxes, old hats, shoes, digging through the closet, looking for what White wanted him to find. Behind him, he could feel White's eyes on him, burning through him.

"Where, where..." Trent growled, reaching high on the top shelf.

There.

Hands trembling, Trent pulled out an old, brown file box. It pulsed in his hands. He looked back over his shoulder at White, who nodded serenely.

"Now," he said, "Put everything back the way it was."

—

At ten o'clock, Ann Marie Landry came into her kitchen for a much-needed break in her work. She loved tending to her garden and her bee hives, and on days like this, when it was sweltering before lunchtime, she had to force herself to take breaks.

She left her dirty shoes outside on the small back porch of her trailer and went into her kitchen. She picked up her cell phone as she drank a cold bottle of water and listened to the one message on her phone.

When the message ended, Ann Marie looked at her phone, not sure about what she had just heard. It was from Ms. Cindy, but it didn't make much sense to Ann Marie. Ann Marie hit the return call button, but Ms. Cindy didn't pick up.

Ann Marie felt the hair on the back of her neck stand on end. It wasn't like Ms. Cindy to not answer

She's probably taking a nap, Ann Maire told herself.

Nonetheless, with shaky hands, she called Ms. Cindy again. And again.

Fifteen minutes later, she was in her car and driving to Ms. Cindy's house.

You're being stupid, a voice in her head said, *totally stupid.*

"I don't care," Ann Marie said aloud to herself in the car, "I'll head over, wake her up, and she'll gripe at me. It's nothing."

—

Duane Thompson pulled up to Cynthia Devaunt's house at 10:40, about ten minutes after Ann Marie Landry had called 911 to report that the older woman had fallen out of her lift chair.

The ambulance was already there.

Thompson nodded to the woman who was sitting in a rocking chair on the front porch crying as he walked up the front steps to the home.

"I'm Officer Duane Thompson ma'am," he said, crouching down in front of her, "Are you Ms. Landry?"

Ann Marie nodded.

"I know this is hard, Ms. Landry, but can you tell me what happened?"

Ann Marie nodded and said through sobs, "Ms. Cindy called me and I didn't hear, I was outside and didn't hear the phone," she hitched a breath, "I called her back, and she didn't pick up so I came to check on her."

"And then you found her?"

Ann Marie squeezed her eyes shut and nodded.

"Ok, ma'am. You just stay right there for now."

Thompson opened the front door, walked in the house, and quickly shut the door behind him.

An EMT stood over the body.

"Hey Duane, how you been, man? You ain't off to the Staties yet?"

Thompson shook the EMTs hand, "Not yet, Sonny. How you been? Just you today?"

Sonny shrugged and smiled sadly.

"It's me and JoAnn out there driving. And I'm better than this poor lady, Duane, I mean godDAMN."

Thompson looked down at the blood splattered floor and wall and at the woman's crumpled, mangled body where it lay still strapped to the lift chair. He looked up the stairs at where the arm of the device was still attached to the wall.

"It must've fallen off, huh Duane?"

Thompson shook his head and put his hands on his hips, "I guess it must've."

Thompson crouched down next to the body, looking at the chair and where it had been attached to the wall.

"I hate to say this Duane, but Je-sus, don't this remind you of that other lady we found out there by the levee?"

Thompson felt his gaze snap up to Sonny's concerned face.

The other EMT opened the door quickly and scooted in, looking at the body and up to the wall.

"Oooo boy," JoAnn whistled through her teeth, "That lift chair company is going to have one hell of a lawsuit."

"Nah," Sonny shook his head, "Ms. Cindy didn't have no family left. Just Ms. Ann Marie out there took care of her."

Thompson looked again from the body to where the lift chair attached to the wall. He carefully stepped across, avoiding any of the blood splatter and walked halfway up the stairs, peering at where the chair detached. He pulled a glove from his top pocket, and after putting it on his hand, he touched the wires protruding from the wall unit and looked back down at the body.

"Sonny, what do you mean it reminds you of the lady we found by the levee? You're talking about Evangeline Nunez?"

Sonny paused, "Yeah, that's her Evie Nunez. Paul's wife."

"But this is different, Sonny. This is an accident."

Sonny sucked his teeth, "Yeah, Duane, whatever you say,"

Thompson turned and gave Sonny a measured look. Sonny rolled his eyes.

"You haven't been up here, have you Sonny?"

"Nah, of course not," Sonny paused and craned his neck to look up at Thompson, "Why?"

Thompson didn't answer as he slowly walked onto the landing at the top of the stairs. He peered into what was the master bedroom, the bathroom, and then into a spare room. The closet door in the spare room was open a crack, and Thompson walked toward it. He opened it all the way and peered at a mess one might expect to see in an unused closet.

Thompson reached out and touched the arm of a coat that was hanging haphazardly on a hanger. He looked at the papers and photo albums crammed onto the top shelf of the closet.

He turned around and looked at the dresser, the bed, a bookshelf, all of which were neat and orderly.

Thompson left the guest room and went into the bathroom, using his gloved hand to open a linen closet. Rows of towels were folded neatly next to a small basket filled with toilet paper and another small basket filled with toiletries.

He left the bathroom and walked into the master bedroom and opened the closet there.

"Duane?" Sonny yelled from below, "Can we get started down here or what, man?"

"Hold up, Son," Thompson yelled back, "Just gimme a second."

The master closet was neat as a pin. Dresses hung from their hangers and shoes were lined up on a shoe rack. Thompson went back into the guest room and looked at the jumble of shoes and hats on the floor of the closet, shaking his head.

"Hey Sonny!" Thompson called, urgently, "Don't touch anything! I think this is a crime scene!"

—

Missy's heart hammered in her chest as they approached the Amite Springs Museum. The large brick building was set off to the side of a large park on the other side of a playground. In front of it was a large gazebo in the middle of which was a dark iron fountain. The center of the fountain was a sculpture of a young Native American girl bent on one knee, her hands cupped under a small plume of water.

Behind them, on a small stage by the farmer's market, a band began to play, the music echoing through a PA system. All three women started at the sound, and Alessandra laughed.

"Sweet Home Alabama," she said, "Truly frightening."

Trenise, however, looked at the fountain.

"What Trenise?" Missy asked as she paused in front of it.

Trenise tried to swallow but her throat clicked from dryness. She licked her lips, "This was an old Choctaw town, you know."

Missy gazed around her, "You mean right here?"

> Trenise nodded, "Mmhmm. The white settlers wiped them out so they could settle here." Trenise gestured at the fountain, "Because of the natural mineral springs."

Alessandra looked at the fountain and reached out, dipping her fingers in the water.

"It's freezing," she whispered.

Missy reached out and dipped her hands in as well, watching the statue of the Choctaw girl as she did.

"That's the burial ground over there," Trenise pointed into the tree line, "and they say there's mounds back there on private property."

"Oh, good!" Alessandra said as she touched the cool water to her temples, "Just in case what's going on isn't terrifying enough, let's add in some pissed off dead Indians."

Missy put her ice-cold hand over both of her eyes, marveling at the feeling of it in the boiling hot midday heat.

Trenise dipped her hands into the fountain, reaching in up to her elbows. She watched as her brown forearms showed brightly against the black iron of the fountain's base and then looked up at the Choctaw maiden's serene face.

Trenise took her arms out and shaking them off pressed her hands over her mouth and the back of her neck.

"She doesn't seem pissed off, Alessandra," Trenise whispered.

"No," Alessandra whispered back, "she seems ok with us being here."

Missy felt strong and calm as she looked at the Amite Spring Museum. Her face was still cool from where she had touched the water from the spring.

"Are y'all ready?" Missy asked.

Trenise and Alessandra nodded and followed Missy as she walked up the stone steps to the museum and pulled the door open.

The cool of the building against the wet from the fountain took Missy's breath away as she stepped into the entry way. An older woman with gray hair sat behind a desk that said "Admission." She looked up and smiled.

"Good morning! If you wouldn't mind signing in here..." the woman trailed off, looking behind Missy.

Missy turned to look at Trenise and Alessandra. Trenise smiled broadly, and Alessandra looked bewildered.

"Trenise Jones!" the woman at the desk yelled, "As I live and breathe! Trenise Jones!"

"Ginny Bourgeois" Trenise said laughing, "Girl, if you're not a sight for sore eyes."

Missy and Alessandra stepped to the side as Trenise and Ginny hugged.

"What are you doing here, Trenise? Just come for the Farmer's Market?"

"Well, kind of..." Trenise trailed off and looked at Missy desperately, not knowing what to say.

"I'm Missy Douglas," Missy reached out a hand, "I'm Trenise's neighbor. I'm kind of new so Trenise has been nice enough to share some local history with me. We figured this was a nice little day trip."

Trenise laughed and looked relieved, "And this is one of my students, Alessandra Sanchez, she lives in the neighborhood too."

Alessandra waved cheerily.

"I'm Ginny Bourgeois, I used to teach with Trenise a million years ago," Ginny beamed at the three of them and gestured them over to the admissions desk.

"I'm paying y'all," Trenise said, trying to sound casual, "How much to get in, Ginny?"

Ginny waved her hands and walked back behind her desk.

"I'm not charging you Trenise, go on and enjoy. And look, there's a new exhibit all the way at the back of local pottery, it's beautiful."

She handed them each a sticker that said 'visitor' and a map of the museum.

Alessandra looked at the map and started walking down the small hallway to the left. Trenise felt her heart speed up as she turned away from

Ginny to watch her walk away. Missy gestured her head in the direction that Alessandra had gone and turned to follow her.

Ginny followed Trenise's gaze, "I won't keep you Trenise- let's have lunch sometime! Give me your number before you leave."

Trenise nodded, "You bet Ginny."

The wide hallway was dimly lit, Trenise guessed to protect the art that hung on the walls and the artifacts that were protected by class boxes. Trenise glanced around at broken shards of Native American pottery, at paintings of Bayous. She felt the woosh of the air conditioning and smelled its slightly stale scent and gripped her dog tags.

Ahead of her, Missy looked around at every painting, every piece of folk art, every artifact while Alessandra next to her was still pouring over the map of the small museum.

"What section do you think it'll be in?" she whispered, "It says here there's a section for folk art from the 1700s, but is a Bible folk art?"

Missy shook her head, "I wouldn't think so. Is there a section for local history?"

Alessandra shook her head and groaned, "It doesn't look like it."

Trenise stood at Missy's shoulder with a copy of the map of the museum held open in front of her.

"It looks like the hallway turns here toward the new exhibit."

"Well, it's not down there, the lady at the desk said that was pottery, plus Ms. Cindy said it's been here since the 1970's."

Alessandra looked to the left and continued.

"It's got to be down there."

Missy looked in the direction Alessandra pointed and saw an ancient pirogue with red ropes around it, a huge taxidermized alligator, more glass boxes.

The lights looked dimmer, and Missy could smell mildew very faintly. There were no windows in this section of the museum, and the hall continued for another 30 feet before turning to the left.

The air was still and strange. The smell of mildew grew, and Missy felt her skin crawl as she looked at the alligator. It seemed incongruous with the rest of the museum.

Trenise moved first, approaching the pirogue slowly. The air conditioning whirred above her somewhere, and she looked over her shoulder. Missy and Alessandra moved behind her slowly. Both wore matching looks of apprehension.

"You don't think there's anything here that could hurt us, do you?" Alessandra whispered, eyeing the taxidermized alligator as they approached it on their right.

Missy shook her head and swore she could see the thing take a breath. She slowed her pace, holding Alessandra at arm's length behind her as the alligator emitted a low growl.

The three of them skittered to the left and gave the alligator a wide berth, watched as it slowly turned its head to watch them pass.

Alessandra moaned and Missy clutched the bag from Rainbow. The alligator lifted just its head and sniffed the air, watching them with its dead glass eyes. It didn't move its body as they passed it quickly and rested its head again on the ground when they moved by.

"We must be close," Missy whispered.

Trenise nodded and tried to swallow but her dry throat clicked.

"Stay together," she muttered.

Alessandra looked around, searching for the Bible, and watched as a painting with a man in a pirogue much like the ancient one they had just passed began to move.

The painting was stationary against the wall, but the colors, the paints, the water in the painting began to move like a slow cartoon. The man locked eyes with Alessandra as he paddled through the bayou.

"Ms. Jones..." she moaned softly.

Alessandra reached out and locked hands with Missy and stretched out her other hand for Trenise.

Hand in hand, the three of them made it to the corner. Trenise held up a hand for them to stop. She peered around the corner quickly, making sure nothing was there. She peered into this new, even darker hallway and saw it was only about five feet long.

Two paintings hung on each wall, and all the way at the end sat a large glass box with a large book opened inside of it.

Alessandra glanced behind them toward the alligator and tugged Missy's elbow. She strained to see it.

Had the fucking thing moved again? Was it closer to them than it had been?

"Missy," she whispered, "I think that alligator..."

"That's it!" Trenise whispered excitedly, interrupting Alessandra, "That's it right there! It's got to be!"

Missy rushed forward, half expecting some invisible force to block her.

"Missy, hold up." Trenise said lifting her eyes and eyebrows significantly, "There's a camera."

Missy glanced up to the corner of the room.

"Shit."

She strolled forward in what she hoped was a casual way and peered into the glass container and then at the small placard next to it.

"The Bible of Reverend Emmanuel White, pastor of the first established Baptist Church of St. Tammanend Parish," Missy read out loud.

She glanced at the painting closest to her right and saw that it was a stone church, painted white. The church stood in a clearing and had a small graveyard next to it.

Trenise followed her gaze and read the placard out loud, "Church of the King, painting by Ezra A. Miller, commissioned by Reverend Emmanuel White 1798."

"You think that fucking camera got that fucking alligator moving out there?" Alessandra asked breathlessly, not taking her eyes from the edge of the hallway. Her heart hammered in her chest.

Trenise shook her head, "I don't know. I doubt it."

"So, what do we do now?" Alessandra asked.

Trenise shook her head, "We can't just break it."

Missy looked from the Bible back down the hallway and back to Trenise, "I have an idea."

—

"Ms. Landry, when you pulled up, did you notice anything unusual about the house?"

Ann Marie looked up at the young police officer, "Unusual? How do you mean?"

"Oh, like a car you didn't recognize or maybe a window or a door opened that shouldn't have been?"

Ann Marie shook her head, "No. No, it looked like it always does."

"You said Ms. Devaunt called you and that's why you came over. What did she say?"

"Well, I didn't talk to her," Ann Marie said, "she left me a message."

"Would you mind if I listened to the message?" Thompson asked.

Ann Marie reached into her pocket and handed her phone to Thompson. He pressed a few buttons and listened. When the message was over, he handed the phone back to Ann Marie.

Thompson gritted his teeth.

What the HELL were these three playing at?

Through his anger, Thompson forced himself to speak slowly and calmly, "She said she needed to talk to you about something she told Trenise Jones this morning."

Ann Marie nodded.

"Do you know why Ms. Jones would've been here? Were they friends?"

Ann Marie shook her head, "I guess they would've known each other from around town, but I don't know why she would've been here honestly."

Thompson furrowed his eyebrows.

"There ain't no way in hell Trenise Jones had anything to do with this," Ann Marie sobbed.

"No ma'am, I don't think she did, but she might've seen something."

Ann Marie shrugged, "What do you mean 'seen something?'"

Thompson shook his head, "I don't know yet Ms. Landry. You're free to go whenever you feel ok to drive. I'll call you within the next few days."

Ann Marie nodded and put her face in her hands as Thompson walked slowly down the porch and over to the ambulance where Sonny was leaning smoking a cigarette.

"You calling people in to process it, Duane?"

Thompson nodded, "About to do that now."

What the FUCK is Trenise Jones playing at? Thompson shook his head angrily.

Who does she think she is? Fucking Scooby Doo and the Gang?

Sonny nodded, "You better come here and talk to this neighbor, Duane. I think you're about to step in something here."

Thompson caught his breath and closed his eyes.

I don't want to be involved in this. I don't want to know what this is.

Sonny threw his cigarette and gestured behind the ambulance. Thompson followed him and came face to face with a man and woman, both in their 60s, who looked as angry as he felt. His eyes flicked from the couple to the well-kept house behind them.

"Tell Officer Thompson what you told me," Sonny gestured at Thompson.

"Well, I'm Janice Floyd and this is my husband Rick," Thompson nodded to them both, noting the man's annoyed look.

"Nice to meet you," Thompson said quickly, "Do you have some information about what happened here?"

The woman looked at her hands nervously, "I think I might. I saw two men in Ms. Cindy's backyard, Officer."

Thompson closed his eyes again.

I don't want to be involved in this.

He opened his eyes and glanced at Sonny, who was looking at him curiously.

"Did you see what they looked like?" Thompson asked the woman.

"Oh, I saw one of them clear as day. Know him too. The other one though...." Janice trailed off.

".... You better be damn sure before you give false testimony to a police officer," Rick Floyd said angrily.

"I AM sure," Janice said, turning a deep scarlet.

"Who was it?" Thompson asked. He had a terrible feeling that he knew what she was going to say.

The woman glanced at her husband, "It was Trent Longue."

Rick threw his hands up and huffed angrily, "God damn it, Janice, you don't KNOW that."

"I DO. I SAW him. I know who he is, I watched him at the damn football games every damn Friday you made me go. I know him from church. I KNOW it was him."

Thompson's hands shook as he took out a small notebook from his pocket.

I don't want to be involved in this bullshit.

He asked Janice Floyd to give him a description of who she saw and wrote as the woman described his build and hair color.

"And I saw his FACE."

"Did you," Thompson looked keenly into Janice Floyd's face, "did you happen to talk to Trenise Jones this morning?"

"Trenise Jones?" Janice looked bewildered, "The basketball coach? No, I haven't talked to her since Evangeline Nunez's wake."

"Ok," Thompson nodded, not sure if he should believe her or not, "What about the other person you saw?"

The woman turned red and glanced again at her husband who was shaking his head.

"This is going to sound crazy."

"It IS crazy.... You didn't see what or who you thought you did."

Thompson ignored the man, "Please continue, Mrs. ..."

"I couldn't see the other man's face because...well because..."

Thompson waited and watched the woman and gestured for her to continue.

"It was almost like..." the woman trailed off, "he almost shimmered. He had on black clothes, he was slimmer than Trent, but about the same height. But I couldn't see his face. Every time I tried to focus on him it was like he...faded away a little."

Thompson blinked rapidly and stopped writing. Unable to keep his frustration out of his voice, Thompson looked at the woman.

"You're telling me you saw Trent Longue and a man with no face?"

"You sound crazy Janice," Rick Floyd said and laughed.

Janice Floyd started to cry, and Thompson thew up his hands.

Like it or not, you ARE involved, came his Mother's voice, strong and clear, *How dare you not help this woman?*

Thompson turned around, chest heaving, almost expecting to see his long dead mother standing behind him.

Rick Floyd had turned his back and marched back toward his porch. When Thompson looked back at Janice Floyd, Sonny had his arm around her and was staring daggers at him.

"You ain't going to help her, Duane?" Sonny's voice was sharp.

Thompson felt himself redden as his mother's voice echoed still in his ears.

How dare you not help these women?

Thompson could almost feel his mother's hand on his arm, her small but strong fingers clamped around his wrist.

"W-where did you see these two men?" Thompson stammered finally, unable to meet Sonny's gaze.

"There."

Janice pointed toward the back of Ms. Cindy's property, "They were walking toward the house."

Thompson nodded and followed her gaze into the backyard.

Like it or not, you ARE involved.

The leaves on the old oak trees swayed and pink flowers on some of the bushes fluttered in the hot breeze. Thompson reached for his radio where it rested on his shoulder, then brought his hand down. He willed himself to just walk the other way, to get in his cruiser, report that Cynthia Devaunt had had a terrible accident, and drive home. He could call in and say he had a stomach virus. Bordelon would handle it.

But he couldn't do it.

Duane Thompson didn't call in to the operator and instead walked alone in to Cynthia Devaunt's backyard, leaving Janice Floyd and Sonny to stare after him.

—

"Whatever we're going to do, I think we need to do it fast," Alessandra said nervously.

She craned her neck around the corner so that she could look out into the main hallway.

The alligator moved slowly, scraping its belly on the wood floor as it went.

Alessandra gasped and covered her mouth. She squeezed her eyes shut for a moment, and when she opened them, the alligator had stopped. She swore it was looking at her.

How long until it makes it down here?

Trenise looked over her shoulder at Alessandra and tried to appear casual. She stepped away from the Bible encased in glass and stood next to Missy.

Missy didn't turn to look at her, but instead stared at the painting in front of her. Her eyes watered as she watched the leaves in the painting sway in some unfelt breeze. Shadows moved over the old churchyard, cast from the big, puffy clouds that moved in the painting's sky.

"Trenise, tell me you see that."

Trenise stared at it and then spoke, "I see it, Missy. Alessandra's right, I think we need to move fast. I'm going to break the glass and take the Bible. You and Alessandra head back up to the front and try to distract Ginny."

"But Trenise you'll be on the camera." Missy said, tearing her eyes away from the painting.

Trenise thought about the Funny Man and the grave in the woods, about Ms. Sarah and Rainbow, and shook her head.

"I don't care."

Alessandra turned away from the alligator, which was now about half way down the hall, slightly beyond the old pirogue.

"Just give us as long as you can Trenise, I'll see if I can figure out something with the cameras."

Missy started to contradict Alessandra, to tell her that she shouldn't be involved and then stopped herself. Instead she nodded.

"I'll distract Ginny, Alessandra, if you're sure you can do something about the cameras."

Alessandra nodded firmly and grinned, "You know us kids and our technology. My mom's always yelling at me to get off the phone."

Alessandra felt her lip tremble as she thought about her mother, far away in Baton Rouge, cleaning toilets and garbage cans. Alessandra hoped she was safe.

Trenise nodded, "Go on. You have ten minutes."

Missy walked to where Alessandra was standing and took her hand. She started to walk forward, and Alessandra pulled her to the right side of the hallway.

"Stay away from it," she whispered, nodding to the alligator.

Missy sucked in her breath, "Alessandra, that's not where it was when we came up the hall."

Alessandra pressed her back up against the wall of the hallway, "I know."

As they approached the motionless alligator, it growled softly again, deep in its throat.

"Jesus Christ," Missy moaned softly.

The alligator's glass eyes watched them go with a slight turn of its head and then looked back down toward the end of the hallway where Trenise stood, watching Missy and Alessandra.

"Wait for me outside," Trenise called down the hallway. She pulled both the sachet from Rainbow and her dog tags out from under her shirt, clutching one in each hand.

"Ms. Jones! You see this fucking alligator, right?"

"I see it, Alessandra. Go on now!"

Missy felt her heart hammer in her chest as she and Alessandra rounded the corner and headed back to the front desk.

"Walk normally," Missy said.

"I'm trying," Alessandra said shakily, "We can't leave her back there with that thing for too long."

Missy forced herself to smile as they approached the front desk and saw to her dismay that there was now a short line. A small group of middle-aged men and women were getting checked in at the desk, chatting amicably to Ginny. Missy tried to slow her breathing as they waited, tried to think of something to talk to Ginny about that would buy Trenise and Alessandra some time.

When the group finally walked away, Ginny smiled happily, "Hello again! Did y'all need something?"

"Actually yes! Where's the ladies' room?"

Brilliant interference, Missy admonished herself.

"Oh, right over there!" Ginny said genially, pointing, "It's a onesie, though! It's an old building, and I guess they were trying to save space where they could."

Missy nodded, "That makes sense."

Brilliant, just brilliant.

"Everything in here needs a remodel. Bathrooms, electrical, everything...we need more room!"

Ginny threw her hands up in mock exasperation.

"Oh Missy, would you mind if I went first?" Alessandra grinned sheepishly to Ginny and then threw Missy a pointed look.

Missy turned back to Ginny and smiled, "Actually, I had a few questions about some of the pieces we saw...."

—

Alessandra stared at herself in the bathroom mirror, trying to keep from panicking. She looked out of the small, curtained window. Ginny had given her an idea, but she wasn't sure that she quite knew how to do it. She pulled herself up on the window ledge, wondering if she could shimmy out.

If she could get out behind the building and find an electrical box, maybe she could cut it and black out the building.

Yeah, and get electrocuted in the process dumbass, she heard Berto's voice laughing at her, *Use your fucking brain, stupid.*

She dropped from the window and looked around the room again. Ginny said the building was old, that the electric needed to be redone. Alessandra's breath caught in her throat.

The wiring. Maybe she could find the wiring not on the outside, but on the inside.

There was a closet marked storage in the corner and Alessandra approached it, breathing heavily. She thought about when she was a child and she would sit happily in her grandfather's garage as he and Berto worked on cars while her mother was at work. She thought about the neatly lined up tools on their racks, the shining ancient toolboxes, the shelves along the wall filled with car parts and engine pieces, and the small metal door that was just above her head when she stood near it.

She remembered opening it one day and asking her grandfather what the little switches did.

"Please," she said softly, reaching under her shirt and gripping her necklace from Rainbow, "Please help."

She closed her eyes and tried the doorknob on the storage door, sure it would be locked.

When it opened, she opened her eyes as well, greedily looking for another small metal door, chest height on the wall, one that she could open and that would be filled with little switches.

There, above a mop and bucket and a stack of toilet paper, Alessandra saw what she was looking for.

She grinned as she reached out and yanked the fuse box door open.

The black switches were labeled, one for each corridor, one marked "BREAK ROOM," one marked "OUTDOOR LIGHT."

All the way at the bottom was a red switch marked, "MAIN."

Alessandra grinned and tried not to think about the alligator as she flipped the red switch and was shrouded in darkness.

"Good luck, Ms. Jones," she whispered into the darkness.

—

The air around Trenise was foul. The smell of mildew was so heavy she thought she would choke on it. Trenise watched the alligator and occasionally looked at her watch.

Missy and Alessandra had been gone less than five minutes.

Give them time, she told herself, *give them time.*

She glanced to her right and saw a portrait of a woman dressed in antebellum-style clothing slowly shaking her head "no."

Trenise felt her chest heave as the woman in the painting smiled and continued to shake her head. The woman was beautiful and sad.

"No, no, Trenise Jones," she seemed to say.

The woman in the picture took a step forward, closer to the foreground so that Trenise could see her full, shining, white face.

Down the hall, the alligator growled again, and the pirogue shimmied in its stand.

Trenise glanced back at the Bible in its case. The paintings in their frames writhed with movement, and Trenise heard the soft sliding of the alligator's dead skin across the floor.

She shuddered and moaned.

Wait, she heard Big John's voice rumble through her brain, *wait.*

"John?" she whispered softly and looked toward the ceiling. Trenise closed her eyes briefly and drew in a slow breath.

As she did, the lights went out and the sound of the air conditioning stopped.

Trenise Jones was alone in the dark.

—

"You see?" Ginny exclaimed.

Missy watched as she threw her arms up in exasperation, just barely visible in the light coming in from the windows at the front of the museum.

The sound of the automated voice began, speaking slowly in between the sound of an alarm.

"Please exit the building!" The alarm said.

"The electrical's going! It went out two nights ago too! Whole place went black! And I was here alone!" Ginny shouted above the alarm.

Missy caught her breath in and shook her head in sympathy. She looked over her shoulder into the darkened museum.

"Must've been terrifying!" she said, thinking only of Trenise.

"It was!" Ginny yelled over the blaring of the alarm, "And you know they say this place is haunted!"

Missy shuddered thinking of the Indian burial ground, and the Choctaw princess, and the dead girl in the woods, and the thing that turned into Wes, and the monster who had pursued them through the French Quarter.

"Haunted by who?"

Ginny started to answer when Alessandra emerged from the bathroom.

"What happened?" she said innocently, raising her voice to be heard over the booming alarm and cutting Ginny off.

Missy smiled at her and felt like her heart would overflow with love for the young blue haired girl before her.

"The power went out."

"Oh jeez louise!" Alessandra exclaimed.

"I'm sorry y'all but there's no telling when it'll come back on, you'll have to leave. I'll have to call maintenance to have them come see if they can fix it again."

Ginny sighed and stepped behind the desk and picked up her phone.

"I can tell you all the ghost stories you want another time," Ginny yelled, laughing, "It must've been the Choctaw Princess playing with us again!"

Ginny laughed merrily and gestured for Missy and Alessandra to move toward the front door.

Missy and Alessandra moved toward the front door, followed by the group of people who had entered only a few minutes before.

"Trenise is still back there though." Missy yelled desperately to Ginny.

Ginny smiled, "There's emergency exits back there. Trenise Jones can figure out how to use one of those, believe you me. You tell her give me a call about lunch!"

—

Trenise's eyes flew open and registered the darkness around her and the red glow of the emergency lights.

An alarm sounded and then an automated voice echoed, "Please exit the building."

She turned and dashed down the dark hallway toward the Bible and pulled the glass case off its stand.

With all her strength, Trenise threw the case down, sending shards of glass all over the room.

The alarm and voice alternated, drowning out the sound of the shattering glass.

"Please exit the building!"

It the darkness, Trenise heard the alligator roar with anger and the pirogue smash to the floor. Trenise bent down and picked up the Bible, wrapping her arms around it.

As she caught her breath, the painting to her right, the one of the church, flew off the wall and smashed into her shoulder. The woman in the other painting screeched and Trenise screamed in response.

Her terror and the force of the painting smashing her shoulder sent Trenise careening down the hall. As she went, paintings flew off the walls, pelting her back and face.

When she rounded the corner, the alligator was there, blocking her way, grinning at her with sharp teeth.

"Please exit the building!" the alarm screamed.

Trenise screamed again and kicked the alligator underneath its chin. She saw one of its glass eyes fly out of its head, glowing red in the reflection from the emergency lights. It snapped at her and then recoiled. Trenise leaped over it, and ran, only looking back to see that it had slowly turned and was trying to follow her down the hallway.

Looking forward, Trenise could see the fallen pirogue silhouetted by the red from the emergency lights. The air smelled slightly fresher as she gasped with fear.

Clutching the Bible, she skittered to the side of the pirogue, and it launched itself toward her feet, knocking her down.

The alligator scuttled closer and Trenise scrambled up, pressed her back against one wall, and looked desperately toward the light of the main hallway.

The alligator slithered around her and stood next to the pirogue, blocking her path to the right, back toward the main entrance.

Trenise lunged left and shoved the pirogue as hard as she could, smashing it into the alligator.

Unable to get back to the front desk, Trenise rounded the corner to go in the opposite direction. Behind her, the alligator growled with fury. About thirty feet down a sign glowed a warm red.

EMERGENCY EXIT, it read.

"Please exit the building!" the alarm blared in Trenise's ears.

"I'm trying!" Trenise screamed back.

The alligator growled again, and Trenise ran, one arm holding the Bible and the other outstretched to push the door open.

Trenise smashed into the door so hard it shuddered on its hinges. As she flew into the sunlight, the alligator snapped again and she stumbled, rolling into the gravel around the back of the museum.

She rolled over and kicked the door shut with both of her feet, closing the alligator inside.

Behind the glass, the alligator growled and shimmied up the door, trying to push it open.

Trenise sat up on her elbows and tilted her head back, reveling in the fresh air and the warm sun on her face. She took huge gulps of the fresh air. She could hear the music from the band in the square as it echoed surreally around her.

With all the noise she'd just made, she was surprised the police weren't there waiting for her to arrest her for theft and property damage.

"Trenise!" Missy whispered hoarsely.

Trenise snapped her head in the direction of Missy's voice and pulled herself to her feet.

"Is that it?!" Alessandra whispered excitedly, pointing at the Bible.

Missy and Alessandra stood next to her and took in the Bible that Trenise held in her hands.

Trenise nodded.

"Now," she said breathlessly nodding toward the glass door to her left, "We got to get out of here."

"What the fuck," Alessandra yelled, stepping back.

Missy clutched Trenise's arm, staring at the alligator as it swiveled its head back and forth to look at them. She could hear it growling even through the glass.

"Jesus, Trenise," she said softly.

"Let's go," Trenise said, climbing to her feet, "I'll tell you about it in the car."

Chapter Twenty One

The Stone River Police station was small and picturesque. There were flower beds in front of it, maintained by a local women's civic group, and behind it there was a park with a playground and a splash pad.

There were only ten deputies on staff, five of whom were close to retirement, and five dispatchers who rotated part time phone duties. The police department delt mostly with traffic stops, breaking up fights at the two bars in town, medical emergencies, and domestic disputes.

The only person in the department who had his own office was the Chief. Everyone else had a desk in one big open room. Because there were so few officers, there were rarely more than one of two people in the open room.

Thompson leaned back in his chair at his desk with his hands cradled behind his head. He thought about the phone call he had made in his car in front of Cynthia Devaunt's house.

If they don't want to look for the Longue kid, then you should be out there looking for the Longue kid, his mother's voice piped up for the fiftieth time since he'd left Cynthia Devaunt's house.

No, I SHOULDN'T, he responded to his mother's voice, *I tried to help, and it didn't work. I tried to help Trenise Jones, and Melissa Douglas, and Alessandra Sanchez. I tried to help Cynthia Devaunt. I need to think about myself and let sleeping dogs lie.*

Oh, you know a lot about lying, don't you?

> Thompson closed his eyes and tried to push the thought away, knowing where it was going. *Like how you lied to everyone about Elise?*

With the Chief of Police out recuperating from open heart surgery, Bordelon had seniority and as a result was technically in charge.

So, Thompson knew it was Bordelon who called off the APB he had phoned in for Trent Longue.

Thompson had always assumed Bordelon was lazy and inept, but now he wondered if it bordered into something else: corrupt.

This is not your fight.

This IS your fight.

Thompson took a breath in and waited, forcing himself to breath slowly, in and out.

When Bordelon walked in finally from whatever call he had been on, Thompson slowly pulled himself to his feet and walked over to Bordelon's desk.

"Why the FUCK did you call off the APB for Trent Longue," Thompson said quietly.

Bordelon looked bored and stared at his computer screen, "That old lady fell down the stairs and you want to accuse Grant Longue's son of murder based on the testimony of a pill-popping neighbor?"

Thompson took a slow breath.

"I'm not accusing him of murder, Bordelon. Someone tried to attack three women two days ago, and one of them said Trent Longue had been harassing her. Then a woman dies today, and Trent Longue was seen at the property. Don't you think we should at least talk to him?"

Bordelon reached into the mini fridge he kept under his desk and pulled an apple out. He took a large bite and chewed slowly.

Thompson waited.

"I just went and talked to the neighbor, Thompson. I know her husband. He told me that she pops herself a few extra Xanax in the morning and then goes and sits in the backyard with a glass of white wine. She also told me she saw *who she thought might have been* Trent Longue with a man who had no face."

Bordelon said this last part in a whisper and then laughed and wiggled his fingers by his ears.

"What's wrong Thompson, she spooked you?"

Bordelon took another bite of his apple and cocked his head, looking at Thompson.

"There's another witness besides the three women. That man who helped the teenaged girl and called 911. We should talk to him."

Bordelon laughed.

"Mike DiCostanza? Yeah, I talked to him, Duane. You want to talk about a troublemaker? He's a damn heroin addict."

Thompson shook his head in exasperation, "And what about Evangeline Nunez?"

Bordelon took another bite, "What about her?"

"I know her autopsy results were sealed. And I know her husband told police that she had told him Trent Longue harassed her verbally on multiple occasions."

Thompson mimicked Bordelon's gesture with his hands.

"Maybe not so spooky, Bordelon."

Bordelon threw the half-eaten apple into his desk garbage can and stood up.

"Trent is a good kid, Thompson. He's rough around the edges maybe, but what boy isn't?"

Bordelon shrugged his shoulders and looked Thompson up and down.

Bordelon stood up and leaned closer, lowering his voice, "I know you want out of here, Duane. We all know that."

Thompson held Bordelon's gaze.

"And hey, that's ok. I get it. You need to think about yourself here, Duane. Grant Longue knows a lot of people. He's not just slim pickings out here in the sticks. He knows people with the state. One call from him to State Police could make or break you."

Thompson stayed silent, listening and waiting.

Bordelon reached out and grasped Thompson's shoulder firmly.

"I'm telling you this as a friend, Duane."

Thompson nodded his head finally making up his mind.

"So, what you're saying, Bordelon, is that you're going to do nothing about this?"

Bordelon's face clouded, and he sat back down.

"No, I'm not."

He looked over at the clock in the corner of the room, pointed to it and grinned.

"You're off duty, partner. You look tired. You should head on home."

Thompson stared at him in disbelief.

"You're off tomorrow too, isn't that right?" Bordelon grinned even wider, "I think a day off is just what you need. Cool your head a little."

Thompson gave him a measured look.

"You understand what I'm saying Thompson? You are off tomorrow. Hell, why don't you take the next two days off?"

"This is bullshit, Bordelon."

Bordelon laughed.

"Now Duane, see? You need to relax a little. I could *force* you to take the next two days off, but that would have to go in your personnel file. I'll tell Janene you're taking some sick time."

This IS your fight Duane.

"Fuck," he muttered to himself as he walked out the front door of the police station.

Duane Thompson in no way wanted to get involved in what was happening here. He didn't want to cross Grant Longue and jeopardize his chances of getting the hell out of Stone River. He didn't want to be lead on some wild goose chase by a bunch of distraught women.

But, came a cool, calm voice from the back of his mind, *you know this isn't a wild goose chase. You know something is wrong here.*

By the time Thompson climbed into his personal truck and pulled out of the parking lot of the police station, his mind was made up.

—

Trent drove his truck up the driveway in front of his home, then over the back lawn, and pulled it next to the shed. The Preacher was gone again, but Trent knew he wasn't far.

Trent wasn't sure when the Preacher left. One moment he was there with him in the old lady's house, they were walking across her back law, and then Trent was alone.

But Trent could feel him. He was angry about something, and so Trent was angry too.

The blood splatter from the old lady was on his hands and shirt and pants, but Trent didn't care. He knew that the Preacher was counting on him. He knew that the Preacher would take care of him and that he, Trent, would be at his right hand when the time came.

Trent would inherit dominion. He would be more powerful than his own father, more powerful than his brother, off at Tulane, the pride of the family. He wouldn't need any of Grant Longue's help. He wouldn't be relegated to the lumberyard anymore. He would be laughed at or rejected anymore by anyone.

Trent laughed and wondered if he had time to visit Lexie before he began his work. He closed his eyes and let the cold air conditioning wash over him.

Trent had been told that he needed to have everything ready by sundown. He opened his eyes and looked at the clock on the dashboard. The sun would be all the way down around 8 o'clock and it was already past 11 am. Nine hours seemed like a lot of time, but Trent wasn't sure he had everything he needed here at the house, which meant he might have to go to the hardware store.

The thought of having to go into public and talk to people he knew was repulsive. How could he make small talk, smile and nod, when he was part of something huge now, something important, something that none of them could even comprehend was going on right in their own backyards?

Trent heaved a sigh and pushed the idea of Lexie out of his mind.

Get the work done first, he told himself, *Lexie will be there.*

Trent laughed to himself as he turned the truck off. Lexie wouldn't matter much after tonight. After this evening, Trent would have everything and everyone he wanted.

—

Duane Thompson lived in a small house on the edge of Stone River, closest to the larger city of Slidell. He did not live in one of Grant Longue's rentals, and he did not live in the large subdivision owned by the Longue family. While he did rent at this point, it was from the family of an elderly woman who had to be put into a nursing home.

Since he started working on the Stone River police force, Thompson prided himself on not being in Grant Longue's pocket in any way. He didn't go to church with him, or rent from him, or live in the subdivision his family had made so much money off.

He didn't work in one of Grant Longue's lumber or shipping yards. He wasn't in awe of Grant Longue as people like Bordelon seemed to be.

When Thompson looked at Grant Longue, heard about either one of his sons, he felt nothing but contempt. He saw nothing but the privilege that came with the legacy of taking advantage of the impoverished and ignorant.

The fact that the Longue family profited from those less fortunate, like his him and his mother when he was a child, was not his business. Thompson didn't blame The Longues for it, but he wouldn't glorify them either.

In Grant Longue, Thompson saw the mask of small-town politics. It was a good ole boy façade that protected corruption and greed on a much larger scale. Bordelon frequently lauded the Longue Family's long history of cultivating political figures through their connections and financial donations.

Thompson didn't know anything about wealth other than it was something he knew he'd never have.

He pulled his truck into the driveway of his house and looked at the neatly cut yard. It looked similar to the house that he grew up in, the one that his mother worked her fingers to the bone to keep, paying an exorbitant amount of money every month to her landlord, a real estate company owned by Grant Longue.

Her landlord who frequently raised the rent, knowing that she would do anything she could to pay it, to keep her son in Stone River and out of Slidell where the schools weren't as good, and the crime was worse.

Thompson thought about the money his mother paid to Grant Longue's real estate company each month, the rent that always seemed to be more and more. Then he thought about every Christmas when a circular would come in the mail with Grant Longue's face with his smiling white teeth on it, asking for donations to the children's toy drive.

What a hero.

Thompson thought about Evangeline Nunez, how she was beaten to death by the side of the road and left for dead. About the whispers of the suspected rape that wasn't investigated.

Thompson knew she had been beaten to death and so did Bordelon. Everyone at the police department did. But it was swept under the rug, the official story told was that Evangaline Nunez been the victim of a tragic accident.

He thought about Melissa Douglas's scared face as she clutched a baseball bat. About the face of the terrified teenager in the back of Bordelon's SUV. He thought about Trenise Jones and how angry she was that someone would terrorize her in her own yard.

He thought about Grant Longue's white teeth and his sons: one a high school football star and the other a high-powered lawyer in training, probably a future politician.

He thought about his mother working at McDonald's and giving every penny of her earnings to Grant Longue.

He thought about his own silence and complacency. He thought about Elise, his last girlfriend, and how he had treated her. He thought about his ambition and how it had blinded him.

Thompson slowly walked into his house and took off his uniform, opened the door to the small laundry room just to the left of the front door, and dropped it into the dirty clothes hamper.

He walked to the back of the small house, past the living room and kitchen, and into the small master bedroom.

He got dressed again in a pair of old jeans and a faded camo tee shirt and sat down on the edge of the bed to put on the hiking boots he wore when he went deer hunting in the fall.

Thompson knew he couldn't take his service pistol with him, and he didn't dare risk bringing one of his hunting rifles, even though hunting was exactly what he was doing.

Instead, Thompson went into the other bedroom in the house, where he kept weightlifting and hunting equipment. He opened the closet door and opened the lid to the large Tupperware container that sat on the floor.

On top was a large hunting knife that Thompson's mother had bought for him when he first became a cop. She had been so proud.

Protect and Serve.

His mother had had the words engraved on the hilt of the knife.

Thompson grabbed a duffle bag from the top shelf and put the knife in. He looked back through the Tupperware container and pulled out a pair of binoculars and a flashlight, testing it to make sure the batteries were still good.

He went to the kitchen and added four bottles of water to the bag. He quickly made himself two peanut butter and jelly sandwiches and threw a few bags of chips into the bag as well.

Thompson walked back out to his truck, feeling the small surge of excitement he always felt at the beginning of deer hunting season. As he felt the heat of the afternoon on his face, he tried to remember the cool clearness of hunting season. The air today was completely opposite.

Thompson opened his car door, placed the duffel bag on the front passenger seat, and then climbed in after it.

Deer hunting took patience, time, and luck. Duane Thompson pulled out of his driveway and sent up a silent prayer for all three.

—

Sweating with exertion, Trent stood in the sunlight of the clearing and looked longingly at the shady spot where he knew Lexie was, wedged between two gravestones just as he'd done with the other girl.

He heaved a sigh and continued his work.

There were some trees down already around the clearing, but not enough for what the Preacher had asked him to do.

Trent started the chainsaw again and walked over to a small group of saplings. He cut them down messily. When he had cut around twenty, he turned off the chainsaw and dragged the trees over to the pile he was making.

He had a vague idea of what the Preacher was planning and tried not to think about it. The Preacher had warned him on their ride home from New Orleans that the Devil would try to put doubt in his mind but that he must be firm in his faith.

Trent threw the logs onto the pile where it sat in the middle of the old ruins.

What does it matter what happens to the other two? You'll have Alessandra and that's what matters. Who cares what happens to Coach Jones and her chubby friend?

Trent wiped the pouring sweat off his forehead, looked again at the cool shade of the graveyard, and went back to his work.

—

Thompson slowly pulled onto what had been Cynthia Devaunt's street. There was no ambulance, no police cars. No police tape.

Thompson took a steadying breath. There should be cops there now looking for prints in the backyard, prints in the house. Someone should be interviewing Trenise Jones, Trent Longue.

He thought about the blood splatter and the way the old woman's legs stuck out at unnatural angles.

Instead of pulling in front of the victim's house, because she *was* a victim Thompson told himself firmly, he pulled in front of Rick and Janice Floyd's house.

Thompson put his truck in park and forced himself to pause. He really had no reason to be at the Floyd's house, no reason to talk to Mrs. Floyd again. On top of that, Thompson knew Rick Floyd would be angry that he was back poking a hornet's nest. He didn't want anyone tipping off Bordelon about what he was doing.

The house looked quiet and the truck that had been in the driveway earlier was gone. Thompson thought for a moment and then pulled his truck up so that it was between the Floyd's house and Cynthia Devaunt's house.

Thompson got out of his truck and went first to Cynthia Devaunt's backyard. Mrs. Floyd said she had seen the two men walk up from the back edge of the yard toward the house.

Thompson walked to the side yard, then into the shaded, slightly overgrown back yard. He relished how much cooler it felt under the old trees and among the tall bushes.

It was a short walk to the back of the property where the lawn met a wooded area.

Thompson peered through the trees and saw a narrow access path that bordered a deep drainage ditch filled with elephant ears, ferns, and debris. He stepped through the trees and brush and onto the path, looking left and then right.

The access path appeared to run behind both the victim's property, the Floyd's property, and the other neighbor's property. Behind the ditch was another shallow wooded area, through which Thompson could see another back yard leading to a behind neighbor.

He followed the path briefly behind the Floyd's house and saw that the ditch wrapped around behind all of the neighbors' houses up the cul de sac and then split and broke to the left.

Thompson put his hands on his hips. In his own neighborhood, as in most neighborhoods in Louisiana, drainage ditches lined the streets so that when heavy rains and the inevitable floods came, the ditches filled and irrigated people's property rather than flooding their yards and homes.

The ditches were at the front of the property, lining the streets.

Here, however, in this neighborhood where homes were expensive, the ditches had been placed behind the houses. Thompson guessed it was so that the wealthy homeowners wouldn't have to look at ratty ditches filled with mucky drainage. The ditches were bordered by access paths for works to travel to and from the different houses, clearing the ditches, reading water meters.

He shook his head and scoffed, then turned and walked back the way he had come, following the narrow path. Thompson followed the path along in the opposite direction and saw the back drainage ditch did the same thing on this side as well.

Thompson wondered if the ditches ran through the whole neighborhood in the same way, effectively creating a mirror image of the streets, a maze behind each house.

He was in awe for a moment, a hunch growing in the back of his mind. Listening to the birds in the trees, to the distant sounds of cars, the sounds seemed to hang in the humid air.

Thompson was surprised there were no clouds yet, the day was so hot he was sure there would be thunderstorms in the afternoon. Thompson looked at his watch. Not quite noon.

Making a mental note to drive around the neighborhood and see if the drainage ditches varied in any section of the neighborhood, Thompson emerged back into the victim's backyard. The Longue house would be to the North of here. If Trent used the paths that ran next to the drainage ditches to get here, he probably came out close to the Floyd property which would explain why Mrs. Floyd saw him.

Thompson tried to remember what Missy Douglas's backyard looked like the night he had run around her house trying to catch the suspect. He hadn't gone all the way to the back of the property, but he would bet there was the same service path and ditch set up there.

Thompson walked toward the Floyd's property line and looked into their backyard. A neat bed of flowers expertly broke the yard into sections. There were stone benches and wrought iron tables and chairs in each section, creating different spots where the Floyds could enjoy either shade or sun. If Mrs. Floyd was working on any of the flower beds, she would have a direct view to the back edge of Cynthia Devaunt's backyard.

Thompson stopped and bent over, scanning the ground below him. Although it had rained hard the day before, the heat evaporated most of the water already. The ground was firm, but Thompson suspected there still might be some footprints.

He silently cursed himself for not thinking to look at the ground on the path behind the house for prints before walking over it himself.

He moved slowly and then squatted down.

Gotcha.

Thompson grinned and then pulled his phone from his back pocket to snap a picture of the partial shoe print left in the moist earth.

He stood and walked in a straight line, looking for more prints. He found two more around the middle of the backyard, which, to the naked eye, appeared to belong to the same shoe. There were no more from the middle of the back yard to the back door of the house.

Thompson squinted and looked back the way he had come from. Janice Floyd said there were two men. One was Trent Longue and the other one's face she couldn't see.

That ain't what she said and you know it.

Thompson jumped at the voice, the voice that belonged to his mother that was suddenly so clear.

He could almost see her, hands on hips, all 5 feet of her small frame pulled up straight. He was taller than her when he was ten but never dared cross her. He loved her too much.

That AIN'T what she said and you know it, his mother's voice admonished him again.

Thompson shook his head.

No, that wasn't what Janice Floyd had said. She didn't say she couldn't see the other man's face. She said he had no face.

Thompson put his own face in his hands and rubbed his eyes.

Maybe Bordelon is right, Thompson thought, this time in his own voice, *maybe Janice Floyd took too many Xanax and hallucinated.*

Somewhere in the back of his head, Thompson could feel his long dead mother, hands on her hips, switch her weight from one foot to the other, looking at him with one eyebrow raised.

You know that ain't true, boy. You know something's wrong here, dead wrong.

"I know, Mama," Thompson whispered to himself.

He couldn't put his finger on it, but just as when he saw Trent Longue in the clearing in the woods the day before, he knew something was wrong. Something was off.

Thompson walked from Cynthia Devaunt's back yard across to where his truck was parked. He opened the door and took a drink from one of the bottles of water and thought.

What he assumed was Rick Floyd's truck was still gone. Thompson closed the door to his own truck and walked up the stone path that led to the front door, hoping Janice Floyd hadn't left with her husband.

Thompson knocked on the front door, rang the bell, and waited. He leaned closer to the door and listened but heard nothing. He knocked a second time, then stepped back and waited again.

After a few seconds, Janice Floyd's face appeared in the narrow window next to the door. She looked surprised and then Thompson heard the sounds of locks clicking open.

Janice looked doubtfully at Thompson, "I...I already spoke to Officer Bordelon...I...My husband said to..."

Thompson held his hands up and shook his head, "It's ok, Mrs. Floyd I spoke to Bordelon, and he told me that you're saying you're not sure of what you saw now."

Janice Floyd looked down at her feet and nodded, "That's right. I supposed he told you all about my medication? My husband loves to tell everyone about that."

Thompson shook his head again and took a step forward, "I don't really care about that right now, Mrs. Floyd."

She looked up at him, doubtful again.

"Mrs. Floyd, when I talked to you a few hours ago, you seemed sure, absolutely sure, that it was Trent Longue that you'd seen."

Janice Floyd looked at him desperately, "You have to understand something...my husband *works* for Grant Longue..."

Thompson nodded, "I get it and for now this is off the record. Was it him, Mrs. Floyd?"

Janice clutched the frame of the door, looked down, and nodded, "I'm sure of it."

Thompson felt his heart speed up, "And the other guy? Can you tell me anything else about him?"

Janice shuddered and whispered, "You're going to think I'm crazy."

Thompson shook his head, and placed his hand over his heart, "I promise I won't."

Janice Floyd lowered her voice and looked over Thompson's shoulder, then back at him.

"I thought I would go crazy looking at him. He was there and he wasn't. He was next to Trent Longue and he wasn't. I could see him but his face was blurred, almost like static on an old tv, but flesh colored."

Thompson nodded and breathed out deeply, "Ok, Mrs. Floyd."

Janice Floyd looked at Thompson desperately, "And there's one more thing."

Thompson waited, knowing from experience interviewing people that they often saved important information to the end of a discussion. It was similar to what doctors called "door knob questions"- patients would wait until their hand was on the door knob to leave before telling the doctor why they were really there, to ask they really important questions.

Thompson watched Janice Floyd as she struggled to get the words out, "I told my husband, and he said I was crazy."

"You can tell me, Mrs. Floyd, I won't think you're crazy."

Janice looked Thompson in the eye for the first time, "He knew I was there, he knew I was watching. He didn't look at me, but he *saw* me."

Thompson nodded, "You mean Trent?"

Janice shook her head, "No, the *other* one."

Thompson took a deep breath, "Ok, Mrs. Floyd. Here's what I want you to do. Is your husband going to be home anytime soon?"

Janice nodded.

"Until he gets home, lock all the door and windows, don't go outside. When he does get home, make sure all the doors are locked again."

Janice nodded her head.

"I'll be back in touch with you soon, Mrs. Floyd." Thompson reached into his pocket and pulled out one of his cards, "If you need anything else, call me."

Janice Floyd took the card from his outstretched hand, "Thank you."

Thompson walked to his car, feeling more certain with each step that Trent Longue was a danger and that he needed to be found.

He started his truck and looked down the street. Melissa Douglas's house sat about a half mile away on the opposite end of the other cul de sac. Thompson could just make out the white of the garage through the trees and shrubs.

He pulled his truck away from the Floyd's house and down the street. The houses were moderately large, each with at least an acre of well-kept yard. Thompson paused before crossing the main road that led out of the subdivision and, hands on the wheel, paused in thought.

He looked to the right, in the direction of the main entrance to the subdivision, though he couldn't see it from here. He knew about five miles away was the trailer where Alessandra Sanchez lived with her mother.

Thompson chuckled to himself and wondered how many of the Magnolia Forest residents balked at the few small trailers hidden down the short road that was attached to their front of their subdivision.

Thompson looked in the opposite direction to where he knew Trenise Jones's large Acadian sat, backed up to the swamp. Based on what the three women had told him the previous morning, his guess was that Trent was after Alessandra and he had added in Trenise Jones because, according to her and Alessandra, Jones had broken up Trent's assault of Alessandra in school that spring.

He still couldn't place how Cynthia Devaunt or Melissa Douglas fit into whatever Trent was doing, except for that Melissa Douglas was a close friend of Evangeline Nunez and Cynthia Devaunt lived on the same street.

When the three women had appeared in his office yesterday morning, Thompson could feel their frustration and fear and anger. They thought Trent Longue was involved in the death of Evangaline Nunez and were afraid that Alessandra was the next target.

Could that make Melissa Douglas a target if she kept pressing into the matter of Evangaline's death, asking for Trent to be investigated? Had Cynthia Devaunt known something about Evangaline Nunez's death and was that why she had spoken with the three women that morning? Was that why she had called her caretaker to come see her- to help track the three women down?

Thompson shook his head with frustration. He needed to find Melissa Douglas, Trenise Jones, and Alessandra Sanchez. He had a hunch that they knew the answers to some of these questions, and he desperately feared they were on some kind of vigilante quest for justice for Evangaline Nunez.

Although Evangaline Nunez's case had of course been assigned to Bordelon, Thompson was there when her body was found. He had been part of the search crew that went out looking for her, thinking she had taken one of the paths that lined the Stone River and had gotten lost. He had thought that night they would find a confused and slightly embarrassed mother and instead they had found a woman covered with dirt, bones broken, bleeding, and barely breathing at the bottom of a small levee.

He had watched as Sonny, who found her first by some miracle, howled his name like an animal, and performed CPR, screaming to Thompson between breaths that he was scared he would puncture her lung with one of her already broken ribs.

When the ambulance had arrived and taken Evangaline Nunez away, and Sonny with her, Bordelon had stepped to the edge of the levee and looked down.

Sitting in his truck now, choking on the memory, Thompson heard Bordelon's voice echo in his ears, saw him shrug his shoulders, "Poor little thing took a nasty fall, huh Thompson?"

Thompson had felt incredulous at the time, just as Sonny had when he spoke with him at the hospital.

"Duane she didn't fall," Sonny had whispered as they shared a cigarette outside the emergency room, "someone *beat* her."

Thompson has heard the rumors swirled around town after she eventually died in the hospital from sepsis, her blood infected after the severe injuries she had sustained. The town whispered that Evangaline wasn't the victim of an accident, but the victim of a homicide.

Thompson also heard that no autopsy had been performed even though the doctors had found evidence of a sexual assault.

They covered it up, his heart had screamed at the time.

But he had pushed the thought away. Pushed it away because if he interfered it would mar his chances of a recommendation.

He now felt nothing but anger. No more indifference. Anger for Evangaline Nunez and her family. Anger at himself for knowing all of this was happening and doing nothing until now.

But that's what you've always done, isn't it? Take the easy way out? Take the way out that's best for yourself?

Thompson thought of Elise again, of how she cried on the phone the last time he had talked to her, when he told her he wanted nothing to do with her or the baby she was carrying.

As he crossed over to Melissa Douglas's cul de sac, the anger mixed with fear and immediacy.

Thompson knew he had to find those three women before Trent Longue did. He had done his soul a wrong by turning a blind eye to what was happening around him. He needed to find the three women and at the very least tell them he believed them, to tell them that they were right.

Chapter Twenty Two

Ms. Sarah sat back, relaxed, in the blue hospital chair. Next to her, her young female attendant stood casually looking out the window.

"This isn't your fight Rainbow, and it's not mine," Ms. Sarah said calmly, "I don't even know if you could help even if you try."

Rainbow protested, asking how she could possibly do nothing, knowing what was happening.

"You *don't* know what's happening, Rainbow."

Rainbow turned slowly to look at her but said nothing.

"If you involve yourself now, you have no chance of not being involved again. You may not be able to see the situation clearly anymore if any of them need your help in the future."

Rainbow rang the button for the nurse.

"If I don't help them, none of them might have a future, Sarah."

Ms. Sarah shrugged and sighed, "That's true, Rainbow. But that's not for the likes of you or me to decide."

"I have to," Rainbow whispered.

Ms. Sarah nodded and slowly stood up. The young woman at the window moved to her side.

Reaching down and gently squeezing Rainbow's hand, Ms. Sarah nodded again, "I know you do."

Rainbow's eyes filled with tears, "Thank you."

When the nurse came in, Rainbow told her she wanted to be discharged.

Thirty minutes later, Rainbow drove her small Honda as fast as she dared across the bridge that spanned Lake Pontchartrain. The sky above her was an ugly black and purple. A line of mammatus clouds hung sickeningly low, indistinguishable from the rolling waves of the water.

Rainbow's head still ached from the concussion, and if she moved her head too quickly her whole world spun. She blinked and forced her eyes to refocus. Rainbow stared at the horizon in front of her. The end of the bridge was still not visible.

Rainbow turned again to look at the churning water below the bridge and pushed the gas pedal down as far as she dared, praying she could find them in time.

—

"So now what?"

Alessandra sat the back seat and stared at the Bible where it lay on the seat next to her.

It looked strange. The oldness of it against the clean black leather didn't look right. Alessandra thought about the ring Frodo carried in *Lord of the Rings* and Slytherin's locket that Harry and Hermione carried in the last Harry Potter book.

Trenise had asked Missy to drive home when they reached her SUV. She sat slumped in the passenger seat, one hand over her eyes, the other clutching the sachet from Rainbow and the set of dog tags. She had her window all the way down and way taking deep breaths.

Missy ignored Alessandra's question for the moment, "Trenise are you alright? Should I call Rainbow?"

"I'm alright, Missy. I just need to get that smell out of my nose," she paused, "Don't call Rainbow. Not yet."

"So..."Alessandra trailed off.

"I say we burn the fucking thing." Missy said, eyes on the road.

Trenise nodded and opened her eyes, "Kind of fits with what he did, doesn't it?"

Alessandra nodded, "Right. Quid pro quo, Clarice."

"Go to my house," Trenise told Missy, "I have lighter fluid."

Alessandra looked again at the Bible and felt nauseated. She thought about the alligator's dead skin, about a dead girl, naked from the waist down and the Thing in the woods that had turned into David, about the bottomless pit in the ground that Trent had dug. She thought about the moment when Baby's ring had connected with Trent's skin the night before and the smell of rotten burning flesh.

Alessandra again thought of *The Lord of the Rings* and how Frodo cast the ring into the depths of Mordor to destroy it and silently wondered if lighter fluid would be enough.

—

Thompson walked slowly around the side of Missy Douglas's house and back to his truck where it was parked in the driveway. Everything looked the same as it had a few nights ago, except for that there were no children's toys out in the driveway.

When he had talked to Missy Douglas, Trenise Jones, and Alessandra Sanchez the previous morning, Thompson remembered she said her children were with her parents in Tennessee and that she was planning on joining them. Although he knew Ms. Douglas had been in Stone River that morning, talking to her neighbor down the street as reported by Ann Marie Landry, Thompson hoped to God she had gotten in her car and driven to Tennessee in between then and now.

Thompson found what he was looking for in his walk through Melissa Douglas's backyard. The same utility path cut straight through her backyard from one neighbor's yard and into the next. He guessed if you followed it all the way around, you'd reach Cynthia Devaunt's backyard, and further down in each direction, Alessandra Sanchez's, and Trenise Jones's backyards.

This is how the little bastard has been getting around with no one seeing him.

Thompson put his truck in drive and pulled away from the Douglas house. As he pulled to the end of Ms. Douglas's street, Thompson opted against driving down the long stretch that led to Alessandra Sanchez's trailer. He seriously doubted the three of them would go there.

Thompson wanted to be conservative, maybe save part of his reputation. He didn't want to do anything illegal when it came to Trent Longue, but, if he couldn't find the three women, his next step would be to follow Trent. Watch what he was doing so that he could intervene if necessary. But that would be his last resort.

Thompson thought Trenise's Jones's house was the most logical place they would use as a sort of home base: she was the oldest, the most educated, the widow of a cop.

As he pulled onto Trenise's street, his heart dropped when he saw that her driveway and the large stretch of road in front of her house was empty.

"Dammit," Thompson swore and shook his head. Nonetheless, he pulled his truck in front of the house and parked.

Thompson looked at Ms. Jones's house again and decided to walk around the backyard just as he had done at Melissa Douglas's house, looking for some clue as to where they were or what they were planning.

As he rounded the house and entered the backyard, the first thing he noticed was that the reeds and brush that lined the property where it met the bayou behind it had been cut back in one large section.

Thompson walked slowly down to the edge of the water.

Overhead, the sky seemed to darken with every step Thompson took down the gentle slope of the neat lawn. There were a few trees and bushes, but unlike Cynthia Devaunt and Melissa Douglas's backyards, Trenise Jones's yard was mostly open space.

Thompson looked up at the thunderclouds as they built above the swamp and felt the press of the humid air as it built around him.

Thunder rumbled.

Thompson peered to his left and right into the neighbors' yards on either side of Ms. Jones's property. There was no need for drainage ditches because these three houses backed directly up to the swamp, but he could see the same utility pathways through the back yards, hidden behind low bushes.

If, as Thompson suspected, Trent was using the utility paths to get around to commit his crimes, it would make sense that he would have to hide behind the brush as the open layout of the backyard wouldn't offer any hiding spots.

Which is why Trenise Jones saw him in the corner by the neighbor's yard and why she cut down a large portion of the brush.

Thompson shook his head and spit, frustrated that he was still two paces behind the three women and about a mile behind Trent Longue.

They knew something he didn't, and Thompson couldn't quiet put his finger on what it was.

Thompson found it hard to admit that he didn't know where to go from here.

Where could the three of them possibly have gone?

Thunder rumbled again and a strong wind made the trees around him shiver.

Thompson put his hands on his hips and let his eyes wander out into the bayou, thick with cypress trees, reeds, and Spanish moss. The tangle of vegetation made it so that he couldn't see very far and Thompson let his mind wander as well, hoping an idea would come to him.

—

Trent lumbered to the graveyard, breathing heavily as he hauled another bunch of cut trees to the growing pile he was making. The air was oppressive with the afternoon heat and Trent again wistfully thought of having a visit with Lexie where she lay in the shade, legs spread and stiff and then walking out of the woods and jumping in the pool behind his house.

He wiped his brow and took a drink of water, admiring the large pile of wood in front of him.

Go.

Trent startled and spilled water down his front at the sound of the voice. He turned and the Emmanuel White was there, standing by Lexie's body.

"I was doing what you said," he said petulantly, looking down at Lexie, "I was doing what you said first."

White looked grim and shook his head.

"Stop your work here," his voice was no more than a whisper, "What you want and what we need is yours to take. Go now."

Trent's heart sped up.

"You mean Alessandra?"

Emmanuel White nodded, "Go. They have something of mine. Get my Bible and the girl and bring them here. The other two will follow."

Trent's hand fluttered to his throat, to the spot where the skin was blistered where that bitch had hit him with her ring.

Emmanuel White watched him closely.

"Be not afraid, child. For I will be with you. Go."

Trent gritted his teeth and nodded, "Where?"

—

Thompson stood and looked out into the bayou. He hoped an idea would come to him that would help him find three living women and find some justice for two dead women.

Instead, the only thought that came to him was about the Swamp Woman stories from when he was a child.

The real part of the story was scary enough. A man, driven by anger that his wife threatened to leave him, kidnapped her, brought her out here into the Honey Island Swamp, and left her there. After he left her, he panicked and tried to go back to find her, but he couldn't.

The man called the police, told them that his wife was lost in the swamp. After a five-day search, the woman's body was found. Covered with bites from snakes and alligators and bugs, bloated from days in the hot stagnant water, the woman's body was brought to the coroner and the man confessed that she hadn't gotten lost, but that he had left her there on purpose.

Then, of course, the stories and legend grew out of the truth. Duck hunters in their boats claimed they saw a woman in the brush but when they got close to her, she vanished. Fishermen said they heard a woman calling for help from the heart of the swamp.

Thompson wondered distantly how many women in Stone River had met terrible ends, just like Cynthia Devaunt, Evangaline Nunez, and the Swamp Woman.

"Hello?"

Thompson whipped around to look behind himself, thinking Trenise Jones must have come home.

The lawn was empty.

Thunder rumbled overhead and Thompson shuddered and took two uncertain steps forward in disbelief.

"Hello?" he responded uncertainly.

Thompson's heart hammered unnaturally in his chest as he strained forward, head turned so that his ear was toward the swamp.

Again, the voice came, louder, out of the swamp, "Is anyone there?"

Lightning flashed overhead and the thunder rumbled.

"Ms. Jones?" Thompson called, cupping his mouth.

The voice came again, a woman's voice, "Please help me!"

Thompson reached for the radio on his shoulder that wasn't there since he wasn't on duty. "Stay where you are!"

"Ok!" the voice called back, "Please hurry! I'm lost!"

Thompson pulled out his cell phone and tried to call the police station, but the call wouldn't connect.

"What the hell..."

Thompson looked around the property, wondering if he had time to run to a neighbor's house.

"Please hurry!" the woman called again, "There's something in the water near me!"

"I'm coming," Thompson called back, "Keep talking to me so I can follow your voice!"

He looked desperately at his phone again as the woman screamed, the sound of it echoing through the bayou in front of him.

There was no dock on the property, but as Thompson stepped beyond the rushes and closer to the edge of the water, he noticed to his right was a small pirogue he assumed belonged to Ms. Jones, an oar clipped to its side. The pirogue was pulled up out of the water, hidden behind the brush.

It looked ancient, the old style pirogue that was made from a hollowed-out tree.

Thompson wondered vaguely if it was watertight as he stuffed his phone back into his pocket and pushed the pirogue into the muddy water, jumping in as he went. He pulled the oar from the side and paddled around the trees in front of him, into the thick of the swamp.

Thunder boomed overhead and he pummeled himself through the water, navigating around the cypress roots as fast as he could.

"Hey!" he called again, "Where are you? Call out to me!"

"I'm here!" the woman's voice sounded decidedly closer, "Please hurry! I've been out here for so long, and I'm scared!"

Thompson swerved around a cypress stump and felt the knees of the cypress, the roots that stuck up above the surface of the water, scrape the bottom of the pirogue.

"Hey!"

Thompson reached a small stretch of open water and pushed the pirogue forward with the oar.

"Here!" the voice echoed across the water.

Thompson turned his head to the right, toward the sound of the woman's voice. In the distance, through a large tangle of cypress trees, he saw a small mound of what looked like solid land, dotted with cypress knees.

The thunder crashed overhead, a large gust of wind pressed Thompson's shirt against his body, and large rain drops began to splash around him in the water and in the pirogue. He lifted one hand to shield his eyes from the drops and squinted toward the small island, no more than seven feet across.

There, he saw a figure clinging to a tree waving its arms overhead.

"Here!" the voice echoed again, just barely audible over the rain and wind.

Thompson rowed toward the mound, his head down against the rain. The pirogue bumped the edge of the island, and he carefully picked his way along the length of the boat. He gingerly reached one foot out to test if cypress knees would hold his weight as it was holding the woman's.

One knee in the pirogue and one foot on the island, Thompson held out a hand.

"Grab on! I don't know if it'll hold my weight!"

Thompson looked up at the trees in front of him, laden with Spanish moss, swaying in the wind and rain.

"Hey lady! Where are you?"

Thompson took his foot off the island and kneeled in the boat.

"Hey!" he called again.

Thompson looked back over his shoulder in the direction he had come from and realized he could no longer see Trenise Jones's backyard. In fact, he couldn't see any land at all aside from the small island in front of him.

Thompson's insides went cold.

Don't panic, he told himself.

The Swamp Woman.

The rain splashed all around him, and Thompson realized his boat was filling up with water. Hurriedly, Thompson used his hands to bail, grabbed his oar, and rowed to the backside of the island.

There was no one there. There was nothing except trees, roots, moss, and vines.

Stay calm.

Thompson rowed all the way around the island, forcing himself to move in slow, even strokes as he tried to see through the rain.

When he got back to the front of the island, the part he had first tested his weight on, Thompson stopped and looked again.

Again, Thompson felt the cypress knees below his pirogue scrape and jostle the bottom. Using the oar, he pushed against the cypress knees surrounding the island to turn the pirogue around and try to head back the way he had come.

He pushed any theories about what he saw and heard from his mind, unable to grapple with the strangeness of it. For the moment, Thompson didn't think about anything other than the Swamp Woman and how desperately he wanted to be away from the little island he had been lured to.

He felt a surge of embarrassment. He had grown up all his life in Southeastern Louisiana, was a fisherman, a hunter, and a policeman and should have known better than to charge off into an unknown part of the swamp in an unknown boat without telling anyone where he was.

Thompson maneuvered the pirogue so the bow was pointed away from the island and dipped the oar in the water to row back the way he had come. He pulled the water with the oar and the pirogue gave a lurch backwards.

Stuck on the fucking roots.

Thompson reached back with the oar, dipped it below the surface of the water, and jabbed down, trying to free the boat. The rain fell in huge drops and the wind blew the bow of the boat to the side, the stern still jammed on something.

Thompson turned and crawled through the pooled water to the back of the boat to see if he could free it by hand. He reached into the water up to his elbow and felt the hard roots from the cypress mixed with the slimy water plants tangled there.

He shoved down and the boat rocked but didn't come free.

Reaching down further, up to his shoulder and wetting his sleeve, face almost in the water, Thompson turned his head to the side against the water and felt the boat lurch and tip out from under him.

As he hit the water, Thompson felt his face scrape along the cypress knees and roots. He sputtered back up to the surface and watched the overturned pirogue float away in the wind.

"No, no, no."

Thompson kicked off the roots below him to swim after the boat and was pulled backwards by the ankle.

He turned, thinking his foot was caught in the roots as well, and screamed at site of the rotten woman standing in the water behind him.

Her eye sockets bulged with fetid green water and the flesh on her face peeled off in chunks. He could smell the putrid rot coming from her body as she reached out again and grabbed his shoulder, pulling him to her.

Thompson screamed again and lashed out, but his arm connected only with rotten flesh. He turned in horror as pus and green algae oozed over his arm and hand.

The woman grinned.

Frozen, Thompson heard the crack and suck of something pulling itself from the mud. He watched as behind the putrid Swamp Woman, the cypress knees pulled themselves up from the mud and slithered toward him like rotten, possessed snakes.

Thompson kicked and sucked in water as the roots pulled him down.

He raised his hand above the water and clawed his face above the surface. He drew in a long breath and screamed for help as the roots tightened and pulled him under the water.

—

Trent pulled his truck off the road and across the lawn of the house that was next to Trenise Jones's house. He thought about Ms. Jones and her bitch friend, about what they had done to him and was filled with hatred.

He touched the blistering skin at his neck again and felt his body heave and shake with anger.

Trent noted that there was a truck parked in front of the house but didn't give a shit who it belonged to. He could feel Emmanuel White's power within him again and wasn't scared.

Stay quiet, the voice came, *Wait, and watch.*

Trent pulled his truck into the neighbor's back yard and walked up to the house, peering in the windows. All the lights were off. Not caring if anyone was home or not, Trent walked back through the yard and stood at the edge of the property behind a large group of bushes.

As he poked his head around to get a better view of Ms. Jones's backyard, Trent sucked his breath in and froze. There, in the middle of the lawn, was the cop who had been at his house yesterday.

Stay quiet. When the time comes, take the girl. She will lead you to what belongs to me.

Trent felt White leave. His mind was silent and strong.

Trent moved backwards and watched as the cop stood by the edge of the bayou and then shouted something. He watched as the cop floundered with his phone and then pulled himself into a pirogue and rowed off into the swamp.

Trent crept forward again, and then immediately stepped back at the sound of a car pulling up the road. He peered out again and saw Ms. Jones's black SUV pull in front of the house and into the driveway.

Trent grinned with excitement.

—

"Now who the hell is this at my damn house?"

Trenise sat up in the passenger's seat and looked at the truck as they passed it.

"You don't know whose car that is?" Missy asked uneasily.

Trenise shook her head and turned to look at the vehicle while Missy pulled the SUV into the driveway.

"Alessandra it's not Trent's car, is it?"

Missy parked the car and turned to look at Alessandra in the back seat.

Alessandra shook her head, "No, his truck is bright red."

"Could be using someone else's though."

Trenise opened her door and pulled herself out, turning back to Missy as she stood outside the car, "Get that bat and come with me."

"What? Oh..."

Missy reached under her seat where she had shoved her brother's bat.

Trenise turned and walked slowly toward the truck parked in front of her house, Missy on the right and Alessandra on her left.

Missy lifted the bat over her shoulder and looked down the back lawn toward the bayou. Wind blew the reeds and hanging moss. The green leaves on the trees seemed electric against the darkening sky behind it. It wasn't raining yet, but Missy could feel the heaviness in the air that meant it would soon.

Trenise reached the car and tried the handle. When it didn't open, she cupped her hands against the glass and peered in. All she saw was a medium-sized duffle bag on the front seat, but no indication of who the truck belonged to.

"Did you hear that?" Missy asked quietly.

Alessandra looked around, "Hear what?"

Missy held one finger to her lips and tipped her head to the side.

"There," she said finally, looking from Trenise to Alessandra.

"I don't hear anything," Alessandra looked around again nervously.

"I heard it," Trenise said.

She and Missy started walking down the side yard toward the swamp.

"What about the car?" Alessandra called after them, "What if it's Trent?"

"Come on," Trenise waved Alessandra, "If it's him, we'll know in a minute."

Alessandra swore and jogged after them to catch up.

Halfway down the lawn, Missy heard it again. A distant yell, a man's voice. She looked quizzically at Trenise.

"What did he say?"

Trenise shook her head, "Sounded like 'stay there?'"

All three waited and listened.

Further up the lawn, behind them, Trent listened too. Then, he retreated and walked back to his truck, looking over his shoulder as he went. He opened the door of his truck as gently as he could, reached into the glove compartment and pulled out the pocketknife he kept there, tucking it into his front pocket.

He knew that White didn't want them followed, and Trent had a simple idea of how to slow them down at least.

Trent crouched down and duck walked back to his hiding spot. Seeing that the women were still occupied in conversation, he crept from his hiding spot over to Ms. Jones's car and pulled the door open.

There, on the seat, was what Emmanuel White had told him he needed. Trent could feel the Bible throbbing with a raw heat and power. As he reached out for it, the blisters on his neck seared and burned and Trent bit his hand to stop himself from screaming.

On the floor of the car, he could see something long and silver sticking out from a backpack. Trent didn't know what it was, but he felt white electricity coming from it. It felt like the homeless girl's hand and the blond bitch's bat.

Whatever it was, it was trying to prevent him from getting the Bible.

Trent felt his eyes tear up as he reached out, trying to stay away from whatever was in the backpack, and snatched the Bible off the seat. He closed the door gently and panted with pain.

He knew he couldn't touch whatever the silver thing was, but he also knew he couldn't let any of them get to it. Trent opened the driver's seat door carefully and snaked a hand in, hitting the lock button as he did.

Trent turned and watched the three women as they talked by the bank of the bayou, then he opened the pocketknife and thrust it into the back two tires of Ms. Jones's SUV. Then, he walked to the street, quickly but quietly, and slashed the tires on the cop's truck too.

Trent had a feeling that the cop wouldn't pose too much of a problem soon, but he didn't want to take any chances.

Feeling calm and confident, cradling the Bible and relishing the feeling of warmth it gave him, Trent walked along the street to Ms. Jones's neighbor's yard to deposit the Bible in his truck. Once that was done, Trent went back to the front of Ms. Jones's house and crouched down behind her car, watching and waiting.

—

The silence before the sky opens on a boiling Louisiana summer afternoon has a life unto itself. The birds stop singing, the air stills for a moment. Then the wind rushes and swirls everything in its path in an instant. The thunder comes from everywhere, ricocheting off the ground, rattling the Earth and sky together. Then the rain comes, hot and steamy as it hits the dirt and grass and pavement.

Missy felt the hair on her arms stand on end as the first crack of thunder broke the silence and purple lightning rippled across the heavy thunderclouds over the cypress trees in the water in front of her.

"I don't think that's Trent out there."

Alessandra shook her head in agreement, "I don't think it is either."

"No. Stay here."

Trenise ran across her back lawn toward the large shed that sat close to Rita's property. She flung the door open and scanning through the scant junk, she saw what she was looking for under a tarp. Trenise didn't keep much in this shed since it occasionally flooded, but she knew the small plastic kayak was there.

Alessandra looked at Missy as they heard the man's voice call out a few more times, nervously glancing up the lawn toward the street.

When Trenise emerged from the shed a minute later, Missy and Alessandra jogged across the lawn to meet her halfway. The first few drops of rain peppered the boat and the thunder cracked again. Together, they dragged the kayak toward the edge of the water.

"There's only room for one of us," Trenise raised her voice over the hardening rain.

Whoever was out there in the swamp screamed and the three of them looked out across the water.

"I'll go," Missy said.

"No Missy, I know the water, I'll go."

Missy shook her head, "Trenise, Ms. Sarah said we're more vulnerable if we split up. And we saw that last night."

Trenise looked from Missy to Alessandra.

Missy nodded, "Right. If Trent comes for Alessandra again, you can protect her better than I can."

Trenise nodded.

"Ok, Missy. Listen, there's a compass on the bow," Trenise pointed into the swamp, "and that's east. When you're ready to come back," she pointed back toward her house, "Come due West and you'll hit land. Either mine or someone else's."

They pushed the kayak toward the water and helped Missy climb in. Trenise unhooked the double-sided paddle from where it was clipped and handed it to Missy.

Missy paddled out into the water, turning to look through the rain at Trenise and Alessandra on the bank.

Alessandra nodded clutching her elbows and yelled, "Beautiful day for a little boat trip!"

Missy laughed in spite of herself.

"Call for us if you need us," Trenise elbowed Alessandra gently.

Missy turned and paddled out into the bayou in front of her, weaving in and out of the trees and trying to keep the long paddle from bumping into the cypress knees around her.

Her heart pounded, and she squinted to see through the rain. When she turned to look behind her, the shoreline was gone, blocked by trees and hanging moss and the general overgrowth of the swamp.

A thick black snake swam away from the kayak and Missy gasped. The rain splashed all around her in the water, bouncing up and hitting her in the soft spot on underneath her arms.

Missy paddled forward, weaving in and out of the growth. She paused and lifted a hand to her brow to shield her eyes. It looked like the trees formed a clearing ahead and Missy paddled toward it.

She wondered desperately what her children were doing right now. She wished more than anything that she was with them, far away from Stone River.

The ring of trees looked identical to the clearing in Trent Longue's backyard. The clearing with the graveyard and the ruins and the grave that opened into nothingness and the thing that turned into her husband when he was still a violent drunk, and the man who raped Alessandra, and child molester from Trenise's childhood.

Instead of the ruins of a church, though, there was a small island.

As she edged herself into the open water, Missy gasped and fell back in the kayak as she heard a man scream for help.

She sat up again, chest heaving with fear, and shielded her eyes to see through the rain. On the opposite end of the clearing, in front of the little island, the water thrashed and swirled.

Missy desperately wiped the rain from her eyes and watched in horror as the knees from the cypress trees pulled themselves up from the mud and slithered into the thrashing water in front of her.

Whoever had yelled was in there.

Missy gritted her teeth and paddled herself as fast as she could toward the opposite end of the pond.

She propelled forward, rushing toward the tangle of thrashing water. She stopped, raised the paddle over her head, and brought it down onto one of the roots. It recoiled and then darted forward and down again.

"Hey!" Missy yelled, "Hold on!"

Missy brought the paddle down again, feeling the kayak lurching sickeningly from one side to the other. The roots recoiled again and then pummeled back down in the writhing melee under the water.

She brought the paddle down one more time and a hand shot above the water.

"I see you!" Missy yelled and pounded the roots again.

This time, the man was able to bring his face to the water, gasping for breath as the roots wrapped around his chest and neck, trying to strangle him and pull him down below the surface.

"My knife!" he screamed.

Thompson pitched to the side, thrusting his hip toward the surface. He prayed the knife was still attached to his belt.

With her right hand, Missy brought the oar down again on the swirling roots and struggled with her left hand to pull the knife from its sheath. A slithering root snapped at her hand and she brought the oar down again, breaking off a chunk.

Thompson, under the water, dug his fingers underneath where the roots bit into his skin, trying desperately to pull them off. He pushed off them to keep his hip to where the person above the water could get his knife.

Thompson felt whoever it was yank and pull on his belt, and his chest seared with the effort of holding his breath, trying to keep steady.

Above the water, Missy yanked again on the knife, finally freeing it. She slipped back into the kayak, feeling it tilt left and then right. She clung to both sides, trying to steady it as she bent forward toward the water, knife overhead.

Dropping the paddle to the kayak's shallow surface, Missy tried to stay away from the man's body as she slashed at the roots.

The roots recoiled and shrank away from the knife, snapping back to the island. The man below the surface of the water gasped for air and outstretched his hand to Missy and she realized with a start that it was the police officer who they had been to visit just the morning before, Officer Thompson.

"Give me the knife!" he gasped.

Missy realized with horror that the roots had wound themselves around his throat.

His eyes bulged and the finger on his other hand tried to dig their way between the roots and his windpipe.

Missy put the knife in his hand and watched as he went back below the surface of the water. The bayou churned, and Missy clutched desperately at the sides of the kayak, trying to keep it steady. The rain pelted her face as tried to see what was happening below her.

Thompson took his hunting knife and slashed the roots at his throat, feeling them shrink away with each cut. As he felt the roots release him, Thompson swam wildly away from the island.

"Wait!" Missy yelled straining to be heard over the rain. She grabbed the oar and paddled after him, looking over her shoulder as she went.

Thompson clutched the knife in his hand, vaguely aware the woman was following him in her kayak, yelling. When he touched a tree trunk with his hand, Thompson screamed and recoiled, finally stopping and treading water.

He was gripped by a panic he had never felt before. What was happening was not in the order of things. The wrongness of it coursed through his muscles, through this screaming throat.

He finally recognized that it was Melissa Douglas on a kayak coming toward him but could not process why she would be here.

"Wait!" Missy called again, "We have to get back to shore!"

Thompson looked wildly up at her rain drops pelting his face, "How do we get back to shore? I don't know!"

Missy looked down at the compass on the front of the boat and pointed to her left, "That way! Can you swim behind me?"

Thompson gasped for air and nodded, looking over Missy's shoulder toward the root island.

"Keep that knife out!" Missy yelled, paddling as fast as she could.

"Nooo," Thompson moaned softly.

Missy felt the kayak lurch sickeningly to one side as Officer Thompson went limp. She turned and looked at his ragged face and followed his gaze back to the little island.

The Swamp Woman, green and rotting, her naked body a torment of oozing pus and dangling skin stood on the bank of the island, watching them. Behind her, the roots swirled.

Missy turned and recoiled, and instinctively clutched the soggy bag of herbs from Rainbow where they hung at her chest.

Thompson held the knife over his head, treading water with his feet.

"Stay back!"

The Swamp Woman snarled but didn't move off the island. The water around it had settled also, and the pond was calm except for the rain marring its surface.

Missy turned and started paddling the kayak in the direction of Trenise's house. Thompson, his limbs moving jerkily with exhaustion and spent adrenaline, followed Missy, watching the Swamp Woman as he swam, knife still held aloft.

The Swamp Woman turned her head slowly and watched them go, her job, for now, finished.

—

Trenise and Alessandra stood helplessly on the bank, soaked with rain, watching the edge of the swamp.

Alessandra started when she heard Missy's voice yell, barely audible above the rain.

"What did she-"

Alessandra cut herself off as she turned toward Trenise. Trenise wasn't looking into the swamp but was instead looking back toward her house.

Halfway up the lawn, Trent stood, smiling, chest heaving. Trenise couldn't understand the person before her, totally unrecognizable from the spoiled teenaged boy she taught at Stone River High School.

Trent looked deranged. She could see the bubbled, burned flesh on Trent's throat and face from where the homeless girl's ring and Missy's bat had burned him the night before.

"Run, Alessandra." Trenise said softly.

"Run, where?" Alessandra asked breathlessly.

"Go around the side," she said softly, eyes on Trent. "Get to the car and get the tool from your Uncle."

"What about you?" Alessandra asked desperately.

Trenise looked away from Trent for a moment and smiled at Alessandra in the rain.

"I'll be ok. Just get the bar and come back to help me."

Alessandra nodded and slowly moved to her left, trying to flank Trent to get to the car.

Trent watched her go and began to move in the same direction.

"Just come with me, Alessandra, and I'll leave them. I already have the Bible. Just come with me."

Trent spoke calmly, and Alessandra thought his voice sounded different. Older.

"Fuck you, Trent," Alessandra spat.

"Hey!" Trenise yelled, and moved forward, "You're not taking her, Trent."

Trent smiled again and advanced on Trenise. Alessandra darted around him, and he lunged for her. As he did, Trenise clasped her hands together creating a large fist and swung them, connecting with the back of Trent's neck.

It was like hitting a concrete pillar. Trenise lost her balance and fell in the mud. She watched as Trent slowed and turned back toward her, allowing Alessandra to run past him up toward the car.

Trent kicked out and connected with Trenise's face with a booted foot. Trenise howled in pain as she felt her nose smash. She rolled away from him and slipped, desperately trying to get away from him as he stomped with his foot. Trent connected again with her stomach, and Trenise rolled herself down the slope of the lawn, using the mud to propel herself away.

He stomped down again next to her, and Trenise felt her head and neck jerk back down to the ground as he caught the dog tags hanging around her neck. She could smell burning rubber and hear the hissing as the metal tags burned through the bottom of Trent's boot.

He pulled his foot back for a moment, then bore down on her again as she desperately used the mud to slip away.

In the driveway, Alessandra pulled the handle of the door and screamed in fury to find it locked. She looked around her desperately, and then ran for the patio under the house to find something to break the window.

Trenise gasped through her open mouth for air and was able to scramble to her feet, backing away from Trent as he mercilessly gained ground on her.

Tasting blood in her mouth and throat from her nose, Trenise put one hand up in front of her face, the guard stance she'd learned in her hand-to-hand combat training and hit out at Trent with her right hand.

She aimed not for his nose or eyes, but for the blisters on his neck. Trenise watched in satisfaction as Trent howled and crumpled, slipping in the mud as she had done. Trenise raised a leg to kick him in the face, but Trent rolled away and with an uncanny speed turned, lifted her above his head, and threw her down on her back in the mud.

Alessandra ran back across the lawn as fast as she could through the slippery mud and grass. She lifted the chair over her shoulder and swung as hard as she could toward the window, connecting with it and only causing a small crack.

Panicking, Alessandra looked down toward the bank of the bayou and saw Trent lift Ms. Jones above his head like a ragdoll. She watched as Ms. Jones thrashed in the air trying to free herself.

Alessandra swung again and connected halfway down the door causing a large dent. She screamed and turned again to watch in horror as Trent threw Ms. Jones down the lawn and toward the bayou.

Trenise felt only the sensation of free falling, felt her body land, and heard her head hit the ground with a thud. She raised herself on one shaky hand, but her eyes wouldn't focus on the world around her.

Instead, she could only turn her neck a fraction to watch as Trent turned away from her and strode up the lawn toward Alessandra.

"Hey, you chicken shit punk!" Trenise yelled, her voice croaking, trying to lift herself up higher, "Come back here!"

She heard Trent laugh, but he didn't stop.

"Alessandra!" Trenise tried to scream, but her voice again was only a croak, "Run!"

Trenise strained to see if Alessandra had managed to get her uncle's tool, but her eyes still refused to focus. Instead, she groaned and pulled herself forward on her elbows through the mud.

Alessandra stood next to Ms. Jones's car. She knew she had to move but her body refused. Her hands gripped the chair, and she watched Trent walk toward her. Her legs felt like jelly and her heart pounded.

"Shit," she whimpered and raised the chair to hit the window again. This time it connected, and the glass shattered.

Scrambling her hand through the open window, Alessandra felt desperately for the lock, turning her head to watch as Trent walked slowly toward her.

She could see Berto's breaker bar but couldn't find the lock.

Trent was a few feet from her when she hoisted herself through the window, fingertips grazing her backpack.

"Gotcha," Alessandra breathed.

"Gotcha," Trent smiled.

Alessandra felt his hand close around her ankle, felt the edge of the car door cut her stomach as she was pulled backwards. The sachet full of herbs from Rainbow ripped and scattered to the ground and were quickly washed away by the rain.

Alessandra yanked the backpack with her, hitting her face and chin on the driveway as Trent pulled her out of the car.

One hand still on the strap of her back, hand only a few inches from the breaker bar, Alessandra rolled over in time to watch as Trent's fist connected with her temple.

Down the lawn, Trenise howled in pain and fear as she watched Trent rip Alessandra from the car, pummel her in the head, and then hoist her limp body over his shoulder.

"You put her down Trent Longue!" Trenise screamed uselessly. She managed to pull herself to her feet, staggered and fell to one knee.

Trent walked in front of her house, and Trenise lost sight of him.

Terrified, Trenise got up again and staggered to where her car was parked just in time to see a huge red truck peel out from the back of Rita's lawn, speed down her street and turn right onto the main road.

—

Missy paddled frantically to the shore, turning to check on Officer Thompson as often as she dared. His face was a tangle of cuts, and bruises were already visible. His skin was waxy and gray in the murky swamp water.

Missy pushed the kayak forward and finally could see the top of Trenise's house. Her arms burned, and the rain lashed at her face.

Through the noise from the rain hitting the water and the splashing of the paddle, she could hear Trenise scream. She noticed vaguely that Thompson was now able to stand and was moving as quickly as he could through the water, half running, half swimming, shoving his hunting knife pack into its sheath as he went, pulling ahead of her.

The muscles in her arms seared with exertion as she and Thompson broke the tree line. Missy scanned the yard for Trenise and Alessandra.

Trenise slumped onto the rocks that lined the plantings around her front stairs. The thunder crashed and the rain pelted her ruined nose, sending shocks of pain through her face and neck.

Missy jumped out of the kayak and into the water, grasping at the mud along the bank to pull herself out. Thompson made it into the yard first, calling Trenise and Alessandra's names as he went.

Sobbing, Trenise turned and watched as Missy pulled herself out of the water and ran wildly up the yard.

"Here!" Trenise yelled, "I'm here!"

"Trenise!" Missy focused on where Trenise was draped into a flower bed and sprinted toward her.

Thompson followed and skidded to a stop, falling next to Trenise.

"Trenise, where's Alessandra?"

Trenise sobbed and clutched her head, "He took her, Missy. Her and the Bible."

Missy wailed and sunk down to her knees, clutching Trenise to her.

Thompson sat helplessly in the mud, watching the two women and wondering at the mess he had stumbled into.

You shouldn't be here, he told himself shuddering. He looked back down the lawn toward the swamp where he knew the Swamp Woman still lingered, somewhere.

"Come on," he finally said to them, pulling them both to standing by the elbows. His hands were riddled with cuts from the cypress roots. Both women let him guide them under the porch and out of the unrelenting rain.

Under the porch, the wind howled, and the sky darkened. Missy jumped as two of the chairs under the porch tipped and fell to the ground with a clatter.

Wispy fine hairs pulled themselves off of Trenise's temples and formed a halo around her head, her normally neat and tidy hair frizzed from the rain and the mud. The hair on Missy's arms stood on end.

"Do you smell that?" she whispered.

Thompson walked to the edge of the house and stuck his head out to look at the sky. The clouds rushed overhead and turned from dark gray to purple to yellow.

"Mammatus clouds," he said out loud in vague disbelief. He felt his legs freeze up and his stomach seize in horror.

Trenise stared at him, "Tornado."

"Alessandra's bag!" Missy yelled, dashing out to snatch the backpack off the driveway as it started to skitter down the slope of the backyard, scooping up the metal bar that had belonged to Alessandra' uncle and grandfather as she went.

The wind picked up again and rushed through the porch, carrying away Trenise's potted plants and overturning the furniture.

"In the house!" Trenise yelled above the rushing wind.

Missy turn to run back under the porch and was knocked down to one knee.

Thompson felt his legs unfreeze and ran out to drag Missy back under.

"Over here!" Trenise yelled, pointing to a section of the porch that was closed off from the outside.

The wind howled. Trenise and Missy braced themselves against the wall and Thompson put his back to the wind to block as much of it as he could.

The air hummed with electricity. Trenise looked out over her backyard at the leaves and trees blowing in the wind, bending in wild ways. Missy followed her gaze.

"Trenise do you see it?" Missy yelled above the wind.

Trenise nodded and nudged Thompson, pointing toward the bayou.

The leaves and trees swirled, twisting back and forth. Missy saw first a vague shape, round, then oblong. The leaves twisted again, the branches swaying dangerously in the yellow light.

A face. Eyes. A mouth. A snarl.

Thompson listened and heard the sound of a train, the telltale sound that a tornado was imminent if it hadn't touched down somewhere already.

He looked in the direction Trenise pointed, expecting to see the funnel cloud and shouted in surprise at the face in the trees.

"Do not follow," The face mouthed, the words all electric.

"Let her go!" Trenise shouted back.

"Don't hurt her!" Missy screamed at the same time.

The face disappeared back into the mass of leaves.

The air thrummed for a minute or two more, the air rushing away from where Trenise, Missy, and Thompson huddled. As quickly as it started, the wind calmed.

The bruised sky hung low overhead and Trenise and Missy, shoulder to shoulder, stepped out from the patio and into the grass. As far as they could see, branches and trees fell across the road, blocking their way out.

"We can make it," Trenise said calmly, "We can't drive obviously, but we can make it."

Missy walked up to the street and looked at the flat tires on Trenise's SUV and toward the flat tires on Thompson's truck.

She held one hand to her mouth, "We couldn't drive anyway."

"We...we can make it." Trenise said again more firmly. Missy looked at Trenise's gray face, saw her struggling to breathe through her nose.

Missy nodded, "We can make it."

"Not that way, you can't." Thompson said from behind them. "There's no way. I can see powerlines down up there."

"We'll go around them." Missy said firmly, nodded to Trenise.

"You'll get electrocuted."

Trenise ignored him and walked to her car. She unlocked the door with the key that had managed to stay in her pocket and pulled the passenger door open. She crawled in and reached under the front seat, pulling out Missy's brother's bat.

She handed it to Missy.

Trenise took a shaky breath in, "Ok what else do we need?"

"Well, we need to pack up-"

"Are y'all fucking crazy?" Thompson interrupted, throwing his hands up.

Missy and Trenise looked at him and Missy drew in a breath to continue speaking.

"-what we need to burn the Bible, water. Do you have a gun, Trenise?"

"A gun? What are y'all saying?" Thompson recoiled from the fear he heard in his voice, "Y'all cannot just hunt down this kid. And after what I saw out there, I don't think a gun would do you any good anyway."

"Thompson," Trenise said calmly, "You can stay here at my house if you want. But we are leaving."

This is not your fight, he told himself again.

"Call the police," Thompson said, wanting more than anything to believe that this wasn't his fight, "Call the police and let them handle it."

"Handle it like they handled what that kid did to Evie?" Missy spat at him.

Trenise nodded and put her arm around Missy.

Thompson stared at the two women in front of him and ran his hands through his hair.

Are you really going to abandon them, came his mother's voice, soft but strong, *just like you abandoned Elise?*

"You can't go that way. It's not just the downed trees. There are powerlines down," Thompson said again pointing down the street, "But I know a way you can go. One where there are no power lines and that might actually be faster than the roads."

Trenise and Missy looked at each other and then back at Thompson.

"Are you going to tell us?" Missy asked impatiently.

"As soon as you explain to me what the actual fuck is going on here."

—

Trent's heart beat uncomfortably fast. He felt invincible.

Look at what you've accomplished.

He grinned to himself, looking at an unconscious Alessandra slumped on the backseat of his truck. It took all of his willpower not to pullover the truck right here and do what he'd dreamed of for months.

He shook his head. That would come soon enough, he knew.

Trent sped through the neighborhood, vaguely noting the gusting wind behind him. He felt like he was flying. He looked in his rearview mirror again, tipping it down to watch Alessandra.

Emmanuel White's voice snapped him back to reality.

"You'll have time for that soon enough. Now you must hurry."

Trent blinked, sure that White hadn't been sitting next to him a moment before.

"You know what to do?" White asked gently.

Trent nodded, eyes on the road. He felt focused and strong. The blisters on his throat barely hurt anymore and his muscles felt comfortably tight.

"Good," White said, "Because they are coming. One by one, I will take them and become stronger with their sacrifice."

Trent nodded again, but when he looked at the passenger seat, White was gone. Trent allowed his eyes to look in the mirror again at Alessandra. He took in her ripped and bloodied shirt and her long bare legs.

He sighed with longing and drove as fast as he could, wishing with all his might that the other two bitches would get to the clearing sooner rather than later.

—

As quickly as they could, Missy and Trenise took turns explaining the strange and terrifying events of the past three days. Their conversations with Rainbow and Ms. Sarah. Trent and the girl in the French Quarter. Stealing the Bible.

"So, you're really expecting me to believe that a murdering preacher from the 1700s has come back from the dead to possess a neighborhood teenager and force him to rape and murder women?"

Missy and Trenise looked at each other and didn't respond.

"Why though? For what end?"

Missy and Trenise looked at each other again.

"We don't know," Missy said again, "And really it doesn't matter right now. Trent is probably going to rape, torture, and murder Alessandra just like he did Evie and that girl in the graveyard. If he hasn't already."

"That's right," Trenise said, voice husky, "And we don't give a shit if you believe us. We're going to get her."

"Wait," he said softly.

He thought about what they had told him about Missy's bat and the girl in the French Quarter's ring. He thought about how the cypress roots had squirmed away from his knife as he slashed them.

Thompson shuddered and touched the knife where it sat on his hip.

Missy crammed a bottle of lighter fluid, matches, bottles of water, into Alessandra's bag.

"We need to go now. Are you going to help us or not?"

Thompson looked down at his hands and then up at the two women standing before him.

Physically, they were as opposite in every way as they could be. One was dark and one was fair. One had loose, lank, blonde hair and the other had black and gray hair, which had been recently tightly coiled into a bun.

But the looks on their faces were the same.

Thompson stood up, again touching the knife on his hip.

"I'm going to help you."

Thompson turned and walked down the lawn looking to the left and the right. Gesturing to Trenise and Missy to follow him.

"The service lanes run behind all the houses in the subdivision. Except for your street, Trenise, because it's the only one that has direct access to the bayou. Everyone else, I'm guessing, is further away from the water, so there's room for the access lanes."

Missy nodded, "Yes, we have one behind our house. The meter readers use it. It's for water and electric."

Thompson nodded, "So we need to walk through Trenise's yard and down toward the Longue property."

Trenise nodded, pointing to the back of a house on the street behind Rita's. She hoisted Alessandra's bag onto her back.

"It's wooded again there. See? It's wet, but it's not the bayou like it is here."

Thompson smiled, "Then we head that way, find the access lane. I would bet anything that it'll lead right back to the Longue house, back to where the churchyard is."

Chapter Twenty Three

They were silent as they picked their way across Trenise's muddy lawn and into the adjoining property. Trenise felt calmed by the weight of Alessandra's backpack. The breaker bar stuck out of one corner and the lighter fluid, grill lighter and matches rested at the bottom next to Alessandra's wallet and makeup bag.

Trenise had only been in Rita's backyard a few times. She had never been invited over and was always careful to stay in her own yard. She'd learned well enough over the years that some people only needed the smallest excuse to bare their teeth.

Rita's yard was as full of trees and bushes as Trenise's was empty of them. They passed by an open space close to the porch connected to Rita's house and Missy pointed to tire marks left by Trent's truck. The rest of the yard, however, was thick with overgrowth. Even at the edge of the yard, it was hard to see the house that was next to Rita's.

About halfway across Rita's lawn, the bayou faded away and the land became dry again. Trenise could just see the back of the house next to Rita's. It was situated at an angle because it was on the next cul de sac.

Trenise had no idea who lived there. The house itself wasn't visible from her yard. Straining to see through the trees, Trenise touched her throbbing nose and pulled her hand away quickly when the pain doubled her vision.

Trenise blinked rapidly trying to clear her eyes and looked curiously at Missy and Thompson. She wondered vaguely if Trent's kick to her head had given her a concussion, because what she was seeing didn't make sense.

Fog happened frequently enough in Southeastern Louisiana, but usually only in the winter when the water was warm and the air was cool (or vice versa). But there, in the middle of the summer, hung a low mist, swirling around the trunks of the trees.

Trenise squinted at the mist and then looked again at Missy.

Missy, however, was walking with her head down, picking her way carefully through the mess of branches and leaves and vines. She thought distantly of her children, who she had only briefly spoken to today, who were safe in Tennessee swimming and eating junk food. The guilt she felt in sending them away swept through her again, and she pushed it away with a fierceness that surprised her.

You wanted to send them away, didn't you?

The thought startled her. Missy supposed she *did* want to send them away.

This was all just an excuse, wasn't it? You wanted them gone.

Missy shook her head angrily and turned her thoughts instead to Alessandra who had been chased, hunted, dragged across glass, thrown into the back of a truck like a dog.

Missy felt her chest heave with emotion and desperation. She wanted to be back with her own children, back to some kind of normalcy. Although after this, Missy wondered what normal could even look like.

If there even is an "after this."

Thompson scanned the area around him, moving his head slowly and methodically. He was ashamed that he couldn't get the image of the Swamp Woman and her cypress root snakes out of his mind. Every time he tried to think rationally about where they were going and what they were doing, her face swam back into his mind's eye.

The wrongness of the situation he was in was maddening. Seeing wasn't always believing, but Thompson believed what he saw back there in the swamp.

He allowed his pragmatic side to overtake his rational side. He had the cuts and bruises on his arms and hands to prove he had been attacked. He knew he was awake and aware when the cypress root snakes attacked him. He allowed himself to accept that it was real. For now.

In the deepest pit of his being, Thompson knew the Swamp Woman was still out there. She was out there, abandoned and angry, waiting for him in the swamp.

Abandoned like you abandoned Elise?

He pushed the thought away. His main concern was finding Alessandra Sanchez and stopping Trent Longue. If that meant holding off his disbelief of the supernatural to do it, then so be it. If that meant coming face to face with the Swamp Woman again, then he would be ready for her.

Trenise finally couldn't take it anymore.

"Do y'all not see that?"

"See what?" Thompson asked quickly, pulling his knife out.

Trenise sucked her teeth, "Put that away for now."

Missy looked up at Trenise and then to where she was pointing in front of them.

"Mist?" Missy said hesitantly, but she knew right away that it wasn't mist. She sniffed the air.

"Smoke?"

Trenise shook her head and whispered, "I don't know."

Thompson looked ahead, not speaking yet. To him it looked like the heat waves coming off pavement on a summer day.

Instead of clear waves, though, they were opaque, and instead of lingering toward the ground, the waves went all the way up to the tops of the trees. Thompson craned his neck and looked one way and then the other. The waves seemed to extend as far as he could see.

"I'll bet it goes all the way to the road," Trenise said, "the road around the corner from me which is, I'm sure, blocked by downed trees and powerlines."

Missy nodded silently, "Yeah you're probably right. We're going to have to go through it."

Thompson looked at the two women as they slowly walked toward the edge of Rita's property line. Instead of following them, he walked further down, looking for where the access pathway might be. If there even was one.

He glanced behind him, back toward Trenise's house and could just make out the edge of the swamp. The water had calmed since the rain and wind had stopped. A few birds sang, but it was quiet.

Thompson guessed the power was out for most of Stone River after the storm. The air had the eerie silence that came when the noise of a bad thunderstorm was over.

Missy and Trenise cautiously approached the edge of the mist and peered through it. The sun had started to come out after the storm passed, but on the other side of the mist it looked darker. The sky still had the bruised look that it had when the tornado had just missed them.

"Oil slick?" Missy asked quizzically.

"An old window, almost. The kind with the wavy glass."

Missy nodded.

"Heat shimmer!" Thompson called up the yard.

Trenise looked down at him and nodded.

Slowly, Missy held a hand out toward it.

"Careful now," Trenise admonished.

As Missy's fingertips approached the shimmer in front of her, she could feel a slow burn of static creep up her arm. She pulled her hand back.

"It's electric. Like an electric fence or something" She said, "There's no way we can walk through it, Trenise."

Trenise sighed and said quietly, "There's got to be a way."

"Don't touch it, Officer Thompson!" Missy called.

She heard him chuckle, and then yell, "I wasn't going to!"

Thompson walked parallel to the barrier, picking his way along slowly. Ahead, he could see the backs of houses on a different street begin to appear, dark and strange looking through the mist-wall.

He strained his eyes to see through it, looking for a cleared area on the other side that would indicate where the access lane was. Finally, behind a large oak covered with Spanish moss, Thompson saw clearly a dirt path in between the trees. He could see a swing set in someone's backyard behind the patch of woods, distorted by the barrier. It wound ahead about fifteen feet and then curved to the left, he guessed following the curve of the street that ran parallel to it, at the front of the house.

"Here!" he called out, "I found the access lane!"

Thompson put his hands on his hips, staring at it the strange, shimmering cloudiness in front of him, and waited for Trenise and Missy to pick their ways down to where he was standing.

As he waited for them, Thompson listened.

Nothing. No sirens, no kids playing, no one outside looking at the damage. Nothing.

Thompson's arms crawled with goosebumps.

Missy and Trenise slowly approached and peered through the mist. The three of them stood shoulder to shoulder, each wondering how they could possibly get through.

"I can try and run through?" Thompson asked, hesitantly.

Trenise and Missy both gave him a withering look and stepped away from him toward the barrier to look more closely at it.

"It's electric of some kind," Missy said shaking your head, "It'll probably kill you."

Trenise nodded her head in agreement and looked in either direction along the barrier. It extended as far as she could see both ways.

"We could follow it and see if it ends?" Missy asked, following Trenise's gaze.

"That's a lot of time to take, Miss." Trenise shook her head.

"Maybe I can touch it with the bat? See if it resists?" Missy asked.

"I don't know, Missy."

"What do you think Officer Thompson?" she turned to look at Thompson to find him standing a few feet behind them now facing back toward Trenise's house.

"Officer Thompson?" Trenise asked.

"Thompson?" Missy echoed.

He held a hand up for them to be quiet and both women froze, searching the area behind Rita's house.

"There," he whispered.

"I don't see anything," Missy said, looking at Trenise.

Trenise shrugged.

"Listen," Thompson said again.

Missy and Trenise looked out into the brush and trees and reached out to each other when they heard it.

"It's her," Thompson whispered and pulled his knife out of his pocket.

The sound was wet and squelching, the sound of mud and muck being moved. Missy thought of the bugs eating each other in her bathtub and retched. The sound echoed, too loudly, from the area behind Trenise's house.

"If either one of you have an idea of how to get through there, you might want to get to it."

Missy turned around and ran the few steps back toward the barrier, glancing over her should as she did. Thompson and Trenise stood shoulder to shoulder, trying to block Missy from whatever was coming.

"Where's little Duane Thompson?" a woman's voice yelled.

Trenise glanced at Thompson and watched the color drain from his face, watched his chest heave.

"Who is she?" she whispered, still scanning the woods for a glimpse of her.

"The Swamp Woman," Thompson croaked, "She was murdered out in the swamp. They...they used to tell me stories about her, my cousins I mean. When I was a kid it scared me and my mom lied and told me it wasn't true."

He glanced at Trenise.

"But it was true, Ms. Jones. It really happened. And that was her out there in the swamp behind your house."

"Little Duane Thompson!" the voice came again, "I'm waiting here for you Duanie! Your mama lied to you!"

The voice laughed.

"Missy," Trenise hissed, "hurry up."

Missy tried to block out the Swamp Woman's voice and focus on the barrier ahead of her, building up her courage.

She lifted the bat and brought it close to the barrier, waiting to see if she felt the same electric current. Instead, she was surprised at the feeling of coolness.

Slowly, Missy touched the bat to the barrier. She felt nothing.

She pressed the bat forward and felt it slowly move through the mist to the other side. Missy held the bat with two hands and made a circular motion. She watched as the bat cut through the electricity of the mist and form a small opening.

Missy pressed harder and tried to make the circle wider, turning the bat slowly and methodically. Watching as the opening she'd created tried to shrink again, she moved the bat faster, making wider circles.

Trenise turned away from the sound of the Swamp Woman's voice again, closer now.

"Little Duane Thompson!"

"Thompson!" Trenise whispered, "Ignore it! Come help Missy."

But Thompson stood, frozen, staring off into the woods behind Rita's house and into the swamp.

"They told me she comes from you when you're lost and alone. That she's rotten and naked and she...," Thompson swallowed with a dry click,

"...she comes for you and takes you away, and you rot away in the swamp forever with the maggots and the snakes..."

Trenise turned back to Missy desperately, watching as the circle she was making with the bat grew slowly wider. It was almost three feet in diameter now and Missy continued her circles making the hole grow larger.

The Swamp Woman's laugh echoed again, and Trenise put her hand on Thompson's arm.

"You aren't alone, Duane," Trenise said calmly, "And you're not lost."

Thompson turned and looked at her desperately.

"I am lost, Ms. Jones. You don't know what I've done."

Trenise nodded at him, "I don't care what you've done. I'm here with you. We're here."

The Swamp Woman's watery, rotten laugh bubbled through the trees again, and Trenise scanned the trees looking for her.

"I know you're a liar Duane Thompson. And a coward."

Next to her, Thompson moaned and choked. He raised a hand and pointed.

"Oh my God."

Trenise gasped at how close she was to them, no more than 20 feet away. She watched as the Swamp Woman slithered along on two legs, moving this way and that like a muddy current.

The Swamp Woman smiled.

"Little Duane. Little Duanie. Why didn't you listen to your mama?"

Thompson moaned, and Trenise pulled him back toward the barrier where Missy was carving the hole.

"I said, why didn't you listen to your mama, Duanie? You know your mama would've been so ashamed of how you left that girl."

"I didn't," Thompson choked again.

The Swamp Woman nodded, "You did. I know you did. She was going to have your baby, and you left her."

Trenise glanced at Thompson helplessly, "Don't listen to her Duane. Whatever you did, you can make amends."

"Tell her it's true," the Swamp Woman hissed.

"It's true," Thompson whispered obediently, "My girlfriend. Elise. She told me she was pregnant, and I didn't want it. I told her abort it. I told her go home to her parents and don't contact me again."

Trenise shook her head, "Listen to me, Duane, you can make it right."

"I told her I hated her," he sobbed.

"Missy!" Trenise hissed.

Missy had the circle opened large enough from the ground up that one of her children could've wriggled through. Sweat poured down her face and she wound her circle.

"Almost there."

The Swamp Woman nodded.

"She didn't go to her parents Duane. She was too ashamed. Do you know what she did instead?"

Thompson sobbed, "Yes. I left her alone. She did it alone."

"Duane, listen to me," Trenise tried to keep her voice calm and even, tried to keep from shaking as the Swamp Woman crept closer to them, "whatever you did, you can make amends later. We need you here now, Duane."

The Swamp Woman laughed again and paused, watching Thompson sob, seeming to relish the pain she was causing him.

Trenise tore her eyes away from the Swamp Woman's rotten body. She was so close Trenise could see the worms writhing through the open pieces of flesh that hung from her deteriorating frame.

Trenise grabbed Thompson by the shoulder and shook him.

"Duane you need to squeeze through the hole Missy made. You have to get away from her."

"You can't get away from me, Duane Thompson."

"You can just get the fuck back," Trenise yelled.

The Swamp Woman turned her eyes to Trenise and growled.

"You know I've always been back there, Trenise Jones?" she croaked, "I've been watching you forever. You and your little girl."

Trenise ignored her and pulled Thompson backwards toward the mist.

"Thompson, come on!" Missy yelled in triumph over her shoulder.

She moved the bat in large circles, watching as the barrier tried to close in on itself with every turn. Missy strained to push the barrier back, her arms aching.

She glanced back as Trenise pulled Thompson back towards her away from the snarling corpse.

"Look, Duane. Look what you made!"

The Swamp Woman stopped, gagged, and doubled over. Trenise tried to pull Thompson toward Missy, she yanked on his shoulder, grabbed his wrist and pulled back, but he shook her off, staring instead as the Swamp Woman gagged and vomited out ropey black slime.

Trenise stopped trying to pull Thomspon's arm and covered her mouth and nose with her hand, gagging at the smell.

The Swamp Woman straightened again and smiled, holding her arms out wide.

"Look, Duane."

Thompson covered his mouth with his hands. He choked and sobbed but couldn't look away as the Swamp Woman's stomach swelled and puffed, rounding outward.

Trenise felt her eyes bulge, and she shook her head in horror and disbelief. The Swamp Woman's stomach swelled to an unimaginable size, filled with some monstrous offspring.

"Trenise! What's happening?" Missy screeched, arms aching from the effort of turning the bat, "Trenise!"

Glancing over her shoulder again, Missy witnessed the Swamp Woman's wretched labor as she strained and pushed. A head appeared first from the Swamp Woman's gaping underside as she squat, a screaming infant made of festering rot.

Missy, Trenise, and Thompson screamed simultaneously, their voices shrill and feral.

The Swamp Woman groaned. The infant fell from her body with a wet splatter, mewling and writhing in the dirt.

The Swamp Woman stepped over the baby and slowly walked toward Thompson, whose eyes were fixed on the creature in the dirt.

"Stay away," the Swamp Woman growled at Trenise as she tried to approach Thompson again.

Thompson stared and remembered Elise's face when she told him she was pregnant. Her hope and fear. Her anger and hurt when he got up and left. How pathetic he had found her when she begged him to reconsider after he told her to go home to Waveland, Mississippi where her parents were.

Thompson tore his eyes away from the Swamp Woman and looked at the woman on the ground behind him, straining to keep a pathway open and to the women next to him who had told him he wasn't alone.

He looked again at the baby in the dirt, covered with the same maggot and rot that its mother was. He wondered vaguely if Elise had terminated his child or not. He didn't know and hadn't cared up until this moment. She was on her own, that's what he had told her.

Not for the first time in his life, Thompson wondered if he was a good man or a bad one.

He reached down and touched the knife on his hip and felt its cool metal.

Alive, his mother's voice whispered to him, *your baby is alive.*

Thompson sobbed as the Swamp woman advanced slowly, not daring to believe it.

"Duane..." Trenise's voice was soft and firm as she repeated, "whatever you did, you can still make amends."

The Swamp Woman was so close to him now that he thought he would vomit at the smell. A worm buried itself into the flesh of her lip, but she didn't seem to notice.

"We didn't deserve what happened to us, Duane. Me or Elise."

The Swamp Woman spoke softly in a voice that almost showed tenderness. Behind her, her child screamed in a watery voice and clawed at the air.

"But you do. You deserve this."

"I can help you," Thompson whispered, "both of you."

The Swamp Woman nodded, reached out and grasped Thompson's hand in her own.

"Come with us," she whispered.

Thompson looked down and watched as maggots and slime crept onto his hand, engulfing it.

He locked eyes with the Swamp Woman, reached down with his free hand, and quickly unsheathed his knife. Calmly, holding his breath, he drove the blade into the Swamp Woman's chest. He held her hand tightly and brought the knife up toward her sternum, trying to make quick work of it, to put her out of her misery as quickly as possible, just as he did after he had shot a deer.

Thompson had prepared himself for the same level of fight as he had experienced back in the water, had prepared himself that she would smother him to death with mud, but that Missy and Trenise would at least have enough time to escape through the barrier.

Instead, the Swamp Woman's eyes grew wide, and the sound of rushing water came from every inch of her body. The screaming infant fell silent and stopped moving.

Thompson cradled the Swamp Woman's body as it crumpled into his own and he gently laid her on the ground.

Missy watched over her shoulder, groaning with the effort of keeping the hole open, as Thompson pulled the woman's corpse over a few feet and gently laid it next to the baby. The sound of water grew louder, and the bodies bubbled and fizzed. Thompson sat beside them and watched as the Swamp Woman and her child disintegrated into the ground.

He sobbed for the woman and her child, abandoned to die in the swamp. He sobbed for Elise and his own child who he had abandoned somewhere out in the world.

Gently, Trenise put a firm hand on his shoulder and this time, Thompson allowed her to guide him toward the barrier.

Missy glanced up at them.

"You two first and then I'll jump in after."

Trenise looked at Thompson, "Are you sure you still want to come with us?"

HE nodded, looking from Trenise to Missy and back behind him to the smoldering wet spot that had become the Swamp Woman's final resting place.

Trenise nodded back, looked at Missy's red, sweating face and shimmied on her stomach through the open space in the barrier. Thompson followed.

Missy angled her body so that she could continue turning the bat as she herself shimmied through. For a moment, she was in the middle of the barrier, seeing the world she knew behind her and, turning her head, saw the world in front of her, covered in a rank mist.

Missy turned her arm in a circle one more time, the muscles in her arms screaming with exertion, and pulled her leg through. She fell on her back, clutching the bat to her heaving chest.

Trenise and Thompson bent over her and helped her to her feet.

Ahead of her, on the other side of the barrier, was a slim path that ran alongside a deep ditch. Here however, Missy could see the same hazy barrier on both the right and left sides of the path.

Trenise noticed her gaze and nodded.

"Only way is forward."

Thompson clutched his knife in his hand, tears still wet on his face.

"I'm going to go first. Missy, keep your bat ready."

Trenise clutched her dog tags in one hand and Missy's elbow in the other, wondering with dread what else lay on the path in front of them, the path she hoped would take them to Alessandra.

Chapter Twenty Four

Alessandra slowly became aware of first her feet, then her legs. She tried to open her eyes, but the pain all over her body, especially in her head, made it impossible.

She was lying on her back and tried to lift a hand to feel her head. Her right hand was caught in something. She tried to roll over, disoriented, wondering vaguely if she was late for work and if she had smoked too much weed the night before, leading to this monstrous hangover.

Alessandra lifted her right hand again and felt her left hand come along with it, her shoulders aching.

"Oh! You're awake!"

Alessandra snapped her eyes open and pulled herself up to sitting, sending chunks of dirt and rocks flying with her feet as she pushed herself away from the sound of the voice. Her back bumped into something solid, and she pushed up against it. Her hands were tied at the wrists, and she strained to pull them free.

"Don't be like that, Alessandra," the voice scolded, "It's ok, really."

Alessandra looked around and recognized with horror exactly where she was. She looked past where Trent was standing in the middle of the clearing and then over her shoulder.

"No," she cried and scrambled on her knees and elbows away from the gravestone she was leaning up against.

She looked at the ground around her, trying to remember where the open grave was, the grave that led into the abyss.

Trent, seeming to read her mind, said quietly, "Don't worry, Alessandra. I already filled it in. See?"

He pointed behind her and then turned his back, heaving chunks of wood into a pile in front of him.

Alessandra breathed heavily and hoisted herself to standing.

"Trent," she said firmly, "You can't do this. Whatever it is you're doing. You can't do this. Please let me go."

Trent stopped throwing the wood and turned to look at her.

Alessandra gasped at the angry blisters all over the side of his face and neck. She put her hand over her mouth when she realized it was the damage from Missy's bat and Baby's ring. She guessed her backpack was long gone and longed with an aching sadness and anger for Tio Berto's breaker bar, wondering if it would have the same effect on the monster in front of her.

"I can do whatever I want Alessandra. And I'm going to."

"Trent, Trenise and Missy probably already called the cops."

"No, they didn't!" Trent said brightly, "They're trying to come find you!"

Alessandra stared at him, "You don't know that."

Trent smiled, "Yes, I do! Which is great! Because either they'll die along the way, or they'll die here."

He shrugged,"

Reverend White says it doesn't really matter either way."

"R-reverend White?"

Alessandra backed out of the graveyard, toward where she knew there was the path that led to the road. She remembered coming down it with Trenise and Missy only yesterday morning.

Trent followed her with his eyes and nodded, "He can tell you about it."

Alessandra turned to run and slammed into a man about Trent's height, but with a slightly smaller frame. He was strong enough to block her path, to place both hands on her shoulders and stop her from running.

"Stop," the man said softly.

Alessandra whimpered and tried to shrink away from the man's grip, but his fingers tightened, and he steered her back toward the cemetery.

Alessandra pulled away again, and the man gestured to Trent to come toward them.

Trent nodded and approached Alessandra calmly, picked her up and slung her over his shoulder.

Alessandra screamed and punched the back of his head. She kicked her legs, flailing, connecting with Trent's chest and neck. She reached around and scratched at Trent's blistered face.

He howled and threw her up against a gravestone, "You fucking bitch!"

Alessandra looked up at him and tried to roll away, to get to her feet to run again.

Trent reached down and pushed on her back, pinning her facedown in the cemetery dirt.

"Better bind her feet as well, Trent," White whispered.

He bent down and put his face close to hers, his blue eyes cold and relentless.

"Stop this now, or I'll kill you."

Alessandra froze as the pressure on her back lessened. She moved slightly, trying to get away again, and the pressure quickly returned as Trent turned and put his knee on the small of her back. Alessandra kicked both legs at him and he squeezed them together. Alessandra felt rope twist around them.

Her chest heaved and she tried to keep her face out of the dirt, scared she would asphyxiate.

Maybe it's a dream, she thought desperately, *maybe I got knocked out in a car accident and I'm hallucinating.*

Emmanuel White brought his face even closer to hers.

"It's not a dream. It's a new world, Alessandra. And you're going to be part of it."

"Fuck you," Alessandra huffed.

White's face remained unchanged, "You don't believe it?"

"I don't give a shit."

"You will. I promise you will."

—

The path was so narrow that they were forced to walk single file. Missy went first with her bat held high over her shoulder, Thompson was silent in the middle, and Trenise was at the back, checking periodically over her shoulder.

She swore twice that something moved from one side of the barrier to the other, scuttling across the path behind them, but she couldn't be sure.

"How long do you think until we get close to the Longue house?" Missy asked in a whisper.

"It's at least three miles to where our subdivision ends and meets the beginning of their property. Past that, I can't say," Trenise whispered back.

Missy quickened her step, "He's got her in that graveyard, doesn't he?"

Trenise hesitated. She watched a shudder rake through Missy's body and the bat dip down for a moment.

"Yes. I think he probably does."

Thompson was silent still, thinking of his own stupidity and laziness. He had been right there, talking to Trent Longue the day before. And he did nothing. He shook his head, furious at himself.

"You ok, Thompson?" Trenise asked softly.

He glared over his shoulder at her.

"No, I'm not."

Missy swept her eyes from one side of the narrow path to the other, trying to see through the mist barrier. The swirling fog that coated the ground seemed to be increasing, creeping up so that it was waist level and then eye level.

"Trenise," Missy whispered urgently as she half-walked, half-jogged, "The fog is thicker up here and there's a bend in the path."

"I see," Trenise called hoarsely, "You want me to go up front?"

Missy guessed the path curved sharply behind the house at the end of a cul-de-sac, just like it did around her own house. She paused briefly, trying to crane her head so that she could see around the bend.

She furrowed her eyebrows, "It looks like the fog is clearing up a little. Maybe it's a break in the barrier!"

Missy darted forward at a run around the bend in the path. As she turned the corner, she gasped and squinted at the sudden bright sunlight. She dropped her bat and shielded her eyes with her hand.

A soft wind blew around her that felt more like spring- cool and dry. Missy heard birds and smelled jasmine. She looked around, dazed by the bright sun, and saw the leaves on the trees were small, half-formed, filled with buds. The lush greenery of the Louisiana summer was gone.

The barrier was gone and so was the path. Trenise was gone and so was Officer Thompson. Dazed, Missy walked forward, looking around her feet at the green grass, the small flowers.

Missy was alone, and then suddenly found herself standing on a stone patio, flat and worn.

"Are you lost, my darling?"

Missy turned her head slowly toward the sound of the voice. The patio where she stood was at the bottom of a wide staircase that led up to an enormous antebellum house.

Missy could see a deep porch wrapped around the front and sides of the house. The porch was shaded from bright spring sunlight and held beautiful sets of white wicker furniture. The plantation-style windows, long and even, were open to let the cool air inside. White, gauzy curtains blew in every window, bright against the green trim of the sills.

"Do you like our house, Melissa?"

Missy looked from the house to the two young women sitting in front of it at the foot of the stairs. A large oak tree hung over the stone patio, its just blooming leaves shading the two women and the white wrought iron garden chairs on which they sat.

"Would you like to come and sit with us, Melissa?"

Missy stepped forward, looking around in wonder at the beauty of the scenery and the women before her. She looked up at the sky and marveled at its blueness. Had she ever seen a sky so blue before?

"It *is* a beautiful day, isn't it, Melissa?" one of the women said happily.

"It is a beautiful day," Missy heard herself repeat with awe.

One of the women gestured to an open chair, and Missy sat down obediently.

She stared at one woman and then the next. They weren't sisters, Missy could see that, but they were equally beautiful. The woman on Missy's left, closest to the oak tree was blond and small, smaller than Missy, with bright blue eyes and a laughing mouth.

On Missy's left, closest to the house, the woman was a dark brunette with large hazel eyes. Both wore dresses that looked like the same gauzy white material of the curtains in the windows. The styles were old-fashioned. High necked, sinched waists, skirts flowing along on the stones below them. The fabric looked soft and cool and blew gently in the breeze.

Missy could feel herself staring and noticed as the women exchanged a glance and small smile between them. The blonde looked familiar to Missy, but she couldn't quite place where she knew her from. Missy looked down, feeling embarrassed.

The brunette reached out and squeezed Missy's hand, "It *is* a beautiful day, isn't it Melissa? And it *is* a beautiful house?"

"Yes," Missy answered, nodding, "You both are so beautiful too."

The blond laughed merrily and clapped her hands together, "Oh I like her!"

The brunette smiled gently, "I like her too, Camille."

Missy smiled at them both and looked again at the house over the brunette's shoulder. She could see now that behind it was a large garden, only beginning to flower. An arbor covered with vines stood at the opening of a winding path.

Missy put her forehead in her hand. A wisp of a memory of another path crossed her mind and then was gone.

She looked up at the two women who were watching her intently.

"Are you alright, Melissa?" the brunette asked.

"Yes. I'm remembering something. I was walking on a path. I think I was trying to go somewhere."

She looked from one woman to the other. Neither spoke, but they watched her with concerned eyes.

"I think I might be lost."

Both women remained silent and Missy looked around herself, wondering where she had come from.

She noticed a swing in the oak tree and grinned.

"I like the swing too," Camille whispered conspiratorially, following Missy's gaze. She smiled at Missy and giggled.

Her face darkened then, like a cloud passing overhead. Camille leaned forward toward her brunette companion, confused.

"My children liked the swing too, didn't they? Where are they?"

"They did like it. But they died, dear. But that doesn't matter now does it?"

The brunette spoke as though talking to an over tired child.

The younger woman settled back into her seat, regaining her cheery composure.

"No, I suppose it doesn't!"

Missy looked from one woman to the other as they spoke but felt delightfully unconcerned. The faces of two children, a boy and a girl, swam into her brain. She strained to remember who they were and found she couldn't. She felt a nagging sensation of worry about something but couldn't quite put her finger on it

Missy felt the soft wind on her arms and legs and looked down at her old workout shorts, dirty and smelly. She felt her cheeks redden. That must be what she had been worrying about. That she wasn't dressed to be in such a beautiful place.

"I wish I had a beautiful dress like yours," Missy said sadly, looking from one woman to the other again.

"Oh! You may borrow one of ours!" Camille said excitedly. "I have a wardrobe in the house full of beautiful dresses!"

The brunette smiled gently, "And you may borrow mine as well."

Missy smiled and wondered if she had ever been so happy in all her life.

"And then," Camille gushed, "We can have cookies and tea on the porch."

Missy felt herself smile and nod, "That sounds wonderful!"

Somewhere in Missy's mind, she remembered having tea with someone else. She thought it might have been important, but the memory slipped away, leaving Missy to blissfully concentrate on beautiful dresses and tea on the porch.

—

Trenise didn't understand how it happened so quickly. One second Missy was there, right in front of Thompson, then she turned the corner and was out of Trenise's sight for a split second.

"Missy!" Trenise yelled, sprinting forward down the path.

The path was straight and empty for as far as she could see. On each side of her, the electric barrier buzzed, and fog swirled on the other side of it, mostly obscuring anything beyond it.

There were no breaks in the thick mist. Trenise and Thompson were alone on path.

"She must've gone through," Thompson said, "You look on that side, I'll look on the right."

He jogged forward, trying to see if there was any indication of where Missy could've passed through.

Trenise leaned forward, putting her face as close as she dared to where the invisible wall blocked them from leaving the dirt path. She shuddered and jerked backwards.

"Melissa!" Trenise screamed.

Thompson turned and jogged back to where Trenise stood.

"Where?" Thompson asked desperately.

"Try to get through, Thompson! Use your knife!"

Thompson fumbled the knife out of its holster on his hip and tried to cut through the barrier as Missy had done with her bat. The knife quivered and stuck as it sizzled in the electricity of it. Thompson gripped it with two hands and tried to pull up.

"It's moving, but not very much." Thompson huffed.

"Missy!" Trenise screamed again.

She could just see Missy through the thick fog walking slowly through a clearing. Trenise couldn't see any houses, no swing set, no garden.

"Where are we?" she asked Thompson, "There should be a house there."

Thompson shook his head and strained against the barrier. He watched as the knife cut through it and then the space closed in behind it.

"It's not working," he said in a panic, "Trenise, the knife isn't working."

"Keep trying," Trenise said, "Keep trying."

Thompson nodded and pulled the knife down instead of up, hoping that would make a difference.

Trenise turned her attention back to Missy, trying to keep her eyes on her. The fog seemed to be clearing from the ground around Missy's feet as she walked further away from the path.

There should be a house there, Trenise thought doggedly.

Trenise squinted, trying to see past where Missy was, but she couldn't make anything out. She heard voices, muffled and distant but couldn't tell if it was Missy's voice or someone else's.

"Missy!" she screamed again.

Missy turned to the left and Trenise could see her mouth moving, as though she were talking to someone who Trenise couldn't see.

"What is she doing?" Thompson asked as he strained to pull the knife through the barrier, trying to make any kind of dent in it.

"I don't know," Trenise said desperately, "It looks like she's talking to someone."

"Is it Trent?"

"I don't think so. She's not even looking for us. What is she doing?"

Thompson looked up from his work, trying to make out what was behind the haze of the barrier, past the cleared area that Missy walked through.

"What is that, Trenise?"

"It looked like a table. She's sitting at a table."

"No, no, to the right of her."

Trenise sucked in her breath.

Thompson looked down at her and back again, "Is it a mausoleum?"

Trenise nodded slowly, "Keep trying the knife, Thompson."

She looked back toward Missy, helplessly.

"Missy!" she screamed, "Whatever it's saying don't listen to it!"

—

"Melissa? Are you alright, dear?"

Missy nodded slowly, wondering briefly what she had been thinking about. It was something about another young woman. She squinted, trying to remember. It was something to do with the color blue.

"I'm thinking about something blue." Missy said uncertainly. Looking from one woman to the other again. "It was something I was looking for, and it was something blue."

"Hmm," said the brunette softly, placing her delicate chin on her hand, "Is it the beautiful blue sky above us, Melissa?"

Camille looked up obediently and leaned back in her chair, smiling.

Melissa looked up as well, taking in the electric blue overhead. Puffy clouds drifted above them, echoing the soft breeze Missy could feel in her hair and on her arms and legs.

"Camille," the brunette said, breaking their silence, "Why don't you and Melissa walk up to the house, so that she can pick which of your dresses she would like to wear."

She looked pointedly at Camille and then over Melissa's shoulder. Camille nodded and stood.

"Melissa, give me your hand," Camille said, smiling, "The house is so cool and calm, and it will feel wonderful to be out of those dirty clothes."

Missy looked down at her hands. She felt like she should have something in her hand, something important. Had she dropped it?

For a moment, Melissa felt like she was going to cry. She didn't want to spoil the beautiful day. She *did* want a beautiful dress. She *did* want to have tea on the beautiful porch.

The feeling that she was forgetting something tickled at the edges of her happiness.

"What's wrong, Melissa?" Camille asked, blue eyes soft and concerned.

"Melissa," said the brunette in a kind but firm voice, "You will feel better once you are changed. Take Camille's hand."

Melissa nodded, knowing she was right, took Camille's outstretched hand, and stood. Camille's hand was cool and dry.

They walked together, hand in hand, toward the house. Melissa could feel the cool air from the darkened plantation creeping down the porch toward her. Closer to the porch now, Melissa noticed a small set of headstones, no more than 10, to her right.

Had they been there all along? Melissa wondered vaguely.

Melissa looked from the headstones to Camille, a question on her lips.

Camille shook her head, and folded her arm over Missy's.

"It's nothing to worry about."

They walked arm in arm toward the porch and Melissa again felt something drift somewhere in her mind. It cut through her happiness and longing to see the inside of the plantation house.

This image was sharper, clearer. A girl lying by a headstone. She was naked from the waist down and her face was gone except for her blond hair.

Melissa stopped and tore her hand out of Camille's, bringing both hands to her mouth in a gasp.

Camille studied her.

"Let it go, Melissa," she said quietly, "You can just let it go."

Missy looked from the house to Camille and then to the brunette, who was now standing next to the little wrought iron table. The woman stared at Missy, her soft dress oscillating in the breeze.

Missy looked up at the blue sky, then scanned around herself, seeing the garden, the gravestones, the large live oaks that dotted the field behind the house. Finally, she turned to see what was behind her and gasped.

Missy looked past the stone patio to the area thick with trees just starting to bud. Fog swirled through the trunks of the trees and beyond that, a haze shimmered and stretched through the woods.

On the other side of the haze, Missy saw two people. One was an older woman with dark skin, with hair pulled into twisted braids flat against her scalp. The other was a very tall young man who was holding a knife. The dark-skinned woman waved her arms urgently, and her lips were moving, but Missy couldn't hear what she was saying. The tall young man was pulling the knife through the haze, his face contorted in concentration

Missy leaned into Camille, clutching her shoulder.

"Who are they, Camille?"

Melissa started at the brunette's voice, close in her ear now, "It doesn't matter. They can't come here."

Missy nodded and smiled and forgot them.

Ahead of her, the crooked gravestones dotted the lawn in front of the large house. Closer to them now, Missy saw that there were more than only a few.

There were stones all the way past the edge of the house and around the side of it. Melissa could just barely read the names on the headstones closest to her.

One said, "Cynthia Devaunt."

She peered at the next gravestone and read, "Alexis Frechette."

Another read, "Alicia Ann Briggs."

The gravestone belonging to Alicia Ann Briggs had a dolphin carved into it.

She took a step forward to read the name on the next closest stone.

"Evangeline Marie Nunez."

The names meant nothing to her.

Missy stopped and saw that there was another gravestone even closer to her, closer to the plantation. The stone was bare. She stared at it for a moment and then back at the screaming woman with the dark skin behind the fog. She looked back in front of her, choosing to ignore the woman as the brunette had instructed.

Camille and the brunette led Missy up the wide white steps of the porch. Missy turned again to look behind her, vaguely wondering at the frantic woman in the distance, trying to make out what she was saying.

Missy put her foot on the first step up to the porch. The faces of two children swirled in front of her eyes. Then the face of a girl with blue hair. Then the face of an old woman, smiling and kind. Melissa faltered and was steadied on either side by Camille and her companion.

"Just let it go," Camille whispered kindly.

The house in front of them felt cool and dry, the white wood and columns gleaming in the shade cast by the roof extending over the wide porch. The tall windows were framed with dark green hurricane shutters on each side.

Missy could see the inside of the house was filled with lush couches, dark wooden tables, and low chandeliers. She smiled to herself, wanting to go into the cool darkness and explore the large rooms.

"Do you like our home?" the brunette asked, as if reading Missy's mind. She held Missy's elbow and three of them stood on the large porch in front of the open door.

Missy looked into the dark house, around the porch that extended the length of the house, and out to the oak trees that surrounded it. She stopped briefly at the sight of the headstones but chose to ignore them.

She nodded and smiled.

"Yes, I do"

"Camille! She loves our house!"

Camille clapped happily, "Will you stay with us Melissa?"

Camille's eyes were wide like a child's and she clasped her hands in front of her chest.

Missy paused and considered the two women and the beautiful home in front of her. Her mind felt clear and empty. She tried to remember why she was there. Did she need a place to live? How had she gotten here?

She looked at the two young women's expectant happy faces and smiled back at them.

"Well, I don't think I have anywhere else to go," Missy said slowly, "So I'll stay!"

The darkhaired woman entered the house first, leaving Missy and Camille on the porch alone.

"Don't worry," Camille whispered, "It doesn't hurt at all."

Missy smiled quizzically.

"It's like drifting away," Camille continued, gazing into Missy's face, "And then you don't have to remember anything anymore."

Missy turned again to look back across the stone patio, to the wood, to the hazy cloud and the screaming woman beyond it. The woman was frantic now, pacing up and down, her face a tortured mask.

"Come with me, Melissa," Camille urged softly, "Sophie is waiting for us inside. And then it will be over."

"Sophie?"

Camille nodded slowly and gestured to the dark-haired woman in the doorway.

"Melissa," Sophie held her hand out, "Take my hand now."

The children's faces swam again, bubbling up from Missy's mind. She saw them clearly now. Sophie. Her little girl. John. Her boy.

Memories flooded back in snapshots. Alessandra's blue hair. Running through the street. An old woman, Cynthia, serving her iced tea.

"Melissa," Sophie's voice was harsh now.

"Sophie, what's happening?" Camille sounded panicked and wrung her hands in front of her.

The woman behind her screaming. The man with the knife. Her brother's baseball bat.

Missy took a step backwards, away from the open door. She turned and looked at Trenise behind her, screaming behind the barrier, gesturing with both hands for Missy to come back.

Turning, Missy leaped off the porch, skipping over all the steps, and landed in a heap in front of the gravestones.

"Melissa, don't!" Camille screamed behind her.

"Melissa!" Sophie's voice was a bark, cold and demanding, "Don't run from it!"

Missy stood and ran back toward Trenise, sobbing. How could she have forgotten her children? How could she have forgotten Alessandra and Trenise and her brother?

"Because of the pain, Melissa!" Sophie yelled from behind her, "Because they are all too painful!"

Missy was close enough to the barrier now to see Trenise a little more clearly. She looked as though she was saying something, but Missy could just barely hear her.

"Trenise!" Missy screamed. She looked over her shoulder to see Camille standing on the porch, face in hands. Sophie was slowly walking across the stone patio, watching Missy intently.

"Get the bat, Missy!" Trenise cupped her hands around her mouth to amplify her voice.

Next to her Thompson had stopped working his knife and frantically pointed at the ground.

Missy turned around and glanced at Sophie as she advanced slowly through the grass toward her. She dove for the bat.

"Missy!" Trenise's voice floated.

"Melissa," Sophie spoke calmly to her left.

Missy raised the bat over her shoulder to swing.

Sophie shook her head gently, "You don't need to do that. You don't need to listen to her."

Missy took a step away from Sophie, backwards toward the barrier.

"You think she wouldn't do the same?" Sophie asked quietly.

Missy shook her head no.

"What are you going to do with that bat?" Sophie asked quietly.

"Just let me go through the barrier, and I won't do anything with it."

Missy looked over Sophie's shoulder as Camille slowly approached to stand behind her.

"I'm not going to let you go, Melissa," Sophie said quietly.

Behind her, Thompson and Trenise stood silent, watching the three women through the barrier.

The birds stopped singing and the air was still. There was no sound except for Missy's own breathing. Then finally, Camille spoke.

"Do it, Missy. Do it now!"

Sophie's face darkened with shock and anger as she turned to face her companion.

Missy heaved the bat across her shoulder and connected first with Sophie's stomach. When she doubled over with a scream, Missy brought the bat up again, hitting her in the face.

Missy expected her to melt like the Swamp Woman or to hear the sickening crunch of bone like when she had hit Trent in the same spots. Instead, Sophie crumbled without a sound and lay in a heap on the grass like a ragdoll.

Camille gasped, knelt down, and cradled Sophie's soft form in her arms.

Missy kept the bat raised above her shoulder, eyes on Camille, as she sobbed.

"Missy!" Thompson and Trenise screamed behind her, "come back through!!"

Missy turned back to look at them and then looked back at Camille. Her blond head was down, and she pressed her cheek up against Sophie's still form. Behind Camille, the white of the house started to turn to gray and then black. The sky overhead turned from bright blue to a dingy yellow. The live oaks drooped, and the buds withered.

Camille looked up at Missy desperately sobbing, "I *remember*."

Missy laid the bat down gently on the grass and watched as the roof of the house shuddered and fell in on itself. A large branch from the oak tree cracked and fell on top of the wrought iron table and chairs.

"Hurry up Missy!" Trenise yelled behind her.

"Will you help me?" Camille asked.

Missy took in a breath and nodded, "What do you need me to do?"

Camille looked behind her out the house and wailed at the sight of it. Missy felt her heart twinge as the porch buckled and fell.

The stillness in the air changed again and Missy felt a hot gust of wind. The yellow sky turned to a dark bruised color as it had earlier at Trenise's house when the tornado came through.

Missy looked at the cemetery by the house.

Missy picked Camille up under her arm and staggered at how light she was.

"Is that where you are, Camille?"

Missy pointed to the rows and rows of gravestones now visible as the house crumbled.

Camille sobbed and nodded. Missy turned her around as though to walk to the cemetery.

"No!" Camille screamed above the wind, "Not without Sophie!"

Missy bent down and picked up Sophie's motionless body, light as a feather. Camille lifted her skirts elegantly and ran ahead of Missy through the graveyard.

Missy watched as Camille looked at each gravestone, reading each name. Finally, almost at the edge of the tombstones, Camille stopped and exclaimed.

"Here!"

Missy skidded to a stop next to her.

Camille slumped down, back leaning up against the gravestone which bore the name, "Camille Constance Louise Girod."

"Give her to me."

Camille held her arms out to Missy, taking Sophie's body from her and cradling her in her lap.

Missy stood, unsure of what to do, as Camille hummed softly, barely audible against the wind.

"Do...do you want me to put her somewhere?"

Camille shook her head gesturing with her chin to the right, "She's there."

Missy looked at the next gravestone. It read, "Sophie Ann Piety Longue."

"Sophie Ann Longue?" Missy said out loud and shuddered.

Camille didn't respond but continued humming and stroking her friend's hair.

"What do I do now, Camille?"

Camille looked up sadly.

"Go now."

She looked towards the house and back to Missy, who hadn't moved.

"Go on," she said again, "Quickly. The house is almost gone. I don't know what will happen to us when it's gone."

"What happened to you, Camille? Was it...him? Was it Emmanuel White?"

Camille smiled sadly, "In a way."

She wailed again as the house folded in once more. Beyond it the fields and flowers turned to yellow dust.

"Go now," Camille said urgently.

Missy nodded, turned, and ran back to the barrier. At the edge of the graveyard, she held out both hands and touched the last four gravestones as she swept past.

Sweeping up the bat, Missy charged at the barrier with the bat in front of her, digging through it with all her strength. A hole formed and Trenise thrust her hands through grabbing Missy by the elbows. Thompson leaned further in, head and torso across the barrier, and pulled Missy by the waistband of her shorts up and through the hole.

The three of them landed hard on the path on the other side.

Missy stood up and peered through the hole as it closed in on itself. The wind tore through the yard that had surrounded the house, demolishing the arbor, sending the flowered bushes into the air. The live oaks toppled.

She saw Camille, motionless, seemingly undisturbed by the destruction around her. Missy's heart wrenched at the loneliness of it.

Camille turned her face bravely into the wind, clutching Sophie's body to her. The sound of the wind was deafening, a howling scream of some childhood monster.

Missy watched as the house crumbled to nothing and only the staircase of the porch was left.

Fog rose up from the ground on the other side of the barrier and the hole Missy had created became smaller and smaller. Missy watched until she could only make out Camille, and Camille alone. She was far off in the distance, a lone figure in a graveyard.

Before the barrier shut itself again, sizzling with electricity as it closed, Camille turned and locked eyes with Missy. Her face with still and solemn as the hole in the barrier closed.

Chapter Twenty Five

Alessandra lay on her stomach, watching. She didn't dare move, so she stayed as still as she could and thought. She watched Trent move from out of her line of vision and then in front of her again, each time carrying brush and throwing it into a pile in the center of the old ruins.

The Preacher, Emmanual White, was nowhere that she could see.

But, she thought to herself, *that doesn't mean he's not here.*

No matter how she looked at it, Alessandra couldn't think of a way out of her situation. Her feet and legs were bound. Her stomach and back ached with the strain of keeping her head up. Finally, Alessandra turned her cheek to the dirt below her, allowing her head to rest on the cool earth.

She turned her head in the opposite direction, allowing the other cheek to rest. Alessandra thought about Trent and what he wanted. A seed of an idea rose in her mind as she asked herself what she would do to live to see her mother again.

Anything, was the answer.

Anything.

Her stomach lurched and Alessandra closed her eyes. She took a long breath in.

"Trent..." she finally called out, softly at first. She took a deep breath and called again, louder, "Hey, Trent!"

His feet came into view.

Alessandra tried to crane her neck to look up at him.

"Can you please sit me up, Trent?"

When he didn't respond again, Alessandra tried to roll over on her side. As she did, Trent bent down and put his hands under her armpits, pulling her up. She sat on her bottom and scooted back toward the gravestone behind her.

"Thank you," she said softly.

Trent crouched down in front of her and ran a finger down the side of her face. Alessandra forced herself not to shudder away. She scanned the area behind Trent and then looked back to Trent. His face looked different.

Last night and this morning he was deranged and terrifying, now Trent looked more like he had in the spring.

"He's gone for now," Trent said with a nervous smile, "He's working somewhere else, putting everything into motion for us."

Alessandra looked at him desperately, "Trent, what does that mean?"

Trent sat heavily in front of her.

"It means that he needs to have strength. He needs to punish the wicked. Like Ms. Jones and her friend."

"...and me?" Alessandra asked.

Trent shook his head, "No, Alessandra. Not you. He promised me."

"But Trent," Alessandra leaned forward, "How do you know he'll keep his word?"

Trent shook his head forcefully, "He will. And he already has!"

Alessandra sighed and tried to inch closer to him.

Trent grinned.

"See?" he said with a laugh, "Here you are!"

Alessandra sighed, "No, Trent. He didn't bring me here. *You did.* Remember? You attacked Ms. Jones, and then you attacked me."

Trent shook his head again, looking at her desperately, "I *had* to Alessandra. I *had* to do that."

"Why, Trent?"

"We needed the Bible that you had, Alessandra. The one you *stole.*"

He pointed behind him to where the Bible rested on the wall of the old, ruined church.

Alessandra nodded, "I know that. But why, Trent?"

"Because that's what's bringing him here, what's keeping him here. Like the paper from the old lady's house."

"What paper, Trent?" Alessandra felt her heart quicken, "What old lady?"

Trent looked at her, "You know which old lady, Alessandra."

"Y-you mean Ms. Cindy?" Alessandra felt a growing dread in her stomach, "What did you do to her Trent?"

Trent shook his head, "You don't understand."

He reached out and touched her face again. Alessandra forced herself to hold his gaze.

"I did all of this for you, Alessandra. So we could be together, so you would understand."

Alessandra inched closer to him trying not to stare at the bubbling wounds on his neck, trying to ignore the stink of sweat, and the bloodstains on his clothes.

"Tell me, Trent. I'll listen."

"I didn't mean to bring him back," Trent whispered, "I really didn't."

Alessandra tried to look sympathetic, "So why is he here Trent? What happened?"

"I didn't mean to. I just wanted her to look at me," Trent's lower lip quivered, "I didn't mean to hurt her."

He lunged forward and threw his arms around Alessandra, sobbing on her shoulder.

Alessandra stiffened and tried not to fall backwards.

"I really didn't want to," he sobbed, "I hit her with the stone I found here when she laughed at me."

"Who, Trent?"

Trent sobbed harder, "Evangeline."

Alessandra sucked in a breath, letting herself be squeezed. Her stomach roiled, and she thought she would vomit. She sobbed with him.

"Trent," she said in a broken voice, "If you didn't mean to...If it was an accident...maybe you can make it right. You can let me go, Trent."

Trent sobbed harder.

"Let me go, Trent, and I can help you."

Trent shuddered against her and pulled back, looking at her intently. Alessandra held his gaze and nodded.

"Just loosen the ropes, Trent, we can leave together."

Trent reached behind her and touched the ropes around her wrists. Alessandra felt a small hope bubble up in her stomach, and she nodded quickly to him.

"Please, Trent."

"I think that's enough."

Trent stood up, wheeling around at the sound of Emmanuel White's voice. Alessandra followed Trent's gaze and gasped.

White stood on the other side of the wood pile. When she had seen him earlier, when Trent's knee was on her back and he had put his face close to hers, she had been terrified by his calm. It seemed unnatural, like a face molded out of resin.

Now, his face was a terror. His eyes bulged and his skin seemed too tight on his skull. The fine blond hair that had been brushed back now hung in frizzy clumps.

"W-what?" Trent stammered, his voice shaking, "What happened?"

Deep red rings were around White's eyelids, making the cold granite blue seem even more striking in his pale face. He heaved a breath and snarled, showing teeth that looked too thick, too long for his mouth.

Trent stumbled forward

"What happened?" he asked again.

White looked past him, staring at Alessandra. She shrunk back against the gravestone, pulling her knees up to her chest.

"They have turned my own servants against me," White whispered, reaching out to Trent, "bring me to her."

Trent put White's arm over his shoulders and helped him limp over to where Alessandra was huddled.

Alessandra looked at White's face and any idea of hope withered. She tried to search for a prayer but couldn't think of one. She tried to think of her mother, but it was so painful she quickly pushed it away.

Instead, Alessandra thought of the girl in the graveyard, the one with no face. Alessandra felt deeply the horror of her death, knowing well both that it had happened either where she was sitting or close to it and that a similar fate probably was waiting for her. Alessandra closed her eyes, took a steadying breath and tried to reach out with her heart to the girl, whoever she was.

Alessandra felt a calm wash over her like warm salt waves. She squeezed her eyes shut even tighter and saw the ocean. She saw a girl sitting in front of the waves, back to her, looking out over calm swells. She could smell the salt air, feel the moisture from the waves on her face. She didn't know who the girl was, but Alessandra could feel that she was waiting for something. Alessandra tried to walk toward her but the sound of someone calling her name pulled her away.

"Alessandra."

When she opened her eyes, Emmanuel White was sitting next to her, his face close to hers again, watching her.

"She can't help you," he whispered, spittle flying from his cracked lips.

Trent looked from White to Alessandra and back at White again, face darkening.

"I need to test your loyalty and strength, Trent." White whispered.

Trent's eyebrows knit together in concern.

"What do you need me to do?"

White looked slowly away from Alessandra to focus on the pile of brush behind Trent.

"I need you to light the fire now."

Trent stood next to White, looking from him to Alessandra.

"Go now, Trent," White said firmly, "Light the fire and then throw in the girl's body from last night."

Trent lingered a moment longer, then turned and walked toward the pile of sticks and logs he had built. He passed it and went into the woods, leaving Alessandra alone with White.

Alessandra felt her chest heave.

"He won't help you, Alessandra," White said quietly.

Alessandra was silent, looking into the woods over White's shoulder.

"Would you like to see what Trent has done to help me? So that you can understand?"

Alessandra shook her head no.

White paused for a moment.

"I think I will show you, Alessandra. You have no faith. You are unclean."

White knelt down next to her.

"It is my job to punish the wicked, Alessandra. I will show you what Trent did so that you know before you die that no help is coming. He won't disobey me. Maybe your suffering will cleanse your spirit."

Alessandra sobbed and closed her eyes.

"That's right," she heard White whisper, "Close your eyes."

—

The world was black. Alessandra saw nothing and heard nothing. She tried to reach out again to find the girl by the ocean and felt nothing. Her fingers and toes felt nothing. She could breathe, was breathing, she could feel her chest rise and fall. Alessandra felt distant, she was *here* but she didn't know what the here was.

The blackness faded from her vision, except for at the edges, as though she were looking through binoculars. It was evening.

She looked down at the ground, but her feet were not there. She held up her hand in front of her eyes, but her hand was not there.

Her brain refused to understand, so instead, Alessandra looked straight ahead. At the trailer where she lived with her mother. Her mother's car was in the driveway. Her own car was in the driveway. She saw herself get out of her car and slowly walk up the stairs to the front door of the trailer.

Alessandra watched herself walk, shoulders slumped, fumbling with her keys and the tote bag she brought to work with her.

As she tried to make sense of what she was seeing, her view changed. Her trailer was gone. Blackness.

When the light crept back again, Alessandra was in front of Missy Douglas's house, close to the window that opened onto the kitchen. Alessandra gasped when Missy's face appeared at the window. Alessandra tried to call out to her, but she couldn't make any sound.

Missy's face was drawn and sad. Her eyebrows drooped and her mouth hung down at the corners. Alessandra could hear children laughing. Beyond Missy, sitting at the kitchen table, was a man who Alessandra assumed was Missy's husband. He had an open can of beer in front of him and Missy turned her head slightly, peering at him out of the corners of her eyes.

Alessandra recognized Missy's hyper vigilance and wanted desperately to walk into the house and sit with her. She felt her heart would break at the despair she could read in Missy's beautiful face.

Blackness again. Alessandra found herself now in Trenise Jones's front yard. She watched as Ms. Jones's SUV, the SUV whose windows she had watched Trent smash, pulled into the driveway. The SUV was pristine.

Alessandra wondered again where she was.

Is this the future? Is it the past?

Ms. Jones opened the door to her car, and Alessandra focused again on her. She looked different than she had this morning. Her hair was different.

How it was in the Spring. During gym class. When she had taken Trent to the office.

Alessandra watched Ms. Jones pull her lunch bag from her car and then a laptop case. Ms. Jones slowly walked up to the steps of her house and paused. She returned to the car.

Alessandra watched as Trenise put her head against the window of the car and muttered to herself.

"It's ok," Trenise said softly. "Go in and turn on the lights."

Alessandra could feel her loneliness and felt surprise at the heaviness of it. She tried to call out to her, to comfort her.

"I'm here, Ms. Jones," she tried to say, *"you aren't alone."*

Again, blackness.

Alessandra saw Evangaline Nunez's house in the evening light. She watched as Ms. Evie opened the front door and turned, laughing, bent down and said something to one of her children and then closed the door.

Alessandra felt the coolness of the evening air around her as she stood on Evie's front lawn. Evie was wearing a bright pink sweatshirt and grey joggers. She put her earbuds in her ears and looked at her phone for a moment. Then, she took a deep breath as she stepped away from her house, walked up the lawn, and out onto the street.

As Evie walked away from her, Alessandra felt herself tugged along behind. She saw the earth in front of her swivel and buckle and shimmer. Evie walked up the street and was about to turn down the gravel path that led behind the neighborhood to a wooded walking area that ran along the Stone River.

Evie held her head high and swung her arms as she walked.

"*Don't go down there, Ms. Evie!*" Alessandra tried to scream.

Alessandra felt another pull and she was on the gravel path behind Evie. She knew what was going to happen and turned around, looking to see when Trent would appear. There, further down the gravel path, Trent slithered through the shadows, eyes on Evie's back.

"*Leave her alone!*" Alessandra screamed helplessly.

Trent came closer until he passed within a foot of Alessandra, but he ignored her scream. He advanced on Evie, reached out and grabbed her shoulder.

Alessandra watched as Evie wheeled on him, slipped in the gravel, and fell on her back. Trent was on top of her in an instant, grabbing her wrists and holding her in place.

Alessandra screamed again and tried to move forward to stop Trent and found she couldn't. She saw Trent's lips were moving, but she couldn't hear what he was saying. Evie screamed and Trent covered her mouth with one hand.

"*That's enough!*" Alessandra screamed, "*Stop!*"

She squeezed her eyes shut and sobbed. She registered a change behind her closed eyelids and felt the blackness was gone. She felt the dirt below her cheek and felt the ropes on her wrists and ankles. Alessandra opened her eyes again and recoiled at the sight of the Preacher's face, still inches from her own.

His eyes were calm and cold.

Trent had returned and was carrying someone over his shoulder. The person was completely nude, covered with blood and dirt. The arms and legs flopped unnaturally, and Alessandra retched. Trent threw the body onto the unlit pyre and Alessandra saw clearly that it was Lexie. The side and back of her head was caved in and there were gashes all over her chest.

"No!" Alessandra screamed, "Trent, how could you?"

Trent looked steadfastly away from Alessandra and returned into the woods.

"Do you see?" White asked.

Alessandra sobbed and nodded her head.

—

Missy walked in the middle with Trenise in front of her and Thompson walking in the back. His knife was out of its hilt now, and he scanned beyond the barrier on either side as best he could. Trenise's shoulders were square and strong, Alessandra's bag swung gently back and forth, and she was silent.

Trenise didn't question Missy about what had happened, and Missy didn't volunteer. Missy's chest felt heavy with shame and sadness. She thought of Camille's face and of her children's faces, remembering how sweet it felt for a moment to forget everything about her life.

Missy shuddered.

"He's come after you two already," Trenise finally said, "So I know I'll be next."

Behind her, Missy and Thompson both nodded their heads. Trenise didn't turn to see the gestures but took their silence as agreement.

"Whenever it comes," Trenise said after a moment, "I want you both to leave me with it and go find Alessandra."

"No, Trenise," Missy protested, grabbing Trenise's shoulder, "I won't."

Trenise gently shrugged Missy's hand off and turned to face her. Thompson loomed behind Missy, silent and listening.

Trenise took off Alessandra's backpack and handed it to Missy by the shoulder strap.

"If whatever *it* is is...the ghost, the energy...whatever it is," Trenise shrugged, "...if *it* is distracted trying to come for me, then you two have more of a chance to get to Alessandra and to get the Bible back."

"Trenise," Thompson finally spoke, "Are you sure?"

Trenise nodded again, "Get Alessandra. Get the Bible and burn it. And if...if I can't...," Trenise swallowed heavily, "You find Jolie for me, Missy. Tell her I love her."

With that, Trenise turned her back on them both and walked down the path again. Missy put the heavy bag on her back and followed her.

Hot tears ran down Missy's face leaving clean paths in the dirt and grime there. She wondered at the choice she had almost made, and Camille's voice floated back to her.

"I had children once, didn't I?"

Behind her, Thompson brushed the sweat out of his eyes and winced at the cuts and bruises left by the Swamp Woman and the cypress roots. He wondered what choice Elise had made and if his child was alive somewhere right now.

—

Trent tried to stop himself from thinking as he dumped can after can of gasoline onto the pile of logs he had made. He was confused, hurting. The burns on his neck felt like they were on fire again, the muscles in his arms and legs were knots.

White slumped against a tree trunk next to Alessandra, watching him.

He didn't want to do this, not at all. His dreams of having Alessandra, every inch of her, all to himself, to have her beg for him, to keep her bruised but alive, not like the other two, crumbled before his eyes.

He thought about Alessandra saying that she could help him. When he had been pressed up against her, Trent felt White's presence drift away. It was terrifying and liberating.

Behind him, Alessandra was silent. Trent stopped working and glanced back at her. His hands shook at the sight of her dark eyes watching him, her feet and hands bound.

She was supposed to be MINE, he thought angrily. He thought about how strong he had been after he killed the transient girl- how easy everything had been.

Trent took a deep breath and steadied himself at the memory. He knew somewhere in the back of his mind that this was about more than just him. It was *bigger* than that. It was about changing everything.

He turned away from Alessandra and struck the first match.

Chapter Twenty Six

The three of them walked, each lost in their own suffering. White wanted them to suffer. He knew it would make their sacrifices even greater, which would in turn make him even stronger. He lingered, unseen, and watched them, relishing their misery.

Trenise didn't bother looking off to the sides into the barrier. She knew that whatever was coming for her would show itself without her having to look for it.

Instead, she kept her eyes on the ground, watching one foot fall after the other. Her body was sore from her fight with Trent, her shoulder especially where she had hit the corner of the bricks around her flower bed. The muscles in her legs were in knots from her run with the alligator that morning and from the night before in the French Quarter.

She pulled her mind away from her aching body and found comfort instead at the thought of her classroom. She thought for a moment of Jolie, her beautiful and kind daughter, but found it was too painful. Her chest hurt and her arm went numb at the thought of Jolie and for a moment she was scared she was going to have a heart attack at the sadness she felt.

So instead, Trenise thought about her classroom.

It was a small room off the gym where she would show videos to her classes on occasion, hold team meetings, meet with parents. It was neat and clean and functional. A UNO Privateers flag hung on the back wall and LSU Lady Tigers basketball swag hung on the other wall.

There was a small couch in the corner and five round tables with chairs around them. The thought of her classroom, the smell of the wax floors and the rubber of the basketballs, the ambient light that leaked through the door from the big gymnasium were all comforting without being painful.

When Trenise looked up finally, the landscape in front of her had changed. Instead of the clear path it had been, mostly straight with a few winding points where it wrapped around different back yards, she was now facing a swamp that looked remarkably like her own backyard.

Trenise wheeled around to find Missy and Thompson were gone. Where her house should have been, there was nothing but more swamp.

No path. No street. Nothing but cypress and elephant ears and overrun wetlands.

This is how it looked before the subdivision was built. Before the houses. How long ago am I?

The strangeness of this last thought pressed on Trenise, and she found her breath was shallow. She placed a hand on her chest and looked around.

If I turned and walked that way, what would I find? A stone church? Women in petticoats and horse drawn carriages?

Trenise pushed the thoughts away and focused instead on her breath and the feeling her hand on her chest rise and fall.

Go slow whatever happens, she reminded herself, *give them time,*

—

Thompson continued his scan of the world beyond the barrier. He didn't think the Swamp Woman would be back for him. He also didn't think that whatever had come for Missy would come back. He couldn't explain it, but he could feel it.

He peered to his right, into the woods there, searching for some kind of clue as to where they were. He knew they must be getting closer. When he turned back, Missy was still walking in front of him, head down, staring at the ground in front of her.

But Trenise was gone.

Thompson stopped and grabbed Missy by the shoulder.

"What-?" Missy wheeled around on him and then looked around, "Trenise?"

Thompson spun in a slow circle, looking off into the distance, beyond the thrumming barrier.

"She was just here!" Missy moaned, "How could that be?"

Thompson shook his head, "Missy, she told us to go."

Missy opened her mouth to say something and then stopped. She looked again into the barrier to the left and then to the right and nodded.

"We must be getting close," Missy finally said, "There's no houses or anything, and the Longue's land is...a lot isn't it?"

Thompson nodded, made to start walking again, and then stopped.

"Do you smell that?"

Missy nodded, smelling the air.

"It smells like smoke."

She turned, scanning the land in front of her and pointed above the tree line. There, Thompson could see thick dark gray smoke billowing into the cloudy sky.

"Come on," Missy said trying not to panic, "I think that's them."

She set off at a run, Thompson at her heels.

—

Trenise stood in her own backyard, but not her backyard, chest heaving in terror. The anticipation was unbearable.

She gripped the dog tags around her neck and felt calmer, their cool metal soothing her aching physical body and her racing mind and heart.

Slowly, Trenise walked down the slope of the lawn toward the watery swamp. The air was silent, stagnant, and Trenise thought of the air in the Amite Springs Museum as she had readied herself to take the Bible.

She thought of the alligator, of its glass eyes and its sharp teeth and slithering belly, and warily approached the murky water in front of her. Its surface was glassy and still.

Trenise scanned the horizon, looking into the trees and thick weeds and swamp growth.

As she scanned the surface of the water, she saw Missy first, then Alessandra, and then Jolie. She was vaguely aware of other people, out there in the water before her as well, but she didn't know them, couldn't know them. She was aware that none of them were there and then they were all there. People filled up the swamp into the distance in front of her.

The dog tags dropped out of her shaking hands at the sight of them, and she drew her hands to cover her mouth as she screamed.

Trenise knew it was Missy in her heart even though she could only see the back of her head and body. Missy was face down in the water and her hands and arms flailed, beating the surface and creating waves around her. Next to her, Trenise saw her children in the same position. Faces down in the water, they flailed their arms and legs trying to lift their faces above the water.

It's not real, Trenise's rational mind screamed, *none of it is real!*

Beyond Missy, Alessandra was naked to the waist and bound to a tree. Trenise could see the ropes were so tight that blood trickled down her stomach into the water. Her eyes were covered with a blindfold, and she whimpered.

Trenise was frozen. Her knees locked and her stomach dropped. She tried to take a step forward and couldn't.

The sound of crying, loud enough to drown out Alessandra's whimpering and the sound of Missy and her children drowning, called Trenise's attention deeper into the swamp in front of her.

Her beautiful Jolie, not as she was now, a grown young woman, but as a child floated in a pirogue with no oars. She was sobbing as only a child can, as though terror and heartbreak would destroy her small body. She stood in the pirogue, wearing nothing but a pink nightgown.

Trenise locked eyes with her.

"Mama!" Jolie screamed in her little girl's voice, "Mama, help me! He'll be back soon!"

At the sound of Jolie's voice, Alessandra screamed, moving her blindfolded head violently as though trying to shake it off.

"Ms. Jones is that you? Help me! He'll be back soon!"

Missy lifted her head out of the water and groped to her left trying to reach for her children.

"Trenise!" she screamed, her voice gurgling, "We're going to drown! Help us! He'll be back soon!"

Missy's head snapped back down to the surface as though pushed by an unseen hand. She beat the water around her, straining to lift her head again.

Beyond Missy, Trenise saw Evie Nunez bound by her ankles and hanging upside down from a cypress tree. She was lifeless and her body swayed gently above the water. Below Evangeline, the body of another young woman lay tangled in the roots of the tree. Trenise didn't know who she was.

The more Trenise looked into the swamp beyond Evangeline's hanging, lifeless body, the more she saw. One tree held dismembered body parts, three heads wedged in the wide base just above the surface of the water. Alligators thrashed and Trenise heard the shrill screams of someone being eaten alive echo from the disturbed water.

"Jolie..." Trenise muttered, her voice a dry croak.

"Mama!" Jolie screamed in response, sobbing harder than ever, "why won't you help me?"

Trenise hitched a heavy breath, "You're not really Jolie. My Jolie is at school."

"Mama!" the child screamed, snot and tears covering her small face, "Please!"

"Ms. Jones!" Alessandra called, voice panicked, "You know what he did to me, don't you? You know what he'll do when he gets back!"

"Trenise!" Missy choked, mouth oozing mud as she spoke, "Why won't you save us?"

Trenise sobbed, shaking her head.

They're not real, they're not real, they're not real.

She squeezed her eyes shut and covered her ears with her hands to drown out their screams, but didn't dare to turn her back on them.

Missy, Trenise thought, concentrating all her energy on the real Missy, the one who she knew was walking down a path somewhere close, *Missy, hurry.*

—

Missy half sprinted, following the smell and sight of black smoke. Behind her, Thompson looked for any break in the barrier where they could slip through into the woods. The air was thick and smelled of rot now, and Missy knew they were getting close.

Missy, hurry.

Trenise's voice was so clear, Missy turned her head to look for her. She could almost smell her crisp laundry detergent.

At the sound of Trenise's voice Missy froze, ducked down, and pulled Thompson down next to her behind a tree.

"Did you hear that?" she asked him, looking into his bewildered face.

"Hear what?" Thompson shook his head and then when Missy made to answer, he quickly covered her mouth with his hand.

A few feet beyond where they crouched, Trent passed close to them on the other side of the barrier.

Missy's eyes got wide, and Thompson removed his hand, pointing.

We're here, he mouthed.

Missy nodded in return and turned her body slowly to try and see through the barrier behind her. Her ponytail stuck to her neck in sweaty clumps. The haze of the barrier made it hard to see much, but Missy could make out Trent's shape sitting about six feet from them. Beyond him was what Missy guessed was the start of a bonfire. It appeared to be smoldering at the bottom, but it wasn't quite catching in the middle and at the top.

Missy inched closer to the barrier and hoped Trent wouldn't turn. She duck-walked closer to the barrier, ignoring Thompson's hiss to come back.

She squinted, scanning the clearing, and finally saw a pop of bright blue moving, just barely visible over the top of a gravestone.

Alessandra.

She leaned against the gravestone facing away from Missy and Trent.

Thompson tapped Missy on the shoulder, making her turn.

"Let's back up a little where the woods are a little thicker. We'll go back through the barrier with the bat. I'll go in and distract the kid. You get Alessandra and do what y'all have to do. Burn the Bible."

Missy thought of what Trent did to the bouncer in the French Quarter, to Rainbow, to Trenise.

"Use your knife if you have to."

Thompson gave her a measured look and nodded.

—

Alessandra scanned the clearing looking for Trent and White. In front of her, the heat from the bonfire burned her face. Sweat poured off her body coating her skin.

Slowly, Alessandra wiggled her hands together behind her back, pausing every few seconds to allow the sweat to pool again. The rope was tight and twisted in three loops. Alessandra couldn't tell if it was sweat or blood or both that she felt as she rubbed her wrists back and forth, but she could feel her left hand start to slip through the top layer of the rope.

She risked a glance over her shoulder and saw Trent sitting about twenty feet behind her, back up against a tree, looking despondent. He stared into the fire.

She didn't see White at all.

Alessandra tried to stay calm as she rubbed her wrists back and forth more aggressively, pausing when she felt her wrists become dry again from the friction.

The heat from the bonfire was unbearable. Her throat hitched and she struggled to breathe. Her wrists weren't coming free and even if she was able to loosen them, she'd still have to untie her ankles and then outrun Trent. Again.

Alessandra felt hot tears stream down her face and thought of Trent sobbing on her shoulder and how different he had looked then. She thought about the look on his face when she said she could help him and that he had done it all for her.

"Trent!" she called raising her voice over crackling fire, "Trent!"

Trent looked in her direction and then stared stonily away from her.

"Trent, please!" she called again. "I don't care what you did!"

After a moment, Trent stood up and walked toward her, his face changing rapidly from anger to sadness. Alessandra could see that he had been crying.

"Trent," she said softly, "I mean it. I don't care what you did."

Trent didn't respond but stood motionless over her.

Alessandra seized on his apparent indecision.

"Trent, untie me. We can run away."

Trent opened his mouth as though to speak and then shook his head.

Behind them, Thompson stood up from behind the tree where he was crouched and drove his knife into the barrier in front of him. He steadied himself to strain against the force of it, as he had done before when he tried to free Missy. This time, as Thompson pulled up, the barrier gave more readily, and Thompson was able to make a bigger hole more quickly.

Missy was next to him and squeezed the bat into the hole he had made, pulling first toward herself to make a circle. Although she still strained to pull the bat through the electric fuzz, Missy felt that it was easier this time.

She tried to move more quickly. Her eyes darted from Jim's bat to the back of Alessandra's bright blue head, which she could just barely see through the trees. Missy pulled up and around, forming the arc of a hole.

She wondered where Trenise was and if the weakening in the barrier was her doing somehow, wherever she was, and whatever she was fighting against.

Missy thought of Camille and the sad beauty of her face as she sat and faced destruction alone, cradling the remains of her lost companion. She thought of eternity in the howling wind, and wound her bat deeper into the barrier, moving in tandem with Thompson.

"I'll go first," he whispered, "You follow. I'll go straight to Trent. You sneak around behind and untie her."

"Ok," Missy whispered, still moving her arms in an arc, trying to get the hole just wide enough for Thompson to fit through.

"Get her and whatever you need and then just fucking run."

Missy nodded.

"Ok that's good," he whispered, pointing a hand at the opening.

—

Just beyond where Thompson and Missy made a hole in the strange barrier, Alessandra nodded.

"Yes. Yes, we can. You just have to untie me before he gets back. We can run away Trent."

Trent shook his head again and whispered, "He'll find us."

"He won't," Alessandra whispered urgently, "There are people in New Orleans who can help us. Ms. Jones's cousin, there's an older lady too..."

Trent swayed over her, still not speaking.

Alessandra sobbed in desperation.

"Please, Trent. I know you're not bad. Just untie me."

"You really don't care what I did?" Trent asked softly.

Behind them, Missy pulled her bat around one more time, and Thompson bent down to crawl through the small space. Missy let him get a few feet in front of her and then followed.

—

Days earlier, Missy Douglas had stood in front of the coffee shop where Alessandra Sanchez was working and had felt as though an invisible force was pulling her toward the door. She had felt as though forces beyond her control were forcing her to walk. Missy was reminded of being pulled toward the darkness of the ocean.

Trenise felt the same way now, as though she were being pulled into a whirlpool of forces she didn't understand.

She pressed her hands to her ears like a child and squeezed her eyes shut trying to block out the sights and sounds in front of her. On the back of her eyelids, she saw mangled body parts.

Behind her hands, she heard her name over and over again.

"Help us, help us, help us."

Below her, seemingly of their own accord, Trenise's feet moved toward the water. Trying not to panic, Trenise opened her eyes and tried to look at the water and ignore the figures occupying the space before her.

She moved her hands from her ears to her chest again and felt the weight of the dog tags. She pulled on their chain freeing the tags from under her shirt and pressed their cool metal into the palms of her hands.

Instantly, the voices of the women in the water dulled. She found that she could stop her feet from moving toward the water. She looked up and saw that the water itself was now covered in a mist, blocking out most of what was happening. She could no longer see Alessandra tied to the tree, or Missy and her children drowning, or Jolie adrift and screaming. There were only shadows.

Trenise took a slow, shaky breath in and squeezed the tags tighter.

The screams and cries from the women in the water got momentarily louder and then dimmed again.

Trenise dug her heels into the soft dirt and began to walk slowly backwards. Her feet felt like there were fifty-pound weights tied to them, but she dragged herself backwards, nonetheless.

Squeezing the dog tags, Trenise looked over her shoulder at the empty landscape behind her, again wondering what she would find beyond the cypress trees and brush.

Trenise looked toward the water again, and her body lurched forward back toward it against her will. Not knowing what else to do, Trenise sunk into the grass and dug her feet into the dirt.

My dirt, she thought, *this is my land. No matter what it was before, this is my land now.*

As if in response to this assertion, Trenise felt herself being pushed forward again toward the water. She cried out in shock, whipped her head around to look behind her, and wasn't surprised to find nothing there. She felt her bottom drag across the grass as the same invisible force that made her feet move was now pushing her forward again.

Trenise dug her feet in again, momentarily halting her forward progress. Ahead of her, the mist that had covered the bayou cleared, and the women appeared again.

Missy moved jerkily, still face down in the water, but her children had stopped moving.

"No," Trenise moaned.

Jolie's tiny boat rocked in the waves created by the thrashing creatures around her, and she screamed and cried in her little girl voice as the boat tipped.

"Mama, help me!"

Alessandra sobbed and squirmed against the tree and the ropes cut deeper into her bare skin. She turned her head to the left and the right, as though listening for Trenise.

Trenise felt her body pull forward again.

It's not real, she told herself, *Jolie is at school. Missy's children are in Tennessee.*

"Mama!" Jolie screamed again, "I *am* here! Help me!"

Trenise looked up and saw her little girl in her pink nightgown tip and fall into the water. She saw her tiny hand shoot up into the air above the water, and then she was gone.

Trenise let go of the tags and sprinted toward the water, screaming her baby's name.

—

Missy watched as Thompson approached the bonfire and tried to creep around behind the small graveyard. The sound of the crackling fire was loud enough that she felt comfortable moving fast, not really caring about how much noise she made. All she could think about was getting to Alessandra. She didn't care about the Bible. She would get Alessandra, then run back to try and find Trenise.

Her skin crawled as she approached the edge of the gravestones, thinking simultaneously of the gravestones next to Camille and Sophie's plantation and of the last time she was in this spot when there was a girl with no face and a thing that had turned into a monstrous version of her husband.

She thought of the gaping pit and wondered if it was still there somewhere, down below the surface of the earth. She thought of the girl with no face and wondered if Trent had thrown her body into that pit.

Thompson made no attempt to hide himself. He walked through the woods around him, glancing only once to his left to see Missy running as best as she could through the trees and bushes that surrounded the small cemetery.

Trent loomed over Alessandra, and she whispered something to him that Thompson couldn't hear. Neither one of them heard Thompson approach until he was almost on top of them. Alessandra saw him first, and he registered the hope in her eyes only briefly before Trent wheeled around.

"What did you-" Trent looked back at Alessandra his face black with perceived betrayal, "-you bitch."

Trent made to lunge at Alessandra, but Thompson caught him around the middle. Alessandra rolled away as Trent and Thompson slammed into the gravestone she had been leaning up against. They smashed through the stone and toppled into the dirt.

Missy seized the opportunity to dart out of the woods and pull Alessandra away from where the two men wrestled. Missy pulled at the ropes around Alessandra's feet, trying desperately to pull them off so that they could run.

"Hurry Missy! He's here!" Alessandra kicked her ankles trying to rub them free.

Missy whipped her head around. Emmanuel White stood over Trent and Thompson, watching them struggle.

Thompson punched Trent in the stomach and chest, but he seemed to have little effect. When Missy dared to look again, Trent was on top of Thompson punching him in the face and torso.

Missy pulled at the ropes now, digging her fingers beneath them and wrenching them off with all her might. If it hurt Alessandra, she didn't show it as the two of them clawed at the ropes in a panic.

White reached down and pulled Trent off Thompson by the back of his neck. He lifted him slightly and looked at him, then placed him on his feet.

"Go and get them both," he said calmly gesturing toward Missy and Alessandra.

"No, no, no," Missy moaned, pulling Alessandra up to standing.

"Go, Missy!" Alessandra howled, "Just go!"

Missy pulled her along under her arms, "No, I won't leave you."

Trent stood watching them, laughing to himself.

"Where are you going?" he asked, throwing his hands up.

Missy tried to carry Alessandra as Trent walked calmly over to them.

"Run, Missy!" Alessandra screamed, trying to push her off. Missy let her and Alessandra fell to the ground in a heap.

Missy reached behind her into Alessandra's bag and pulled out her bat from where she had stowed it. She stood over Alessandra and swung at Trent as hard as she could. With a laugh, Trent knocked the bat out of her hand with his fist. She smelled the sizzle of his skin burning, just as it had in the French Quarter, but he was ready this time.

The bat flew into the woods, and Missy tried to run after it. Trent grabbed her easily and carried her as she screamed and kicked back to the small cemetery. Alessandra tried again to free her hands and feet.

White stood with his foot pressed against Thompson's neck. Missy sobbed and hit Trent as hard as she could, watching as Thompson's face turned from a deep red to an ugly purple. She watched as Thompson struggled with one hand for the knife on his hip and as White casually reached down, grasped Thompson's hand in his own and squeezed.

Thompson opened his mouth to scream, but no sound came out.

Missy heard the sickening crack of bones as White broke Thompson's hand.

Trent threw her down and held her with one foot as she struggled to wrench herself free. He casually reached into a pile of tools near her and pulled out a small length of rope. He tied her feet first and then her hands.

"Let him go!" Missy screamed at White.

To her shock, White took his foot off Thompson's neck, and Missy watched as Thompson fluttered his eyes and took large gulping breaths. Thompson rolled in the dirt still gasping for air, and Trent threw a writhing Alessandra next to her. As best as she could, Missy inched closer to Alessandra, touching her shoulder with her own.

Behind White, the flames of the bonfire seemed to grow and grow. Missy felt her skin burn in the heat from it and felt Alessandra huddle next to her.

"Whatever happens, we'll be together." Missy whispered.

Alessandra put her head on Missy's shoulder and nodded. She squeezed her eyes shut and prayed it would be over quickly.

Chapter Twenty Seven

Slowly, Emmanuel White walked toward Trent and embraced him.

"You are like Peter," he whispered in Trent's ear, "But just like Jesus, I will forgive you. For my mercy is infinite."

He smiled as he looked down at Thompson. White crouched down, pulling Trent gently with him. White reached out and pressed the back of his hand to Thompson's forehead and then each temple.

Thompson still gasped for air, clutching his throat. He pulled himself up to sitting.

White nodded at him.

"I can see inside your heart Duane Thompson. I know how you feel about *them*," he nodded toward Missy and Alessandra.

Thompson pulled in another long breath.

"I know that you agreed with me that these women need to be stopped. That they need to be silenced. They forced their way into your mind and turned you away from what is right."

Thompson looked at Missy and Alessandra and back to White. His throat felt scorched and raw, every bone in his body throbbed from the beatings he had taken.

"They are *liars,*" White continued, "just like Elise."

Duane looked at him with a start.

"I know. I know she lied to you too."

"Don't listen to him, Officer Thompson," Missy hissed.

White locked eyes with Duane and waved Missy away.

"I know the Swamp Woman," White paused and smiled, "as you call her, told you about your child. I can give her to you. You and her mother. You can have them both. Just as I will give Alessandra to Trent, as promised."

Trent started, "Wha-what?"

White nodded and clamped a hand on his shoulder. He pulled Thompson close to him in an embrace.

"She is alive," White whispered, "your child is alive. What you choose to do with her mother is up to you."

Trent looked from White to Thompson, thunderstruck.

"I'm sorry," he stammered, "I'm sorry I doubted you."

White stood up abruptly and ignored Trent.

"We still have work to do before I can give you both what you want."

HE held his hand out to Thompson.

Duane thought about the Swamp Woman and her baby. He thought about Elise and his baby, his daughter, according to White. He thought about Alessandra and Missy and Trenise Jones, out there somewhere. He thought about Cynthia Devaunt. He looked at the pyre behind White. He looked at Alessandra and Missy, who were both watching him intently, red-faced, bruised, and bloodied. Desperate and pathetic, their eyes pleading with him.

"Officer Thompson..." Alessandra said simply, eyes watering with frustration and despair and the heat of the fire.

Thompson thought about his anger that he had been drawn into this mess, that these women wouldn't listen, and that they had taken it upon themselves to cause all of this. If they hadn't stuck their noses where they didn't belong, none of this would have happened. He wouldn't be here. He wouldn't have crossed Bordelon and jeopardized his whole career to come and find them.

He wouldn't have known about Trent, or Emmanuel White and what their horrific partnership meant for the world around him.

He wouldn't have known about Elise or her baby.

Thompson looked back to White and grasped his hand.

"But I don't understand," Trent said, "I thought you said we have to...you know...," he gestured with is head at the fire, "to Alessandra... for you to come back."

"I said we needed another life Trent," White said patiently, "and we'll have one shortly."

Trent looked quizzical.

White nodded slowly and then gestured to Missy.

"And then another one after that."

Trent nodded and swallowed heavily, "So, Ms. Jones is...?"

White smiled.

"Trust in the Lord God."

Thompson surveyed the fire in front of him and tried not to look at Missy and Alessandra, keeping his face stony. His right hand ached and throbbed where White had broken it. He didn't think it would be much use at this point, but he tried anyway to clench and unclench it.

"You fucking bastard," Missy sobbed.

Thompson glanced at her and took a step forward next to Trent who laughed gleefully.

"Stop it now," White hissed.

White's calm demeanor changed abruptly. He looked into the woods, and Missy saw rage twist across his face again.

"I don't care what you do with them, Trent," White barked, "but keep them bound."

White turned to look at Missy and Alessandra where they lay in the dirt, and Missy groaned at his monstrous appearance. She watched as he faded to the same mist that made up the barrier and then was gone.

"Ms. Jones..." Alessandra whispered.

Trent loomed over them, and Alessandra tried to squirm away.

Missy rolled away from him the best that she could, well aware that there was little she could really do to stop him from doing whatever he wanted.

She looked up defiantly at Trent and then watched in shock as Thompson stepped up behind him and stabbed him in the neck.

—

The water was endlessly deep. Trenise could see that now. There was no bottom. Below her, Jolie sunk and sunk, her small hand outstretched, her pink nightgown rippling around her, as she reached up to Trenise. Trenise swam down headfirst, pushing the water away with her hands.

She felt the dog tags pull at her neck.

She saw the alligators and snakes swarming, coming for her daughter. Jolie's sweet face was slack, her eyes closed.

Somewhere in her mind, Trenise knew that this was not Jolie. Jolie was a grown woman, away in Washington D.C. Still, she propelled herself down, following her baby as she sunk.

—

It had been years since Rainbow had been to Trenise's house. As she pulled off the exit to Stone River, Rainbow realized the last time she had been there was for a memorial for the ten year anniversary of Big John's death. Her head pounded and her eyes ached with pain and sadness.

She tried to let her body take over, to guide her to where she needed to go. Steering the car on instinct, Rainbow looked around in horror at the destruction around her.

There were downed power lines, trees in the road, debris scattered across lawns.

"What happened here?" she said out loud to herself.

The hair on her arms stood up and she tried to maneuver her car faster, finally turning into Trenise's subdivision.

The destruction was worse here than on the main road. Rainbow pulled her car to the side of the road to make room for the crew of men who were trying to clear the debris.

One of them approached her driver's side window.

"Do you live here?"

"No," Rainbow shook her head, "I'm trying to get to my cousin's house. I haven't been able to contact her, and I'm worried."

The man sighed.

"Yeah, I'm not surprised you can't reach her. A tornado came through here about an hour ago. We're going as fast as we can. Does your cousin live close?"

Rainbow felt her eyes fill with tears and desperation, "No, Trenise lives far back. Please, she's all by herself, is there anything you can do?"

"Trenise?" the man's voice perked up, "Trenise Jones?"

Rainbow nodded.

The man grinned.

"That's my daughter's basketball coach! Listen, leave your car here, I'll give you a ride in my truck as far as we can get, ok?"

"Yes, thank you so much!"

"Now listen, you may have to walk some. I hear it gets worse closer to the Stone River."

Rainbow nodded and followed the man to his truck.

—

Thompson's grip on his knife faltered as it connected with the side of Trent's throat. He felt his broken fingers crumble. and although the cut briefly looked deep enough to incapacitate Trent, Thompson groaned when the teenager wheeled on him, screaming in anger.

The knife fell as Trent tackled him, knocking him to the ground. Missy watched for a moment as they fought. They were so close to the fire that she was sure one or both of them would fall in.

"Missy, the knife!" Alessandra hissed.

Missy searched the ground around her and saw it glittering in the light cast from the fire. She inch-wormed closer to it and rolled to one side, desperately trying to reach for the hilt rather than the blade.

"Come closer!"

Alessandra bucked herself toward Missy, feeling the ground below her baking in the heat. Sweat dripped into her eyes, and she blinked it away.

Turning her back to Missy, Alessandra kept her eyes on Trent and Officer Thompson as they moved further and further away from them.

"He's moving Trent away, Missy! Hurry!"

Missy tried to stay calm as she sawed first at the ropes around her own wrists, gave up, and began sawing at the ropes at Alessandra's. Finally, she felt them start to give and her heart leapt when Alessandra screamed in triumph as her hands came free.

"Where's the Bible Alessandra?" Missy asked as Alessandra worked to free her.

"It's there on the wall!"

—

Rainbow walked as fast as she could for the last stretch of road that led to Trenise's house. The kind man who had given her a ride was long gone. She could hear no sounds other than the distant buzz of chainsaws. There were no people. No birds sang. No dogs barked.

Rainbow looked around, astounded at the path the tornado had taken. There was debris scattered across the road, and Rainbow two times had to go onto someone's lawn to weave around large fallen trees.

When she finally found her way to Trenise's street, Rainbow sobbed and desperately tried to walk faster, ignoring the pounding in her head and that her vision kept trying to cut in and out.

The destruction here seemed total. Houses were missing their roofs, trees and cars were overturned.

Could they have even survived this?

As Rainbow rounded the corner and stepped onto Trenise's street, she could see that Trenise's house was still standing- a brilliant white against the still gray sky.

Rainbow laughed and wiped her eyes and thought about what Trenise had told her Ms. Sarah had said the night before at Razoo.

If there were dark forces here, maybe there were light too.

Rainbow walked as fast as she dared, hoping that whatever force had kept Trenise's house standing would also help her find Alessandra, Missy, and Trenise before it was too late.

—

Thompson knew that he couldn't keep up this fight for much longer. His eyes were almost swollen shut and his body coursed with venom after Trent's last punch landed directly to his liver. His broken hand screamed in agony and he desperately tried to fight southpaw, blocking Trent's blows with his right forearm.

The desperate need for redemption was all that Duane could think of. The thought of the two women curled up and bound in the dirt propelled him forward. Remembering what Missy and Trenise had told him about the young woman in the graveyard, the girl with no face, drove him toward Trent even as it became obvious that Trent was only playing with him.

But it was the thought of Elise and what he had done to her that helped him to keep lifting his arms, to keep trying to find some way to stop Trent. Thompson felt the weight of what he had done to her.

He didn't allow himself to think beyond this moment, but he knew in his heart that this wasn't just a fight to protect Missy and Alessandra, it wasn't just a fight for justice for the girl with no face, or for the old woman Trent had thrown down the stairs, or for Evangeline Nunez. He knew this was a fight for his own soul, to prove that he was his mother's son and not the version of himself who had turned lazy and indifferent to the hurt and pain in the world.

Thompson stumbled and fell and grasped for Trent's leg, trying to pull him down to keep himself in the fight.

Trent stood over him and laughed, kicking his hand away.

When Trent bent down over him, Duane tried to swing again and found he couldn't lift his left hand any longer.

"It's ok!" Trent said brightly, "I think it'll be great that you can watch while I throw the blond on the fire!"

"Fuck you, kid" Duane croaked.

Trent laughed again, then quickly stood, suddenly growing serious.

"Hey!" he called, "What do you two think you're doing?"

Thompson rolled over and tried to follow Trent's gaze. He smiled at how far he had been able to move Trent away from both the fire and the graveyard. He smiled more broadly as he saw that Missy and Alessandra had managed to free themselves and that Missy was holding a large brown book in her arms.

"Where's Trenise?" she yelled.

Trent eyed her and inched closer.

"If you throw that in, He will be gone. And she's with him now! She'll be gone too!"

"You're lying Trent!" Alessandra screamed.

Trent took another step towards them and Missy extended the Bible out toward the fire. Trent froze.

"I'll do it, Trent!" Missy screamed, trying to buy herself time to think. If Trent was right, then destroying the Bible would destroy Trenise as well.

Alessandra's chest heaved, and she looked from Missy to Trent.

Ms. Jones, she thought desperately, *Ms. Jones where are you?*

—

Trenise's lungs were almost at their limit. Her chest was on fire and her nostrils burned. She knew she wouldn't be able to hold her breath much longer but desperately swam deeper.

Jolie's outstretched hand was so close she swore she brushed her small fingers.

Ms. Jones, where are you?

Though Trenise was far underwater, the voice echoed clear.

Alessandra.

What are you doing? Trenise's rational mind screamed.

She looked at Jolie's waxy face below her in the water, sinking lower and lower, and then looked above her trying to find the surface.

That thing isn't Jolie!

Trenise clawed and kicked her way up, trying to ignore the burning in her lungs. She could see the light grow brighter above her.

But the distance she seemed to be closing wasn't moving her body fast enough. The surface seemed to stay the same distance away no matter how hard she tried to propel her body.

I'm not going to make it, she finally realized.

Nonetheless, despite realizing really and truly that she could never get to the surface in time, Trenise Jones continued to swim with all her might.

She wondered distantly if anyone would ever find her body or if Jolie would be left wondering forever what had happened to her.

—

"Hey!" Rainbow yelled, stumbling onto Trenise's front lawn, "Trenise!"

While there were branches and debris, including broken glass from Trenise's car window, there was no sign of Trenise, Missy, or Alessandra.

Rainbow looked up at the dark house. If they were inside, they would have come out at the sound of her voice.

"It's Rainbow!"

She paused and listened. Her brain felt slow and untrustworthy, but she tried to reach out with her heart and her spirit. All she heard was water. Drips of water from the trees, water running down Trenise's backyard to the swamp behind it.

Rainbow followed the sound and looked toward the swamp. There was a mist rising from the water and slowly creeping up the bank.

Rainbow sniffed the air and recoiled at the foul smell of it. As she took a step closer to the water, down the slope of the backyard, Rainbow noticed a kayak tipped over close to the edge of the water.

She furrowed her brow and looked around into the swamp, wondering what it was that felt wrong, what felt off.

The moss hanging in the trees blew softly, then seemed to swirl and shake. The trees waved their branches in warning. The water in the bayou bubbled and the mist increased.

"You don't belong here, witch."

The voice came from everywhere and nowhere and Rainbow covered her ears, eyes wide, watching in front of her.

Rainbow ignored the voice and stepped forward.

"You can't hurt me!" she screamed and rushed toward the water.

She stumbled and fell close to the edge and frantically waved her arms through the mist, trying to scatter it. As she waded into the swamp, quickly going in up to her waist, Rainbow registered that the wind became stronger and that branches snapped off the trees around her.

Rainbow knew with all her being that Trenise was in the water somewhere. She closed her eyes as the wind rushed around her. Finally, she took one more step and plunged her hand below the surface.

Here, the water felt ice cold compared to the stagnant warmth of the rest of the water she'd waded through. Rainbow plunged her hand as low as she could, trying to feel for the bottom. Finally, she turned and put her face in the water, opened her eyes, and screamed silently.

—

I'm hallucinating, Trenise thought before she lost consciousness.

As she kicked and flailed, finally succumbing to drowning, she thought she saw Rainbow's face and outstretched arm.

Rainbow's silent scream bubbled to the surface as she saw the depth of the water below her, extending down into nothingness. She plunged her torso downward, careful to keep her footing, grabbed Trenise by the hair, and pulled up and backwards as hard as she could. She grabbed Trenise's shirt and pulled her up and out of the water, away from the cold and into the warm air.

Trenise sputtered and grabbed her shoulders, trying to stand.

"Rainbow," she sobbed, "Rainbow are you real? Is it really you, Rainbow?"

"It's me, Trenise. I promise it's me."

The two women stumbled out of the water and up the bank.

Trenise closed her eyes, sucked in air through her mouth, and lay on her back in the mud. She wanted more than anything to go find a phone somewhere and call Jolie, make sure she was ok.

"Trenise, where are Missy and Alessandra?"

Trenise's eyes shot open.

"Rainbow, we have to go."

Rainbow tried to climb to her feet and found she couldn't. The world turned around her and she slipped back onto the ground.

"I can't, Trenise. I can't."

Trenise nodded and hoisted Rainbow up to standing. She slung one of Rainbow's arms over her shoulders and the two of them slowly made their way up the lawn and under the deck. The wind had knocked the couches out of their normal spots, but Trenise laid Rainbow down on one of them as gently as she could.

"Thank you, Rainbow."

Trenise squeezed her cousin's hand gently.

Rainbow nodded and motioned for Trenise to go.

Trenise took another look at her house and took off at a run down her back lawn.

—

Thompson groaned and tried to crawl after Trent.

"Throw it in Missy," he croaked.

Missy looked briefly at him, thought of Trenise's kind face and of the last words she had spoken to her. She looked at Alessandra's look of terror as Trent bore down on them.

Not knowing what else to do, without any other options, Missy threw the Bible as hard as she could toward the fire.

—

Trenise's entire body felt broken. She could barely breathe through her broken nose, and her throat ached from holding her breath for so long under the water. Her eyes ached and her left knee popped uncomfortably every time she took a stride as she ran.

She ignored all of it. The haze that had blocked their path was gone as she crossed into Rita's lawn. The access path was now filled with a low smoke, and the barrier that had been on either side was only barely visible.

Something felt different.

Trenise kept her pace and jogged as fast as she dared.

—

In the clearing, Trent felt a small surge of hope as he watched the blonde throw the Bible underhand toward the fire.

It's over, he thought to himself grimly.

But instead of landing in the fire, the Bible ricocheted off the air in front of the flames and fell to the ground.

Trent lurched forward, sprinting to grab it and threw his body into the dirt on top of it.

"You failed."

Trent looked up at Emmanuel White as he stood over him.

Alessandra clutched at the blond woman, trying to pull her back and away.

"You *failed,*" White said again.

Behind him, Trent heard the cop groan.

"Hey!" the cop croaked, crawling toward them, "Hey, asshole!"

White turned and growled at him, an inhuman sound that issued from his whole being.

"Coward," he breathed, "traitor."

Then he turned to Trent.

"You know what to do know, Trent."

Trent nodded solemnly and walked over to the cop, wondering how long he would scream when he was thrown into the fire.

Thompson waited and let Trent get close. He waited with eyes closed, curled up in a ball, feeling what must have been the last of his adrenaline pound through his body. Finally, he opened his eyes and saw the toes of Trent's shoes only inches from his face.

Hoping he still had some element of surprise, Thompson used the last of his strength to wrap his arms around Trent's thighs, wrestling him to the ground once more. He felt Trent drop the book and hoped he could give the women enough time to try again to throw the Bible in the fire.

—

Trenise heard Missy's voice clearly. It wasn't in her head, some echoey version of telepathy. It was her voice, screaming.

"Get the Bible, Alessandra!"

Trenise clutched the dog tags that bounced at her neck and silently prayed that whoever had been watching over them all this time would be there to help her now.

"I'm coming!" Trenise yelled.

—

Missy knew her bat was gone, lost somewhere in the woods. She had no idea where Alessandra's bar had gone to. All she knew was that by the look of him, Thompson had very little fight in him.

In a split-second decision, Missy rushed Trent, bowling him over. The distance wasn't far, and she screamed for Alessandra to get the Bible as she ran.

Missy landed in the dirt, close to the fire. Her shoulder screamed from where she connected with Trent's strong body. She lay there, dazed for a moment, and heard Trenise scream in the distance.

Missy hoisted herself to her feet, scanning around her.

Trent on his feet, trying to push past Thompson and get to where Alessandra crouched, clutching the Bible. Alessandra cowered as White bent over her, whispering in her ear.

Alessandra's face was white and she sputtering noiselessly.

"Missy!"

Missy looked past White and saw Trenise burst from the woods. Missy ran towards Alessandra, meeting Trenise there.

White, startled, and looked at them, and sneered.

"Throw it in!" he howled with rage, "The righteous will always triumph!"

Trenise pulled Alessandra to her feet and Missy grabbed the Bible from underneath her. Trenise held Alessandra's arm at the elbow and put her hand on the small of Missy's back.

Missy stepped closer the·flames and threw the Bible again. The Bible flew into the fire, past Trent and Duane. Trent tried to grab it and missed.

The last sound Missy heard was an earth-shattering scream before her body was blown backwards.

—

The screaming shocked Alessandra's eyes open. She leapt to her feet, looking around her, and quickly realized something had knocked her backwards, away from the flames. Trenise was closest to her, with Missy slightly to her right.

"No!" Missy yelled running forward.

Trenise stood as quickly as she was able and followed Missy.

Alessandra scanned the clearing in front of her, trying to get her bearings. White, Officer Thompson, and Trent were nowhere to be seen. The flames from the bonfire had grown taller and wider. The trees and bushes around her were singed and black. Smoke filled the clearing.

"Grab his feet!"

Alessandra watched as Missy and Trenise reached close to the fire and heaved backward, pulling someone out by their legs.

The screaming continued. Alessandra rushed forward and realized that it was Officer Thompson who Missy and Trenise pulled out of the flames. His face was black, and his clothes were burnt.

Alessandra walked past Missy and Trenise where they huddled over Thompson's charred form. When she reached the edge of the flames, she peered deeply into them. The screaming continued.

Trenise bent down and tried to feel if Thompson had a pulse but pulled her hand away from the heat of his body. She tried to put her hand on his chest to see if he was breathing.

Alessandra stared into the flames. In the center, the fire seemed to burn more slowly, glowing an ugly green. On the ground, Alessandra could see that it was the Bible on fire, growing smaller and smaller as it was consumed by the flames.

Close to the burnt remnants of the Bible, Alessandra could see what she thought was a human figure. It writhed and screamed one more time and then was silent.

Alessandra knew that it was Trent, destroyed by the fire he had made to destroy her.

She felt Missy and Trenise stand next to her, both watching as the Bible burned down to nothing.

"Duane is dead." Trenise finally said with a sob.

"So is Trent," Alessandra answered.

"White seems to be gone."

Trenise looked over at her, "Seems to be."

The flames appeared to slack and Alessandra tilted her head, listening.

"Is that sirens?"

Trenise and Missy stood and listened, both nodding.

"We need to leave now," Trenise said.

"But what about White? Shouldn't we wait and make sure?"

"There's no time, Missy. You want to be here when the cops show up because of all this smoke and explain two dead bodies?"

Missy shook her head, then reached down to squeeze what remained of Duane Thompson's hand.

Alessandra took her hand and followed Trenise back to the access path, moving quickly as the sound of the sirens got louder and louder.

Looking back over her shoulder, Alessandra thought she saw the of a shape of a man moving in front of the fire. She almost told the others to stop but when she looked again, the shape was gone.

Epilogue

"We're Stone River Strong is what we are. No tornado or tragedy will stop our spirit!"

"And that was Mrs. Judy Frechette speaking to us on the six month anniversary of the tragic Stone River Tornado that caused so much destruction. She is the mother of the young woman who was tragically lost in a bonfire accident along with her boyfriend and local quarterback Trent Longue, son of prominent businessman Grant Longue, and police officer Duane Thompson on the same day as the tornado."

"That's right Kelsey. To have two young lives and the life of a first responder, who we assume was attempting to save them, all lost and on the same day that a tornado tragically wiped out so much of Stone River and Amite Springs, including the museum, seems just so unfair and heartbreaking."

"It really is unbelievable, John. But like that grieving mother said, they are Stone River Strong..."

Trenise shut off the tv, picked up her cup of coffee and walked out onto her front porch. It was much smaller than her porch at her old house in Stone River, but the view was beautiful. Just over the horizon, Trenise could see the ocean.

In the months after the day of the fire, Trenise knew she could no longer live in Stone River. She sold her house as quickly as she could and bought this much smaller cottage in the small beach town of Bay St. Louis in Mississippi.

Her days were quiet and slow. She spent time combing the beach for shells, visiting the library, volunteering at the animal shelter. She tried as best as she could not to think about what had happened to her, what it all meant for her world view, what the implications were of the supernatural events she had witnessed.

Some nights she barely slept. The supplements Rainbow made for her helped some, but they weren't perfect. She dreamed about the alligator, about drowning. She woke up in a cold sweat, clutching her soaking wet sheets.

She knew that Jolie worried about her, but when she came to visit, Trenise sent her back to Washington D.C. as soon as she could. She didn't want her baby anywhere near Stone River.

Trenise frowned and pressed her palm to her forehead, allowing the cool ocean air to wash over her.

Alessandra was the closest to Stone River still. Her mother couldn't afford to move very far, so they were in the next town, Slidell. Trenise called to check on her weekly and was happy when Alessandra started working part time for Rainbow. Trenise knew Rainbow didn't need any help but was doing it so that she could watch over Alessandra.

Trenise sat on the small wicker glider and rocked, running her hand over her cropped hair.

When Missy is gone, I can rest, she told herself again, *once she's back in Tennessee, I'll feel better.*

Like Trenise, Missy couldn't stand the thought of living in Stone River after what had happened. Her husband had agreed that he would keep his job offshore and drive back to Tennessee when he was off.

Missy told Trenise about their small house in the suburbs of Chattanooga.

"With no trees or swamps," Missy had told her over the phone, "there's not one tree on my property, Trenise, I had them all cut down."

They both had laughed, but there was a flint to Missy's voice.

Last week, Missy had called Trenise to tell her she would be in Slidell to sign the last bit of paperwork to sell her house.

"How about I swing by before I head back to Tennessee?"

Trenise smiled now while she sat on her porch, waiting anxiously for Missy's car to pull into her driveway.

—

Missy shuddered as she pulled away from the realtor's office. The bright Christmas lights that decorated the outside of the office, which were still on in the daylight, seemed garish and strange. It was cool and overcast, and Missy hustled to her car to turn on the heat.

Her cheeks hurt from forcing a smile during her meeting. She nodded along as the realtor noted the amount of business they'd done with people coming and going after the tornado and "the terrible tragedy."

Although she talked to Alessandra frequently both on the phone and via text message, Missy still desperately wanted to see her.

"You know I'm already working for Rainbow," Alessandra had told Missy the week before, "but her friend Ms. Sarah, you know, the one you and Trenise met in the French Quarter? She owns an Apothecary and kind of like...New Age store in the French Quarter. You know, books, gifts, stuff like that? Well, I'm supposed to start the day you'll be in town!"

"That's great, Alessandra!"

"Do you want me to try and move it? Start another day?"

Missy had of course told her no, but her heart was scared. She knew that Trenise was still struggling with what happened and so was she. Alessandra, on the other hand, seemed unbothered by the events they had been a part of.

No mention of bad dreams, no fear.

Missy hoped it was a combination of youth and her newfound purpose working for Rainbow...and now Ms. Sarah.

Missy shuddered again.

At a red light, she looked in the rear-view mirror at her drawn face. She'd lost 15 pounds since the summer and still had no interest in eating. As she drove toward Trenise's new address in Mississippi, Missy's mind returned to the now familiar loop of worry and fear.

—

Trenise rocked and remembered the aftermath of that Saturday six months ago. It was a story she revisited frequently in her mind.

Missy had walked down to the road, flagged down a parish worker and told them there were four injured women who were unable to make calls out. A short ambulance ride later, and they were in St Tammany Parish Hospital.

"This is the second hospital I've been in in one day," Rainbow had remarked absently.

The four of them had huddled together with the other people who had been injured in the tornado.

Trenise remember Missy jumping a mile when her phone rang. She had looked at it bleakly, marveling that it was working again, and answered. She tearfully told her mother the story they had agreed on. They had tried to take shelter in Trenise's house but were injured before they could. Simple. Technically not a lie.

Alessandra's phone had rung next, and she told her mother she was in the hospital with her teacher from school.

"My mom's on her way," Alessandra had told them. Her whole body shook, and she started to sob.

Trenise's phone didn't ring until much later, when word finally got to D.C. about the tornado in Stone River. At the sound of her sweet girl's voice, Trenise had finally broken down.

Trenise smelled her coffee deeply, rousing herself from the memory. She turned and saw Missy's small car turn onto her street. She stood and waved.

—

It wasn't a long visit. As they sat on Trenise's porch, the two women tried to read one another, to get a handle on the other's mental and emotional state. Each was shocked by the change in the other: Trenise by Missy's weight loss and Missy by Trenise's short gray hair.

Finally, Missy reluctantly said that she needed to leave to make it home by nightfall.

Trenise followed Missy down the short few steps to her car, waiting while Missy opened the door.

> Missy paused, finally deciding to broach a subject she had been avoiding for six months. She turned back to look at Trenise.

"What about whatever Trent took from Ms. Cindy, Trenise? What are we going to do about it?"

"Nothing, Missy," Trenise responded sternly, "We're not going to do *anything.*"

"Ok Trenise...." Missy let her voice trail off.

"There's nothing we *can* do, Missy."

Missy nodded again and watched her friend.

"I'm going to miss you, Trenise."

Trenise laughed a little, "I'm going to miss you too, Missy."

"You keep in touch with me, Trenise. And if anything happens, you call me."

Trenise nodded solemnly, "I will, Missy."

Missy gave Trenise's hand a squeeze, closed her car door, and pulled out onto the street.

Trenise watched her drive away, and then stood there, gazing down to the ocean. It glittered in the winter sun, calm and gray. Pelicans stretched their wings and soared in and out of the water, looking for fish.

There was peace here somewhere, Trenise could feel it. Every time she touched it, though, it seemed to slip away from her, to drift down a bayou clogged with cypress knees and secrets.

About the Author

Meghan Flewellyn lives in the greater New Orleans area with her family. She enjoys taking long walks and watching for what lurks in the swamp by her home.

www.ingramcontent.com/pod-product-compliance
Lightning Source LLC
LaVergne TN
LVHW090548110826
845146LV00001B/60

* 9 7 9 8 9 9 3 3 0 4 9 1 5 *